Mary
and the
Captain

A PRIDE AND PREJUDICE CONTINUATION

NANCY LAWRENCE

ALSO BY NANCY LAWRENCE:

Regency Romances:
A Scandalous Season
An Intimate Arrangement
Miss Hamilton's Hero
Once Upon a Christmas

Regency Short Stories:
A Bewitching Minx
The Notorious Nobleman
One Dance with You
Sweet Companion

Jane Austen Inspired Fiction:
Mary and the Captain

THANK YOU ...

... to the exceptional people at FanFiction.net, for your suggestions, feedback and, most importantly, your generous encouragement.

1

Captain Robert Bingley returned his dance partner to her mother's side and made a short bow. "Thank you for the dance, Miss Garfield. It was a pleasure."

In truth, the ordeal of dragging the young lady through the steps of a polonaise had been far from pleasurable, but good manners and a keen self-control born from years of military training helped him hide his true feelings from both the lady and her mother.

He offered her a smile, which his sister Caroline had often complimented as having just the right combination of civility and aloofness, and asked after the health of Miss Garfield's father. For answer the young lady's mother launched into a catalog of her husband's medical complaints that lasted several minutes. Robert listened patiently and murmured appropriate words of sympathy, giving the ladies his undivided attention until the orchestra sounded the chords of the next dance. It was his signal to move on.

He bade them a good evening and was just beginning to

make his way through the crowded ballroom when he caught sight of his sister Caroline moving purposefully in his direction.

Miss Caroline Bingley was in excellent looks. Her gown was, as always, exquisitely cut of fine silks, and her dark curls were arranged most becomingly about her pretty face; but he saw in an instant that there was a light in her eyes he had not seen earlier when he left her side to search out his dance partner. Caroline was up to something.

As soon as she reached his side she threaded her gloved hand through the crook of his arm and directed his steps toward the opposite end of the ballroom.

"I have been looking everywhere for you," she said. "What on earth were you doing with that tiresome Louisa Garfield?"

"Partnering her about the dance floor. I believe you were a witness to it."

"Yes, but, *why*, I should like to know, when there are so many more *desirable* young women here tonight?"

"And so many more ladies who wish to dance than there are men to partner them, as is often the case. As a gentleman, it is my duty to dance with as many as I am able."

"Oh, *duty*," Caroline said, dismissively. "While you were busy giving consequence to the unworthy Miss Garfield, *I* have been working diligently on your behalf."

"Have you? How so?"

She looked up into his blue eyes and smiled enigmatically. "Sowing seeds, dear brother, sowing seeds. Do tell me you are not engaged to dance the next with some undeserving—and equally forgettable—miss."

"On the contrary, I have pledged the next dance to your friend, Miss Paget, and was about to go in search of her."

Caroline's expression brightened. "Twice in one evening, Robert? I begin to think you have developed a *tendre* for my dear friend."

"Would it surprise you? I think you are aware Miss Paget is by far the prettiest woman here, and certainly the sweetest in temperament."

"You have stated the very reasons I decided to take her up. Oh, this way," Caroline said, applying pressure to Robert's arm to right the direction of his steps.

Robert tolerantly allowed her to steer his course. "Clearly you have a destination in mind for us. Where are we going?"

For answer Caroline stopped walking and faced her brother. She looked up to examine his face, from the neat arrangement of his dark brown hair to the firm line of his chin; from there her gaze traveled over his broad shoulders and the polished medals fixed to the red tunic of his officer's dress uniform. How handsome he looked! And how much she wished he was not so tiresomely independent. If he would only learn to lean on her and allow her to manage one or two small things in his life, he would thank her for it later, she was certain.

Hadn't her instincts been right about his military career? Hadn't she predicted that some horrid colonel would whisk him away from the bosom of his family as soon as he purchased his commission? And so it had been, for no sooner had he been gazetted than Robert's regiment was immediately despatched to Turkey—or was it Egypt?—she had never been quite certain.

She had been against his joining the army from the start, insisting that Bingley men should use their wealth to purchase memberships at White's, not military commissions; and predicting that living in encampments would rob him of his good manners and make him fit only for mingling with the fish mongers at Billingsgate. Robert had listened patiently, and called her Mother Hen; then he promptly joined the Hussars and reported for duty with a stunning swiftness that almost made her head spin.

That had been over two years ago, and in that time the Bingleys had seen nothing of Robert as he traveled to the far reaches of the world. But now he was back in London, having returned in August; and if she had her way, she would see to it that he never left the family fold again.

She brushed an infinitesimal bit of lint from the shoulder of his tunic, and said, "You must not blame sisterly pride when I say you are quite the handsomest man here tonight. I have noted the admiring glances of every eligible young woman who has had the privilege to see you pass by—not to mention the calculating looks of their mothers! You must promise me you shall resist them all."

"All?"

"With the exception of Miss Paget, of course. After all, she *is* my closest friend—so close that I often think of her as a sister, and have to remind myself there is no blood between us. Still, we enjoy the deepest sister-like devotion."

"Caroline . . ." he said, in a mildly warning tone.

"You are right, of course, that Miss Paget can never be a *true* sister to me—only a sister-*in-law*, much like our dear Jane. It was a lucky stroke for all of us when Miss Jane

Bennet married our brother Charles, and have we not welcomed her to the family as one of our own? I suppose," she said, allowing a hint of tragedy to tinge her tone, "it is too much for me to hope that the same may one day be said of my dear friend, Miss Paget."

Robert's expression was wary but tolerant. "When did you become such a calculating minx?"

"I?" she said, with innocently wide eyes.

"Allow me to conduct my own flirtations, Caroline."

"Of course—but only if you will tell me that my instincts are correct in this. Have I accurately gauged your feelings for Miss Paget?"

As soon as those words left her lips, Robert's expression changed; the look of affectionate amusement disappeared with the finality of a curtain dropping on the last act of a play. "May I give you a hint, Caroline? Soldiers are trained to be lead, not pushed."

"I meant it kindly, brother."

His expression softened slightly. "Of that I have no doubt."

"Can you blame me for wanting to see you happy and settled in life?"

"That depends on how you intend to accomplish the thing."

"I shall tell you, though I hadn't meant to say a word about it until I was certain every detail was arranged."

"Are you about to finally describe those seeds you said you were sowing on my behalf?"

"Indeed, I am," she answered, with a coy smile and a dip of her head that caused the jewels in her headdress to glitter beneath the ballroom's candlelight. "You see, I have become so fond of Miss Paget that I begin to think it a shame that we must spend Christmas apart."

"But you and I are to spend Christmas at Netherfield with Charles and Jane. We have planned it so."

"And Helena is to go to Essex to her sister and brother-in-law. She has mentioned to you, has she not, that her sister is soon to deliver her first child? Helena's mother is determined to be in Essex for her lying in."

"Yes, she told me."

"Did she also mention she is not keen on the idea? Of course she wishes her sister well and hopes she delivers of a fine, healthy child, but Helena cannot like the idea of burying herself in Essex for two months."

"Just what, exactly, are you up to, Caroline?" he asked in a tone of affectionate suspicion.

"I have been busy with Charles and Jane. *They* wanted to spend a quiet family Christmas at Netherfield with you and me and Jane's sisters—"

"I did not know Jane's sisters are to be there. I look forward to meeting them."

"Don't," Caroline recommended. "Oh, I know you are the model of good manners, but you will waste such efforts on those Bennet girls. Promise you will pay them no mind."

"Ignore my sisters-in-law? Caroline, you cannot mean it!" he protested, unsure if he should laugh at her or scold her.

"You say that only because you have never met the creatures."

"But they are Jane's younger sisters, are they not?"

"Yes, but a last name is the only thing they have in common. They are nothing at all like our dear Jane."

He looked down at her, frowning and smiling at the same time. "How can that be?"

"You will learn soon enough. They have nothing of Jane's temperament and no accomplishments to speak of. One of them—Kitty, they call her—runs after officers. She is quite shameless about it, so beware she doesn't set her sights on you."

He laughed outright at the notion. "And the other sister?"

"Mary is even more trying. She imagines herself a talented musician, but the truth is she has no ability whatsoever, yet the family *will* encourage her. Your regiment marching down a dirt road has a finer sense of musical rhythm than Mary Bennet can ever hope to achieve."

"If they are Jane's sisters, they cannot be as bad as you describe," he said, in good humour. "Why, Jane is dear and sweet—I could not have wished for a better match for our brother Charles. I think these sisters must be more like Jane than you are willing to admit."

"I assure you, they are not."

"Still, I will be happy to make their acquaintance. But what have they to do with those seeds you have been sowing?"

"Nothing at all and I assure you, they will never figure in any of *my* plans."

"And those plans are . . . ?" He was beginning to wonder if Caroline would ever tell him what plots and ploys she had set in motion.

"I believe I can convince Jane to invite Miss Paget to

spend Christmas at Netherfield with us."

Robert was still for a long moment. His heart, which had beat so strongly and steadily a mere moment before, now began to thump crazily beneath the gleaming medals pinned to the tunic of his uniform. Christmas with Miss Paget? It was almost too much to hope for. From the moment Robert had made the acquaintance of Miss Helena Paget he had been smitten as never before. He had met her in August after his regiment had returned to England; Caroline had introduced her as one of her dearest friends, and that alone would have disposed Robert to think well of her. But it also happened that she was the most bewitching young woman he had ever met.

At twenty years of age she was delicate and sweet, quick to smile and possessed of an engaging dimple and an equally engaging wit. He had first been attracted to her beauty; but after ten minutes of conversation with Helena, he found himself completely beguiled by her many charms; so much so that when he discovered his regiment had been ordered to Kent, he was besotted enough to consider the idea of resigning his commission, just so he could remain in London by her side.

He had not done so, but leaving Helena behind had been one of the most difficult things he had ever done—far more difficult, he began to think, than facing an enemy on the battlefield. Under this strong emotion he entered a new and extraordinary phase of his life, where the military career he had always enjoyed and celebrated suddenly began to chafe. Where once he had been content to concentrate on obeying orders and going where his king and colonel commanded, he now found his thoughts consumed by the date of his next scheduled leave and the quickest route back to London and Helena's side.

When he was with his regiment he relied on Caroline— good sister that she was—to keep his memory fresh in Helena's mind until the next time he was able to see her. But now, it seemed, fortune had smiled on him. Thanks to his sister's machinations, he might actually have two uninterrupted weeks with the lovely Miss Paget at Netherfield, his brother's country estate. Two weeks in which he would be free of his regimental duties. Two weeks in which he could court her as she should be courted, and make his feelings known to her. Two weeks in which he would have ample time to secure her promise to marry him.

On an impulse he gave his sister a quick kiss on the cheek. "Oh, you dear little schemer! You cannot know how happy you have made me, Caroline."

"Stop that," she said, embarrassed but pleased. "You may thank me by putting your time at Netherfield to good use and making my friend Helena your wife. But I beg you will not mention the arrangement until I have secured Jane's agreement. You know how Jane is—she hesitates so over the smallest decisions that you or I would have settled in an instant. We are decisive by nature, you and I—the sensible members of the family."

"How will I ever thank you?"

"By dancing with Miss Paget, of course." With a slight, graceful gesture she directed his attention to the far end of the ballroom. "You will find her there, with her mother and father. When I left them, they were standing between the door and the potted palm."

Instinctively Robert's head turned that direction, his eyes scanning the assembled crowd from his advantage of height; but the ballroom was filled to overflowing with guests, making it impossible for him to single out one petite young woman.

"And may I give you another hint, Robert? She is wearing her mother's sapphire tonight. I find it gaudy, myself, but I daresay it would mean much to her if you were to compliment its color and size."

Robert dipped his head to murmur close to her ear, "Mired in the details, as always, are you? No, no, I mean to compliment you, for you have managed us all very well tonight, I think. What would I do without you?"

"Without me you'd still be dancing with the Miss Garfields of this world. Now go, do! The beautiful Miss Paget awaits."

Caroline tarried just long enough to see Robert escort Helena Paget onto the dance floor before she joined her brother and sister-in-law. She found Charles and Jane in close and happy conversation, their attention devoted only to each other in the midst of the overcrowded ballroom. After almost a year of marriage they were still in the throes of first love and had not yet progressed past the newly-wed stage of affection. Caroline often wondered how two grown people who spent every waking hour together could remain so besotted with each other, but Charles assured her that she would no doubt feel the same when Cupid's arrow struck her. Caroline pledged to evade all such arrows aimed her direction. But when it came to matters regarding *Robert's* heart, she was quite happy to help Cupid's dart find its target.

She purposefully stepped between Charles and Jane to ensure she had their full attention, and said, complacently, "Tell me, please, you have noticed that our brother is dancing a *second* dance with Miss Paget."

Neither Charles nor Jane had noticed it. Indeed, they had eyes for no one but each other, but at Caroline's invitation they dutifully directed their attention toward the dance floor.

"What do you see?" Caroline asked.

"A very creditable cotillion," Charles answered, promptly. "Robert always was an excellent dancer."

"And what of my dear friend, Helena Paget?"

"She is a charming young woman," Jane said. "I am so glad to have made her acquaintance. You are blessed with a delightful friend, Caroline."

Caroline's expression revealed none of the impatience she felt. "But what do you *see* as they dance *together?*"

Both Charles and Jane studied the couple as they moved through the figures of the set. At last Charles said, "They dance splendidly together. I always liked a cotillion myself! Jane, we must have a cotillion or two played at the New Year ball. You know we are planning to have a ball at Netherfield right after the New Year, don't you, Caroline? We must have mentioned it. Nothing too lavish—just an excuse, really, to have our Netherfield neighbours about us and welcome in a New Year together. Jane has been planning the thing for weeks. Tell her, Jane."

"I look forward to hearing all the details," Caroline said, before Jane could reply, "tomorrow, perhaps. Now do look at

Robert and Helena again. What do you notice?"

"They look as if they are enjoying themselves," Jane ventured.

"Enjoying themselves?" Caroline repeated. "Yes, I dare say they are, but look again. Oh, for heaven sake, can you not tell they are *in love?*"

Jane and Charles immediately looked surprised, then turned as one toward the dance floor, watching in earnest as first Robert then Helena executed a very graceful allemande.

"Only see how he looks at her, how soft his expression," Caroline said. "I do believe he can barely take his eyes off her. And see how sweetly Helena blushes whenever her gaze meets his. It is plain to anyone who looks their direction they are in the hopeless throes of a romantic attachment."

"Goodness!" Jane said, as the truth of Caroline's words dawned upon her. "Can it be? They have known each other only since August."

"That is nothing, my dear," Charles said, "for I knew I was half in love with you the night we met at the Meryton Assembly."

"Then you agree with me," Caroline said quickly, before her brother could indulge in further memories. "You do see, as I do, that Robert and Helena Paget are in love?"

"I do, indeed, now that you mention it," Jane said. "Oh, I hope Robert will be happy!"

"He will be, I am certain . . . once he proposes marriage. But he has not done so yet."

"What is keeping him?" Charles asked. "It is not like Robert to hesitate. Always forward, always marching toward the future, that's him!"

"He has been waiting for the right time and the right setting. You know how difficult it has been for him to find two days together in which to see her. His regiment gives him leave to come to London, but then orders him back to ranks before he has a chance to press his suit."

"I see what you mean," Jane said, with a small frown marring her lovely features. "That is always the way for poor Robert. Sadly, tomorrow he must return to his regiment and we shall not see him again until Christmas Eve, when he joins us at Netherfield."

"But there he may stay for two uninterrupted weeks," Charles added, heartily. "We Bingleys shall have a nice long stay at Netherfield before Robert must report for duty again."

Caroline nodded, making the jewels in her headdress sparkle. "Very true, brother. Robert will be at Netherfield for two weeks—just long enough, in my opinion, for him to properly court Helena and press his suit with her, *if* she were invited to Netherfield, too. I am certain with two weeks at his disposal, Robert will propose marriage to Helena Paget, and she will accept. Oh, do say you will invite her to Netherfield for Christmas! I think the thing may be easily done. Look, there are her parents, standing just a little by the door. It would be a simple matter for you to go to them now, Jane, and beg the favor of allowing Helena to come to us for Christmas. She can travel to Netherfield with us in our carriage. Won't that be cozy?"

Jane frowned slightly. "Do you really think their regard for each other has advanced to such a degree?"

"I am certain of it. Why do you hesitate? Do you dislike Miss Paget?"

"Indeed, we like her very well," Charles said, quickly. "She is very charming."

"And she is the niece of an earl," Caroline added, meaningfully, "as well an heiress in her own right. Of course, that sort of thing is beside the point when it is clear Robert's heart is engaged. What do *you* think, Jane?"

"Like Charles, I think Miss Paget is charming. And now that I understand how highly Robert regards her—Oh, Caroline, if I hesitate, it is only because I had planned a small *family* Christmas at Netherfield. You know my sisters Mary and Kitty will be there, and I was so looking forward to pampering them a bit before we remove from Netherfield for good."

"And so you shall!" Caroline said, in the tone of a parent coaxing a reluctant child. "And at the same time your Mary and Kitty may become acquainted with the young woman destined to be their future sister-in-law. Now, isn't that the model of a true family Christmas? Oh, what a lovely time we shall all have together!"

Jane looked at her husband, her expression still doubtful. "Charles, what do you think? Should we expand our Christmas plans to include Miss Paget?"

Before he could reply, Caroline said, "Oh, if you think it best to confine our Christmas to only Bingleys and Bennets, there is no more to be said. I was thinking only of Robert, you know. But, as you say, there is probably no reason to exert an effort on *his* behalf. He must learn to be satisfied with the little crumbs of happiness he can find here and there in life; and when he leaves us to fight again in some God-forsaken land from which he may never return, we will have our cozy little family Christmas to look back on."

Charles gave Jane an earnest look. "It seems Caroline may have a point. Perhaps we *should* invite Miss Paget to Netherfield. If she is to join our family as Mrs. Robert Bingley, it will be the perfect chance for all of us to get to know her better. What do you say, Jane?"

"You are correct, as always," Jane answered, reaching out to place her gloved fingers on his arm. "I think Kitty and Mary will like her very well. Yes, I do believe our family Christmas can include one more near-relative."

Caroline smothered a triumphant smile. "Then let us go to Mr. and Mrs. Paget now, Jane. I see them there, just beside the open doors. We will beg the favor of allowing Helena to travel to Netherfield with us. They cannot refuse, I am certain, for they, too, must have remarked on their daughter's partiality for Robert; and if they haven't, I mean to point it out to them—subtly, of course."

And with this stream of words, and many more like them, Caroline led Jane Bingley to the very field in which she had sown those seeds on Robert's behalf. She would tell Robert about it presently, for she knew he would appreciate her efforts. For now it was sufficient to know that her plans concerning her brother were about to bear fruit. Miss Helena Paget was to spend Christmas at Netherfield, just as Caroline designed. It only remained now to find a way to somehow rid Netherfield of Mary and Kitty Bennet and the Bingleys would be able to enjoy a lovely Christmas, indeed.

2

The Bennet Home
Longbourn, Hertfordshire
December, 1814

Mary Bennet traced her tongue across her suddenly dry lower lip and gathered her courage together. From experience she knew nothing good could come from trying to reason with her mother; and when Mrs. Bennet was distracted and rushed—as she was on this December morning as she packed her travel trunks with haphazard abandon—the chances of her considering anyone's wishes but her own were almost non-existent. Still, Mary felt she had to try.

"Mama, are you listening to me?" It was a rhetorical question for Mary knew her mother was too occupied with the task of packing to pay close attention to anything else.

"Of course I am listening," Mrs. Bennet said, impatiently. "Why must you ask such questions? Just read the letter, Mary."

"I *did* read the letter," Mary answered, looking down at the page of closely written lines set in her sister Jane's neat handwriting.

"Then read it again. I couldn't hear a *thing* you said because you *will* insist on mumbling so. Read out, Mary! Read out!"

There was no point in arguing. Mary drew a deep breath and began to read her eldest sister's letter again while her mother moved restlessly around her bedchamber.

It had been agreed weeks before that Mr. and Mrs. Bennet would spend Christmas at Pemberley with their daughter Elizabeth and her husband, Fitzwilliam Darcy, while Mary and Kitty Bennet stayed with Jane and Charles Bingley at Netherfield. The morning mail had brought a letter from Jane—who had been residing in London with her husband for the last six months—in which Jane outlined a slight change to the plans. That change, of which Jane wrote so casually, greatly upset Mary. She wanted to tell her mother of her concerns, but Mrs. Bennet was more absorbed in the business of packing than she was with her daughter's clearly worried expression.

In true form, Mrs. Bennet had delayed packing for her journey to Pemberley until the day before she was due to depart, and on this morning she was in a frenzy, ransacking her dressing table, selecting a number of dresses to add to the trunk only to change her mind moments later, and driving her housekeeper Mrs. Hill—who was doing her best to make order out of the chaos her mistress created—to utter distraction. It was in this environment that Mary read her sister Jane's letter aloud a second time.

When she finished she looked up to see her mother standing before the wardrobe, its doors thrown wide as she studied the contents. Then, with a quick movement, Mrs.

Bennet reached inside and began to rifle through the neatly arranged clothes. Mary wished she would look at her instead.

"Mama, I don't *want* to go to Netherfield. I want to go to Pemberley with you and papa."

"Don't be ridiculous, child!" Mrs. Bennet turned around, but her attention was focused on her best silk shawl, which she held out at arm's length, the better to admire it. "Just look at the colours," she murmured. "I am certain Lady Lucas has nothing like it." She tossed the shawl into the open trunk in which Mrs. Hill had just finished placing her mistress's gowns with great care.

"Mama, I want to go to Pemberley," Mary said, firmly.

"No, no, child! Pemberley will not do. Of course you and Kitty must spend Christmas at Netherfield. What good can come of your going to Pemberley, I should like to know?"

"But I shall be more comfortable at Pemberley. Lizzy promised a small family gathering and that is exactly what I would like most."

"Nonsense! Pemberley is the *worst* place for you to be!" Mrs. Bennet scooped up the contents from a drawer in her dressing table and dumped the lot on her bed. "How on earth are you ever to meet a rich husband if you hide away for three weeks in Derbyshire with only your family about you?"

Mary felt the familiar flutter of panic rise in her chest, as she always did when her mother raised the topic of marriage and rich husbands. She looked down at the letter from Jane that she held in her hand and saw that her fingers were trembling.

"But a quiet family Christmas is what I should like most of all—"

"And, of course, *that* must settle the question! Whatever Miss Mary Bennet wants *must* prevail! It makes no matter, I suppose, what your father and *I* may plan—thinking only of our daughters' futures! Perhaps if I were a less loving and devoted mother I could understand when one of my daughters is deliberately inconsiderate of my efforts to see her happy and settled in life. It's a thankless task, I must say!"

"I don't mean to be ungrateful, mama—"

"Oh, no, no, Hill, not the *grey* gloves!" snapped Mrs. Bennet as the housekeeper began to wrap a selection of gloves in silver paper before stowing them in the trunk. "Oh, all of this packing should have been done *hours* ago. I daresay Mr. Bennet is at this very moment wondering why I have not finished."

"He is, indeed, wondering that very thing," came Mr. Bennet's voice through the open doorway to the bedchamber next door.

Mary instantly moved toward the sound of his voice, hoping her father would be more willing than her mother to listen to her pleas.

"Papa, may I go with you to Pemberley? I am certain Kitty shall have just as nice a time with Jane and Bingley if I am at Pemberley with you."

"What did your mother say when you applied to her?"

"But no one shall *miss* me if I go to Pemberley," she said, ignoring his question.

Mrs. Bennet looked up from where she was sorting gloves and ribbands into a muddle of confusion on top of her bed. "Don't be silly! Your sister Jane shall miss you, for I finally secured her promise that she will do her duty by you at last. She has been most selfish, I must say—Married for almost *a year* to Mr. Bingley, and she has yet to introduce you or your sister Kitty to a *single* gentleman of fortune! *That* is a situation she will remedy, mark my words!"

"Please, papa?" There was a note of urgency in Mary's voice now, as a sudden vision flashed through her mind of the fate before her if her mother got her way: the long formal dinner table at Netherfield where she would be seated with male guests to her right and left, who must be spoken to throughout a meal of several courses. The drawing room filled with people who were virtual strangers, where intimate conversations must be conducted with wit and aplomb. She had never mastered the art of carrying off such social niceties. She would stutter and stumble, or—even worse—sit in strangled silence, unable to conjure up a viable thought to add to a conversation.

"*Please*, papa?" she said again, prepared to sacrifice her dignity by begging, if required.

Mr. Bennet came through the open doorway to pat her shoulder with an uncertain hand.

"There, there, Mary. When you are older and have been married as long as your mother and I have, you will understand peace comes from shared sentiments."

"Are you saying you *agree* with mama?"

"Indeed I do."

"But you know the entire time I am at Netherfield I shall be miserable."

"But your mother will be content, and *I* shall enjoy a quiet drive to Pemberley." He rolled his eyes toward his wife as he spoke, in a way that would have evoked a smile of understanding from his daughter Elizabeth, had she been there. But Lizzy Bennet was *not* there, for she had been married to Mr. Darcy and mistress of Pemberley for almost a year. Unlike Lizzy, Mary saw nothing humorous in her father's remark; nor did she feel like smiling when her father brushed aside her concerns, as he so often did, with no more compassion than he might feel as he flicked a bit of fluff from the velvet cuff of his favorite coat.

"Hill, *do* be careful with that bonnet!" Mrs. Bennet said, almost gasping, as the housekeeper carefully placed the silk and lace confection on the bed beside the ribbons and gloves. "That bonnet was a gift from Lizzy and if even *one* of those silk flowers on the brim is crushed, I shall not be able to wear it. Although, to be sure, Darcy can afford to buy me another, for he is *that* rich, but I daresay Lizzy would expect me to take some care with it. Be certain to pack it in the original hat box—No, no, the one with the *label* on it so everyone can see it came from a *London* milliner."

"Mama!" Mary said, trying to get her mother's attention once more.

"Honestly, Hill, sometimes I wonder if I am the *only* person in this family who understands our social position. You would be astounded if you knew how often Lady Lucas compares *her* son-in-law to *mine*—to his detriment, of course. Naturally, *her* Mr. Collins can never compare to *my* Darcy and Bingley. Why, just the other day Lady Lucas actually said . . ."

Mrs. Bennet's voice droned on, and Mary recognized her mother's tried-and-true method for ignoring a conversation she did not wish to have. She spun around to speak once more to her father, and saw that he had retreated to his own bedchamber and quietly shut the door behind him. How like him! And how like her mother! Was there no one to listen to her? No one to understand how much she would suffer if she were forced to spend Christmas at Netherfield?

Anger and a good deal of frustration welled within her. She clenched her fingers, crumpling the letter in her grasp. Had her temperament been more akin to her eldest sister Jane's, she would have retreated to her room and gained solace in quiet contemplation. Had she been more like her sister Elizabeth, she would have immediately quit the house and set off on a brisk walk through copse and meadow, returning home exhausted and in a quieter frame of mind. But she was just plain Mary Bennet, and in her nineteen years she had found only one satisfying outlet for her emotions.

She left her mother's room and flew down the stairs to the spinet in the drawing room, where she threw back the cover from the keys with a resounding bang. Her fingers, which moments before had crumbled her sister Jane's letter in frustration, began to pound out the chords of a concerto almost before she sat down before the instrument.

Her younger sister Kitty was in the drawing room, seated at a table near the window. She looked up from her fancy needlework and frowned. At the first opportunity in which she thought she might be heard over the crashing chords, she said, "Mary, *must* you pound the keys so hard? I can hardly hear myself think!"

Mary stopped playing to glare at her sister. "What is

there to think about? You are netting a bag! *That* takes no very great care. It's not as if you were totting numbers in your head."

"No, but it is much nicer to net a bag with pleasant music to listen to. What are you so angry about, anyway?"

"Netherfield." In that single word Mary laid her problem before Kitty, who had read Jane's letter earlier before Mary delivered it to their mother upstairs.

"I see," Kitty said as she turned her attention back to her needlework. "I suppose mama would not agree to your plan?"

"Mama wouldn't even *listen* to my plan. Kitty, what am I to do? If I have to go to Netherfield for Christmas I shall be miserable the entire time. I want to go to Pemberley."

"If anyone is to go to Pemberley, it should be *me*. When Lydia went to Brighton, I had to stay at home. And when Jane went to London, where was I? At home. And Lizzy went first to Hunsford to visit Charlotte Lucas, then to Derbyshire with our aunt and uncle. Everyone goes everywhere except me. I think it's time I went *somewhere!*"

"Then go to Pemberley. Go to Netherfield—go to *London*, if you wish! I shall stay here."

"No, you won't."

"I assure you, I shall." Mary's chin went up.

"And spend Christmas with none but servants? That will not be pleasant for you."

"I would rather spend Christmas alone in a cave than have to spend it with strangers."

"Not everyone at Netherfield will be a stranger. You will have Jane, and me, and Bingley—You like Bingley, don't you?"

"Yes, I like him well enough."

"He has been very kind to you and me, and I'm certain he will be as welcoming and loving toward us as he always is."

"That is as you say, but Jane and Bingley will not be the only ones at Netherfield. Jane writes—" Mary paused as she took up the letter she had dropped on top of the spinet, and smoothed the wrinkles from the page with her fingers. "Jane writes that Charles Bingley's sister Caroline will join them, and she has invited other guests, as well."

"Netherfield is large enough to accommodate a dozen guests, I daresay."

"But does one of the guests *have* to be Caroline Bingley? She doesn't like me. She doesn't like either of us."

"No, but only because she is the type of person who must look down on someone else in order to make herself feel higher. Lizzy said so. I don't pay attention to it."

"But in her letter Jane said there will be other guests besides Caroline. *Strangers*," Mary said meaningfully.

"The guests will be Bingley's brother and a friend of Caroline's. That is not so bad. I am certain Bingley's brother will be just as kind and pleasant as he is."

"And Caroline's friend will be just as *un*pleasant as Caroline is."

"You don't know that. Besides, we will not be with them often, I daresay. And if Caroline insists upon making things uncomfortable for us, we can always excuse ourselves and call on Lucas Lodge. You know Mariah Lucas will welcome us," Kitty said, reasonably.

That much was true enough, thought Mary. Mariah

Lucas had been a life-long friend to Mary and Kitty, despite Mrs. Bennet's often harsh criticisms of the Lucas family.

Mary closed the keyboard with much more care than she had used to open it, and crossed the room to sit at the table with Kitty.

"I was hoping our Christmas at Netherfield with Jane and Bingley would be a nice, quiet family visit. That was Jane's original plan, and I am sorely disappointed to read in her letter that she has now invited scores of other people to join us."

"How you exaggerate, Mary! There will not be *scores* of people at Netherfield. Jane has invited three people besides us."

Mary's nose wrinkled with distaste. "Caroline Bingley and her friend."

"And Bingley's brother. Did you read how Jane described him in her letter?"

"Yes. He's a soldier in the Hussars."

"An officer!" Kitty said, pausing her stitches to flash a look of delight at Mary. "Only think! I am certain he must be very dashing and handsome to be a captain in the Hussars."

Mary frowned discouragingly. "Do not tell me you mean to fall in love with him."

"No, I intend that *he* shall fall in love with *me*," Kitty answered with an impish light to her eyes. "I wonder if he is as rich as Bingley? Did Jane ever mention whether he has a fortune? Never mind, I shall soon discover the truth of the matter. In the meantime, it will be nice to see a red coat in the county again."

"I hope you will not devote all your time to chasing after

Bingley's brother."

"Why shouldn't I?"

"Because I need you to help *me*."

"Help you with what?"

"*Talking* to them. You know what it is like for me to meet someone new. I am introduced, then there follows a period of anguish while I try to think of something to say. It's like drowning in a quicksand of speech."

"Oh, that. Of course I'll help you, if I can. And you must know Jane will do her best to make you feel at home."

"Yes, I know Jane will help." The thought made Mary relax a little.

"Still," Kitty said, "it might be a good idea for you to take some of your sheet music with you, just in case you cannot hold a conversation. Then you will have your music to play, and no one will expect you to talk. And Bingley has a fine pianoforte—not like our old spinet. You'll like that, won't you—playing Bingley's pianoforte, I mean?"

Mary's spirits lifted a little. She always enjoyed playing the beautiful instrument at Netherfield whenever she had the chance. Oddly, she felt calmer after talking the matter over with Kitty; and after admitting to herself that she really would not like to pass Christmas alone, she slowly resigned herself to the prospect of going to Netherfield, after all.

"Very well," she said, after a few minutes of thought, "I shall go to Netherfield. And I shall do my best to enjoy myself."

"And I shall go to Netherfield, too," said Kitty, "and I will do my best to win the heart of Captain Bingley. See if I don't!"

3

The drawing-room at Netherfield was an elegantly appointed apartment with a southern aspect. Along the main wall, tall cased windows looked out upon a well-manicured garden, beyond which was a cunning pond of perfect dimensions set in an idyllic meadow. The eastern windows afforded a view of the main gate and the parkland, which was, on this Christmas Eve, still showing patches of green in the bright winter sunshine. Mary Bennet did not think the weather at all conducive to the spirit of Christmas, for, thus far, their winter had been mild, with temperate weather during the day and little rain or snow to impede forays into the out-of-doors. Not that Mary spent much time out-of-doors even in good weather, for she had always been one to stay at home with a book or a bit of needlework while her sisters visited the neighbourhood. She employed her time in the same manner at Netherfield, where she found contentment exploring the interesting titles displayed in the well-stocked library, or playing the pianoforte to her heart's delight whenever she thought her music would not disturb anyone else in the household.

By Christmas Eve Mary and Kitty Bennet had been three days at Netherfield. In that time they had been warmly welcomed by Jane and Charles, made the acquaintance of Miss Helena Paget, and renewed their acquaintance with Caroline Bingley.

Caroline had greeted them with a good deal more tolerance than she had been wont to exercise on previous occasions; but though her manner was somewhat conciliatory, her words held a sting the Bennet sisters had come to expect. When Kitty complimented Caroline's gown, Caroline looked down at the afternoon dress she'd worn many times before, and said in a dismissive tone, "I am certain you have seen me wear this gown on other occasions."

"I have, but that does not mean it is any less to be admired," Kitty answered. "It is very fine. I should like to have a gown like that myself."

"Oh, I am certain there are lesser copies of it to be had," Caroline responded, loftily, "but my London *modiste* designed this gown exclusively for my taste and figure. I doubt it would look half so well on a woman of shorter height and more common bearing. Let me encourage you, Miss Kitty, to keep to your own style of dress."

As for Caroline's friend, Helena Paget, Mary and Kitty found her to be just as intimidating as Caroline, but for a completely different reason. Helena Paget was a dauntingly attractive young woman, a delicate little doll of porcelain and silk. Within seconds of making Helena's acquaintance, Mary realized that she was looking at a flesh-and-blood Helen of Troy; the kind of young lady whose looks and nature attracted beautiful women and handsome men to orbit about her—to the exclusion of all others whose features were of the more common variety. Mary knew her own features fitted into the latter category. She had no illusions about her looks, having realized long ago that her older sisters Jane and Lizzy were the beauties in the family. And she had no pretensions toward vivacity of spirit, for her younger sisters had laid claim to those charms in their childhood.

But upon Helena Paget had Nature bestowed the gifts of both beauty and vivacity, and Mary knew from experience that, when placed beside a young woman of Miss Paget's resources, Mary Bennet tended to fade to the background and become almost invisible. She didn't do so on purpose; she simply fell into the trap of comparing herself with the object of beauty and, finding herself falling short, shrank a bit inside herself. She tried to do so immediately after making Helena's acquaintance, but Helena would have none of it.

"Oh, Miss Bennet," she said upon making Mary's acquainttance, "I understand you are a musician. I dearly love music, and I hope I will have the pleasure of hearing you play."

This unexpected compliment surprised Mary so much, she flushed to the roots of her hair. "I—! Yes—! That is, if you want me to."

"Indeed I do. And if you will allow me," she added, with a demure look that caused her lovely long lashes to fan coyly over her fair cheeks, "I hope we may one day play a duet, although I dare not consider my talent equal to yours."

From that moment of their first acquaintance Helena had disposed herself to be kind to both Bennet sisters, but to Mary in particular. Mary marveled over it, and wondered, several times, that a girl used to mingling with the *crème de society* should be so determined to be on friendly terms with herself and her sisters.

But on this Christmas Eve, even Helena was subdued. The much-anticipated day of Captain Robert Bingley's arrival at Netherfield was creeping relentlessly toward its close, with still no sign of the captain.

By late afternoon, when the party assembled in the drawing-room for tea, everyone was in a quiet mood. Charles and Jane had invited Mr. Penrose, the vicar of Meryton, to join the family circle, and that young gentleman did his brave best to raise the family's spirits, with limited success. Though conversation never waned, it was clear that there was an undercurrent of worry in their assembly. Even Helena Paget's lovely brow was marred by the hint of an anxious frown.

Caroline, too, was not herself. She could not keep still, but traveled the room, her carriage erect, her movements graceful; but when she stopped at one of the eastern windows from which she could view the gate where the neatly-graveled drive to the house left the public road, she gave the window hangings an impatient twitch. "Oh, where *can* he be?"

"Caroline, your tea will be cold," Jane said, coaxingly. "Do sit down and join us."

"Why isn't he here?" Caroline demanded, ignoring Jane's

invitation. "It is not at all like Robert to be late. He promised to arrive this morning. His letter stated so."

Indeed, Robert's letter to Charles had said to expect him in the morning, and Charles had declared how much he was looking forward to sharing a Christmas Eve with the people he held most dear. Jane spent the early hours of the day with her housekeeper, ensuring that Robert's bedchamber was well appointed, and that the first footman who was to serve as the captain's valet during his stay was fully aware of the responsibility of such an undertaking.

A long-cart bearing the captain's trunks and cases arrived mid-morning, leaving the Bingleys and the Bennets to believe that Robert would soon follow; but every moment they anticipated seeing the captain's carriage sweep up the drive to the house was a moment of disappointment.

"Oh, I'm certain he will be here soon," Charles said over and over; but with each utterance the brightness of his expression dimmed just a little.

A planned excursion into the countryside to gather evergreen boughs and branches with which to decorate the front hall and drawing-room was discarded, for no one wanted Robert to arrive at Netherfield while the family was away from the house.

At luncheon each member of the party took a turn casting a look of longing toward the empty place setting at the table; and when the tea tray was delivered to the drawing room late in the afternoon, a distinct pall of unspoken concern had settled upon the group.

Caroline left the window and slowly made her way back to her chair near the tea tray.

As soon as she was settled, Mr. Penrose attempted to draw her into the conversation by saying, "I have just explained to your friend Miss Paget that it is a Meryton tradition to hold vespers on Christmas Eve. I hope I may see you there this evening."

"I cannot speak for others," Caroline replied, barely looking at him, "but I could not consider leaving this house until I see my brother safely arrived."

Mr. Penrose smiled kindly. "Is there a better place in which to pray for his safety than in a church?"

"If you can guarantee that my prayers will be better heard there than here, I will run to the church right now," Caroline retorted.

"There is no need to run," he replied, pleasantly. "A good, brisk *walk* will get you to the church in due time without the risk of losing your breath."

Caroline scowled at him, prompting Jane to say, in an apologetic tone, "We are all a little on edge, Mr. Penrose."

"It's very understandable, Mrs. Bingley. Yet from all I have heard of the captain, he sounds like a most capable young man. I quite think that if he does not present himself very soon, he will at the very least send word."

"That is what I thought," Charles said, with a strained smile. "But the thing of it is, he's so dreadfully late, that I can't help wondering why he has not sent a message by now. It's not like Robert to be behind-hand in anything, you know." His gaze strayed toward the clock on the mantle—not to note the time, but to calculate instead how late the afternoon had advanced from the appointed hour his brother had been due to arrive.

"Surely a captain in the king's army has many duties to perform," Mr. Penrose suggested. "Perhaps he did not leave his regiment this morning as planned."

"Then why did his trunks arrive earlier today?" Caroline asked, rising as she did so to move back to the window. "I am certain he would not have sent his things unless he intended to follow them immediately."

Kitty asked, hopefully, "Will he be wearing his uniform when he arrives, do you think?"

"Why, pray, is *that* important to ask?" demanded Caroline, turning to look at her from her post by the window.

"Because I've never seen a regimental uniform," Kitty said, reasonably. "I have seen only the red coats of the militia before, and none of them had braided knots or medals. I think I would like very much to meet an officer who has been decorated for bravery as often as your brother has."

Helena Paget set her cup and saucer down on the table and said, "May I venture to offer my opinion on the matter? You see, I have met Captain Bingley in London several times in the last few months, and I believe I may say with authority that he is, indeed, an impressive figure in his regimentals." Having spoken her peace, Miss Paget blushed becomingly. The bloom of colour accentuated the perfect symmetry of her delicate features, as she gazed at the assembled company with eyes the colour of a spring sky.

"Thank you for saying so, my dear Helena," Caroline said. "I share your opinion of my brother, but had *I* offered it, it would have sounded like boasting."

"Oh, no, my dear Caroline, it would not be boasting at all. Captain Bingley is exemplary in every way and has earned our good opinion."

"How well do you know the Captain?" Kitty asked, delving to the heart of the matter.

Helena blushed again, and looked at her from under her long lashes. "Well enough to know he is possessed of an admirable temperament. He has traveled widely, you know, so his knowledge of the world is quite impressive."

"He cannot be *that* clever about the world," said Kitty, "or he wouldn't be lost right now."

"Kitty!" Jane said, in a mildly scolding tone.

"Well, if he isn't lost, where is he, I should like to know? You said he was due to arrive hours ago, and we even held luncheon for him until it was plain we could hold it no longer."

"He will be here shortly," Charles said, in a falsely bright voice. "I assure you, only a matter of great importance would have kept him from arriving on time. My brother is very punctual—it's his military training, you know."

"Perhaps," Mary murmured, "he has been set upon by pirates." She thought she had spoken in a voice low enough to be heard by no one but Kitty, who was seated beside her; but no sooner did those words leave her lips than she heard a chorus of protests.

"Mary!" said Jane.

"Preposterous!" said Caroline.

"My dear Miss Bennet, you cannot mean it!" begged Mr. Penrose.

Kitty said, scoffingly, "Don't be silly, Mary. Pirates plague sailors at sea. It is *footpads* who accost travelers on the roads. Captain Bingley has probably been set upon by *footpads.*"

"Of all the utter nonsense!" Caroline said, indignantly. "Why, my brother Robert would never fall victim to a common footpad! He could fight off a *dozen* footpads at once and not suffer so much as a single scratch. He served in Brussels, then Egypt alongside the Mamelukes, so his bravery cannot be disputed."

"I never said he wasn't *brave*," Mary answered, defensively. "I only meant—"

"We know what you meant, thank you, Mary," Jane interrupted her. "I think I can say with confidence Captain Bingley has fought neither pirates nor footpads today."

"Then what could be keeping him?" Kitty asked. "What reason could he have for being late?"

"'Better three hours too soon than a minute too late,'" Mary quoted.

Caroline shot Mary a look of deep disgust. "*Must* we endure yet another reading from the gospel according to Mary Bennet?"

There followed a long moment of silence in the room, during which Mary knew not where to look. Her cheeks flushed scarlet with embarrassment. She had done it again; in her quest to find something suitable to say, she had uttered the wrong thing, and had earned the scorn of those around her. It was her worst nightmare come true; and for a moment she toyed with the notion of fleeing, until Jane reached over to grasp her hand in a comforting grip.

"Pay her no mind, Mary," she said in a voice that was barely above a whisper; yet the hateful silence stretched on as Mary's discomfort increased.

Mr. Penrose left his chair to join Caroline at the window. For a while he was silent as they stood side by side, gazing upon the view of the parkland. Finally, he said, in a low voice, "I know I am an outsider here, Miss Bingley, but may I talk to you as a friend?"

"If you mean to *scold* me, Mr. Penrose, for speaking as I did to Mary Bennet, you may return to your tea."

"Scold you? Oh, no, that is not my intention at all. I was thinking instead that you are, without doubt, the very person to lead the people gathered here through this very troubling afternoon."

She turned her head to look up at him in surprise. "Lead them? What *can* you mean?"

"I mean that you appear to me to be a woman of good sense who can keep her emotions in check when necessary. I see by your expression you think me impertinent," he said, in a tone that conveyed the fact that he was not at all bothered by her opinion, "but in my profession I meet a great variety of people, and I've learned to sketch their characters reasonably well. Take Miss Mary Bennet, for example. Normally, I would recommend she leave the sermonizing to me, but I can see her heart is in the right place, even if her words are ill-chosen."

"And now, I suppose, you mean to give an account of *my* character?" Caroline said, as she turned her angry eyes once again upon the view.

"Why, yes, I do mean to do just so," he answered, amiably.

"Oh, *pray*, continue! The opinion of a country vicar is of the *utmost* importance to me." She said this in a tone of withering sarcasm, but Mr. Penrose's expression of mild unconcern did not alter.

"Very well. Let me begin by saying that, although our acquaintance is of short duration, I think I can safely conjecture that you are a woman of vast fortune—and not just in monetary wealth. You, Miss Bingley, have been favoured with an excellent education and an enviable station in life. Your intelligence, disposition, and charm of manner must be admired wherever you go—which makes me wonder what you gain by speaking in a manner calculated to send Mary Bennet into the depths of shame."

Caroline's head turned sharply to look up at him, but he said, before she could utter a word of protest, "Yes, I admit, she does tend to blurt out the greatest absurdities from time to time, but we both know she is shy by nature, and has not your facility for clever conversation. Does she not, then, deserve our patience and kindness, rather than our censure and scorn?"

She frowned at him, not quite believing what she had heard. She was far from impressed by Mr. Penrose; he was too young, for one thing, to be telling anyone else what to do, and he was too tall, for another. His features were far from handsome—although he did have a kind expression in his hazel eyes—and his manner was impertinent. No one had ever spoken to her in such a fashion, and she was decidedly certain she did not care for it one bit. To be scolded . . . by a *vicar!* It was too much to be borne!

She said, witheringly, "*I* am not responsible for propping up Mary Bennet's ego."

"I agree with you. But I do think you are responsible for

helping your family—the people I am convinced you love very much—through a difficult time of waiting for news of Captain Bingley's safety. Won't that task be accomplished more readily by keeping everyone's emotions on an even level? Take Mrs. Bingley, for example. Don't you think her worry for the captain is now compounded all the more because she knows her sister Mary is distressed?"

That suggestion surprised Caroline very much. On impulse she turned and looked over her shoulder to see Jane doing her best to comfort Mary. In Jane's expression she saw concern and worry; and while she watched Jane murmur comforting words to Mary, she realized how distressed Jane must be to see her sister so perilously close to tears.

That was a circumstance she had not anticipated. She genuinely liked Jane, although she had, from the first moment of their meeting, been repulsed by the rest of Jane's family. She had never considered that her actions toward Mary might hurt Jane, too, and she was a little sorry for having spoken so harshly—not because Mary did not deserve censure for being so ridiculous, but because her hasty words had clearly upset Jane.

But even in this realization, Caroline's chin went up. "I suppose you will next demand that I apologize to Mary."

"No, for only you can determine how best to assuage your conscience. I am merely suggesting that you use your intelligence to manage everyone here a little bit better. You're the strong one in the family, and if *you* set the tone for calm hopefulness regarding Captain Bingley's safety, the rest will follow, I am convinced."

"Me? But doesn't the offering of hope and sympathy fall

under *your* realm, Mr. Penrose?"

"They do, indeed, but the sun is setting, Miss Bingley, and I must return to Meryton and prepare the church for evening service. But I think I can make my good-byes to everyone with a clear conscience if I am certain I can rely on your kindness and strength to help them through the remainder of the day—whatever the day may bring. Please tell me I have not misread your character."

Caroline trained her gaze upon the view from the window. A breeze had begun to blow outside, and every now and then a strong gust made claim to the fallen leaves and sent them skipping across the lawn or twirling and dancing in mid-air. She felt very much like those leaves, for after Mr. Penrose's words, she knew not what to think. He'd confused her greatly. Some of the words he'd spoken had *sounded* flattering, but he'd delivered them in a tone that was more impertinent than deferential. He had praised her good judgment, yet made her feel contrite for following her instincts. What a contrary man he was!

She lifted her chin. "You may rely on me, most certainly."

"Thank you. You are very good, Miss Bingley. May I escort you back to your chair?"

"No, thank you, Mr. Penrose. I believe I will remain here a moment longer."

"Then I will bid you good-day, Miss Bingley; and I will trust you to deliver everyone to Christmas service in the morning." He sketched a very civil bow and returned to his chair beside Jane.

She passed the vicar a fresh cup of strong tea, liberally sweetened and with a bit of milk, just as he liked it, and asked, "Will Miss Bingley join us?"

"I think not. She is on the watch for her brother and engaging in a little bit of self-reflection."

"I hope you were not very severe with her."

"Not at all. Still, I think you will find her in a more genial mood when next she speaks." He took a sip of his tea, and gave a sigh of great satisfaction. "No one makes a cup of tea as well as you do, Mrs. Bingley. In fact, you have made me so welcome here, I am reluctant to leave—but, unfortunately, the time has come when I must." So saying he glanced up at the clock and rose from his chair. He turned toward Charles and said, "The sun has begun to set, and I must go. I regret I was unable to make your brother's acquaintance this afternoon as planned, Mr. Bingley, but perhaps I shall have the pleasure tomorrow? Christmas service in the morning, you know—I shall see you all there, of course."

"You shall, indeed," said Charles. "Here, let me walk with you to the door."

Charles went with the vicar to see him safely on his way, and Jane glanced over to where Caroline remained steadfastly at the window.

"Caroline, won't you join us?"

"No, I—" She stopped short, as she recalled the assurance she had given Mr. Penrose just a few minutes earlier. He was right; the family needed direction and a steady hand if they were to set aside their worries and remain hopeful of Robert's safe arrival—and she was the one to provide that leadership. There was no one else present who possessed such strength of character—on that point she was in solid agreement with the vicar. As much as she would have liked to remain at the window, hoping—nay, *willing*— for Robert to appear at the gate, safe and sound, she knew where her duty lay. Her duty lay in supporting Jane and amusing Helena and, yes, in being polite to the Miss Bennets, as much as that thought must jar her sensibilities. But such was her duty and she would not shirk it. She raised her chin a notch and slowly walked back to her chair beside the tea tray.

"Yes, dear Jane," she said in a gentle tone, "I will join you. And I will take another cup of your excellent tea."

4

At first Captain Robert Bingley thought himself very
fortunate to have come upon an inn just as the evening
temperature was beginning to fall; but as he pulled his horse
up in the yard of the Bark and Bull, he found himself
wondering which would be the worse fate: to ride on in the
cold night—even though he knew himself to be hopelessly
lost—or spend the night in such an unattractive and dismal-
looking place as the Bark and Bull.

A sudden gust of cold wind blew through the yard. His
horse, Ibis, reacted with a small movement of her feet and a
slight flick of her tail, yet her movements told Robert all he
needed to know. His horse was tired, and so was Robert.
He'd been riding for hours, anxious to reach Netherfield and
spend Christmas Eve with his family and Helena. But Fate
had not treated him kindly that day. Last minute regimental
duties had caused him to start his journey much later than
planned; then, in his haste to make up for lost time, he had
taken a wrong turn somewhere on the road, and his instincts
had deserted him when he tried to right his course. Now he
was in the middle of heaven-knew-where with darkness
falling and the cold December temperature beginning to

drop.

He looked over the ramshackle inn with distaste. It would be a simple matter to merely ask for directions and continue on until he found a more comfortable looking inn; but then he thought of Ibis. Ibis had carried him through two campaigns and eight battles, never once shying from danger, always finding the strength to push on when other officers' mounts were too exhausted to carry their riders another step. He owed his life to Ibis, and if she wanted rest, he would gladly give it to her.

He patted her neck with his gloved hand, and Ibis exhaled a deep, fluttering breath through her nostrils.

"All right," he said, "we'll stay here. You deserve a good dinner and a night's rest in a warm stable."

He tossed the reins to a waiting ostler and slid down from the saddle.

"See that she gets a good brushing and a hearty dinner, will you?' he said as he strode toward the door of the inn.

He entered the public room to find it empty except for a boy who was busy stoking the fire in the great hearth. Robert couldn't tell how old he was, but the boy's age mattered not. He was simply one of those urchins that often hung about such places, ready to hold a horse or carry a valise for a penny.

Robert drew off his gloves, though the room seemed only a trifle warmer than the fast-darkening December night, and deposited them on the table, all the while watching the boy.

"If you throw some of those smaller pieces on the fire, it will burn bright more quickly," he said, in a pleasant tone.

The boy almost jumped. He looked up, his eyes wide and

startled, and he stared at Robert a moment; then he carefully set aside the heavy log he had been about to add to the fire and selected a smaller piece of wood instead. With great care he tucked some twigs around the fresh log and watched the meager fire flare up in a bright spurt of light and heat.

Robert smiled slightly as he swept his hat from his head. Out of the corner of his eye he saw the boy was still crouched close to the fire, warming himself. He didn't mind; he could tell the boy's clothes were too ragged to provide much warmth, so if the lad wanted to huddle beside the heat of the fire for a few minutes, he'd make no objection.

He was placing his hat on the table beside his gloves, when the muffled sound of "Ooomph!" caused him to turn about.

He took in the situation in a flash. A man was standing over the boy in a menacing pose, having obviously just kicked the child away from the hearth.

"Haven't I told you not to let that fire go down? Well, *haven't* I?" the man demanded angrily. Then he turned toward Robert and bowed, his expression softening into an obsequious smile. "Welcome, me lord. Pay no mind to the stupid boy—he'll do better at keeping the fire burnin' for you, I'll see to that."

Robert instantly felt a lump of loathing rise in his throat. "Have you a room?" he asked, coldly.

"Of course, me lord. I've a fine room for you, me lord. Shall I take you up?"

"In a moment. I could use a hot drink, first. It's devilish cold outside, you know."

"I've got a nice hot punch for your lordship. I'll get it

44

meself."

When he was alone again with the urchin, Robert unbuttoned his greatcoat, revealing his riding attire underneath, and said, genially, "Between you and me, I'm not a lord, but I daresay it doesn't hurt to let *him* think so, eh?"

The boy was about to leave the room, but at this he turned about, his expression an odd mixture of fear and understanding.

Robert shrugged out of his coat and threw it over the back of a nearby chair. "Well, you've done a fine job of coaxing some life into the fire. I feel warmer already." It was only a slight exaggeration, but he moved closer to the hearth and made a great show of holding his hands out toward the dancing flames. "I hope that 'fine room' the landlord has allotted me has a good fire in it. You'll see to it for me, won't you?"

The boy kept his eyes trained on the floor, and answered in a low voice, "Yes, sir." Then he darted from the room.

The hot punch the innkeeper served him a few minutes later had no resemblance whatsoever to any punch Robert had ever tasted before. He suspected its chief ingredients were rum and some other alcohol the innkeeper brewed in a tub behind the stables; and he could detect no hint of Madeira or citrus in the few sips he took. But it was hot, and before long he began to feel the warming effects of the drink.

By the time the landlord served Robert his dinner he was in a more charitable mood. He was also hungry, and he was certain he could do justice to any meal the landlord might place before him. He sat down at the wooden table close to the window and removed the covers from the dishes. There was a bowl of some kind of soup with a layer of grease on top, bread with a hard crust spread with an oily substance that was probably meant to pass for butter, a half of a chicken, warm applesauce, and a pudding that had not set properly. Robert blanched as he surveyed the unappetizing dishes. He pushed every dish away except the plate of chicken and the bowl of applesauce.

He took a small, wary bite of the chicken and looked idly out the window. The boy he had seen before was outside, walking across the yard, his breath leaving small wisps of frozen moisture in his wake. Robert frowned. The child was wearing no gloves or hat, no muffler about his throat to keep the cold away. He was wearing breeches and torn stockings and a jacket worn thin at the elbows from wear; and when he walked Robert could clearly see that the sole of one of the boy's shoes was loose, for it flapped with every step.

"He must be freezing out there," he murmured, as the boy disappeared around the corner of the stable. The boy reappeared a few minutes later with a load of wood in his arms. Robert watched him with interest; not because of what the boy was doing, but *how* he was doing it. He carried the armload of small logs as if his task were a great secret, is if he were smuggling gold bricks instead of fuel for a fire.

When the boy disappeared again from his line of sight, there was nothing outside the window to hold his attention, so Robert concentrated on choking down the rest of the dry chicken. Next he took up his spoon and the bowl of warm applesauce and moved over to a chair by the fire, where he soon placed the empty bowl on the stone hearth.

He had but one more task to perform for the night. He donned his coat, hat and gloves, and made his way out into the cold night. In the stable he found the ostler brushing Ibis, as he had requested, and doing a reasonable job of it. Next he inspected the feed trough and decided that Ibis had probably enjoyed a better dinner than he had. Ibis gave a soft nicker of recognition, and Robert went to her, resting his chin for a moment against Ibis' long nose.

"I know, girl," he murmured, "but it's just for one night. We'll be on our way early tomorrow, mark my words."

Robert returned to the inn, stopping downstairs just long enough to light a taper to carry up to his bedchamber. At the top of the narrow stairs he came upon a scene that was by now a little too familiar to him.

The boy who had tended the fire in the public room was on the floor, the landlord standing over him with his fists clenched. Even in the dim light afforded by his candle, Robert could see the boy's lip was bleeding.

"What is this?" he demanded in a tone that made the landlord's aggression evaporate.

He turned to Robert and said, in his toad-eating voice, "Why, nothin' to worry your lordship."

"On the contrary, it worries me a great deal whenever I see someone who has done me a service forced to the ground like a dog. I'll ask again: What is going on here?"

"Him? He's never done a service for nobody. Why, I just caught him stealing."

"Stealing what?"

"Firewood, me lord. I've got a strict allotment of wood I use for each chamber, see, for economy sake, and this boy

47

defied my rules and carried off more than allowed."

"Did he?" Robert stepped past the man and flung open the door to his bedchamber. Inside the fireplace blazed with a bright fire, and on the hearth was a neat stack of wood waiting to be added to the fire as needed through the night. "Is that the missing wood?"

"Oh. Well, he never said what he *done* with it. I only know he *took* it."

"For me. He took it for me," Robert said, wishing it were within his power to teach the repellant landlord a lesson he would never forget. "I asked the boy to see that I had a hearty fire in my room because when I was up here earlier I saw that someone had lit an insultingly pitiful fire that wouldn't burn a bandbox."

The landlord paled. "Well, now, how was I to know that was his purpose for stealing the wood?"

"Did you *ask* him?"

"Now, why should I, I'd like to know?" the landlord said, in a tone that was becoming churlish. "He's a thief and—"

During their exchange Robert had removed his gloves and unbuttoned his great coat. Now he reached into the pocket of his waistcoat and extracted the first coin his fingers touched. He tossed it to the landlord.

"Here! That should cover the cost of the extra firewood I requested."

"Thank you, me lord. Why, that's most generous of you. Most generous, I must say!"

Robert's lip began to curl and he fought against it. "I can be very generous when I wish to be. If you want me to grease your fist once more, you'll ensure I never see you again until

I leave in the morning and pay my reckoning. Do you understand?"

The landlord frowned. "But who will attend to your—?"

"Anyone but you."

"But who will serve your—?"

"Anyone but *you*," Robert said again, with emphasis. He could tell by the landlord's expression he was weighing his options: in the end, the lure of earning a healthy gratuity overcame any objections the landlord might have had to having his place usurped.

"Very well, me lord. The boy can look after your needs."

"Very ably, I am certain. Oh, and innkeeper," Robert said, halting the man's steps when he would have made a retreat. "If you strike or harm this child again in any manner, you will answer to me. Do you understand?"

The landlord looked startled, then his eyes narrowed slightly. "Here, now, I won't be threatened by nobody in me own house."

"You mistake; I didn't threaten you. I simply explained to you the consequences should you choose to act in a way that offends my sensibilities. I trust we understand each other. Good-night, innkeeper." The landlord's expression twisted into something dark, causing Robert to say, in a genial tone, "Tut-tut! Remember the gratuity I promised! Now, do be sensible and say good-night."

The reminder of another promised coin mollified the man a great deal. He bit back the harsh words that hovered on the tip of his tongue, and, without another word, he turned and stomped down the stairs.

Robert looked down at the boy, who hadn't moved an

inch since he had first come upon him. "Are you badly hurt? That lip will swell if you don't apply a cold compress right away." As soon as he said the words he realized how inane they were. This boy looked as though he had little comfort in his life, and he sincerely doubted that there was a kind person to whom the boy could turn to tend his injury. "Come, now, on your feet," he said, encouragingly. "Let me see your pluck!"

He stepped back to give the boy room, and was rewarded by the sight of the lad scrambling quickly to his feet. He would have scampered off had not Robert moved to block his path to the stair.

"Not so fast, young man. I want to be certain you heard what I said just now. I'll allow no one—neither father nor stranger—to strike you or any other child while I am in this house. Do you understand me?"

The boy kept silent and looked down at the floor.

"I think you do. I've seen enough of brutes and tyrants in this world, and I won't sanction one here—not while I am under this roof." He watched the boy thoughtfully for a moment, and said in a softer tone, "If that man lays a hand on you in anger, I want you to tell me. Will you do it?"

The boy stood perfectly still for a long moment, but after some consideration, he gave his head a slight nod.

"Very well. Off with you now. I am leaving at first light tomorrow and I need my sleep." He moved closer to the wall to allow the boy to rush past him with surprising speed; and Robert didn't see him again until the dawn broke on Christmas morning.

Robert was dressed and downstairs by the time the sun peaked over the horizon. He had slept well, despite a lumpy bed, and now he was eager to be on his way. His first thought when he awoke that Christmas morning was of Helena— lovely Helena—waiting for him at Netherfield. He imagined she was wondering what had become of him, for he had pledged to be with her no later than Christmas Eve, and the fact that he had been unable to keep that promise weighed heavily with him. He had much to tell her, much to explain. And much to ask.

In the public room he rang the bell. Within minutes the boy came in bearing a tray laden with dishes. He watched as the boy arranged the plates and bowls on the table near the window, and his sharp gaze took in the boy's appearance in a glance. He saw no fresh bruises or other signs of mistreatment. There was that cut on the boy's lip, which had healed somewhat overnight, though it still appeared a bit swollen. But it was when the boy lifted the covers from the dishes of toast and eggs and bacon, drew a deep breath, and actually trembled that Robert gave him a good, steady look.

Ye gods, is the boy hungry?

Robert sat down at the table in front of the food. "You must tell the landlord for me that he serves a good breakfast, but the truth is, I could never eat so much so early in the day. Here, be a decent sort and eat this bread for me, won't you?" He singled out a thick slab of bread with a hard crust, the very same variety that had been served to him the night before, and pushed it across the table.

The boy stared at it a moment, swallowed, and slowly shook his head.

"I must beg you to reconsider, young man. You'd be doing me the greatest of favors. You see, I can never eat all this, and I hate the notion that such good food will be simply thrown away, or worse, fed to the livestock. Be a good lad and help me! I'd do the same for you."

The boy inched forward and took the bread.

"Now, there is one more service you can do for me, if you are willing." He waited expectantly, then asked, "*Are* you willing?"

The boy nodded, his mouth full of bread.

"Very well. I'll confess to you that I made a wrong turn somewhere on my way from here to there. In other words, I'm hopelessly lost. Are you familiar with the roads? Perhaps you can tell me where I went wrong. At the very least you can tell me if I'm in Hertfordshire. *Am* I?"

The boy nodded as he chewed his bread.

"Then I'm not doing as badly as I thought. Do you know a town called Meryton?"

Another nod from the boy.

"Even better. I'm on my way to my brother's for Christmas, and I thought I knew the way. My brother is the master of Netherfield Park, near Meryton. Do you know it?"

The boy nodded again.

"How far out of my way did I go, do you think?"

The boy muttered something unintelligible owing to the quantity of bread in his mouth.

"I beg your pardon, young man. I didn't understand you."

The boy swallowed and said in a voice loud enough to be

heard, "Netherfield is but six miles or so, sir."

"Is it? Then I didn't make too great a muddle of it after all. Can I rely on you to set me on the right road this morning?"

"Yes, sir."

"Thank you, um—Here now, I can't keep talking to you this way without knowing what I am to call you."

"Daniel." At last he dared look Robert in the eye for the briefest of moments. "My name is Daniel, sir."

"I'm Captain Bingley. Very well, Daniel, I'll trust you to get me off in the right direction this Christmas morning. I'm anxious to see my brother and sister. They're hosting a small house party, and there is one guest in particular—her name is Helena and—" He stopped short, realizing that he had been prating on unnecessarily. "Well, suffice it to say I shall be happy to get to Netherfield. Christmas with family, that's what's important to me." He was feeling in high spirits and was talking a good deal more than he would have if his mood hadn't been so festive and his anticipation of seeing his beloved Helena weren't so keen. "What about you?" he asked. "Will you have Christmas with your mother and father?"

"Yes, sir. When I get to heaven."

Startled, Robert's eyes flew to his face. "Oh!" was all he could manage to say. Then his expression softened and his blue eyes searched the boy's features. "Are you telling me the landlord is not your father?"

Daniel shook his head.

"Then, how did you ever come to live—? Never mind. So your mother and father are gone, are they? I'm sorry for you, truly I am." He pushed the plate of inexpertly cured bacon across the table so it would be within the boy's reach. "Here, you can eat this, too. Share it with the ostler if you like."

Daniel hesitated only a moment before he grabbed the plate and ran from the room. Seconds later, Robert looked out the window to see Daniel run across the yard with the treasure, the sole of one shoe flapping crazily with each step, before he disappeared inside the stable.

Though he was hungry, Robert abandoned the rest of the unappetizing meal. A half hour later he was ready to leave. He paid his reckoning with the landlord, along with the promised gratuity, and stepped out into the cold but bright sunshine. The ostler led Ibis over to the mounting block and Robert took the reins.

"Whoa!" he said, as Ibis danced and curveted as soon as he made a move to slip his booted foot into the stirrup. "None of your nonsense this morning, you imp. Stand still, can't you, until I'm mounted?"

The horse answered with two mincing steps sideways, causing Robert to take two inelegant one-legged hops of his own before he could get both of his feet firmly back on the ground.

In an instant, Daniel was there at the horse's head, catching the bridle up with a firm grip.

"Thank you, Daniel," Robert said, swinging himself up into the saddle. "Now, tell me, which way?"

The boy pointed toward the north. "That way, sir, until you reach the dog's leg and stay to your right. Right again and you'll be on the road that will take you straight to Meryton. Netherfield Park is just beyond."

Robert smiled at him, and leaned down to shake hands. Daniel reached up, and, to his astonishment, came away with a half crown in his hand.

"Don't show that to a soul," Robert whispered so the ostler wouldn't hear. "Hide it, and at your first opportunity, buy yourself a pair of shoes and a good coat. Oh, and a hot meal. Be sure you get a hot meal. Will you do that for me?"

Daniel looked up at him, his brown eyes wide and suspiciously moist. "I'd do anything for you, sir."

Robert straightened and waved him away from the horse's head. "Keep a brave heart and do your father proud, even though he's no longer here. A happy Christmas to you, Daniel!"

Then he turned Ibis about and galloped out of the yard, north toward Netherfield and Helena Paget.

Daniel's directions proved as true for Robert as the North Star. In little more than an hour he reached Meryton, which appeared to be a charming place, but he was of no mind to linger there. He pressed on, and soon had his first glimpse of Netherfield. How much more welcoming was the large, stately house than was that tumble-down inn where he had been forced to spend the night; and inside that house was his family and dear, sweet Helena. With this thought he urged Ibis to quicken her pace, and soon he was mounting the front steps of the house. The great doors opened magically at his approach, and he entered the bright, warm hall to find a footman ready to relieve him of his coat and hat.

It was early; the family was still abed, and Robert petitioned the footman to say nothing of his arrival.

"I am in no looks to meet my brother or his guests," he

said. "Give me the opportunity to make myself presentable before you announce me, please."

The footman showed Robert to a large comfortable bedchamber, where he was relieved to see his luggage had arrived before him. He called for a bath, hoping to scrub off all reminders of the dirty little inn, with its greasy dishes and unkempt rooms. A mere thirty minutes later he was immaculately groomed, fashionably dressed, and ready to do justice to a hearty breakfast.

From his previous stays at the Bingley's London townhouse, he knew his sister-in-law's breakfast table would be filled with all good things. He could practically smell the savory aroma of well-seasoned eggs, sweet-cured ham, jellies, creams, and breads as he made his way down the stairs.

A footman directed him to the family dining-room. He threw open the door and entered, then came up short. He had anticipated an empty dining-room at that hour of the morning; instead, he found himself looking into the surprised expression of a dowdily-dressed young woman, who was already seated at the table.

5

The last thing Mary Bennett expected on Christmas morning was a handsome man bursting upon her as she enjoyed her breakfast in the family dining-room. Certainly Kitty would have deemed his sudden appearance a Yule gift of the very best kind, but Mary's first reaction was startled silence.

Breakfast was the one daily occasion when Mary could enjoy a meal in peace and quiet, with a good book arranged to her liking on the table beside her plate, and no requirement to engage in small-talk with family or acquaint-ances. From experience she knew the Bingleys kept town hours and rarely presented themselves until well after nine o'clock; and since the only other person who was expected in the house was sure to be attired in military regalia, she could not work out in her mind why her morning custom should be breached by a handsome stranger.

And handsome he was. He was tall with an athlete's figure. His light brown hair was attractively arranged a lá Brutus, and his blue eyes were bright and friendly, once he overcame his initial surprise at finding Mary seated at the table before him. But more than his physical niceties, Mary recognized in the man the distinct air of a finished gentleman; a man with confidence and bearing; a man who might cause others to unconsciously step a little to one side to let him pass.

He stopped short, examined her quickly with a flick of his blue eyes, and said, genially, "I beg your pardon! I had not thought there was anyone awake in the house at this hour. I have come for my breakfast, too, you see."

Mary slowly closed the cover of her book as she came to the awful conclusion that, if the man intended to stay, she would have to make some sort of conversation with him. She felt the muscles in her body stiffen at the thought.

He came closer and said, "Under the circumstances, I think we must forego the usual etiquette. Shall I introduce myself? Or shall you? I'm a little unsure of the proprieties!"

Mary slowly rose to her feet and executed a simple curtsey. "I am Miss Mary Bennet."

Another look of surprise crossed his face, but it was gone as quickly as it came. "Miss Bennet, I have looked forward to our meeting with great anticipation. Your sister Jane is very dear to me, and I am anxious to call you sister, as well."

"Oh!" she said, feeling suddenly stupid. "Then you are—? Are you—?"

"Captain Robert Bingley, at your service, ma'am. No, don't apologize," he said, after watching the color quickly rise in her face, "for you couldn't have known. Did you expect me to be in uniform?"

"Yes, I did, and so did Kitty. She will be vastly disappointed." This blurted confidence made his eyebrows go up a little.

"Poor Kitty! But I'm on leave, you see, and plan to dress the role of a country gentleman for the next two weeks. I hope, under the circumstances, Kitty—Can that truly be her name?—will be generous and forgive me."

"Kitty is my sister. She is named Catherine, but we call her Kitty." Her hand fluttered nervously near the base of her throat before it fell to rest on the cover of the book she had been reading. Thoroughly bemused, she sank awkwardly back down onto her chair.

"May I join you?" he asked.

She nodded, but she had the feeling he would have served himself from the dishes arranged on the sideboard whether she gave her permission or not.

He claimed a chair directly opposite her at the table. "Shall I assume you and I are the only members of the family who do not keep town hours?"

"Yes," Mary said, her eyes on her plate.

"It is impossible for me to lie abed that late, I fear; my military training forces my eyes open by dawn each morning." He looked at her, awaiting a reply, but on hearing none, said, pleasantly, "I doubt, however, the same can be said of you, Miss Bennet. You, I feel sure, have no military training. May I assume, then, you are an early riser by nature?"

"Yes," she said again, as her fingers surreptitiously dragged her book from the table and hid it beneath the tablecloth on her lap. She saw that he was looking at her expectantly. Clearly he expected more of an answer from her, so she offered up the first thought that came to mind. "I like mornings. Quiet mornings. Before the busy currents of the day intrude."

"Then we have something in common, which is always a good way to begin."

Mary sat quietly at the table, listening to his easy talk and watching the play of expression on his handsome face. Any other woman, she told herself, would respond to his well-meaning words with equally well-meaning conversation; yet Mary could not think of a word to say on her own. The most she could achieve were terse answers to his questions.

Simple conversation had always been her torment; shyness made her agonize over every word spoken to strangers; but on this morning she felt an added pressure, for she could not recall a time when she had ever found herself conversing with a man as handsome as Captain Bingley. Handsome gentlemen typically ignored her, but this one seemed to be making a push to be very agreeable to her, indeed. That was a novelty; but instead of feeling flattered by his attention, Mary felt her body tense, and she was faced with the same old dilemma: should she remain quiet, say nothing and *look* like a fool? Or say the wrong thing and *confirm* she was a fool?

She decided to take a gamble. "I like to read in the morning." Despite her efforts to sound conversational, her voice sounded tight and uncomfortable, even to her own ears.

"An excellent occupation, and one in which I often indulge, myself. Tell me, what do you like to read?"

Oh, dear, thought Mary, as her fingertips brushed across the cover of the book resting on her lap. Should she confess that she had been reading Reverend Fordyce's *Sermon's for*

Young Women only moments before? Her sisters had often remonstrated that her choice of reading material was dull and uninspired, and she didn't wish to create such an impression with the handsome captain.

"I read a great *variety* of books," she said. It was really only a slight stretch of the truth; but she was saved from having to expand on her reply when the door opened. Charles Bingley entered in a rush, his blue eyes anxiously searching the room, overlooking Mary's presence.

"Brother!" he exclaimed; and he barely gave Captain Bingley a chance to rise to his feet before he clasped him in a tight, brotherly embrace. "You cannot know how relieved I am to see you! Why, when you didn't appear yesterday—! Mary, tell him how worried we were!"

She was given no chance to tell him anything of the kind as both brothers began to speak at once—Charles with questions and exclamations of relief; Robert with answers and laughing admonishments that his older brother worried too much over his welfare.

"How can I not worry? Mary, do you know this brother of mine has an adventurous streak? Why, just a few months ago he was in Egypt, where he was made to fight in one skirmish after another. The letters he wrote me with tales of the fighting alongside those unruly Mamelukes were enough to curl my straight hair, I can tell you."

"I see I shall have to edit my letters more carefully in future," Robert said, teasingly.

"It's just like you to rush headlong from one scrape to another; and when your luggage arrived yesterday and you did not—Well! I imagined you were waylaid by the most ridiculous of reasons. We *all* did."

Robert laughed as he looked at Mary. "What reasons did you imagine?"

"Footpads and pirates," Mary said, flushing slightly. "It was only a bit of nonsense. Pay us no mind!"

He laughed again. "Your imagination is much more interesting than the truth."

"Then what *did* happen to you?" Charles demanded. "Why did you not arrive yesterday as planned?"

"I simply got lost. There, you have it! I found my way to Egypt and back without incident, but I couldn't navigate my way from the barracks to Hertfordshire. I ended up spending the night in a wretched posting inn that I hope I shall never have reason to see again." He resumed his seat at the table, intending to do justice to the food that remained on his breakfast plate. "Tell me, Miss Bennet, aside from the footpads and pirates, were there any other interesting theories offered to explain my absence yesterday?"

"No," she said with a little shake of her head and a shy little smile; and this time, she didn't blush when she answered him. When he'd first entered the room she had been startled and uncertain, as overwhelmed by his personality as she was by his handsome features; but now, seeing him beside Charles, who was the dearest and best of brothers to her, she saw that Robert Bingley was very like his older brother. They shared the same firm jaw, the same aquiline nose. Robert's blue eyes, like Charles', were lit with the same amiable candor that invited confidences and friendships.

This quick assessment flashed through Mary's mind as

she watched the brothers' easy camaraderie; soon she was smiling at their banter, and feeling that it just might be possible to be as comfortable in Robert's presence as she was in Charles'.

"I hope I won't disappoint you," Robert said, "by confessing I have never had a skirmish with a footpad before. Is it too much to hope that I came out the victor in that imaginary encounter?"

"Oh, yes," Mary said, promptly. "Caroline assured us you could thrash a dozen footpads at once without suffering a scratch."

"That's Caroline for you," he said, approvingly. "Sisterly devotion, through and through."

"She said you were brave enough to fight—" Mary's words halted as the door opened. Helena Paget entered the room, and the remainder of Mary's words were abandoned, for it was clear to her that no one—especially Captain Bingley—was listening any longer.

He looked around, and instantly leapt to his feet, his fork clattering onto his abandoned plate. In an instant his eyes took in Helena's appearance, from her shining head of golden curls to her daintily shod feet. She was dressed most becomingly in a pale blue gown that set off the color of her eyes; and in her hair was threaded a ribbon of soft pink that delicately highlighted the purity of her porcelain complexion.

He drew a breath that was audible even to Mary, and he stepped forward, saying, in a soft, ardent voice, "Miss Paget! I am delighted to see you again."

Helena curtsied, then impulsively extended her hand to him. "Will you forgive me if I say how relieved I am—How relieved we *all* are—to see you safely arrived?"

Robert's eyes never left her face as he took her hand and bowed low over her delicate little fingers.

Charles, observing the interplay with brotherly satisfaction, said, "He has assured us, Miss Paget, that his delay was by accident, not design, and certainly not the work of footpads. Here, Miss Paget, do take this chair. What may I serve you?"

"Oh, nothing," she said, as she gracefully alighted on the chair beside Robert's. "I had a bit of toast and coffee in my bedchamber and I simply could not eat another morsel."

This innocent-sounding speech caused Mary to recall the hearty breakfast she had just finished consuming. She knew herself to be nothing like the beautiful Helena Paget, but she had not realized *how* different until she saw Captain Bingley's reaction to Helena's unexpected appearance. She believed it must be plain to the most casual observer that he was a man in love, and Helena was a woman who invited his attentions; but in Mary's mind, it was more than that. To Mary, the captain's attraction to Helena was almost palpable; it seemed to fill the room, to the exclusion of everything and everyone else.

The door opened once again, and this time Jane, Caroline, and Kitty entered, all talking together as they exclaimed over Robert's long-looked-for presence, questioned his delay, and marveled over his appearance of good health.

He greeted each of them, and when Jane introduced Kitty, he said, affably, "I hope you are not too disappointed in me, Miss Kitty?"

"A little," she answered pertly. "I was hoping you would

be wearing your uniform when we met."

"So I was told. What a very disobliging man you must think me, but I brought only my dress uniform, you see."

"Oh, then you will certainly wear that to the ball."

Robert looked over at Jane, a question in his eyes. "The ball?"

"Our first ball at Netherfield since our marriage," Jane answered, with glowing happiness. "We thought it would be a pleasant way to welcome the new year with our friends and neighbours."

"We mean to make it an annual event," Charles added.

Caroline waved her hand dismissively. "Oh, the Bennets hold with many traditions, I have learned, and Charles is willing to fall into step with them. You will be interested to know, Robert, they give their servants a half-holiday on the morrow."

"Do they? That is generosity, indeed."

"I hope you will remember that sentiment," Caroline said, ominously, "when you sit down tomorrow evening to a cold supper."

"Surely Robert has suffered greater hardships than a cold supper," Jane said, scoffing. Then she had a sudden thought and looked at him anxiously. "You do not dislike aspic, I hope?"

"Dining *a la Greque*, are we? It sounds delightful," he answered.

By this time they were all seated at the table, and Caroline was able to give her older brother a frank, measuring look. "I must say, you do not seem the worse for having kept us waiting on pins and needles for your arrival."

"You must forgive me, Caroline, for I alone am to blame for losing my way. Once I left London proper and found myself in the gently-rolling hills of Hertfordshire, I took a wrong turn. The mischief was that I wouldn't acknowledge my mistake until it was too late. I ended up staying the night at an inn that was far from welcoming. I can't begin to describe the wretched dinner and breakfast I was served. The only bright spot in the entire ordeal was the boy I met there."

"Boy? What boy?" asked Kitty.

"Daniel. He worked at the inn, and I don't think I ever had anyone try to please me more. He was very young, yet he seemed to know a great deal about the area. He was certainly smart enough to give me fair directions, or I might still be wandering the countryside around Meryton."

"You attach too much importance to the circumstance, I am certain," Caroline said. "Everyone knows the boys who hang about posting inns are too dull and stupid to do anything else."

Without thinking, Mary said, solemnly, "Young minds ought to be encouraged. In every young mind there is something good."

It was a passage from Reverend Fordyce's *Sermons for Young Women* that she had been reading but a few minutes before, and she thought the sentiment timely; but she instantly realized that no one else agreed with her assessment. Everyone in the room regarded her with either confusion or censure, and she knew that, yet again, she had uttered something inappropriate.

"Robert," said Caroline, breaking the silence, "I beg you to forget all about the wretched place you spent the night.

You are at Netherfield now, and I am certain you will enjoy it immensely, although there is little society to speak of."

"That's not true," Kitty said, defensively. "We have many friends in the neighbourhood, and I am certain they will call upon you, Captain Bingley, once they have seen you at church."

His brows went up in surprise. "Are we going to church? On Christmas morning?"

"We are pledged to attend. Miss Bingley promised the vicar."

"Did she? That was handsome of you, Caroline."

"I cannot take credit where there is none," Caroline replied. "The truth of the matter is that I promised the vicar—Oh, what *is* his name?"

"Mr. Penrose," Kitty said helpfully.

"He and I made a pact: he promised to pray for your safe arrival at Netherfield, and I promised to deliver us to church this morning to hear him preach something. I can only suppose he held up his end of the bargain, for here you are; so I must uphold mine."

Robert laughed and gave her a quizzing look. "Dear Caroline! I think you would make a pact with the devil if it meant you could keep your family safe and sound. Very well! I shall happily help you meet your obligation and attend services with you this morning. What time shall I be ready?"

It was soon decided among them the time of departure; and, having partaken of her breakfast, Mary sensed an opportunity to beg to be excused. She was burningly aware that she had already annoyed Caroline with one ill-judged comment, and she had no intention of annoying Caroline—or anyone else, for that matter—again that day if she could help it. It was her object to pass a peaceful Christmas, and to that end she was determined to say as little as possible.

She clutched her book and left the room, intending to retreat to her bedchamber until it was time to leave for the church; but as she crossed the hall to the staircase, she heard Kitty call her name.

"Oh, Mary! Are you going upstairs? Wait, and I'll go with you. That dining-room is frightfully cold this morning, and I must have a shawl." She fell into step beside Mary and asked, "What do you think of Captain Bingley? He is very handsome, is he not?"

"He is, indeed."

"I like the look of him, though I am disappointed he does not wear his regimentals."

"He said he will wear his dress uniform at the ball."

"But what will he wear until then, that's what I want to know. Did you see his smile? It is vastly charming, and I think I saw the merest hint of a dimple when he smiled just now. Did you see it, too?"

"No, I did not."

"His manners are very nice. Why is he in the military, I wonder? What do *you* think, Mary?"

"I think he is very engaging. I am certain he will make Miss Paget very happy."

"*What?*" exclaimed Kitty, rounding on her in surprise. "Do not tell me—! Is Captain Bingley *engaged* to Miss Paget? I won't believe it! Mary, I beg you not to jump to conclusions again. You have heard no announcement of an engagement, I am certain."

"No, I have not—not yet, at least; but I think it is plain they are very much in love."

"Are they? Oh, I cannot credit it! Mary, how could you possibly know such a thing?"

"It is hard to explain." In truth, however, she had gauged the state of Robert's heart when Helena first entered the room and Robert, in one mortifying instant, had forgotten Mary's very existence. Thereafter, it had been plain to Mary that, though he spoke ably with Caroline or Jane or Charles, Robert's gaze never strayed for long from Helena's lovely face.

"But that isn't fair," Kitty said, in deep disappointment. "No one said a word about his having an attachment before this."

"I'm afraid there is no planning affairs of the heart," Mary said, reasonably. "I would not be surprised if Captain Bingley proposes marriage to Miss Paget before his visit here is through."

Kitty was vastly disappointed, and made no effort to hide her feelings when she followed Mary into her bedchamber, forgetting all about her shawl and the breakfast awaiting her downstairs. "It seems very unjust that Captain Bingley should be practically engaged to Miss Paget before we even got a chance to meet him."

"Did you think he was obliged to meet the Bennet sisters before he fell in love?"

"No, but he is the first handsome young man to make our acquaintance in some time. I vow, Mary, that it is very trying to never meet anyone new. No interesting families ever come into the neighbourhood, and I am never allowed to travel outside it. I could not be more vexed!"

"Perhaps Captain Bingley will introduce you to some of his officer friends."

"I have little hope of that, when he is not even obliging enough to wear his uniform. I swear, Mary, my visit to Netherfield is turning out to be nothing as I imagined, for it is five times more boring here than it was at home."

"You must learn to look on the bright side of things, Kitty. Only think: later today we will gather in the drawing-room to celebrate Christmas; and tomorrow we will be back at Longbourn to make a merry Boxing Day for all the labourers and tradesmen and servants. You'll enjoy that—you always do."

"Yes, I dare say I will, but now that you have told me Captain Bingley's heart is engaged—! Mary, I refuse to believe it—not until I see proof of it myself."

6

Robert was in the great hall alone, standing in front of the large fireplace, which was burning brightly. Over the mantle hung a large tapestry, and he was examining the details of the woven figures as he waited for the rest of the party to assemble before driving to the church. He had already donned his greatcoat, and he carried his gloves and hat in his hands.

A slight sound from behind caught his attention; he turned in time to see Helena Paget descend the last steps of the staircase. In an instant he took in every nuance of her appearance, and wondered if he would ever cease to be enchanted by the picture of beauty and grace she presented. She was dressed for the out-of-doors, having donned her bonnet and gloves upstairs; and her pelisse of dark blue velvet accentuated the blue of her eyes.

He went to her immediately and offered his arm. "Let me take you a little closer to the fire, Miss Paget. It is easy to become chilled in a large hall such as this."

She willingly allowed him to lead her toward the warm fire. "Is it very cold outside, I wonder? It is so hard to tell merely by looking out the window."

"It is, but I have already spoken to the grooms. They have supplied everything needed to make your drive to Meryton as warm and comfortable as possible."

She looked up at him questioningly. "Will you not ride in the carriage, as well?"

"There is not enough room. The ladies will have the carriage while I will ride with Charles. He has purchased a new curricle and pair, and is anxious to show me his driving skills."

"A curricle? Oh, you are very brave to ride in an open curricle on a December morning!"

"It is not so very cold as you imagine. Besides," he said, earnestly, as he took a step closer to her, "I am much more concerned that you are warm and comfortable during the drive. Only tell me what you require and I shall make it so."

She blushed charmingly but made no effort to move away. "I wonder what can be keeping the others?"

"Would you like them to appear? Only say the word and I shall bang the gong to summon them all . . . but I hope you won't."

"I shall say nothing of the kind, Captain," she answered, with a light in her eyes that captivated him, "for I do not wish you to send the entire household into an uproar. There will be time enough to spend with Jane, and Caroline and the Miss Bennets."

"How do you get on with them all? No need to tell me! They must love you by now."

"We go on very well together, I think. We sit in the drawing-room most evenings and talk and play cards. Sometimes Mary Bennet plays the pianoforte."

"Does she play well?"

"No, not at all, but I *tell* her she does."

He said, a little startled, "Indeed? Why would you do such a thing?"

"Do you think me wrong to do so? You see, I am trying to instill a bit of confidence in her."

"Confidence?" he repeated, mystified.

"She's very shy, you know."

"Yes, I noticed."

"And you will soon observe, if you have not already, that she often says unfortunate things."

He recalled Mary Bennet's utter lack of conversation at breakfast that morning in the dining-room. "She did appear a bit dull and unremarkable. Perhaps she is simply uncomfortable with strangers."

"Oh, her discomfort is not limited only to you. She is uncommonly shy, but I have pledged to be kind to her. It has become my habit to invite her to sit with me, and I do my best to engage her in conversation. I hope she will eventually perceive I am a friend, and I may draw her a little out of her shell; then perhaps she will learn from me and gain a bit of polish."

His expression changed rapidly from confusion to admiration. "You are very kind, Miss Paget! I knew you were possessed of a generous heart."

"It is nothing," she murmured, blushing prettily.

"It is more than others would do, I dare say. There are not many young ladies of my acquaintance who would go out of their way to champion Mary Bennet, and I admire your courage."

"My courage?"

"Why, yes. It takes considerable courage to take on such a challenge. If Mary Bennet is as timid as you say, I fear you have a formidable task before you, if you mean to bring her into fashion."

"Oh, I doubt I shall transform her, but I hope, at least, to help her out of her shyness. You see, I have such an appreciation of beauty that I cannot help but do my best to make little changes where I can. The question is, with so much in Miss Bennet that needs improvement, where shall I concentrate my first efforts?"

"May I make a suggestion? Begin with appearance. It is, after all, the first impression one makes on a new acquaintance."

"That is an excellent suggestion. Yes, I think I shall try to influence Mary Bennet to make one or two changes to her appearance. Do you know, when I first met her, I could hardly credit she was Mrs. Bingley's sister."

"And I, upon first making her acquaintance, thought she was a governess, or a companion of some sort. I couldn't have been more surprised when she introduced herself to me."

"You need say no more, Captain Bingley. I shall follow your guidance and make altering her appearance my first priority. It is, after all, important to me that the Miss Bennets and I are friends; for if they are dear to you, they must, of course, be dear to me."

Her words had a powerful affect on Robert; he hardly knew whether to revere her or take her into his arms and kiss her soundly. At the very least her words confirmed that her feelings for him were all he had hoped they would be; and he resolved to speak to her more plainly at the first opportunity.

He was prevented saying more when Charles and Jane descended the stairs and joined them in front of the fire. Soon the rest of the party was assembled and they were ready to drive to the church. With the utmost care Robert conveyed Helena to the carriage and handed her in; and his memory of the charming smile she bestowed upon him in return served to keep him warm during the entire drive to the church.

"She is the loveliest girl I ever beheld!" Robert said, as he climbed up into the phaeton beside his brother.

Charles couldn't help but laugh. "Those are the very same words I used to describe my Jane when I first met her."

"Then you know very well what I'm feeling. Helena Paget is everything I could want in a woman: she is charming and considerate, graceful and endearing. Only think how well she will fit in with the other officers' wives."

With a flick of the reins Charles set his horses in motion, and they proceeded down the drive with the carriage following close behind. "You surprise me," he said, as he focused his attention on guiding them safely through the gate and onto the road."

"In what way?"

"I had not thought Miss Paget would like the idea of life as an officer's wife."

"Why wouldn't she?"

"No reason that I know of. But she is a rather delicate-looking little thing. I never considered she would be willing to follow army encampments and live in tents—nor did I think her parents would allow it."

"She is not such a faint-heart as you imagine! You'll see, she will come to love army life as much I do."

"If she intends to leave her comfortable existence to gad about the world with you, then she must truly be in love with you, I think."

Robert favored him with a dazzling smile. "I cannot wait to make her mine. I have been entranced since I first looked into her lovely blue eyes."

"I first fell in love with my Jane's nose," Charles said, teasingly.

"And I admire her sweetness and intelligence. Do you know, she is determined to help people? Why, just this morning she told me of her efforts to help bring Mary Bennet a little out of her shell."

"Did she? That is curious, for I do not think Mary Bennet is in need of a champion. Mary is shy, to be sure, but I also know that she can be a very determined young woman, when she wants to be."

"Yes, yes, but my point is that Helena's heart is just as beautiful as her face and figure. With her by my side, how can I ever be anything but happy in this life?"

"You are beginning to sound like a poet."

"I hope I may soon sound like a husband."

"Then I wish you well, and once you tell me I may call Miss Paget my sister, I will wish you joy together."

And with this promise ringing in his ears, Robert once again resolved to ask Miss Paget to be his wife at his very earliest opportunity.

When the service was over, the Netherfield party stepped out of the church into a day of bright sunshine. They had been enjoying several weeks of inordinately mild weather, and Charles, who always preferred the out of doors, paused beside their waiting carriages. He looked down at the sun light shining off his wife's hair and said, "It is such a pleasant day, Jane; let us walk for a bit. What do you say?"

"An excellent notion," she said, readily. "I should be glad of some fresh air. Caroline, will you join us? Miss Paget?"

Caroline agreed, as did Kitty and Mary.

Miss Paget was the only member of the party to hesitate. "I do like to walk . . . within reason. Tell me, Captain Bingley, do you think it is safe?"

"Safe? In what way? Surely you do not fear footpads on the streets of Meryton?"

"Oh, no, I do not fear that," she said innocently, even as her blue eyes scanned the surface of the road.

"Then what troubles you?"

"I do not like puddles."

This made him smile. "I do not see any standing water on the road ahead, but I will remain on watch, and if we do come across a puddle, I promise to sound the alert. Will that satisfy you, Miss Paget."

"Oh, yes," she said, blushing prettily. "Thank you, Captain. You are very considerate."

With this plan in place, Charles and Jane set a leisurely pace for their guests to follow.

"Do they not look well together?" Caroline asked, as she walked beside Charles and Jane. She gave a quick look over her shoulder to where Robert and Helena had naturally fallen into step together. "I never saw a more handsome couple."

"I, for one," said Charles, "am happy he arrived at Netherfield safe and sound."

"And now he is here he may court Helena in earnest. I will counsel him to make fervent use of the time he has. He must concentrate on wooing Helena without veering off on one of his tangents."

"Caroline, I hope you do not mean to push them together. Let them plot their own course."

"Push them together? I have no intention of doing any such thing, for there is no need. You have seen how he looks at her; now tell me, does he not appear to be a man in love?"

"I agree there is a remarkable attraction between them," Jane said.

"Oh, there is more at work here than mere attraction! Naturally they will be married in London. In the spring, I think. The wedding, I assure you, will be everything it should be, for Lord and Lady Berkridge will insist on having only the *crème de society* in attendance." She lowered her voice and said, archly, "Have I mentioned that Helena's uncle Lord Berkridge is great friends with a certain *Royal* Duke? Just think of it! If a Royal Duke were to attend my brother's wedding, I may die happy."

Charles laughed. "My dear sister, what would we do without you to manage us all?"

Caroline chose to interpret his remark as a compliment,

and continued to spin her web of plans and schemes. Once or twice she glanced over her shoulder to satisfy herself that Robert and Helena were still engaged in conversation; and that Mary and Kitty, walking several steps behind them, did not try to interfere. Her only complaint was that Robert and Helena were conversing quietly in tones too soft for her to overhear.

Their conversation was not of a deep variety; Robert remarked that the day just might prove to be very warm for December. Miss Paget replied that she would be happy when Spring arrived.

"Why Spring? Are you a student of the Earth's annual rebirth?"

"No, but in winter I dislike drafts and cold; and in summer I dislike the heat."

"Then Spring must be for you a perfect time of year."

"It would be were it not for the rain. I detest the rain, for it makes a horrid mess of my skirt hems, and it has ruined more pairs of shoes than I care to admit."

"Ah!" he said with dawning recognition. "The puddles! Now I understand your concern, Miss Paget."

"You must think I am very silly."

He looked down at her with a gleam of appreciation in his eyes. "I think you are delightful."

She favored him with a shy smile; but in the next instant her smile disappeared, and she let out a small exclamation.

In a flash, Robert's hand was at her elbow to prevent her from falling, but her circumstance was not so dire. She did not fall, nor did she stumble or even lose her balance. Still, she stared down in dismay and said, in a plaintive little voice,

"Oh, it is too, *too* bad!"

"What has happened?" he asked, concerned that she might have sustained some unseen injury.

"My shoe!"

He was doing his best to understand her, but had to admit, "I do not see any harm. Has the heel broken?"

"No, but look there!" she said, pointing down at the tip of one shoe. "It is a smudge of dirt. Can you not see it?"

He had to look very hard to detect the merest evidence of damage. "Yes, I do see a bit of dirt, but surely your maid will be able to brush it out."

"I suppose so."

"For myself, I am thankful you did not turn your ankle or suffer some other injury. Shall we walk on?"

"I think not. You may consider it a trifling matter, Captain, but the thought of walking further with a ruined shoe has swept away all my enjoyment. Please," she implored, prettily, "will you escort me to the carriage?"

"Of course," he said, though he was hard pressed to understand her thinking. He held up his hand to signal the carriage, which until this point had been following them at a discreet distance, and he called out to his brother. "Charles! Miss Paget prefers to ride. I wonder, would any of you other ladies care to join her?"

They did not, but they were too polite to say so. Jane and Caroline murmured words of sympathy as they stepped into the carriage, while Kitty and Mary kept their silence.

Once the ladies were comfortably settled in the carriage, Charles and Robert boarded the curricle, and in short order, the entire party was on their way Netherfield.

Immediately after their return from church the Netherfield party gathered in the formal drawing-room to celebrate Christmas. In front of the Yule log that blazed bright in the hearth they wished each other good health and a happy Christmas. Their mood was festive, and after they had toasted the day with a cup of punch, Jane and Charles surprised them all by bestowing upon each of their guests a small gift by which to remember the day.

Mary immediately retreated to a quiet corner with a long-wished-for biography of John Locke—a gift from Charles—and Kitty declared that her new bonnet—a gift from Jane—far outshone that old thing Maria Lucas had bought in London the summer before.

Charles watched them all with an indulgent air, until his attention was caught by the sight of his brother standing silently by the hearth, looking down into the burning fire. He went to him, and said, "You are very quiet here, brother."

"Am I? I don't mean to be."

"You've been staring down into the flames for several minutes. Is something troubling you?"

"Not at all. I was just considering how fortunate we are to spend Christmas together in a comfortable home with people we love."

"Come, come! Be honest with me! You were looking a little too melancholy just now to be thinking such warm thoughts."

"Perhaps I was indulging in a bit of moralizing about the difference four-and-twenty hours can make."

"How so?"

"The difference is that yesterday at this time I watched a boy at the inn try to warm himself in front of a fire very like this one."

"That's the second time you've mentioned that boy to me. It seems very odd. What could have occurred to make your thoughts dwell so much on a stable boy?"

Robert shrugged his broad shoulders. "I cannot say anything extraordinary happened. Perhaps because I was the only guest at the inn I had plenty of opportunity to observe him. He was very ragged and I am certain he was cold and hungry, yet he bravely went out in the cold night air to gather wood to build up the fire in my room."

Helena was seated nearby, admiring the beautifully painted fan Jane had given her; but at this she looked up at Robert. "Brave? Captain Bingley, I think you may be guilty of attributing a virtue where there is none."

"How so, Miss Paget?"

"She means," said Caroline, "that if the urchin was tasked with getting wood for your fire, there is no more to be said. Why attach bravery to a deed that he was compelled to perform in the first place?"

"And besides," Helena said, in a voice as charming and sweet as a silver bell, "the boy did not feel the cold, I am certain of it. Boys like that are used to being in the elements."

Robert stared at her, a little stunned. "On the contrary, Miss Paget, it is my experience that people are very much the same. There is no difference between the skin of a wealthy boy and that of a poor boy; both are equally able to shiver in the cold winter air."

"Of course Miss Paget knows that," Charles said, quickly. "I'm certain the boy felt the cold, whether there was a coin in his pocket or not."

"He may not have had a coin when I arrived," Robert said, "but he certainly had one when I left. I made certain of it."

"Oh, Robert, you didn't!" said Caroline, scoldingly. "You know better than to give a boy like that a coin. What on earth will the boy do with *money?*"

"He can buy some clothes and shoes. And he can certainly buy a hot, nourishing meal, which, I am certain, he has not had in an age."

Helena's lovely blue eyes widened. "Goodness! How is so much to be bought with just a penny?"

"I did not give him a penny," Robert said. "I gave him half a crown." From the advantage of his height Robert could see everyone's reaction to this admission. They each looked back at him with an expression of surprise, with the exception of Miss Mary Bennet. In her face he saw a look of censure. It was nothing more than a quick, frowning flash, and then it was gone, as Mary dipped her head and focused her attention again on her book; but Robert saw it clearly, and he felt his resentment rise. He didn't like the fact that she would take his measure and find him wanting; and when he considered the fact that Mary Bennet must have a very hard heart indeed to begrudge a poor, hungry, and cold boy a bit of money that might relieve some of his suffering, he could feel his resentment rise further.

"Miss Bennet?" he said, with a challenge in his voice. "You do not agree? You think I should have given him *more* than half a crown?"

She looked up and answered slowly, "No. I think you gave him *too much* money."

"There!" said Caroline, triumphantly. "Miss Bennet is correct, and I could not agree with her more."

"Well, I *don't* agree," Robert retorted. "It seems very easy to pass judgment on a situation you know nothing about. If you had only seen the boy in his ragged clothes and shoes— shoes that were almost *falling* off his feet—!"

"You mistake me, Captain Bingley," Mary said, quickly, stemming his words. "My opinion—for what it is worth—is that you behaved very honorably toward the boy. If I am concerned, it is only because of the amount of money you gave him. You see, I cannot work out in my mind how he will be able to spend half a crown without calling attention to himself. Won't the landlord notice if the boy should suddenly appear wearing new clothes and shoes? Won't the landlord wonder where he came by them?"

Robert stood very still, looking at her, realizing, with astonishment, the sense of her words. In a rush he recalled the boy's bruises and swollen lip, all inflicted by the landlord. If the man was violent toward Daniel when he thought he had stolen a crust of bread or a bit of firewood, what was he capable of doing if he suspected Daniel of stealing clothes and shoes? Worse still, what would he do if he suspected Daniel of stealing half a crown?

He said, in a tight voice, "I apologize, Miss Bennet. You have made a very good point. I see now that, in my attempt to be helpful, I have probably made matters worse for him."

"I cannot see how," Helena said, reasonably. "A half-crown would be a fortune to such a boy."

"You don't understand." He took a seat very near hers and looked earnestly into her eyes. "I saw the landlord kick the boy, and another time I came upon him right after he had struck Daniel hard enough to send him to the floor."

"Perhaps the landlord felt he deserved to be punished for some misdeed," Helena suggested, artlessly.

"I think," said Jane, who had been silently watching the Captain's forehead furrow into a worried frown, "Robert fears the landlord will mistake the matter, and he'll punish the boy for stealing."

"Oh," Helena said, and she turned her attention back to studying the delicately painted figures on her new fan.

Robert looked up at his brother. "What do you think, Charles? Did I put the boy in danger?"

"That is a difficult thing to tell. I daresay the boy is fine. Nothing to worry about!"

"But how can I know for certain?"

Jane reached out to lay a comforting hand on Robert's sleeve. "You are very good to concern yourself over the boy's plight."

"That is not of the moment," Robert said. "What is important is what Miss Bennet said—that I might have added to the boy's troubles instead of alleviating them."

Caroline directed an accusing look at Mary. "*Now* see what you've done!"

Mary looked up from her book again, uncertain whether she should defend her words or apologize for them.

"It isn't her fault," Robert said. "She only pointed out the very thing I should have reasoned for myself." He soon fell into a mood of abstraction. Caroline tried her best to coax him into conversation, and though he answered her politely, his former brightness had been diminished, and it was clear his thoughts were still distracted by his memory of the boy at the inn.

Helena then asked shyly if he would like her to play the pianoforte, saying she had learned a charming song that had made her think of him the first time she heard it.

"Yes, I should like to hear it very much," he said, instantly; but he made no attempt to abandon his contemplative mood or his seat by the fireplace.

This was an unexpected turn for Miss Paget, for she was used to young men leaping at the chance to gallantly squire her to the instrument, and stand by in silent admiration as she plied her nimble fingers to the keys. In the end, it was Caroline who walked with her to the pianoforte and ensured she was comfortably seated on the music stool.

"I cannot think," Helena said, in a low voice that did not carry to the group of people by the fire, "what has come over Captain Bingley. What does he mean by sinking into a fit of the dismals over a stable boy?"

"I cannot explain it myself," Caroline murmured, "although it does seem to me that he was in fine spirits until Miss Mary Bennet opened her mouth. You will have learned by now, my dear Helena, that the Miss Bennets are forever blurting out one bit of nonsense after another. I must urge you once again to have little to do with them."

"You make an excellent point, but I do so want Captain Bingley to see that I am making a push to be cordial. They are, after all, practically his sisters."

"Sisters-in-*law* only," Caroline replied with emphasis. "When we are returned to London you will have no cause to think of them again. I assure you, *I* never do."

"I wonder if it would not be a good idea if you and I were to keep the Miss Bennets away from your brother as much as possible. That way they will have no opportunity to say things that upset him."

"Dear Helena, may I tell you how much it warms my heart to hear you say so? What a loving and comforting wife you will make. What a help you will be to my Robert."

Helena's porcelain cheeks bloomed with soft color, as she said, demurely, "You know, more than anyone, how hopeful I am in that regard. But I cannot think Captain Bingley will be brought to the mark and propose marriage to me if others are intent on distracting him."

"What you need, Helena, is time alone with my brother."

Miss Paget gave this recommendation some thought. "I suppose I could invite him to walk about the grounds with me, if the day is warm enough; but what if the day is cold? I do not like to be cold, dear Caroline."

"Nor should you be. A woman sufficiently chilled to have goose-flesh is a woman not fit to be seen."

"Then how am I to accomplish it?"

"I think I may have the answer. Tomorrow Charles and Jane and her sisters have planned to be away most of the morning. They go to Longbourn to deliver Boxing Day gifts—yet another of their ridiculous traditions. I had planned to remain behind to keep company with you and Robert, but I have a thought . . ."

"Yes, Caroline?" Helena prompted her.

"If I were to beg a place in the carriage, I am certain Jane and Charles will oblige me and allow me to accompany them. During our absence you will have Robert all to yourself, with no one to interrupt you in any way."

Helena clasped her hands together and said, her eyes shining, "Dare I? A morning alone with Captain Bingley?"

"It is a bold plan, to be sure."

"My mother would never approve. And if ever my aunt, Lady Berkridge, should hear of it—"

"But she will never know. How can she? I dare say Robert will never speak of it, nor will Jane and Charles; and the Miss Bennets will never be introduced to the Countess of Berkridge, you may be certain. Well, my dear Helena? What do you say to the scheme?"

"I must say . . . I must say, yes, of course! Oh, Caroline! You will do that for *me?*"

"At great personal sacrifice, yes, my friend, I will do that for you. Now, play. Let us see if you cannot soothe Robert's nerves a little with your music, and show Miss Mary Bennet how a pianoforte is *supposed* to sound."

7

After luncheon the ladies retired to their rooms to change clothes for the afternoon, and Robert found himself alone in the drawing-room with his brother. He challenged Charles to a game of chess, reminding him that they were once equally matched in their youth; and they were soon agreeably situated at the chess board.

They played in silence for several minutes; then Charles said, with an eye to his brother's reaction, "You are quiet again. Still thinking of that boy at the inn?"

"If I am quiet it is because I am trying to make sense of your strategy. I thought you were employing the French Defense, but then you moved your bishop to D7. What the devil do you mean by it?"

"I mean to throw you off your game, of course. But I don't think that's what is bothering you."

Robert scowled at him. "Are you going to talk or play?"

They lapsed into silence again, but when Charles captured his rook, Robert looked up in surprise.

"How did you manage that?"

"It's easy enough when only one of us is concentrating on the game. Admit it! You are thinking again of the boy."

"I am, and regretting that I ever gave him that half crown."

"You meant well."

"I meant to assuage my conscience by giving him a bit of money. I was so selfishly consumed with reaching Netherfield that I left that boy behind. I, who knew he was being mistreated! What if Mary Bennet is correct? What if that brute of a landlord should punish him because of my actions?"

"Of course you must be concerned, but I wonder ... is that *all* that is bothering you?"

"Certainly," Robert said stiffly, and he bent his attention once again upon the chess board. But after a rather long silence, during which time he made only one move, he said, in what he hoped was a casual tone, "Miss Paget seemed to have some very decided opinions on the matter."

"Yes, she did," said Charles, trying his best to sound equally uninterested.

"*Boys like that*, she said. I don't mind telling, you, I was never more astonished."

"Nor was I."

"Then what the devil did she mean by it, do you think?"

Charles gave the question some thought. "I have been trying to explain it myself, and the only thing I can offer is that she is very young and impressionable. Perhaps she was simply repeating something she once heard someone else say."

"I confess I do not understand it. Just this morning she spoke with such tenderness about befriending Mary Bennet; but after her comments about Daniel—I hardly recognized her as the same person. How is it possible for her to be so kind one moment and speak so cruelly about a poor stable boy the next?"

"I don't know," said Charles, who was watching him intently, "but having heard your concerns, I cannot help but wonder: are you quite certain Miss Paget is the woman you wish to marry?" He saw Robert's sudden frown and said quickly, "I do not know her well, I'll grant you, but it seems to me you have very little in common with her."

"I cannot agree with you there; since the moment I met her we have spent a great deal of time together and enjoyed each other's company immensely."

"Under the eye of her watchful mama! But here at Netherfield she has no one to manage her tongue or tell her what to say. She is free to utter any thought that comes to her mind; which reminds me—That shoe business this morning was very odd."

Robert thought so, too, but since he could neither explain nor defend Miss Paget's conduct in his own mind, he did not try to do so for his brother's benefit.

Charles, warming to his theme, said, "Here's what bothered me most about it: if a bit of dust on her shoe will upset Miss Paget to such a degree, how will she behave when she is faced with some true hardship? You know very well what her life will be like as an officer's wife. Why, had she been with you in Egypt she would have ruined a dozen shoes in a week, and she cannot cry and moan over them all."

Robert thought there was a good deal of truth in what his brother said, but he was given no opportunity to say so.

The door opened to admit Caroline and Helena. Both

ladies were in fine looks and were in the process of charming the men away from their game, when Jane joined them. She begged them to excuse her and her sisters for the afternoon while they attended to another matter.

Her request did not sit well with Caroline. "This is most extraordinary, Jane. What *are* you and your sisters doing that you cannot join us?"

"We are in the morning room, assembling Boxing Day gifts."

Helena looked up, for though she had but a vague understanding of Boxing Day, she had a keen and happy mastery of the word *gift* and was curious to learn more. "May I see?" she asked, prettily.

"Why, yes, of course!" Jane answered, pleased by her interest. "Come with me."

In the end, the entire party followed Jane to the little morning-room, which was pleasantly situated on the south side of the house. Tall windows ensured plenty of natural light, even on winter days, making it one of Jane's favorite rooms. It was here that she had made the most changes since becoming mistress of Netherfield; the chairs she selected were stylish, but more comfortably upholstered than those found in the more formal drawing-rooms; the writing desk was delicately sized to be suitable for a lady's use; and throughout the room she had added bits of comfort: favorite books, pots of trailing English ivies, and warm shawls that could be drawn across a lady's legs to protect against draughts or simply to nestle under on a chilly afternoon.

In the center of the room was a round table on which was spread a variety of items, among them, coins and children's toys, wines and crocks of chutney. At the table stood Kitty and Mary, busily sorting the objects.

Helena's eyes brightened at the sight. "My goodness, Mrs. Bingley, you have a great many things here. Whatever are they for?"

"They are our gifts for Boxing Day," Jane said. From Helena's expression she perceived that more was required. "Tomorrow is Boxing Day, a day when we give gifts to our servants and the tradesmen who wait upon us throughout the year."

"Goodness! How generous you are! I have never given a gift to a servant in my life."

"You can rectify that easily enough," Kitty said, "if you will help us."

"And you do this every year?" Helena asked, ignoring Kitty's comment.

"*Every* year," Kitty said, significantly. "It is a Bennet tradition."

Helena looked at her in wide-eyed wonder. "I cannot see the sense of it. Surely you do not hold to perpetuating this sort of thing year after year?"

"It is important," said Mary, stiffly, "for families to uphold traditions wherein the small sacrifices made by others are acknowledged and appreciated."

"Do you not *pay* your servants, Miss Bennet?" Helena asked.

Mary frowned. "Of course we do."

"Is that not sufficient? I cannot think it a good thing to bribe servants to perform the very duties for which they are already paid."

"But, Miss Paget," Jane said, gently, "these are not bribes, but gifts. As Mary said, they are simply our way of showing how much we appreciate the care and attention others give us throughout the year."

Helena watched as Mary placed several coins in a pouch, which she then deposited in a large wooden box along with a number of other items. "You give all that to a servant?"

"To the servant's family," Jane answered. "We do our best to assemble boxes or pouches that are particular for that servant or tradesman. Some receive boxes, while others receive a small gift, or simply a pouch of coins."

"And tomorrow," said Kitty, "we will go to Longbourn to distribute them all."

This last step in the process seemed to Helena to be an extraordinary measure that was most unnecessary. "It seems to me that if servants must have such gifts, they could at least come to fetch them and save you the trouble of driving to Longbourn. What do *you* think, Captain Bingley?"

Robert had been viewing the collection of toys on the table, and had just picked up a bilbo-catcher to examine more closely; but finding himself thus appealed to, he said, thoughtfully, "I think it is a fine thing. We Bingleys can be counted on to throw our coins in the alms box on a Sunday, like everyone else; but there our charity with the world ends. I rather like this Bennet tradition. Here, Miss Bennet, let me help you with that," he said, as Mary tried to pick up the large wooden box she had just finished weighing down with food and coins and toys.

He picked the box up easily and carried it across the room where he placed it on the floor at her direction. "What family will receive this?"

"Our cook's family."

"And the bilbo-catcher? That's a toy that will make some fine young boy very happy."

His words sounded casual enough, but Mary had been watching him, and saw his amiable expression fade as he looked over at the table where he had left the toy. She had a sudden thought that he was thinking once again about the boy at the inn and the ill-judge words she had spoken earlier in the day.

"I see you are still worried about the boy," she said, in a low but urgent voice, "all because of me! Please, will you forget what I said earlier today? I never meant to give you cause to worry needlessly."

His blue eyes met hers. His lips parted to answer her, but he was prevented speaking his mind when Caroline recalled his attention.

"Robert! Robert, come here; I have need of you."

Whatever he had been about to say to Mary was lost forever. He drew a steadying breath and turned toward his sister with a cordial expression. "How may I be of service, Caroline?"

"I have changed my plans for tomorrow. I believe I shall go to Longbourn." This announcement earned Caroline looks of patent surprise from the Bennet sisters.

"Are you certain?" Jane asked, unsure she had heard correctly. "You intend to go *with us to Longbourn?*"

"I believe I just said so."

"I wonder," Kitty ventured, "if you know what we intend to *do* at Longbourn?"

"I have a clear understanding, I assure you."

"But we intend to distribute the boxes tomorrow—to *servants and tradesmen*," Mary said, meaningfully, as she returned to her previous place at the table. "Is it your intention to help us do so?"

Caroline hesitated. She was willing to sacrifice her notions of decorum by accompanying the party to Longbourn, if it meant Robert and Helena could be alone for the better part of the morning; but the mere thought of having to converse with the Bennet servants, or, worse, having to be close enough to hand one of those beings a box filled with paltry trifles was more than Caroline could contemplate.

She raised her chin and said, "I may have spoken hastily. I wonder if it would be a good idea for me to intrude on what is obviously a special time for you to carry on your unique tradition. Perhaps it would be better for you to set me down at Lucas Lodge as we pass. I should be glad to spend an hour with Sir William and Lady Lucas while you distribute all these . . . these *things*." She had a sudden thought, and said quickly, "You *will* be no more than an hour, I hope?"

"I'll go to Longbourn, too, if you'll have me," Robert said.

"Certainly not!" Caroline retorted, instantly. "There is not enough room in the carriage."

"Then I will follow the carriage on horseback. Ibis can do with a bit of exercise."

"And will you abandon Miss Paget to amuse herself for the entire day?"

He flashed a quick look at Helena. "I beg your pardon. I had not thought of that."

"Then it is settled," Caroline said, with authority. "Robert will remain here to entertain Miss Paget."

Robert said no more, but he took a place at the table between Mary and Kitty, and allowed himself to be pressed into service. Soon he, too, was filling boxes, counting coins into pouches, and performing any other service that was needed. Charles helped as well, while Helena and Caroline claimed chairs near the fireplace and watched the proceedings with interest and an occasional comment.

In short order all the boxes had been packed save one. It stood open on the table as Mary surveyed the remaining few items left to be included.

"Who will receive this box?" Robert asked.

"Mrs. Doyle. She does our laundry," which remark was met with a decided snort of derision from the direction of the fireplace. Mary ignored it. "Mrs. Doyle is a widow with three young children."

"Boys or girls?"

"Two little girls and an infant boy." She carefully placed a wooden cart and horse in the box; to that she added a child-size set of nine-pins, and a wooden-peg doll dressed in a printed muslin gown. She reached out to add the bilbo-catcher, too, but she saw that Robert was studying it, and she stopped, her hand poised in mid-air as she sent him a questioning look. It was clear to her that he was deep in the throes of solving some great puzzle.

He frowned, his blue eyes still trained on the toy, then he straightened his shoulders and said, suddenly, under his breath, "By God, I must!"

"You must what?" asked Mary.

He looked at her then, but instead of answering her question, he turned toward his sister and said decisively, "I fear I cannot remain here tomorrow, after all, Caroline. It pains me to disappoint you, and I heartily beg your forgiveness, but I am determined to leave first thing in the morning to go back to the inn."

His announcement drew a chorus of protests. Caroline scolded him immediately for allowing sentiment to rule his common sense. Even Charles recommended he reconsider his plan.

"I know you do not understand my feeling," Robert said, "but I cannot be satisfied until I know if my actions endangered the boy."

Next, Helena tried to dissuade him by saying, in her most beguiling tone, "I wish you would not worry yourself into such a state. I think you forget that there are certain people who must be left to the lives they've chosen."

"I think this boy did not have the luxury of choosing his life. It was *thrust* upon him."

"How do you know?"

Her question surprised him. "Well, I—I *don't* know—not to a certainty."

"And isn't that the point?" she asked, in a tone that sounded reasonable, even as her words did not. "That kind of person can always find a way to live, if it is meant to be. And if not . . ." She gave a delicate wave of her hand to complete her thought.

Robert looked at her in consternation. "It is no use arguing. I cannot settle my conscience until I see the boy with my own eyes."

"And what will you do when you see him?" Charles asked.

"I will ascertain his health. I will ensure he is no worse off than he was when I left him."

"And if he is not, what then?"

"I—I don't know," Robert said, in some confusion. "I hadn't thought that far. But if I see signs he has been mistreated again, I cannot in good conscience leave him there to be kicked and beaten. He's only a child."

"Then you will need to take the carriage," Jane said, thereby becoming the first member of the party to ally herself with his cause, "in case you need to remove the boy from the inn."

He looked at her with an expression of warm relief. "Thank you, dear Jane. That is an excellent suggestion, but I fear the carriage will be too slow."

"Then take my curricle," Charles said. "You rode in it this morning, so you know it is built for speed. And those new chestnuts I purchased to draw it—they're wonderfully spirited and will take you there and back in a trice, you'll see."

This suggestion proved too much for Caroline. In an instant she was on her feet, saying fiercely, "Robert I absolutely *forbid* you to go! You may think you can run riot over all of us, but I will not have it. And when I think of the *ungentlemanly* way you have behaved toward Miss Paget, I could shake you. No brother of mine has ever treated a young lady so shabbily—leaving her to roam about this vast house by herself while you drive off on some crack-brained quest!"

"She needn't remain here by herself, Caroline. You could invite Miss Paget to accompany you to Longbourn—"

"There is no room in the carriage for her!"

"Then you could stay here with her."

"No!"

"Then she'll come with me," Robert said, impulsively. In an instant he covered the distance to the fireplace and knelt down on one knee before Helena. "Will you do it, Miss Paget?"

"Me?" she asked, stunned as much by his question as she was by the urgency of his tone.

"You have a kind heart, Miss Paget—I have seen the evidence of it—and your sympathetic nature has earned my admiration. If you could only see this child, I know you would open your heart to his plight. Come with me."

Her initial surprise had by this time evaporated into practicality. "Drive six miles out and back on a cold winter morning? No, I thank you!"

"It will not be so very cold outside, and I will make the journey comfortable for you, I swear."

"No, I say! I shall stay here at Netherfield, and so should you."

"Won't you reconsider?"

She looked at him sternly. "No, I won't, and I don't see why you are so intent upon wasting an entire morning chasing after a boy who doesn't need your help at all! His circumstance cannot be so very bad, you know, for he has a roof over his head and employment to keep him from trouble. Those kind of people do not need more; they have a way of making the best of their lot, if only you will see it."

He stared at her for a long moment, hoping to hear one word of sympathy from her temptingly soft lips. "You cannot think," he said, at last, "that a child relishes being struck to the ground, my dear Miss Paget."

She flushed with angry color. "It matters not what *I* think, for I am *not* going to ride in an open carriage on a cold winter day to some horrid inn you described as a little more than a shanty! If you are determined to waste *your* time on such a venture and must insist upon company, I suggest you take Mary Bennet with you! It was, after all, *her* doing that put the notion in your head in the first place!"

Mary had been tucking the last items into the box for Mrs. Doyle, but at this she looked up and found six pairs of eyes trained on her.

"Well?" demanded Helena in a challenging tone, as patches of angry color stained her fair cheeks. "Are you going to accompany Captain Bingley to the inn or not?"

Then Mary Bennet did a most surprising thing. She looked back at Helena, lifted her chin little, and said, calmly, "Yes, I will. I'll be ready to go at first light."

8

"Oh, Mary, I do wish you would reconsider this scheme of yours," Jane said later that night as she, Kitty and Mary climbed the stairs together to prepare for bed. Her usual calm demeanour was marred by an expression of mild worry. "I cannot think it a good idea for you to drive alone with Robert."

"But he is your brother-in-law, is he not?" Mary asked. "There can be no question of propriety, I think."

"Caroline thinks it *most* improper," Kitty said, with a hint of glee. "Didn't she look as angry as a *hornet* when Mary agreed to go? I am certain she was trying to trick Captain Bingley into spending tomorrow alone with Miss Paget."

As much as she wished to scold Kitty, Jane could not, for she had entertained similar thoughts of her own. "It was too bad that we should have ended our Christmas with angry words and arguments."

"It was Caroline who did the arguing," Kitty said, as she followed her sisters into Mary's bedchamber. "Meanwhile, you were splendid, Mary. I must say, I was never more shocked when you answered Miss Paget so confidently. What got into you, anyway?"

"Nothing got into me," Mary said. "I only wished to be of help to Captain Bingley. My words were to blame for his worries; I simply wanted to right the wrong I did him."

"You'll be driving six miles to the inn and six miles back," Kitty said, as she took a seat on the bed, very much as she was wont to do at home in Longbourn. "Mary, what on earth will you find to talk about with Captain Bingley?"

"Goodness, I hadn't thought of that!" Mary said, as the possibility dawned on her for the first time.

"Well, you better *start* thinking about it," said Kitty, "for twelve miles will pass slowly without some conversation between you."

Mary instantly felt a trill of alarm. "But what shall I say? What shall I talk about?"

"How should I know? Speak of the weather, if you like, for that is often a good way to start."

"I may start so, but what comes after? You know how hard it is for me to speak to strangers."

"But Robert is not a stranger," Jane said, gently. "He is my brother-in-law and a member of our family. Perhaps if you think of him in that way, you will find yourself more comfortable in his presence."

"Whatever you do," recommended Kitty, "do not mention any of your old books, and do *not* quote from them."

"If not for quoting from books," said Mary, in rising panic, "I will have absolutely nothing to say."

"Then if you must quote from books, do not quote from that horrid old book of Fordyce's sermons! Quote from something else."

"Like what?"

"Like *Evelina*."

"Quote from a *novel?*" Mary said, scoffing. "I would never do so—chiefly because I have never read it."

"I cannot think Captain Bingley has read the novel, either," Jane said, with some authority, "but it matters not, for he is a gentleman, and *he* will start the conversation, Mary. You have simply to listen carefully to what he says and follow his lead. Can you do that?"

Mary replied that she would certainly try, but Jane was not through dispensing sisterly advice. "Holding a conversation is one thing, but there is more to consider here. I understand you wish to be of help to Robert, but how will you accomplish it? When you arrive at the inn and see the boy for yourself, what then?"

Mary hesitated. "I don't know. I suppose I shall follow Captain Bingley's lead in that, too."

"Perhaps that is best, but I want you to remember that you have a sensible head on your shoulders. I know I can rely on your good judgment to make sound decisions and help Captain Bingley do the same." But even as she spoke these words, Jane looked uneasy.

"Are you worried about the landlord, Jane?" Kitty asked. "He sounds like a blackguard to me. I hope Captain Bingley takes his sword along and runs the landlord through."

"Kitty, you do not mean it," Jane protested.

"I cannot think anything will be accomplished with violence," Mary said, "and I will strongly encourage Captain Bingley to leave his sword behind."

"Well," said Jane, with a look of resolution, "if you are determined to go with Robert tomorrow, then you must be properly prepared." She opened the clothes press and, withdrawing Mary's pelisse, held it up for examination. "Is this the warmest you have? I fear you shall be very cold in an open carriage. I will lend you my heavy cape and hood for the journey. Where are your gloves?"

Mary dutifully produced them, and calmly accepted Jane's assessment that her gloves were too thin to guard effectively against the cold morning air.

"I would lend you *my* gloves," Kitty said, "but your fingers are longer than mine and you will stretch them out."

"You will take my ermine muff, too," Jane said, decidedly. "It will help keep your hands warm, and I will lend you my Kashmir shawl. If you drape it over your head, and pull the cape hood over it all, I think your neck and ears will be warmer than if you wore your winter bonnet."

In the end, Jane and Kitty selected several layers of garments in which Mary was to array herself in anticipation of a chilly morning drive with Captain Bingley.

She had agreed to be ready to travel at eight o'clock, weather permitting. As Mary looked out her window the next morning to watch the sun rise in the eastern sky, she could see the morning dawn clear. It was a good sign, she thought, for though the lack of clouds foretold a frosty morning, there was an equal chance the bright winter sun would warm the day to a tolerably comfortable temperature.

She presented herself downstairs just as the tall case clock in the hall was striking the hour. Robert was waiting for her.

He looked up as she descended the last steps, and said, with mild surprise, "Good morning. Eight o'clock precisely. I wasn't sure if I should expect you."

"Why not?"

"Because it's devilish cold outside, for one thing. Besides, I wouldn't blame you for thinking I'm about to set out on a fool's errand. Miss Paget certainly thinks so."

She heard no bitterness in his tone, but she guessed the captain was still smarting from some of the arguments leveled against him the night before. Caroline and Helena had been united in their efforts to convince him to abandon his plan to return to the inn. Helena had prettily begged him to reconsider, reminding him in the gentlest of terms that remaining with his family was far more important than setting off on some quixotic journey inspired by a troublesome urchin he didn't even know; and Caroline had alternately raged and threatened in her efforts to change her brother's mind. In the end, Robert stood strong, although Mary had detected a good deal of anger in the way he had clenched his jaw and replied to his sister's criticisms with clipped, emotionless words.

Mary looked up at him, and said, "I do not consider it a fool's errand at all; and you must know by now that I feel a good deal responsible for having put worrisome thoughts in your head. I cannot rest easy until I know you have seen the boy and are satisfied."

"I dare say you will find it extremely cold outside."

Mary was wearing her warmest gown and pelisse; over all she had donned Jane's shawl and heavy, hooded cape, and she carried Jane's warm ermine muff to preserve her gloved fingers from the cold. In all, she had thought herself well prepared, but now she frowned.

"Am I not sufficiently dressed? I can go back and add another layer of garments, but I do not think my elbows will be able to bend, if I do."

He smiled slightly. "No need. I have done what I can to make us both comfortable. Shall we go?"

Mary led the way outside and immediately felt the effects of the frigid morning air on her cheeks. Robert handed her up into the curricle, where she found a hot brick for her feet and a large, heavy carriage blanket at her command. It took her only a moment to cocoon herself in its warmth; then she adjusted the hood of her cape so it fit more closely over her ears, and pronounced herself ready.

The little curricle heaved slightly as Robert climbed up beside her. He drew another blanket across his legs, took up the reins, gave a flick of his chin to signal the groom to stand away, and gave the chestnut ponies the office to dash through the gates and onto the road.

For the first mile or two they were both silent as Robert concentrated on controlling his horses in their head-long rush. Presently he asked, his eyes still trained on the road ahead, "Are you cold?"

"No, thank you."

They didn't speak again for several more minutes, when Robert slackened the horses' pace; then he leaned back slightly, and relaxed his hold of the reins. He stole a quick look at Mary, and smiled. Sometime after they set off, she had pulled the heavy blanket up to her chin, so only her face was visible. He saw that her cheeks, nose, and ears had gone pink from the cold. He also saw a light in her hazel eyes that made him take a second look.

"If I did not know better, Miss Bennet, I would say you were enjoying yourself."

"I have never ridden in a curricle before," she answered, candidly. "It's almost like flying, isn't it?"

"That is a very good likeness. This little curricle is built for speed, and my brother has chosen a pair of sweet goers to draw it. I must remember to congratulate him when we get back." He gave her another quick glance. "May I ask, what is your usual mode of transportation—if not a sporting curricle?"

"My feet," she replied, primly.

"Not a carriage?"

"My father keeps a carriage, but the horses that draw it serve double duty on the farm; therefore, I must rely on myself to transport me wherever I wish to go."

"Walking is an excellent exercise."

"For me it is a necessity, unless I resolve to be content to spend my life within the confines of Longbourn."

"Have you traveled much, Miss Bennet?"

Here Mary made a strategic error by turning her head and looking at Captain Bingley. His attention was still trained on the lively pair of chestnut horses as they neared a dense grove of trees, but the sight of his handsome profile made her lips go suddenly dry. Of a sudden she was conscious of her situation: she was driving through the countryside in a small curricle beside a very handsome man. Though moments before she had been reveling in the excitement of hurtling forward at, for her, a breath-taking speed such as she had never encountered before, now her

excitement disappeared and was instantly replaced by suffo-
cating shyness.

She forced herself to look straight ahead, and said, in a
tight little voice, "No, never."

"Would you like to travel?"

"No."

That single word sounded rude, even to Mary's ears. She
knew Captain Bingley was doing his best to draw her into a
conversation, but that realization immediately sent her into a
panic that robbed her of any ability to respond in kind. As
usual when she found herself sinking into the quicksand of
shyness, she struggled mightily to find something to say, and
after casting about in her mind for several precious seconds,
she hit upon the happy thought of asking his own question
back to him.

"I have not—That is, have *you* traveled, Captain
Bingley?"

"I have, indeed."

"Where?"

"From Dorset to Egypt, and almost everywhere in
between. I go where my king commands me."

His mention of Egypt reminded her of something he had
said in passing the day before. "I think my sister told me you
returned from Egypt a few months ago. Is that where you
learned about Ibis?"

"That is where I *bought* Ibis. She is my horse, you see—a
beautiful roan, bred by the Mamelukes. I brought her back to
England with me."

"Oh. You must think her very intelligent."

"I do, but I'm curious why you would say so."

"Her name is Ibis—named for the Egyptian god of knowledge, I think."

He allowed his gaze to flick over her briefly, before he returned his attention to the road and his horses. "So you know something of Egyptian mythology, do you?"

Mary pursed her lips together. Only the night before she had promised Kitty not to speak of things she had read in books, yet she could not in honesty deny to Captain Bingley what she had learned.

"I know a little," she said, carefully.

"What else do you know?"

"I know Ibis was the symbol for a male god, yet your horse is a female."

He looked at her again, this time a little longer. "Very impressive, Miss Bennet. You can thank the Mamelukes for that. They prize female horses above males—unlike we English—and bestow their most treasured names on the mares."

"Why are mares prized so highly?"

"Because they show exceptional courage in battle. Ibis has carried me through many battles, and never once did she shy from danger. I often think I owe my life to her."

"That is praise indeed. Where is Ibis now?"

"When last I saw her, she was eating a leisurely breakfast in her warm stall in the Netherfield stables." He looked over at her. "Did you have any breakfast this morning?"

"None at all."

"Are you hungry?"

"No."

"I didn't think so. At least, you don't *look* hungry yet."

Her brows went up. "How does a hungry person look?"

"You shall see for yourself when we reach the inn."

She watched his features cloud a little, and she said, quietly, "You are thinking of Daniel, aren't you?"

"Yes, I am. And I hope you will allow me to thank you, Miss Bennet, for being the first of my relations to understand that the child has a name—that he is not simply *that urchin*."

She judged the bitterness of his tone to be a product of the furious debate that passed the previous evening between Robert and his sister. She said, a bit impulsively, "I wish to be of help to you. Tell me, what is your plan? What shall we do when we reach the inn?"

"That is a good question. I suppose we should first find Daniel."

"May I make a suggestion? If Daniel is not in plain sight when we arrive at the inn, I propose we separate. I will search out the boy, if you will engage to keep the landlord busy."

"A bit of divide and conquer, eh, Miss Bennet? I suppose that will work as well as any plan. If you find him before I do, you will bring him to me immediately, won't you? I must see for myself that he is no worse off than when I left him yesterday morning."

By this time they were driving through the grove of trees; the branches were dense, weaving spindly, leafless webs above and beside them. As he spoke, Robert reached up to catch a low-hanging branch in his hand, and he held it out of the way so it wouldn't graze against Mary as they passed beneath it.

The gesture surprised her and thrilled her at once. How very gentlemanly Captain Bingley was! She had thought him handsome from the first moment of their acquaintance, before she ever heard him utter a kind word for an unfortunate boy that others cared not one whit for. His concern for Daniel had earned her admiration; and now, watching him exert himself for her comfort in so gallant a way, she felt her heart respond. She had never been the recipient of such thoughtfulness before, and she had to wonder if Miss Helena Paget realized how fortunate she was to have secured the affections of such a man.

When they cleared the grove of trees Robert increased their speed and they flew down the road at a pace that made Mary thankful for the heavy carriage blanket that protected her from the cold.

They arrived at the inn without incident, and she had her first glimpse of the ramshackle place Robert had described so thoroughly. The yard was deserted at first, then an ostler appeared from the direction of the stable to take charge of the horses. When questioned, he assured Robert that he would find the landlord inside.

"And the boy? Where is Daniel?"

The ostler looked innocently back at him. "Dunno, yer lordship."

Robert reached up to assist Mary down from the curricle, saying, in a grave tone, "It seems impossible to me that one child can be so much neglected. We shall have to search for him, I think."

"I will look in the stable first. If I find him, I will bring him to you inside." She was rewarded with a grateful look and the slight pressure of his fingers on hers before he released her hand.

Robert gave the ostler a quick instruction to water and turn his horses, then he strode purposefully into the inn.

Mary set off toward the stable and stepped inside to find a young boy in one of the stalls. He was intently wielding a broom that was easily twice his size as he tried to arrange a meager amount of fresh hay over a soiled layer that had clearly been used on previous days.

"Good morning. Are you Daniel?"

He spun around with a jerk, his eyes wide with alarm. There was a red mark on his chin, and a deep bruise near his eye that Mary judged to be fresh; and she could tell he had been crying from the tell-tale signs of tears having trailed down his dirty cheeks. He looked to be about nine or ten years old, but his face was so thin, she could not trust her instinct. His clothes were little more than filthy rags, and his thin, red fingers were so cruelly exposed to the cold, she wondered how he could possibly hold on to the broom. All this Mary observed in an instant, and a fierce indignation swelled within her. She drew a deep breath to steady her rising emotions and asked again, in a gentler tone, "Are you Daniel?"

He didn't answer. Instead, his eyes darted fearfully about the stall, seeking out possible avenues of escape; but there were none, for Mary blocked the only way out.

"Don't be afraid," she said. "I am here on behalf of your friend, Captain Bingley."

With these words his eyes flew to her face. "Who?"

"Captain Bingley. You remember him, don't you? He spent Christmas Eve night here and you served him admirably. He told me all about it, and he has come back to see you. Will you come with me and say hello to him?"

Daniel stared at her, his expression an odd mix of wonder and suspicion, as he considered her question. After a long moment he gave a curt nod of his head, but he remained stock still, clutching the broom.

"I will take you to Captain Bingley, if you will allow me."

This invitation brought the fearful expression back to his eyes. "No, I can't. I've work to do, and if I don't do it just so, Meeks will . . ." His voice trailed away, and Mary took a step toward him.

"Is Meeks the landlord or the ostler? The landlord? Then you have nothing to fear for Captain Bingley is with him now, and he shall see that no harm comes to you. Now tell me, where is your winter coat?"

He looked down at his dirty clothes. "I haven't a winter coat."

"Very well," she said, falsely bright, though her heart was breaking a little, "I will take you to Captain Bingley now. Here, hold my hand, if you please."

Slowly, he propped the broom against the wall and took two tentative steps toward her; then he stopped and rubbed the palm of his dirty hand against the even dirtier leg of his ragged trousers, before he tucked his fingers confidingly in hers.

Mary led the way into the inn. She discovered Robert in the tap room with the landlord, and said, "I have found

Daniel, and he is most happy to make your acquaintance again."

Robert looked around, and his eyes fell on Daniel. He examined him quickly, and though his blue eyes clouded a little as he inventoried the child's injuries, he said, in a pleasant voice, "Here you are at last! I am happy to see you again, Daniel—although the innkeeper just swore to me that he knew not where you were."

"But I swear, I *didn't* know," protested Mr. Meeks. "I don't know nothing about him ever."

"Perhaps," Mary said, in a voice of barely-controlled contempt, "Mr. Meeks is so much in the habit of striking children he cannot keep track of one over the other."

Robert's attention remained with Daniel. He had assessed his appearance in an instant, noticing the new marks on the child's chin and cheek. His gaze traveled down to Daniel's feet, which were still clad in the pathetically inadequate shoes that he had been wearing the day before.

"Tell me, Daniel," he said, in a quiet voice, "when we parted yesterday morning I gave you something. Are you still in possession of the item?"

Daniel focused his gaze on the floor in a guilty way, prompting Mary to sink to the floor beside him.

"Will you show me your pockets?" she asked, in a gentle voice.

Wary but obedient, Daniel first turned the pockets of his trousers out, then he did the same with the pocket in his coat, all three of which proved to be empty. Mary glared up at the landlord. "You took the money from him, didn't you? You, sir, are little more than a thief!"

"Not at all," said the landlord, in a smug tone. "I took it. I had to. It's evidence."

"Evidence of what?" demanded Robert.

"Stealing! And I mean to hand him over to the magistrate for it."

"If what you say is true," said Robert in a tone of deep suspicion, "and you think this boy is guilty of a crime, why haven't you delivered him to the magistrate before now?"

"Seemed to be no sense spoilin' the magistrate's Christmas—not over a boy like that."

Mary was again on her feet, and clasped Daniel's hand in a firm grip. At the mention of the magistrate, she could feel him tremble slightly, and she didn't know whether to cry for Daniel or rage at the landlord. "What do you mean, *a boy like that?*" she asked, with deep offense.

"Oh, he can pretend and put on airs, right enough. That's what comes of me doing my Christian duty and taking in a vicar's brat, for all the good it's done me. And besides, he owes me that and more for all the care I took of him, and all the dishes he broke, and the food he ate."

"Do you wish me to believe that this child somehow *owes* you the money you took from him?"

"Indeed he does," Mr. Meeks said, lifting his chin to a defiant angle. "He eats my food, doesn't he? And I give him a place to sleep. Why, he has it just as good as if he were a paying guest in one of my rooms."

"I can attest to that," said Robert. "A night in one of his best chamber is little better than a night in his stable."

Until this point Mr. Meeks had maintained a polite, but defensive air. He recalled the healthy gratuity he had received from the gentleman only the day before and he was, frankly, hoping for more; but he did not relish being insulted, especially in front of such an ungrateful brat as Daniel had proved to be. His expression darkened.

"I keep a respectable inn, and respectable workers, and if one of 'em don't toe his line, I'm within my right to make him do so."

Mary said angrily, "Is that how this poor child came by the red mark on his chin? You struck him, didn't you! Tell us, if you dare!"

He did not dare; instead, he narrowed his eyes at Daniel, and said, "Get back to your work."

Daniel almost jumped, and would have rushed toward the door had Mary not stopped him by tightening her hold on his hand and holding him fast. "You stay right here, Daniel, and don't be afraid." She looked up at Robert and whispered, "What shall we do?"

For answer, Robert took a firm hold on Daniel's arm and led him outside to the yard. In one quick movement, he pick-ed the boy up—for he weighed little more than a feather— and tossed him up onto the curricle bench.

Mary followed close behind, thinking all the time that Jane had exhorted her only the night before to use her good sense this morning. She was uncertain that Jane would approve of what Robert planned to do; taking Daniel with them to Netherfield was a wild notion, at best—an overstep of the conventional ways of doing things; but Captain Bingley seemed determined, and she could not bear to thwart him— on the contrary, it was all she could do to keep from cheering as she watched him climb up into the curricle beside the boy.

"Here, now, you can't do this!" Mr. Meeks complained loudly, as he followed them outside. "He belongs here with me!"

"Does he? I wonder if he will agree," Robert said, looking down at the boy. "Do you wish to remain apprenticed to this man here, Daniel? Or would you like to come and stay with me?"

Poor Daniel didn't know what to think. His gaze veered between Robert and Meeks, fearing the consequences of choosing one over the other. He murmured something incoherent; Robert was about to ask him to repeat himself when he felt Daniel clutch at the sleeve of his coat, and he had his answer.

"He prefers to go with me, I think."

"Well, he can't," Mr. Meeks said, his temper now flaming. "He's mine. I'm the one that's fed him and kept him out of harm when no one else would. Why, he owes me, true enough, for the food I give him and the roof over his head, and he must work in kind."

"How much?" Robert said, turning to look at him with an expression of loathing.

"Huh?"

"How much does he owe you for his *work in kind?*"

"Well, I haven't totted up the numbers—"

"Then name a figure, and be done with it."

The landlord thought a moment, then suggested an amount that to Mary sounded exorbitant.

But Robert didn't hesitate. He reached into the depths of his greatcoat pocket and produced a small purse, out of which he selected a few coins to toss down to the landlord.

"I shall not see you again. I hope we understand each other." He turned his back on the man while he enveloped Daniel in the blanket he had employed earlier; then he reached down his hand to Mary. "Miss Bennet?"

She placed her fingers in his and allowed his strong pull to guide her up into the curricle. It was a tight fit, but she managed to sit down on the bench, wedging Daniel between herself and Robert, who drew the remaining blanket across her legs.

"Ready?"

She nodded.

The horses broke into a canter; at the road they lengthened their stride to a gallop, and their drive back to Netherfield was commenced.

Mary grasped the side of the curricle to preserve her balance and asked, with a glowing look at Robert, "Do you realize what we have just done?"

"I have a general idea," he said, calmly, "but the enormity of it has not yet occurred to me."

"What will you do with Daniel when we arrive at Netherfield?"

"I haven't the faintest idea, Miss Bennet." He looked at her over the top of Daniel's head. "I'm hoping you will advise me."

"Me?" she asked, surprised.

"Most certainly. You and I, Miss Bennet, are in this fix together—partners and co-conspirators!—and I dare say, with your intelligence, you will have many more practical suggestions for Daniel's future than I will ever have."

Mary felt the familiar heat of a blush mantel her cheeks, but this time the blush was not the result of embarrassment; rather, it came from the knowledge that Captain Bingley had paid her a compliment. It was certainly unexpected, and for a moment she had no idea how to respond. In the end, she decided no response was necessary, for he was absorbed with managing his horses, and she was happy to revel in the warmth of his flattering words.

Their drive back to Netherfield was much different than their drive to the inn. The morning, which had begun so promising, now began to cloud, blocking the sun and turning the day colder still. Sitting in the curricle, traveling head-long at a breath-taking speed through the cold air, Mary made up her mind not to let her teeth chatter. It wouldn't do to betray her discomfort when, really, she was in the middle of what seemed very much like an adventure, and everyone knew that adventurers did not complain. So she sat back in the curricle, appearing to look at nothing and be interested in nothing, when all the while her heart was singing. Whatever happened next, she decided, she had, for the first time in her life, done a most remarkable and unexpected thing.

About a mile after they commenced driving they were forced to stop to attend to Daniel, who was wholly unused to their high speed of travel, and developed an unfortunate and violent case of carriage-sickness. Mary climbed down from the curricle unassisted, while Robert held the horses. She helped Daniel to the ground and stayed with him as he lost the meager contents of his stomach in the dirt on the side of the road. She did her best to comfort him, kneeling in the dirt beside him, laying her hand on his back, only to find herself close to tears when she felt the distinct impression of his ribs through the thin fabric of his shirt and coat. From her reticule she produced a clean linen handkerchief, which she used to tenderly mop Daniel's face before she helped him back up into the curricle. Then she took the heavy carriage blanket she'd been using and wrapped it as a second layer about Daniel.

"You'll freeze to death without something over you," Robert said, with a small frown.

"If you can stand it, Captain Bingley, so can I. Besides, at the pace you drive we shall be back at Netherfield before I have a chance to know I'm cold."

He said no more, but there was an odd little light in his blue eyes as he watched her drape her arm protectively around Daniel's shoulders.

They set off again. Mary dug her free hand deep into the warmth of her fur muff, while she continued to hold onto Daniel with the other. Soon he fell into an exhausted sleep against her, wrapped comfortably in his cocoon of blankets. She held him tightly, trying not to shiver, and marveling that the child could sleep so soundly while being jostled over rough country roads.

They covered the next few miles in silence, which Mary used as an opportunity to apply her mind to the riddle of determining Daniel's future. In the end, she came to no distinct conclusion and, sighing, glanced casually over at Robert.

Without warning, he turned to her; their eyes met and held for an instant.

"What is it?" she asked, blankly.

"Nothing . . . just, *thank* you."

The warmth of his tone surprised her just as much as the unreadable look in his eyes. Her breath caught in her throat and she turned away in a flurry of confusion, vowing not to look at his handsome face again until they reached Netherfield.

9

In the drawing-room at Netherfield the Boxing Day party was just returning from their morning at Longbourn. Jane, Kitty and Charles had dutifully carried their offerings to the Bennet family home and distributed them to the family's servants and long-time retainers. Next they had stopped in the village, where tradesmen received tokens of the family's esteem and best wishes for a new year of health and happiness. It had been, in their opinion, time well spent; and Charles had declared that—excepting the day his beloved Jane had agreed to be his wife—this was quite the happiest time he had ever spent at Longbourn.

"Does that mean," asked Kitty, "that you will continue the tradition? It would be very nice, I think, to celebrate Boxing Day in the same way at Netherfield in years to come."

Charles hesitated a moment, then said, "I should like to carry on the tradition at Longbourn or Netherfield . . . or wherever I make my home."

They entered the drawing-room to find Caroline and Helena seated together near the fire. Caroline assured them that she had been busy on their behalf during their absence, saying, "I know you will not mind when I tell you, Jane, that

I have sent an order to Meryton for bees-wax candles. They are a necessity for the ball-room, you know."

"That was kind of you," Jane answered, "but I already have enough candles for the ball."

"But they are not of the right size, I fear. I spoke to your housekeeper this morning and she told me you have laid in a supply of short tapers, which will never do. Why, they will be burnt to the socket in no time, and your footmen will be changing them out three times over before the evening is done. You will recall when my brother held the ball at Netherfield before you were married, I used only long tapers in the ball-room girandoles. They worked splendidly—you must have remarked on it."

Jane wisely chose not to argue the point—although the cost of bees-wax candles was very dear—and conceded that Caroline was probably right. She thanked her for her help, assuring her that she could not properly plan a ball without her.

"I have a suggestion to make, as well," Helena said.

"By all means," Jane said as she claimed a chair near hers, "please share it. I welcome any proposal that will make the New Year ball a success."

Helena clasped her hands together and said, with a bright smile, "Fresh fruit! Only think! Wouldn't fresh fruit be a surprise in the middle of winter? My aunt—the Countess of Berkridge, you know—served fruit last Christmas from the hot house at their country seat, and it was a special treat."

"But Netherfield does not have a hot house," Kitty said.

"Oh, but you can certainly find one, I am sure. Fresh fruit in January is the height of luxury—my aunt Lady Berkridge swears by it. Perhaps if we inquire in Meryton, or send away to London, we can find someone who can accommodate us."

Jane silently thought that the prospect of serving a delicacy like hot house fruit in January sounded like an expensive proposition, indeed; and she had just decided to try to steer the conversation down a different path when she caught the sound of hasty footsteps in the hall, and male voices raised in exclamation.

The next instant Mary burst into the room, still clad in her cape and carrying her muff, saying, "We are back! And you must not be surprised for we have brought Daniel with us, and he is in dire need of your warm fire!"

No sooner did she impart this warning than Robert appeared in her wake. He was not alone, but had under his control what looked very much like a walking mound of carriage blankets, which were wound so snugly about Daniel's body and head that only the child's eyes were visible. Robert, still in his greatcoat, hat and gloves, had a commanding hand on Daniel's shoulder as he guided him toward to the fireplace.

"Daniel!" exclaimed Kitty, as Robert pulled an upholstered bench close to the hearth and bade Daniel sit down. "Is that the boy from the inn? Why, he is shivering so!"

"We're all frightfully cold," Mary said. "Had it not been for Jane's heavy cape about me, I think I would have frozen into a block of ice!"

"And so it would have been your own fault," Caroline said, curtly. "Did we not warn you it was too cold to go off in such a way? Oh, Robert, this is too bad of you. Why on earth did you bring that boy here?"

"Because Mary's fears proved correct—he has been sorely mistreated since I saw him last, and I could not leave him there a moment longer."

"Good heavens!" uttered Helena, faintly, as, with a pained expression, her blue eyes flicked over the boy.

Charles instantly moved toward the bell-pull. "We must get him warm at once. A hot drink will help—some punch, I think."

"Oh, no," Jane said, when a footman answered the summons. "A punch will do nicely for Mary and Robert, but we must not serve that to a child. Bring a pot of hot chocolate, just the same as my maid serves me in my chamber before breakfast."

"Thank you, Jane!" Mary said, warmly. "You see how he is—cold to his very bones, I should guess, and hungry, too. The innkeeper did not treat him well at all."

Jane and Kitty, who were very fond of children and enjoyed excellent relations with their young cousins, moved a little closer.

"Hello, Daniel," Jane said. "I am Mrs. Bingley and this is my sister, Miss Catherine Bennet. May we sit with you?" She did not wait for an answer, but very cautiously claimed a place beside him on the bench.

While Jane and Kitty made their overtures with Daniel, Caroline rose to her feet with a great deal of dignity and went to her brother. He was near the window, having discarded his hat on the top of a nearby table, and was in the process of removing his greatcoat and gloves.

"I want you to know," she said, in a low voice, "I do not blame you for this. It isn't your doing, I am certain."

"What, bringing Daniel here, do you mean? Of course it was my doing. Don't tell me you wish to rain criticism down on Mary Bennet's head."

"How like you to defend her! But, of course, *she* was behind it all. I know you would never inflict such a creature on us unless she talked you into it."

"What a very frippery fellow you must think me! Do you honestly believe me capable of looking the other way when an injustice is being done? Neither you nor I was taught to do so—only think back to our father's principles, Caroline."

"Do not speak of our father to me; I am quite aware of his so-called principles. And why speak of injustice? What injustice has to do with this situation, I cannot see."

"Then you aren't looking very hard. Let me make it plain to you; I could not, in good conscience, leave that child with a master who mistreated him. I like to think you would not do so, either, Caroline. Please tell me I am not mistaken."

"But why bring him *here?*" she demanded, ignoring his question. "There must be some place you can take him that will be better suited for a such a boy."

"Like a parish charity? Perhaps that is the best solution— but I intend to weigh all the options first before making any decision, and that may take a little time."

"How much time? And what will you do with him until then?"

"I haven't the faintest notion, my dear Caroline! But any fate I can think up for the boy will be, I am certain, ten times better than the fate he would have suffered had I left him at the inn."

"But I cannot understand you! You have seen impoverished stable boys before. Pray, what is so remarkable about *this* one?"

"Nothing, except that he seemed to me to be in dire need of a friend."

"He has no place here," she said, with rigid disapproval. "He should never have been brought into the house."

"But you are not mistress here, my dear sister, so he shall remain until *Jane* tells me he must leave. Then, of course, I shall remove him immediately . . . but not before."

Caroline meant to argue more, but the distinct sound of a gasp made her stop short and turn to discover the source.

It was Jane. She had been making some progress in be-friending Daniel, and had gently coaxed him into loosening the blanket that had covered his head and face, thereby gaining her first look at his cut lip, and bruised cheek and chin. Her gasp had been involuntary; she winced at the sight of his injuries, and murmured, "Oh, you poor, *poor* child! Charles, do you see this?"

He did, indeed; and he frowned as he watched Jane examine Daniel's face with sympathy.

"Now you know," Mary said, "why we thought it best to take him away from that horrid place."

"You did right, Mary," Charles said. "I'm proud of you."

"As am I," Jane added, though her sympathetic gaze never left Daniel's face. "Now, Daniel, I have a question for you. Now that you and I are friends, will you be kind enough to stay here as a favor to me? Please say you will. You shall sleep in a grand bed with a nice fire to keep you warm all night long."

This suggestion was too much for Caroline. "Jane! You

cannot be thinking of installing that . . . that *urchin* in one of your guest chambers!"

"I agree," Kitty said. "I think he will be more comfortable in the family quarters."

"That was not my meaning at all!" Caroline retorted, rather furiously, as she went back to her chair, which was thankfully placed a good distance from Daniel.

A footman entered with a tray bearing cups and saucers, a bowl of punch and a pot of chocolate. Mary immediately poured out a cup of the chocolate and offered it to Daniel, saying, "Here, drink this. It will warm you, and I dare say you shall like the taste of it very much."

He obediently loosened his hold on the blankets to take the cup from her. The blankets fell away, revealing his dirty clothes and matted hair and unwashed hands. In all, his appearance could not have been in starker contrast with the exquisitely perfect décor of the Netherfield drawing-room.

At the sight of him Helena uttered a sound that matched her expression of horror, and she averted her gaze, while beside her Caroline fairly trembled with disapproval.

Daniel saw only the cup. He wrapped his fingers—each of which had a line of caked black dirt beneath his torn nails— around the delicate bit of china and cautiously raised it to his lips.

"Sip slowly," Jane murmured. "You must be very careful, for the drink is hot, and you don't want to scald your mouth. Yes, yes, that's the way." She looked up at Robert, who had taken a position on the other side of the hearth, the better to watch Daniel. "We shall have him warm soon enough."

"Thank you, Jane. I had planned to throw myself on your

mercy and beg you to let the boy stay here."

"There's no need," Charles said, with a steely look in his eye. "He'll stay here until some arrangement can be made."

"But not in a guest chamber," Robert said. "It was generous of you to offer, but I fear it might be too much for him. After all, he's a stranger in a strange land right now. I don't want him to be frightened by being made to spend the night alone in a large bedchamber in an unfamiliar home."

"What do you suggest?" Jane asked.

"Well, Daniel and I are old friends now. Perhaps it would be best if he stayed in my room, if no one objects. I should think it would be a simple matter to have a trestle bed brought into the room, don't you?"

"Would you like that, Daniel?" Jane asked. "You will stay here with us and sleep in your own bed near Captain Bingley. What do you say to that?"

Daniel considered the matter carefully. "I should like it fine, for then I will be able to tend his fire in the night." He directed wide eyes up at Robert. "Should I gather the wood for it now, sir, or wait until you are ready to retire?"

This suggestion left everyone in a state of stunned silence for a long moment until Robert said, in a gentle voice, "No, my lad. In fact, I dare say you shall never have to gather wood for anyone's fire ever again."

"You should not make such promises," Caroline said, though her tone held none of its previous censure.

"If Daniel is to stay," said Kitty, who had been examining his tattered clothes with interest, "he shall need something to wear. And shoes and warm mittens and hats and—oh, he needs everything!"

"You may leave that to me," Charles said. "I shall ride to Meryton directly and visit the shops. I'm certain I can buy some decent clothes for the boy."

"I'll go with you, Charles," Kitty said, "if you will allow me. I helped my Aunt Gardner pick out a suit of clothes for one of her sons last summer, and he liked it very well. Besides, if I go along, I can make some inquiries while we're in Meryton."

"Inquiries about what?" asked Caroline.

"About Daniel. Perhaps someone may have heard of him or knows something of his history."

"I doubt it, for Meryton is nowhere near the inn where he was living. Besides, his history is of no importance. If he has relations, they would have claimed him by now. If you really want to be of service to the child, you will immediately turn him over to some family that will take him. A farm family is probably best, where he can earn his keep and learn to support himself in future. Believe me, that is the best solution."

Mary's eyes flashed with sudden alarm. "And run the risk of throwing him under the power of another Mr. Meeks? Pay her no mind, Daniel. You are staying right here until we have had a sensible discussion and decided the right course of action."

Daniel wisely refrained from answering, concentrating instead on draining the last of the chocolate from his cup while the conversation swirled around him.

"I think he's hungry," Kitty said, still studying him, "but luncheon will not be served until one o'clock."

"No matter," Jane said. "Pull the bell, Mary, and I will

ask for a little bread and cheese. That should tide him over."

"No!" Caroline exclaimed, before Mary had a chance to move. "I beg you do not serve him anything here."

"Why not?" asked Kitty.

"Because he is filthy! It is bad enough to have to *look* at him, but to watch him eat—! Oh, I cannot permit it!"

Helena, who was still unable to bring herself to look at the boy, said in a low voice, "I must agree with Caroline. Please don't feed him here. I cannot think he knows how to eat—in company, I mean. Perhaps he should eat in the stable, instead."

"What, out of a *trough?*" Kitty demanded, indignantly.

"Oh, you misunderstand me, of course! I simply meant there are other places he will no doubt be more comfortable, with people of his own kind. If you really care about the boy you will not force him into a realm to which he is not accustomed."

Mary took the cup from Daniel's hands. "Come with me."

"Where you are you taking him?" Robert asked.

"To the kitchens to get him something to eat."

"Oh, Mary, do let him remain here where it is warm," Jane said, as Mary gathered up the heavy blankets and wrapped them around Daniel again.

"I'll keep him warm, never fear; but he must have some food and I will not make him wait until luncheon." So saying, she took Daniel by the hand and led him toward the door; but as she guided Daniel away from the hearth, she thought she saw Helena clutch her skirts and move them aside as Daniel passed. Mary's face flushed with resentment, and she was sorely tempted to turn back and make a fuss until she recalled Daniel's hand in hers. If he did not notice the slight, she would not point it out to him, for heaven knew he had suffered enough indignities for one day.

Charles and Kitty went away to prepare for their drive to Meryton; and Jane departed to meet the housekeeper in her sitting-room to discuss the many arrangements she wanted to make for Daniel's comfort.

Thus it was that in very short order Robert found himself alone in the drawing-room with Caroline and Helena—and neither lady looked the least bit happy.

10

W ell!" Caroline said as soon as the door was closed. "This is a turn of events I never could have predicted!"

"Frankly, nor could I," Robert said. "I have a fair idea of what you wish to say to me, Caroline, and I think I'll need some fortification first. May I serve you some punch, as well? Miss Paget?" He handed both ladies a cup of the warming brew before he poured out a cup for himself; and after taking an initial sip and finding the taste and potency of the punch quite to his liking, he said, "Very well, I'm ready now. Fire away, Caroline!"

"I don't intend to fire at all—and I beg you will not use your soldiers' cant with me!" she retorted, with much dignity. "I will admit that I was very much surprised when you first brought that boy into the room—"

"Stunned!" interjected Helena.

"—but now that the initial commotion has subsided, I believe we can discuss the matter calmly. I know you will deny it, but I cannot think this affair is entirely of your choosing. I am certain Mary Bennet imposed upon your kind nature. The Bennets, I fear, have some very strange opinions about treating people of all classes in a very pert and familiar manner."

Robert resumed his post beside the mantle, his drink in his hand. "I told you earlier that it was my decision to bring Daniel here, and I meant it. That boy has been on my conscience since the moment I first saw him, and I won't desert him now."

"It is too bad of you! Had you only thought for a moment—had you only *considered* the consequences, you would never have brought him here."

"Would you have me leave him back at that inn? You would not think so if only you had felt the poor child's bones through his clothes, as I have!"

"But what will you do with him now you have got him?" asked Helena.

"I don't know," he said, sincerely, "but I shall find some suitable situation for him. Caroline's suggestion to hand him over to a local family may prove to be the best course of action."

"And in the meantime?" asked his sister. "Robert, only think—Charles and Jane have not yet set up a nursery, so there is no one in the house to care for a child. You cannot leave a boy—especially one as undisciplined as he is sure to be—alone to run riot over the grounds of Netherfield. Who knows what mischief he will get into if he is left unattended?"

"Undisciplined?" Robert considered the word carefully. "He doesn't strike me as undisciplined at all. In fact, now that I think on it, he seems to be an extremely well-mannered little boy."

"A very *dirty* little boy," Helena said, as she curled her

pretty nose. "I confess I could barely bring myself to look at him."

"That is because," Caroline said, "you have been carefully nurtured and have never had to come in contact with such a nasty little creature before. Why, when I had my first good look at him, I was almost driven to distraction!"

Robert gave her a resentful look. "Perhaps he did not look his best today, but such will not always be the case. I am certain there must be soap and bathing tubs somewhere in this house just waiting to be used."

"Oh, yes," said Caroline, "you may clean him up and dress him in new clothes, but he will *still* be nothing but a stable boy!"

"My only aim is that he shall be a stable boy who does not fear being mistreated."

"That is magnificent talk, indeed! How lofty that sounds! But in the meantime you haven't the faintest notion what to do with the child, admit it!"

"I shall find a home for him."

"You say that as if it were the simplest thing in the world!" Caroline retorted.

"Isn't it? How difficult can it be to find a home for a boy who isn't afraid of hard work and only wants a bit of kindness in return? And in the meantime he will stay here; I am certain I can arrange matters so he will not be in the way to anyone."

"But there are places for him to go, surely," Helena suggested.

"There are . . . and *this* is one of them."

"Oh, you know very well what I mean," she answered,

coaxingly. "I see you have a sincere heart in this matter, Captain Bingley, and your intentions are commendable, but the world is full of unfortunate creatures, and you cannot save them all, you know!"

"No, I cannot; but I don't *know* all of those unfortunate creatures of whom you speak—I only know Daniel, and I *can* help him."

"But how will you go about it? You will turn your brother's house upside down by making it into an orphan asylum."

"My dear Miss Paget, do you really think I am in danger of doing any such thing? Does Netherfield *look* like an orphan asylum?"

"No—not yet, at any rate. But only imagine some rough boy banging doors and shouting through the halls and stamping dirt into the carpets. Little boys are always awkward, and they pick up all kinds of ill manners so easily."

"If you are so firmly set against Daniel being here, I will gladly remove myself and the boy to the inn at Meryton," he said, coldly.

"You are deliberately misunderstanding Miss Paget," Caroline retorted. "Of course she is excessively sorry for that boy's situation, and I am astonished you would speak to her in such a manner."

"And I am a good deal surprised to find any female with so little compassion for a child as wretchedly situated as Daniel has been!"

Helena stared up at him in stunned surprise. It was a new experience for her to discover that anyone could find fault with her character, and the realization robbed her of speech for a long moment. Then her wide blue eyes slowly filled with tears, as she said, "This is a strange world, indeed, when speaking sense should be rewarded with criticism. I assure you, no one has ever accused *me* of lacking compassion before—why, simply *everyone* of my acquaint-ance knows me to be wholly unselfish. I am certain no one has a kinder disposition than I!"

The sight of her tears took a good portion of the angry wind out of Robert's sails. He had never intended to speak so harshly, and he apologized immediately, begging her forgiveness in the humblest of terms. When she didn't reply he added in a well-controlled voice, "You must know how sorry I am for speaking so hastily. Please, won't you let us continue this discussion in a calmer, more deliberate manner?"

"No. I hate discussions," she answered in a small voice. "Discussions are some masculine trick to make women feel like fools. 'Let us talk about this calmly,' men will say, when all the time they really mean that women are simpletons who should not offer an opinion in the first place. I *hate* discussions!"

Robert stared at her. A dull colour crept into his cheeks as he struggled to find something to say; but her petulant outburst had banished all reasonable thought from his mind. He knew she was young; knew, too, that her parents had raised her in a bubble of protective love. Hadn't her beauty and simple nature been the very things that had attracted him in the first place? Yet in all his dealings with the fair Miss Paget, he had never before been caused to wonder if the depth of her character was entirely limited to thoughts of her own comfort and well-being . . . until now.

"Of course I will not force you into a conversation that can only be distressing for you," he said, formally. "Here, let me serve you a bit more punch."

She handed her cup to him, but said, as she rose to her feet, "No, I thank you; I do not want more. You'll forgive me if I return to my room. I am certain it must be time to change for lunch."

It was clear to Robert by the wooden manner in which she carried herself to the door that he had hurt her deeply, and he was genuinely sorry for it. He left the cup she had handed him on the mantel, and sank down onto a chair near Caroline.

"Well, I made a great mull of it all, didn't I? You must know I never meant to let my temper run so. Is she very angry, do you think?"

"I cannot speak for Helena," she replied, grimly, "but *I* am very angry indeed, and I don't believe I could forgive you if you begged me on your knees!"

"You? Why would I want to beg *your* forgiveness?"

"Because you are teetering on the brink of ruining us all!"

"You're overstating things a bit, aren't you? I admit I lost my temper with Miss Paget, but I cannot think the situation is as tragic as you describe."

"It will take more than a simple apology to patch things up with her. I heard the accusation you hurled at her, and I saw the look on her face, poor girl! I shudder to think what your marriage shall be like after witnessing the spectacle you just displayed. And what shall her family think?"

"Her family? What the devil have they to say to anything?" he demanded, impatiently.

"You can hardly expect Mr. and Mrs. Paget to turn a blind eye to the way you have treated their daughter! Why, I am certain Helena is in her room this very moment writing to her mother of the scene you just enacted. You have placed your betrothal to Miss Paget in the greatest peril—and all because of that boy!"

"She will forgive me," he said. "I shall make her forgive me."

"You had better—and quickly, too. Why, we are this close—*this close*—" she repeated, almost pinching together her thumb and forefinger, "to having an earl in the family."

"So that's what this is about—not about my happiness or Helena Paget's compassion, but your own desire to have a peer to call your own! I had not thought you so ambitious, Caroline."

"You call it ambitious now, but you were not so critical when I first introduced you to Helena. And I didn't hear a peep from you about principles when she spoke of introducing you to her uncle, Lord Berkridge! The fact is, you were just as desirous of marrying into the Paget family as I— the difference is that you chose to cloak your desire in the language of love!"

"If you doubt my feelings for Miss Paget, Caroline, there is nothing more to be said!"

"How can I help but doubt them? You have been more concerned with lifting a stable boy beyond his station than you have for poor Helena's feelings. And if she should warn her parents that Captain Bingley has taken a crack start into his head and adopted a dirty stable boy, they will descend upon us and carry her away before we know what they are about. *Then* where will you be?"

"But I haven't adopted him. And if I ever utter a plan to do so, you have permission to have me placed under immediate restraint!"

"Do you think her parents will care for the fine distinction? They will only know that you favoured an urchin above their daughter, and treated her shabbily in the bargain!"

He made an impatient gesture. "Then what do you advise?"

"Get rid of that boy. Send him away immediately."

"You know I cannot."

"You *must*. Simply take him back to where he came from," she said with finality.

"Rather like a pair of cufflinks I've taken in dislike."

"Unjust, Robert."

"Is it?" He looked at her a long moment; then, to her very great surprise, he leaned forward and claimed her hand in his. He said, earnestly, "There was a time when you and I were once devoted to each other. We thought exactly alike; we finished each other's sentences. Do you remember?"

She tried unsuccessfully to pull her hand away. "Of course! Aren't we close still?"

"Not like when we were children. Back then we were the best of friends, in fact. We did everything together equally; and we suffered equally when we were caused to be separated—me at Harrow and you at that ladies' seminary in London. I have never forgot it, you know."

He knew by the way she immediately averted her eyes that she had not forgotten either. Somewhere beneath sister's very elegant silk gown and Brussels lace and society manners was the young girl who had been his best friend and greatest ally when he was a child. And when she had gone off to a London boarding school and he to Harrow, their frequent letters to each other had been filled with confidences and expressions of loneliness. But more importantly, their letters had traded pathetic accounts of the treatments they were each made to endure by their fellow students. He had long suspected that Caroline felt her classmates' snubs and sneers far more keenly than he ever had. He knew, too, that she never really forgot what it was like to be afraid and in a strange place; or how it felt to know she was unwanted and shunned by other girls simply because of the means by which her father had gained his fortune. "I think—No, I am certain of it—that somewhere, deep in your memories, must reside even now a spark of compassion for Daniel. He's simply an unfortunate child who is feeling very much as you did so many years ago: friendless and lonely. You see that, don't you? Can't you show him a bit of the compassion you desperately wished someone would have once shown you?"

Caroline pursed her lips together to fight against the memory his words had conjured up, but it was too late; he had already seen her reaction. The tip of her aquiline nose coloured the faintest hue of pink, her chin trembled for the merest second, and a suspicious sheen of moisture gathered in her eyes. He had hoped to rekindle her memory, but even he had to marvel over the fact that after so many years, the simple mention of the hurts of her childhood still had the power to bring tears to her eyes.

She covered her emotions as she always did, by lifting her chin and saying, in a steely voice, "You seem to forget there is to be a ball at Netherfield in less than a fortnight's time."

"I have not forgotten."

"That boy must be gone by then."

"Why?"

"Because the ball is too important to Charles and Jane; and they will not be able to enjoy the evening as much as they would like if they are worried about that child."

"You may be right."

"Of course I am right!"

He smiled softly. "Very well, my dear sister, you have my promise: Daniel will have a new guardian and a new home by the day of the New Year ball."

"I shall hold you to that."

"I won't disappoint you," he said, impulsively planting a kiss upon the back of her hand; "not my best friend."

Now she did snatch her hand away, but the sudden colour in her cheeks bore witness to the fact that she was just as pleased by his gesture as she was embarrassed by it. "You would be better off murmuring your words of love in Miss Paget's ear than mine."

"I shall be her devoted slave at tea time, I promise. That and a heart-felt apology should set her pretty little nose back in its joint," he said as he rose to his feet. "I'll see you at tea, Caroline; but right now I have some work to do, if I am to find a home for Daniel."

He left her then, intending to go in search of the kitchens, but since he had no experience in the lay-out of the house, and no knowledge whatever of the servants' nether-world, that proved easier said than done. He was obliged to ask the assistance of a footman, who led him to a dark corner of the main hall, through a half-concealed door, down a steep case of stairs, and into a cavern of bustling servants that rivaled the traffic of Piccadilly.

The housekeeper had earlier intercepted Mary and Daniel on their way down those very same stairs, and had spirited them away from their original destination and into the small, cramped room from which she directed the business of the household. She had already been apprised of Daniel's presence, for news of his arrival had raged like wildfire through the servants' hall within seconds of Daniel's passing through the front door of the house; and being possessed of a kindly disposition, she desired to shield the poor little boy from the patent stares and encroaching comments of the footmen and maids. She therefore ushered Mary and Daniel into her office, drew two chairs up to the table that served as her desk, and begged them to be seated. Then she disappeared, only to return minutes later with a tankard of fresh milk, and a plate of chicken, bread and cheese.

It was thus that Robert found Mary and Daniel. Mary had tucked a large table napkin into the collar of Daniel's soiled and tattered shirt as if his clothes were made of costly fabrics that needed protecting. Robert entered the office just as Daniel was taking a drink of milk; and as soon as he set the tankard back on the table, Mary tenderly dabbed at his mouth with the napkin and adjured him not to drink too fast, for it would never do to upset his stomach again.

"Here you are. How do you go on?" Robert asked, as he closed the door, shutting out the curious looks of the servants milling in the hallway outside the housekeeper's office.

Mary looked up. "We are doing very well, I think." She watched Robert pull a chair forward, and asked, "How are *you?*"

"I have had a very thorough trimming," he said pleasantly, "but that is not important now."

"Miss Bingley and Miss Paget were very surprised, I dare say."

"They were." He was thoughtful for a moment, then said, "You must make some allowances for Miss Paget, you know. She has not had the experiences in life that you and I have had. She's very young and ignorant of the ways of the world. I fear that by protecting her, her family have shaped her to hide her naturally kind heart, and she cannot express her generous spirit very well."

"I hope you told Miss Paget and your sister this entire affair is my fault."

"I did not."

"But it was I who caused you to worry about Daniel in the first place. Were it not for me, you never would have been forced to bring him here."

"Forced? My dear Miss Bennet, I am a captain in the Hussars. There are very few people—outside my regiment—who can force me to do anything I am not willing to do on my own."

"Is that true? Then you are fortunate, indeed, for I find that I am constantly being told what to do."

He gave her an odd little smile. "That does not necessarily mean you do not have a mind of your own. I have seen how your eyes sparkle when you defend someone you care about."

She looked at him in surprise. "You have?"

"You are certainly Daniel's greatest champion, I think. Here now, how much of that chicken has he eaten?"

"Almost half. He has a healthy appetite, which is a good sign, I think." She watched Daniel take another drink of milk, and murmured, "His fingers are so thin. I cannot help but compare them to my young cousin's—*His* hands are plump and dimpled, as all children's should be."

"Daniel's hands will soon be plump, as will the rest of him. It must be so. I might as well tell you now, Miss Bennet, that I have promised Caroline that I will find a new home for Daniel right away."

She looked at him with surprise. "But I thought Daniel would stay with you!"

"Impossible. I am in the army and go with my regiment I-know-not-where. I can't have a child hanging on my neck."

"But you will not always be in the army."

"Of course I shall."

"But Caroline said you will leave the army as soon as you are—"

"As soon as I am . . . ?" he prompted, after realizing she was not inclined to voice the remainder of her thought.

"As soon as you and Miss Paget—That is, Caroline sounded very definite," Mary finished, in some confusion.

"Did she? I will thank you not to listen to everything Caroline says. She is very good at managing a great many things, but I am not one of them!"

Mary was not so certain, but declined to say so. Instead, she used the corner of the napkin to dab at Daniel's mouth again, and said, gently, "If you could choose anywhere at all, Daniel, where would you like to live?"

"What kind of a question is that to ask a boy?" Robert interrupted.

"Don't you think he should have a say about where he lives?"

"Not if his answer is that he wants to live on the moon."

"But that is nonsense! No one can live on the moon."

"You said *anywhere*, Miss Bennet; and I'm sure if I were a boy and could choose anywhere I wanted to live, *I* would choose the moon."

"I would, too!" said Daniel, surprising both of them.

Robert's brows went up, "And if ever I have a chance to fly to the moon, you shall be the first person I invite to come along. In the meantime, where would you like to live?—And do try to limit your fancy to the confines of Hertfordshire!"

Daniel's brows knit together as he gave the question some thought. "A house?" he suggested.

"I am certain I can find one of those. What else?"

"A house with children."

"A tall order, but I dare say there are plenty of those to be had. What else?"

Daniel thought for a moment. "A mother?"

This simple request almost proved too much for Mary. She dipped her head so neither Robert nor Daniel could see the pity in her eyes; and when she looked up again, she found Robert watching her.

She said, in a steady voice, "It may take a bit of time to find a place that meets that criteria."

"But we don't have a bit of time. That promise I made to

147

Caroline—I have given my word Daniel will be in a new home by the night of the New Year ball."

She stared at him. "But the ball is less than a fortnight away!"

"I know. But the lad cannot live in limbo forever. The sooner a proper home is found for him, the sooner he can settle into his new life."

Mary hoped her countenance did not betray her as she said, in a bright tone for Daniel's sake, "Well, then, we have much work to do. What shall we do first?"

"I can't help thinking," said Robert, "the first thing to do is to make Daniel look as smart as possible. You must be excessively uncomfortable in those clothes, young man."

Daniel looked down at the napkin that covered a good deal of his ragged clothing. "This is all I have, sir."

"Yes, but my brother has gone off to Meryton to buy you a new suit of clothes and shoes and smalls and whatever else you require. And clean clothes must be worn by a clean person. Do you understand me?"

Daniel made a face. "Must I take a bath?"

"Before the clock strikes the hour, if I have anything to say about it."

Since Daniel had finished his meal by this time, there was no excuse for him to tarry longer in the housekeeper's office. He slowly pulled the napkin from his collar and deposited it upon his plate, and was getting up from his chair when Mary stood up, too.

"I shall go with you and help," she said.

Robert shook his head. "Thank you, Miss Bennet, but no! You will be shockingly in the way."

"But I have bathed children before."

"Not in my bedchamber, you haven't. If I find I need assistance I shall call on that footman who acted as my valet this morning." She pursed her lips into a mulish little line, prompting him to add, "Yes, I know, you don't want to leave Daniel at the mercy of a bachelor and a footman, but we will take excellent care of him. When next you see him, I dare say you won't even know him, and I shall have to introduce him to you as Master—" He stopped short and looked down at Daniel. "By the way, what *is* your last name?"

"Westover, sir."

Mary, still with the mulish look about her mouth, had gone to the door; her hand was on the knob, but her progress was arrested upon hearing those two words. She turned quickly; her eyes, wide and questioning, flew from Daniel's face to Robert's.

"Yes, Miss Bennet?"

"Oh, nothing. I simply thought—It is nothing."

"Is it?" Robert asked, looking steadily at her. "You look as if you have had a revelation."

"Oh, no. Nothing like that, only—Please excuse me!"

In the next moment she was gone, leaving Robert to wonder why the name *Westover* had the power to evince such a strong reaction. The question was on the tip of his tongue, but he thought better than to call after her. There would be time enough later to quiz her, but right now he was committed to seeing to Daniel's needs. Still, he could not help thinking of the look of surprise in her hazel eyes; and he resolved that as soon as his young charge was bathed and dressed in fresh clothes, he would seek out Miss Mary

Bennet and demand an honest explanation for her very singular behaviour.

11

It was almost eleven o'clock in the evening by the time Mary finally found the book she required. She had lit a single candle in the library, and though its dim light did not reach the far corners of the large room, it cast just enough light for her needs. She knew the Netherfield library well; many times she had established herself in one of its comfortable chairs and lovingly lingered over the pages of a book. She had studied with pleasure the pictures and charts and maps that hung on the walls, and committed their details to memory; and in the center of the room, where a large table resided, she had explored the base of the table with delight, opening its drawers to expose their mysteries, and reaching into its pigeon holes, hoping to find therein some long-forgotten treasure. It was a library composed of all things she liked most, and she resolved that when she had a home of her own, she would have a library just like the one at Netherfield.

But on this evening she had no time for leisurely reading or exploring the delights of the room; she was on a mission to find a particular book, and she was having a difficult time of it, indeed. She thought she had spied the title on an upper shelf a few days before; and to that end she had wheeled the

library ladder along its rail to the location as she remembered it; but in the shadows of the upper shelves, she could
not find the book.

Her search was a tricky business. She was obliged to hold
on to the ladder rail with one hand and handle the books
with the other; and once, when she thought she found the
book and tried to pull it from the shelf to better read the title
on the spine, the book proved to be heavier than she anticipated, and her slim fingers could not hold its weight, causing
it to fall to the floor with a loud, echoing thud.

Seconds later she heard the door open. She looked down
from her perch to see Captain Bingley standing just inside
the room, a look of concern on his handsome face.

"Miss Bennet? What on earth is going on? That sounded
very much like a gunshot!"

"A book just hit the floor. Forgive me if I disturbed you."

"I was on my way upstairs when I heard the noise." He
closed the door and came further into the room, his attention
firmly fixed on her. "Miss Bennet, what are you doing up
there?"

"I'm looking for a book, naturally."

"But why are you throwing them down on the floor?"

"I didn't throw it. It fell, quite by accident, you can be
sure. You see, I have only one hand to hold onto the ladder
and one hand to pull at the books to read their titles, and the
thick ones will insist on falling if I do not have a good hold of
them."

"But why are you up there? Won't reading one of the
books on these lower shelves prove just as satisfying?"

"No, they won't do at all. I have already determined the

book I am looking for must be up here on one of these shelves. If I were at home I should look at my father's copy, but since I am here . . ." She turned her gaze back upon the rows of books before her. "Oh, there must be an edition of it somewhere—I am certain a library of this size must have one."

"Have what?"

"A *Debrett's Peerage.* I thought it would be easy enough to find, but nothing seems to be in any order that makes sense. I tell you, I am just *itching* to catalog all these books and put them in their proper place. Only see—here is a copy of Dante's *Inferno* shelved right beside Shakespeare's *Sonnets.* Have you ever heard of such a thing?"

Perceiving that she actually expected an answer, Robert said, "No, I have not. But what is so important about reading *Debrett's* now when there are hundreds of other books here from which you might choose?" He cast his gaze about until it lit upon a familiar title on a nearby shelf. "Why, here is *Gulliver!* Now, *that* is a book worth reading. It is one of my favorite novels."

She looked down at him in surprise. "It is?"

"Certainly. Don't you like it?"

"Why, no—I mean, I didn't think men read novels," she said, thinking back to something she thought Kitty had told her.

"I assure you, men do. In fact, it was a novel that made me want to join the king's army. This novel, to be exact— *Gulliver's Travels.* Do you know it?"

"I have heard of it."

"Then let me recommend it to you. It's a fine book, full of

adventure and descriptions of exotic lands." He paused as Mary pulled another book from the shelf, sending a shower of delicate dust into the halo of the candle's light. "Let me also recommend that you come down from that ladder, Miss Bennet. I should not like you to fall."

"I won't."

"But I cannot be easy seeing you up there. Besides, I want to talk to you about Daniel."

"I can hear you quite well from here. What is it you have to say to me?"

"Only that I saw your reaction earlier when Daniel told us his last name. Why did you look so astonished?"

Instead of answering his question, Mary gave a small shout of triumph. "Oh, there it is!"

She stretched her arm out toward the book she was seeking, but the short little volume stood tantalizingly just out of reach. Standing up on her toes did not cure the problem, and she was about to place her foot on the next rung up the ladder when Robert said, in a commanding voice:

"Don't do it!"

"But I must get just a little higher if I am to reach it."

"Come down now, Miss Bennet, and allow me to retrieve the book for you." She hesitated, causing him to say, "If you do not come down this instant, I shall come up there after you."

There was something about Captain Bingley that made Mary think that he was the type of man who was prepared to act on any threat he made. He was certainly a good deal taller than she was and would be able to reach the book with ease.

"Very well," she said, beginning a slow descent.

Once her feet were safely on the floor, he handed her the *Gulliver's Travels*. "Wouldn't you like to read this book instead of the *Debrett's*, Miss Bennet?"

"No—I mean, yes, I will read it on your recommendation, of course! But I still need the *Debrett's*."

"As you wish." He set his foot on the first rung of the ladder, but paused, and looked down into her eyes. "I have a deep suspicion that you make it a practice never to read novels, Miss Bennet."

"That is true."

"What *do* you like to read for pleasure, if you don't mind my asking?"

"Pepys and Pope, usually."

He made a face. "Diaries and poems? I suppose they are all very well, but would you call them inspiring? Surely there must be times when you want to read something that fires your imagination."

She tried to think of such an example, but couldn't. "My sister Kitty reads novels. She swoons over *Evalina*."

"Miss Bennet, don't you think it is time you swooned, too?"

Mary looked up at him, on guard for any sign of mockery in his eyes; instead she saw that his expression was somewhat measuring, and that he was half-smiling at her in a way that was really very charming. She could not help responding to it, even as she wondered whether he meant his words as a compliment or a criticism.

He climbed the remaining rungs with the alacrity of a

sailor climbing a mast; and once he was in position, he reached up and easily took possession of the book she required.

"I never knew," he remarked, after he climbed down the ladder and handed it to her, "that a dull list of the peers of Great Britain and Ireland could excite such enthusiasm in a young lady."

"That is because—Oh, I wasn't going to say anything to you until I was certain, but now I think I may as well tell you as not, though I fear you may think me very foolish."

He smiled at her sudden rush of words. "I can think of nothing that would ever make me think *that*, Miss Bennet."

Slowly she moved to the center of the room where she carefully laid the book on the table, conscious of the fact that he had followed and was standing very close beside her. "The reason I wanted to find this book is because I rather suspect it will benefit Daniel."

"How so? Do you wish Daniel to find employment in the house of a peer?"

"No, but maybe—Oh, it is really too fantastic to consider, but it may be *possible*."

"*What* may be possible?"

"What the landlord said at the Bark and Bull. It was just a mention said in passing—but in the midst of his ridiculous complaints, I heard Mr. Meeks say that Daniel was a *vicar's brat*."

In the dim light of the candle, she could see the sudden recognition in Robert's eyes. "Yes, I heard that, too, now that you have reminded me. But what of it?"

"Well, it got me thinking, for there have not been that

many vicars in the county, and a few years ago our vicar had to go to Hammersmith because his mother fell ill."

"Your vicar," Robert repeated, conjuring an image of the man he had met on Christmas morning. "You mean, Mr. Penrose?"

"No, Mr. Penrose only came to us last spring. I'm speaking of the vicar who had the charge of Meryton *before* Mr. Penrose—but that is not to the purpose, for the important thing is the man who took our vicar's place while he was gone. And then, when Daniel said his name was Westover, why, the entire thing made sense."

"Perhaps to you, but I must say that so far it makes no sense to me at all. Enlighten me!"

"The young vicar who came to us—his name was Mr. Westover!"

Robert's brows went up. "Interesting. Do you imagine the young Mr. Westover who came to Meryton was Daniel's father?"

"I think it is possible."

"Possible, perhaps—but how can we know for certain?"

She tapped her finger against the hard cover of the book. "I think the *Debrett's* may help."

"You think . . . Wait! Are you honestly telling me you think that substitute vicar—your Mr. Westover—was a peer of England?"

She heard the doubt in his words and felt her own cheeks flame in response. He probably thought her foolish; perhaps he thought her idea a preposterous flight of fancy. Oh, how she wished he had never joined her in the library!

"No, not a peer—I simply thought—If we could *just* look

at the page—!" She wasn't certain if it was the doubt in his tone or the nearness of his handsome face to her own that made her feel so befuddled, but she heard her own words dissolve into a morass of stammering speech and knew she would never be able to explain herself. There was nothing for it but to test her theory. She opened the book and flipped to the last page of the alphabetic index of names, and traced her finger down the list.

"Westcote, Westmeath, Westmoreland . . . Westover! Page sixty-seven." She turned to the proscribed page.

"Good God!" said Robert, under his breath, as page sixty-seven proved to contain a good number of revelations, beginning with the title printed at the head of the page:

MARQUESSES.

"Goodness!" Mary added. "I thought it possible for Daniel to be related to a baron, perhaps, but a marquess—!"

She was still digesting this bit of information when she realized that Captain Bingley was already reading aloud the entry printed mid-way down the page:

> QUINTON NUGENT TEMPLE WESTOVER, Marquess of RAINHAM, Earl Cottes, Viscount Tremont, Baron Cottes; of Cottesmere, Lord Lieutenant, and in right of his wife, Hereditary High Steward of Derbyshire.

"I suppose," Robert said, after a long moment of quiet thought, "with a name like Westover it is possible Daniel is related to Lord Rainham, but his must be a distant relation at best, don't you think?"

Mary looked up and was surprised to find that when he

leaned down to read the page, his handsome face was on a level with—and very near to—her own. "The *Debrett's* will tell us." She dared not say more, but deliberately forced her attention back to the book.

There were several paragraphs of text attached to Lord Rainham's entry, and she quickly found the information related to his lordship's progeny. In all, the marquess had nine children—six daughters and three sons—and the *Debrett's* dutifully listed each in turn, along with their dates of birth. Beside each daughter's name was listed her date of marriage and husband's name; for the sons, the content was decidedly more meager.

Beside the name of his eldest son and heir, Thomas, was printed the name of Thomas' wife and the date of their marriage, but no children were listed. The second son was shown to be deceased when he was still in his youth; but it was the information about the third son that caused Mary to stare:

> Daniel Eames Westover, born Jan 19, 1780; married April 10, 1802, Anne Montgomery, daughter of William Montgomery, bart. by whom he had issue, Daniel, born Feb. 1, 1804.

Even though she had suspected there was a chance Daniel Westover—the humble little boy she and Robert had rescued from the inn—could count a peer among his family, she never imagined that peer might be a marquess. She was a bit stunned, and was trying to collect her thoughts when Robert said, "But this is astonishing! How did you *know?*"

"I didn't know, I assure you."

"Then you must be some sort of seer. Why else would you

think to look in this book?" She didn't answer, and he said, "I won't be satisfied until you tell me. Why did you think Daniel was related to a peer and not simply the son of a tenant farmer from the next county?"

"It was something my aunt once said."

"Your aunt? I confess, I am more at sea than ever, Miss Bennet."

"If I tell you, you will know my Aunt Phillips for a gossip."

"Who am I to judge? Besides, I sometimes think what civilians call *gossip* is the very same thing we in the military call *intelligence gathering*. Either way, it can often provide valuable information."

She gave him a shy smile, for there were times when she very much liked the way he said things. "You are very good, but I cannot deny my Aunt Philips *is* a famous gossip; however, I don't suppose, now that I think on it, that there is any reason why one more person should not know it. But the thing of it is, when Mr. Westover came to us that time our own vicar was called away, my mother told my sisters and me that Mr. Westover was the son of a peer, and *she* had the news from her sister, Mrs. Philips."

"But how did your Aunt Philips know about Mr. Westover's family relations?"

"Oh, she knows everything. She lives in Meryton and on most days her drawing-room sees a steady stream of callers, starting with elevenses; that's where she hears all the choicest bits of gossip. And on the front of her house is a great bowed front, and from that window she can see all the way up High Street. That is how she knows who is having a leg of lamb delivered or who has had the doctor in."

"Your Aunt Philips could have a position in the Foreign Office. She sounds like a very busy woman, but I don't think we should rely on rumours told in her drawing-room to establish Daniel's history."

"I agree, but I would like to do a bit of research before we discard the story out of hand."

"What kind of research?"

"I will visit my aunt and ask her if she recalls how she came by the story."

"A sensible course of action. Perhaps you will allow me to go with you."

"Oh, no! You mustn't!"

He was a little startled by the look of mild panic in her eyes, and said, quickly, "I beg your pardon! I didn't intend a breach of etiquette."

"It isn't that. It is only—I have already mentioned how much my aunt loves gossip, and if I were to call upon her with a *gentleman* there is no telling *what* she may think . . . and if my mother should hear of it—!"

"Yes, I see," he said, with sudden understanding. "Well, if I am not to make an appearance before the famous bow window, I will have to content myself with waiting for you to report back to me. In the meantime, perhaps there are one or two things I can do to discover Daniel's past."

"Such as?"

"Well, I can ask him, for one thing. He seems like an intelligent sort of boy, and, hopefully, he knows his father's name; and if that name is Daniel Eames Westover," he added, reading the name from the page of the book, "then it is yet another bit of evidence that Daniel may be related to Lord Rainham."

"He may be more than simply a relation; he may be Lord Rainham's grandson."

He looked down at Mary for a thoughtful moment, and said, in a low voice, "That is an extraordinary possibility. We shall have to be very careful in our proceedings, you and I."

We. You and I.

He said the words so casually, but to Mary they implied so much: a partnership, a secret, an intimacy that he shared with no one but her. The notion thrilled her and frightened her at the same time, for she could feel her good sense eroding as she stood shoulder to shoulder with Robert in the pale light of a single candle in the vast, darkened library. The tenor of his softly-spoken words had an almost hypnotic effect on her, and she had to struggle to find something sensible to say.

"I . . . I don't think we should mention this to Daniel," she said, in a breathless voice.

"No, nor to anyone."

"Perhaps soon—once he realizes he can trust you— Daniel will be inclined to speak of his family and you can coax him into telling what he knows."

"But you'll help me with that, won't you?"

She had the odd sensation that her heart was thudding against her ribs—whether from his nearness or the tenor of his voice, she could not tell. She was obliged to look down at the book so he wouldn't see her reaction. "If you'd like."

"I'm relying on it. Like it or not, Miss Mary Bennet, you and I are in this together. Now," he said as he closed the book, and, taking hold of her wrist, placed the *Debrett's* in her hand, "hold on to this. Keep it somewhere safe, for I have a feeling we may have to refer to it again."

His simple touch on her wrist left a burning sensation that sent her instantly into a flutter of shyness. Gone was the easy intimacy they had shared, replaced by wave after wave of blushes and the old complaint of finding her tongue tangled in a quagmire of words. "Yes. I—somewhere safe. I—of course!"

He smiled slightly and picked up the candle. "Let me take you back to the drawing-room—"

"No!" The word came out a little too strong, but she couldn't take it back. Nor could she ever explain to Captain Bingley that the thought of going back to the drawing-room and seeing him and Helena together was more than she could bear at that moment. "I beg your pardon. It's been a long day. I think I will retire instead. Will you make my good-nights for me?"

"Certainly." He walked with her to the door and opened it for her. "Good night, Mare—Miss Bennet."

"Good night, Captain Bingley." She passed into the hall, expecting the captain to walk with her as far as the door of the drawing-room before she continued on her way to the stairs. Instead she heard the quiet click of the library door closing behind her, and knew that he had elected to remain there alone. She wondered what he meant by it, but her curiosity was quickly supplanted by the realization that he did not intend to return to Helena's side in the drawing-room. That thought—as perverse and small as it was—made her climb the stairs with an unexpected lightness in her step.

12

The next morning Mary stepped out-of-doors to a day of sunshine. Of a certainty, the day was cold, but since she was attired in her warmest winter pelisse, gloves, and hat, she was not uncomfortable.

She had begun the day as she had ended the evening before—in the library. There she had retrieved the *Gulliver's Travels*, which she found on the table where Captain Bingley had left it. She had never been one to read novels before, nor had she ever been one to relish descriptions of adventure and derring-do; but the mere fact that Captain Bingley had recommended the book to her instantly made it in her eyes the most desirable volume in the house. She had secreted it away to her bedroom immediately after breakfast, and now she was prepared to cut short her morning exercise in order to return to her room and begin reading the book just to please the captain.

She left the house with the intention of taking a brief walk about the grounds, but as she started down the drive, she heard the sound of a child's voice coming from the direction of the stables. On a whim she altered her course, and when she rounded the end of the stable block, she saw

Robert riding a beautiful roan-colored horse around the paddock. Daniel was there, too, shrouded once again in a heavy blanket, and standing at the rail fence in the company of an elderly man she recognized as Abbott, the head groom.

"Good morning," she said, as Abbott politely doffed his hat and made a short bow. "Hello, Daniel. Tell me, how did you sleep last night? Well, I hope."

"Yes, ma'am," he said, his thin cheeks glowing in the chilly air. "I had a bath!"

"Did you?"

"Yes, ma'am. See?" He dislodged one of his hands from the folds of the blanket and held it out that Mary might admire his clean and neatly-manicured fingernails.

She clapped her gloved hands together. "How lovely!"

"And look!" He stretched his arms out to his sides to hold the blanket away; beneath it he was dressed in a new suit of clothes—a warm jacket and pants, with sturdy stockings and shoes. Over all was a serviceable winter coat; around his neck was wrapped a woolen scarf; and on his head was a winter cap that fitted snugly over the tips of his ears.

"How handsome you look!" she said, approvingly. "Tell me, are you warm enough? The morning is rather chilly."

"Yes, ma'm. I'm helping with the horses."

"Are you?" She directed an inquiring look at Abbott.

"There's a brazier burning in the stables, miss," said Abbott, "and that's where he's been most of the morning. We kept him as warm as a bite of toast while Captain Bingley took his daily ride. He's only been out here since the captain returned with Ibis."

"I helped while I waited for him," Daniel said, clarifying

the matter.

"How did you help?" she asked.

"I put corn in the trough and I swept the floors."

"He's a fine sweeper, miss," said Abbott, with a paternal air. "As fine as ever I did see."

Daniel's eyes shone bright with the compliment, and Mary couldn't help but contrast his carefree manner on this morning with the fearful little boy she had first met at the Bark and Bull. He was an altered child as he stood at the rail fence, asking intelligent questions of Abbott while his gaze remained focused on Robert and Ibis.

When Mary had first joined them, Robert was putting Ibis through some paces for Daniel's amusement—curveting and prancing, Ibis moved with agile grace around the corner of the yard; but as soon as Robert noticed Mary's presence, he wheeled Ibis about and rode over to the railing.

"Good morning!" he said, as he touched his gloved hand to the brim of his hat. "Will you ride this morning, Miss Bennet?"

"No, thank you, for I do not ride," she said, quickly. "I was about to set out on a walk when I heard Daniel's voice and came to investigate."

"If you ever change your mind about riding, you have merely to say so. You can trust Abbott to select a suitable mount for you. A nice, gentle mare, perhaps—nothing like my Ibis." As if on cue, Ibis rounded her neck and rhythmically lifted each of her legs in a playful little piaffe.

"She is very beautiful," Mary said, and meant it; but she had never been comfortable around horses, and the idea of attempting to ride even a docile old mare was beyond her imagination. Even now it was difficult for her to watch Ibis. The gleaming horse was not as large as Mary expected, but Ibis was a well-muscled and spirited animal. Watching her antics, Mary had to resist the impulse to take a few cautious steps backwards.

Robert threw his leg over the pommel and slid down to the ground. He grasped Ibis' bridle near the bit and led her close to the rail, saying, "Here, Daniel, what do you think of my horse? You met her before, you know." He watched Daniel reach up to run his fingers down the length of Ibis' nose.

"She nickered at me!" he exclaimed, with wonder and delight.

"She remembers you, I think, and she never forgets a friend. Would you like to know a secret about her?"

Daniel nodded.

"She's a foreigner—an Easterner, though you can't tell by looking at her."

Daniel's eyes widened. "Do you mean she's from Essex?"

"No, she's from Egypt," Robert answered, trying not to laugh. "It's a place very far away. Have you heard of it?"

Daniel shook his head. "No, sir."

"In Egypt the desert stretches as far as you can see. They have trees shaped like umbrellas, and no one who lives there has ever seen snow before."

"She is very far from home," Daniel murmured, as he stroked Ibis' nose in the precise manner calculated to make her his abject slave. "She probably misses her mother." This he said in a low voice and with a tender emphasis on the word *mother* that went straight to Mary's heart.

"It is her good fortune to be among friends who love her," she said, "and who will always treat her with kindness. You'll be her friend, won't you?"

"Oh, yes." Daniel touched his forehead to Ibis' nose. "She likes me already, and I like her."

Robert watched him for a moment, then said, "She had a good amount of exercise this morning, and it's time for her first brushing. Would you like to help?"

"Oh, yes!" he said, with a bright look in his eye.

"Off with you, then. Abbott will show you the way."

Daniel hesitated. "But I would rather *you* showed me."

"Why learn from me when Abbott is the expert on horseflesh? Everything I know about horses I learned at Abbott's knee—starting, I think, when I was about your age."

Daniel looked a little doubtfully at Abbott. "Is that true?"

"It is, Master Daniel, and I feel sure you'll learn just as quick as Captain Bingley ever did." He laid a protective hand on Daniel's shoulder, and began to gently usher him toward the stable. "You pay attention, now, Master Daniel, and I'll show you the very brush Ibis likes best."

Robert handed the reins to a waiting groom, and said, as he watched Daniel disappear into the stable block with Abbot, "He looks like a very different boy this morning, doesn't he?"

"He does, indeed. Tell me, how did he fare last night?"

"Rather well, until he saw the preparations for his bath, then he got a little nervous. I was finally able to convince him to get into the tub by holding his hand alongside mine and letting him see how much dirt was accumulated beneath his fingernails compared to mine."

"That was very clever of you," she said. "After a nice warm bath, he was probably very tired and ready for his bed."

"Well, now, that's what I thought—especially after he admired his little cot for a full two minutes at least before he climbed into it. At first he seemed happy enough, and quite enjoyed nestling down beneath the bed clothes, but when I awoke in the night, I found him sleeping on the floor in front of the fire."

"On the floor! That must have been very uncomfortable for him."

"On the other hand, sleeping on the hard floor is no doubt what he is most used to."

"Yes, that is probably true, but that does not make it right. Oh, when I think about what that poor child has been made to endure, I don't know whether to be angry or sorry."

Robert rested his forearms on the top rail of the fence. "There's a good deal of cruelty in this world. It is up to each of us to decide how much of it we will tolerate . . . or not."

There was something in his tone that reminded her very much of the manner in which he had spoken to her the night before, and that was something she had been trying not to think about. From the moment of their acquaintance she had felt that attraction any woman must feel for a man blessed with a handsome face and pleasing manners; but last night in the library, she had felt something more, and that, she knew, was dangerous. When she had taken time to consider it, she realized that her feelings for Captain Bingley had been subtly changing with every encounter between them; little by little she had grown to admire his frankness. She liked the smile in his blue eyes, and his ready courage to shoulder the responsibility for a little boy who was in desperate need of a champion. In Captain Bingley she recognized an innate sense of nobleness that colored everything he did or said or looked. It was in the very set of his head and shoulders, and in his walk, and in the open and trusting way he dealt with everyone he met.

But there was something else, too, that she was almost fearful to admit to herself; for—as fantastic as it seemed—their encounter in the library had convinced her that there was an expression in his eyes that was reserved only for her. She had not seen that same look on his face in his dealings with Charles or Jane; and there was no hint of that look when he spoke charmingly to Helena Paget. It was an expression she found hard to describe, a mixture of intensity and softness; but when he had looked at her in just that way and spoke softly to her of partnerships and secrets, she knew he was sharing with her a portion of himself he shared with no one else. How could she not be beguiled by it all? No man had ever paid her such attentions before; and she had gone to bed savoring and turning over in her mind the memory of every moment of their encounter in the library.

But in the bright sunshine of a December morning, Mary's rational nature returned. A darkened library, a handsome man, a few murmured words spoken in a soft baritone—all the things that had conspired to put romantic notions in her head the night before looked very different in the glaring light of day. However much she liked and admired Captain Bingley, she knew he was a man whose heart was already engaged. He was to marry Helena Paget—

both Charles and Caroline had been very clear about that—
and whatever emotions she felt for him must never be
revealed to anyone. She had too much common sense to
allow it, and too much pride, too, for anyone to discover that
she was fast falling in love with a man already promised to
another. So she deliberately focused her gaze on the toes of
her kid boots, and said:

"I wonder if Daniel realizes yet how fortunate he is that
you stumbled upon that horrid inn on Christmas Eve."

"I have the distinct feeling he does not yet appreciate his
present circumstance. Not, at any rate, after the way he was
treated when we arrived yesterday."

"But Jane and Charles and Kitty were sympathetic. We
can count on their support, at least."

"At least." He repeated the words with emphasis. "No
need to remind me that Caroline and Helena Paget were
noticeably unsupportive. Frankly, they baffle me!"

She immediately regretted her choice of words, and tried
to erase the look of consternation on his face by saying,
quickly, "Your sister and Miss Paget were simply shocked—
They all were! I cannot blame them for being so, can you?
Why, I am certain I have never seen a ragged and dirty little
boy in any other drawing-room before. What a sight we must
have been!"

He smiled slightly. "A sight, indeed! You and I were both
wind-tossed and pink from the cold!"

"And I had dirt on my skirts from my knees to my
ankles—which I didn't even notice until I went to my
chamber to change for tea."

He laughed outright. "I thought Caroline was going to

have an attack of the apoplexy!"

"And I thought Miss Paget was going to jump up and flee the room," Mary said, joining his laughter. "I hope they will forgive us."

"They must. I can't go back on my actions now."

"Nor should you. But today is new and fresh, and I am certain by this morning both Caroline and Miss Paget have had time to regret their actions. Today they will be more tender-hearted."

He raised his eyebrows and gave her a measuring look. "Rainbow chasing, Miss Bennet?"

"I hope I am always optimistic," she said, a bit defensively.

"Yes, I rather think you are."

"There are worse things to be."

"Self-centered and mean-spirited come to mind—Two qualities I hope I shall not see again where Daniel is concerned." He was quiet for a moment, then said, "Forgive me. I should not have said that."

"Your feelings are understandable. You have grown very protective of him in a short amount of time."

"I have, but there's a danger in that. I don't want him to become too attached to me."

"Your concern comes too late, I fear. Perhaps you have not noticed the way his eyes follow you wherever you go. He looks to you as his hero; you cannot fail him now."

"I have no intention of failing him, Miss Bennet." He pushed himself away from the fence rail and said, in a rallying tone, "I have finished exercising Ibis, and Abbott can be relied upon to keep Daniel busy for the next hour or two.

Will you walk with me to the house?"

She dipped her head in assent. He placed one booted foot on the lower rail then leapt gracefully over the top of the fence.

He fell into step beside her as they began a slow progress toward the house. "I have been thinking of what you said to me last night, Miss Bennet—were I not a soldier, I might be inclined to keep Daniel with me."

"I did not mean to imply a criticism."

"Nor did I infer one; but a soldier's life is not his own. Caring for a child would be impossible, I think."

"Do you ever find military life difficult? I am certain there are many hardships in your way."

"There are, but there are benefits, too. I have been fortunate to travel the world, and I've seen many far-away places."

"While I have only *read* about far-away places," she said, sensibly. "There is only so much one can learn from reading a book. To truly appreciate a place—its history and architecture and unique culture and, oh, so many other things!—one really must visit a place."

"I could not agree more. I hope you will have the chance to travel to exotic lands some day. It is not a life for everyone, but I think you have it in you to be a great adventurer."

"You do?"

"Of course. Tell me, if you could go to some exotic location anywhere in the world, where would you go?"

"To Derbyshire."

Her reply surprised a laugh out of him. "Derbyshire does not meet the definition of an exotic location."

"It does if one has never been farther abroad than Hertford."

"A point taken, Miss Bennet. But why Derbyshire?"

"I have a sister there I have not seen since her marriage a year ago."

"Very well, I will allow your first destination to be Derbyshire. Where next would you like to go?"

"Anywhere, I suppose, and everywhere. China or Burma —perhaps the New World!"

"America? Would you really go there?"

"Yes. Wouldn't you?"

"Indeed I would, but it's all very wild there, you know. I hear their cities are civilized enough, but between them is a great deal of wilderness."

"Wilderness just waiting to be explored."

"I think," he said, looking down at her appreciatively, "you are an adventuress at heart." He saw the protest form on her lips, and said, quickly, "Yes, I know, *adventuress* is not a word ladies of quality usually like to have attached to their names, but between you and me—If I may be so bold to suggest it—I have often thought that ladies have just as much right to see the world as we men do. As you say, there is only so much that can be learned from a book. I suppose you may read on the printed page a description of a Bedouin's tent, but until you can see it for yourself, and touch it and feel the heavy coarseness of the fabric, you can never really appreciate what it is like to live as a Bedouin does."

"That is my thought exactly," she said, wondering how this man—who had been a complete stranger to her two days before—could state so clearly what was in her heart.

"I hope you get your wish, Miss Bennet, and travel to exotic lands. It is not a life for everyone, but I think you have it in you to be a great explorer."

This, she decided, was a compliment out of the common way. She blushed slightly, and tried hard not to reveal how pleased she was by his words. When next she looked up at him, she was ready to be practical again, and said, "I noticed Daniel had no mittens this morning. My sisters and I are driving to Meryton today to visit the shops, and I'll purchase one or two pairs for him."

"Will Caroline and Miss Paget go with you?"

"Yes, and that makes the excursion a bit tricky. I had hoped to have the chance to call on my Aunt Phillips, but now I don't see how I can."

"What will prevent you?"

"Caroline and Miss Paget. Neither is known to my aunt, although my aunt would not object to receiving them, if they cared to call."

"And therein lies the rub, for I cannot imagine either lady engaging in such a breach of etiquette. Tell me, what is your Aunt Phillips' situation?"

"Her husband is an attorney."

"A noble profession to be sure, but I dare say my sister would not care to pursue the acquaintance." He slowed his pace a little and said, somewhat carefully, "Caroline was not always so, you know. There was a time, years ago, when her manner was more accepting, and she was more willing to be pleased."

"What circumstance changed her?"

"I do not think I can point to a single event; it was a series of little things that she seemed to take very hard—things that did not impact Charles and me in the same way. Beneath her airs and her prideful demeanor she is still possessed of a sensitive nature, I think."

Mary thought Caroline made excellent work of hiding her sensitivity—if, indeed, she had any. She said, diplomatically, "Perhaps one day she will consider making the acquaintance of my aunt and uncle, but for today I would be glad to call on them alone. If I have a chance to get away without exciting anyone's interest, I will visit my aunt."

"I know you'll be careful in what you say to her. It would never do to have our suspicions revealed before we have a chance to first make one or two inquiries."

"I will be *very* careful," she promised.

At the house they separated; Robert remained in the hall where he handed his coat, hat, and gloves to a waiting footman, and Mary mounted the stairs to her bedchamber.

She had just finished laying off her things when Kitty knocked on the door and entered without waiting for answer.

"Mary, are you going with us to Meryton?"

"Yes, I am. Do you know what time Jane plans to set out?"

"Soon, I think, for everyone has had breakfast by now. I'm going to buy some ribbons to wear in my hair at the ball. What will you buy, Mary?"

"I don't know. I suppose I shall do the same—ribbons for my hair. And I think I will buy some mittens for Daniel."

"But Charles and I bought gloves for him yesterday."

"Yes, but he needs warm mittens to cover his hands out

of doors."

Kitty sat down on the edge of the bed and asked, in a tone of concern, "Mary, what you going to do about that boy?"

"I don't know yet. I believe Captain Bingley plans to find a suitable home for Daniel."

"He shall have to find one soon, for I don't think Caroline or that horrid Miss Paget will stand silently by if Daniel remains in the house for long."

Mary frowned. "What do you mean?"

"Oh, nothing. I refuse to say more, for it appears Captain Bingley means to marry Miss Paget, and though I cannot like it, I suppose we must endure her if she is going to be part of the family."

"It is not enough to *endure* her, Kitty; you must be polite to Miss Paget."

"But I'm *very* polite. I have been the *pink* of politeness, but I cannot figure her out. She is sweet and dear one minute, and prickles and thorns the next. You must have noticed."

Mary had, but she chose not to say so. In the first days of their acquaintance Helena Paget had gone out of her way to be kind to her, prompting Mary to form the opinion that Miss Paget just might prove to be as pure-hearted as she was beautiful; but Miss Paget's behavior toward Daniel had wrought serious injury to that belief. She hoped she was wrong; she hoped that she was simply witnessing Miss Paget's shocked reaction to an unusual circumstance, and that Miss Paget did not mean to behave so unkindly toward Daniel. For Captain Bingley's sake, she prayed that was the case; but in the back of her mind she couldn't see how a young woman possessed of so many fine qualities could be so lacking in compassion for an ill-treated little boy.

The ladies drove to Meryton in high state, with a coachman and two grooms to attend them. Before Jane's marriage to Charles Bingley, the Bennet sisters often visited Meryton to shop or call on their aunt, but on such occasions they had been obliged to walk the distance between Longbourn and Meryton. But on this morning they were at all times under the care of the Bingleys' dedicated servants. Jane ushered the ladies from store to store very much like a mother hen might pilot her chicks, while footmen waited outside, ready to carry their purchases as soon as they emerged from the shops. This, to Mary, was luxury indeed; and as she had never before traveled any farther than Meryton in her life, she had no basis for comparing that town's shops with any other.

But Helena Paget and Caroline Bingley had both made it a practice to shop in the best establishments London had to offer. Both ladies were used to the finer things in life, and quickly realized that the wares offered in a town like Meryton were not at all similar to the quality of wares to which they were accustomed.

They had just emerged from the first shop where Mary and Jane had purchased two pairs of mittens for Daniel, when Helena's attention was caught by an item in the milliner's window.

"Why, do my eyes deceive me or is that a coquelicot ribbon on that bonnet in the window across the street?" She became very animated, saying, "And a feather, too, of the same color! Who would have thought to see such a fashionable bonnet in a little market village like Meryton!"

Kitty remarked, with a great deal of annoyance, that Meryton was not a village, but a town; and she was sure the bonnets to be had in Meryton were just as fashionable as those found in London; but Miss Paget did not attend her. She stated her intention to enter the shop, and just as everyone else began to follow her across the street, Mary saw an opportunity to slip away.

She said, very quickly in Jane's ear, "I'll just run in to call on Aunt Phillips for a few minutes. I shall meet you presently!" And she hurried away before Jane had a chance to stop her.

This Caroline deemed very questionable behavior. "Where is Mary going?" she asked, as she and Jane hastened to catch up to Helena and Kitty, who were already entering the milliner's shop.

"She has gone to call on our aunt," Jane answered. "She will join us later."

"Does she normally traipse about the village in such a manner?"

"How do you mean?"

"She is a young, unmarried woman. Certainly she should not be allowed to go about unchaperoned."

"You are right, of course, but in a town like Meryton we are quite comfortable. And besides, my aunt's house is just down the street a little ways. You can see her bow window from here. I am certain she is standing there now watching our progress down the street."

This disclosure made Caroline look up at the bow window in some alarm. "You mean she is watching us from her window at this very moment?"

"I cannot say for certain, but she often does."

"Will you call on her?"

"Not today. Mary will make our apologies."

By this time they had entered the shop, where Helena had already instructed the proprietor to have the bonnet with red ribbons removed from the window so she might try it on.

Caroline did not join her; instead she moved idly about the shop, running her gloved hand over a fur muff, pulling at a ribbon of decorative tape, and, in general, touching bits of merchandise without really seeing any of it.

Kitty joined her, and said, in a challenging tone, "I don't suppose you will find anything here you will like."

"Why do you say so?" Caroline asked, with mild annoyance.

"Because you are used to frequenting London shops, and I dare say you will find nothing in Meryton that you would consider purchasing."

At first Caroline did not answer, then she met Kitty's eyes and said, loftily, "On the contrary. I have just thought of something I liked very much in the first shop we visited. I have half a mind to go back for it."

"Do you? Then I am surprised. I will tell Jane—"

"No, don't bother her. I will go myself to fetch it and will be back before you know it. Tell Jane not to wait for me. I shall meet you at the carriage in a little while."

With a determined set to her chin she slipped through the shop door and out onto the street, intent upon engaging in the very same behavior she had condemned Mary for but moments ago. Caroline had been watching for an opportunity to slip away without being noticed, and with Jane and Helena distracted by the bonnet, this seemed as good a time as any.

One of Charles' well-trained grooms stepped forward to assist her, but she waved him away, for she wanted no one to gauge her intention. Instead, she made her way down the street to the next corner, where she quickly made the turn, following her instinct and a vague memory of the tall church spire she had seen peaking above the treetops on their approach to Meryton.

She walked quickly and soon found herself on the lane that led to the church, and the gothic-style vicarage just beyond. She mounted the stone steps and sounded the knocker in an imperative manner.

The door opened slowly to reveal an elderly woman with a flushed face, wearing an apron on which she was wiping her hands as a sign she had just come from the kitchens. Surprised, the woman's gaze rapidly took in every detail of Caroline's appearance, from the curled feathers of her fashionably high-crowned bonnet to her expertly tailored pelisse and expensive kid boots.

"Good morning," Caroline said, in the same tone she used when addressing any servant. "Is Mr. Penrose at home? Good. You may give my name. Miss Caroline Bingley is calling."

So saying, she stepped past the astonished woman into the reception hall, and waited expectantly for her name to be announced.

13

What on earth could the woman possibly be doing? Caroline waited in the entry hall with a mounting sense of impatience. She was not a woman who was used to being kept waiting; this fact, combined with a keen awareness that Jane and the other Netherfield shoppers might at any moment begin their search for her, caused her impatience to soar. She simply *had* to be allowed to speak to Mr. Penrose without further delay.

There were several doors that led off the main hall, and she had watched the housekeeper disappear behind one of them. Caroline moved toward it; the door was slightly ajar and beyond it she heard the murmur of a man's voice in conversation with the housekeeper's.

In Caroline's mind there was nothing worse than to know she was being discussed by others in a less than favorable light; from there it was no very great leap to imagine that Mr. Penrose meant to instruct the housekeeper to express his regrets and claim he was not at home to receive her. That was behavior not to be borne. She was determined to have her way and speak to the vicar without delay. She squared her shoulders and purposefully pushed the door open. In the next moment she was in the room, surprising both the vicar and his housekeeper into startled silence.

Mr. Penrose was standing behind a large, old-fashioned oak desk. He was in his shirt sleeves, having draped his simply-tailored black coat over the back of a nearby chair; and his momentary surprise allowed Caroline the opportunity to note every nuance of his appearance. Though they had met previously, she had never taken his measure before; she had thought him simply another village vicar of modest dress and unremarkable manner; but seeing him in the thin lawn of his dress shirt, she couldn't help but notice that he was tall and lean, with narrow hips. He was also a good deal younger than she had first imagined, for the beams of sunlight that streamed through the window fell on the smooth planes of his face, betraying his youth and bringing rich highlights to the waves in his brown hair.

Mr. Penrose quickly took up his coat, shrugged his arms into the sleeves, and tugged the lapels into proper order over his chest. "Miss Bingley! This is an unexpected surprise. I did not hear a carriage pull up in the drive."

"I walked here," she said, curtly.

His brows went up. "From *Netherfield?*"

"Certainly not! I am come from High Street. I am supposed to be shopping with my sisters-in-law, so you will forgive me, I know, for coming to you this way; but I assure you, I am here on a matter of grave importance that cannot wait."

He murmured something to the housekeeper as he came around the desk to place a chair for her. "Please sit down, Miss Bingley. Tell me, how may I be of service to you?"

She didn't answer right away, but waited for the housekeeper to leave before she made an answer. She rather liked the fact that the vicar was ready to get right to the meat of the matter—no prevarication, no needless declaration about the honor of receiving an unexpected call from such a distinguished lady. He was, she could tell, a sensible man who would know just what to do. Yes, she was quite satisfied with him, and she felt confident he would agree to her plan.

She folded her hands in her lap and looked across the desk at him. "I am come to request your assistance, Mr. Penrose, on a very delicate matter. You see, my brother Captain Bingley is soon to be married."

"And may I assume the young lady in question is Miss Paget?"

"You may; but how did you know?"

"Simple observation, Miss Bingley. I have a very clear view of my parishioners from the elevated perch behind my pulpit. During the service on Christmas morning it was not difficult to see that Captain Bingley and Miss Paget were quite smitten with each other. Tell me, when will the marriage take place?"

Since Caroline was rather certain Robert had not yet officially asked Miss Paget for her hand in marriage, she found this question difficult to answer. "No specific date has yet been named. There are some details that must be gratified first."

"Ah! And you wish me to read the banns?"

"Good heavens, no! In fact, I want you to promise me you will refuse to render such service if it should be asked of you."

"May I ask why?"

"I will not have my brother married here in this *wilderness*. He will be married in London in the spring, when Miss Paget's uncle, Lord Berkridge, is in town."

"And Lord Berkridge's attendance at the wedding is important to you?"

"It is vital," she replied, thinking of the many social advantages that would result from such a connection.

"Is that what your brother wants?"

"My brother wants what is best for the family; and, of course, he is keen to please Miss Paget. *She* is a young woman who demands only the best, and why shouldn't she? The Pagets are well-established leaders of society."

Mr. Penrose looked at her for a thoughtful moment. "I stand ready to be of service to you, Miss Bingley, but so far, I know not how."

"Allow me to speak plainly, please. What I am about to impart may very well shock you, but I am determined to lay the case before you with all honesty."

"Very well. I am prepared to be shocked, Miss Bingley."

He did not look ready to be anything of the sort; in fact, she had a strong suspicion that he was doing his best not to laugh at her. She raised her chin and said, majestically, "My brother has assumed responsibility for a child—a stable urchin for whom he allowed himself to feel sorry; and in a rash and unfortunate flight of fancy, he took possession of the child." She had the satisfaction of seeing his expression change from one of mild amusement to genuine surprise.

"Took possession?" he repeated.

"Yes. Robert removed the child from his . . . *stable* and

has installed him in the drawing-room at Netherfield!"

"Has he indeed? That suggests to me that your brother has a rather deep altruistic streak."

"I know."

"And you wish he did not?"

"No! Oh, you have quite mistaken my meaning. I do not fault Robert for showing kindness to strangers, but you must agree that he has gone too far in this case."

His brows came together slightly. "And you wish me to counsel him?"

"No, I wish you to take the child."

Now he really was astonished, and repeated, in a tone of disbelief, "*Take* him?"

"Yes, take him and do something with him."

"Such as . . . ?"

"Whatever it is that vicars do with orphans," she said, impatiently.

"Vicars do not, as a rule, do anything with orphans," he said, in a reasonable tone, "other than tend to their souls."

"But what of the poor? Surely you have methods for helping the poor."

"I do, but my methods as a vicar are no more than any individual possessed of a serviceable conscience may employ—in fact, I'd venture to say my ability to help is considerably less."

"But you're a vicar! You are supposed to aid widows and orphans."

"Aren't we all, Miss Bingley? Certainly those people possessed of wealth and means are better situated to offer relief to the less fortunate among us."

Caroline's fingers, still clasped in her lap, tightened until her knuckles showed white. She was becoming quite exasperated with Mr. Penrose, but she was determined not to reveal her feelings for fear she might dissuade him from her purpose.

"Perhaps I have not made my intentions clear," she said, in a calmer tone than she had used before. "I am not asking you to assist the child in a monetary way. But certainly you know the neighborhood, and you are well acquainted with the people of Meryton. There must be some family—some person who would be willing to take the child. Here is my suggestion: I will bring him to you. He will stay with you, allowing you the opportunity to know him and sketch his character. That, I am certain, will greatly assist you in selecting the right family that will take the boy on a permanent basis."

"That is an interesting proposition, Miss Bingley. But would the matter not be equally settled if the child were to stay at Netherfield while I make inquiries about the neighborhood?"

"No, it would not. The child must be gone from Netherfield as soon as possible."

"May I inquire the reason for such immediacy?" She hesitated, prompting him to ask, "Does the boy possess a defect of character that gives concern? Come, come, Miss Bingley, you might just as well tell me the whole of it rather than a piece. Why are you so intent upon immediately removing the child from Netherfield?"

"Because that boy is slowly driving a wedge between my brother and Miss Paget." She had the satisfaction of seeing another flash of surprise in his hazel eyes. "It is difficult to understand, I know, but my brother has never been one to do things by halves. He rescued the child from a cruel innkeeper—At least, that is the story my brother has circulated—and until he can find a home for the child, he is determined to have the care of him. You must realize that every minute Robert spends with that boy is one less minute he spends with Miss Paget."

"Am I to understand that Miss Paget does not share your brother's views toward charity?"

"Oh, she has a very kind heart, to be sure; but she is well aware that nothing good can come from elevating a stable boy beyond his natural sphere in life. Why, yesterday that boy took tea with the family in the drawing-room! Certainly you can see how much harm that will do the boy in the long run."

"That is Miss Paget's opinion?"

"It is."

"And do you share in this opinion, Miss Bingley?"

"My chief concern is and always will be the welfare of my family," she said, in a lofty tone.

"That is an admirable sentiment, to be sure."

She waved her gloved hand in a dismissive gesture, for she was determined to keep the conversation on the subject of her choosing. "Then you understand why the boy must be removed from Netherfield immediately. Now, will you take the child or not?"

He looked at her for a long moment as he considered the question. "May I ask the age of the child?"

"I have no notion of it. He may be nine years of age—

perhaps ten."

"And what is his history? Who are his people?"

"They may be gypsies for all I know! Why do you ask such questions? Surely you must suppose that if he had any relations I would petition *them* to take charge of the boy."

"Yes, I've no doubt you would. Well, Miss Bingley, you have certainly presented me with a fascinating puzzle this morning. I cannot think when I have had a more stimulating conversation with a more intriguing person. I shall certainly give your request my utmost consideration."

"But how long will that take?" she asked, unable to hide her disappointment. "I was counting upon your immediate assistance. Time is of the essence in this matter."

"Yes, so you have said. Very well; allow me to suggest a course of action. I propose calling upon you at Netherfield so I may see the child for myself, after which I will be in a better position to determine whether it is in the best interest of everyone concerned for me to take charge of the boy."

"Then I must insist you call at Netherfield this afternoon," she said with finality as she stood up and prepared to leave.

"As you wish . . . with one condition."

She stopped short and looked up into his eyes as he, too, rose to his feet. "And what condition is that?"

"Nothing to cause alarm, I assure you. But you will recall that you and I struck a bargain upon the occasion of our first meeting. Do you remember? I promised to pray for your brother's safe arrival at Netherfield on Christmas Eve, and in exchange, you promised to appear at church on Christmas morning."

"Oh," she said, with some relief, "and I suppose you want me to attend church service again on Sunday?"

"That would be quite satisfying, Miss Bingley; but, no, that is not the condition I seek."

"Then what it is you want of me?"

"My proposal is this: I will call at Netherfield to meet the boy, and I will consider your request that I find a home for him. In exchange, you will call here again tomorrow, when I will show you the life children lead when they are thrown upon the charity of the Parish."

This was a surprising proposal, to be sure, and Caroline did not know what to make of it. She suffered an odd sensation that there was some hidden danger in his plan—that by agreeing to his offer she would find herself in uncomfortable territory. But he stood watching her with an expectant look in his hazel eyes that held no trace of malice or cunning. She lifted her chin a little.

"Very well," she said. "I agree to your terms. You will call at Netherfield today in time for tea. And I shall return here again tomorrow, but for what purpose I cannot imagine."

"Shall we say, after lunch?" he asked, ignoring her implied complaint.

She gave a curt nod of her head, then waited as he circled the desk and opened the door for her. "May I have your assurance, Mr. Penrose, that our conversation today will be kept in the strictest confidence?"

"Unnecessary to ask, Miss Bingley, for I hold all conversations with my parishioners in the strictest confidence. I see by your expression you are not convinced," he said, with that light in his eye she had come to believe was a sign he was possessed of a very freakish sense of humor. "Very well—I give you my oath that I will not divulge to anyone the subject of our meeting today." He opened the door then, and smiled at her. "Good day, Miss Bingley. I have enjoyed your visit, and I shall see you again presently."

Mary was alone in the drawing-room, playing the piano-forte when Robert came into the room. She stopped playing immediately, telling herself that it was only polite to offer him a proper greeting upon seeing him for the first time that day; but in truth, she stopped because her senses had been arrested by the look in his blue eyes. He was happy to see her, of that she was certain; and no sooner did that realization spring to her mind than her fingers began to tremble, and any thought of playing on quickly evaporated.

"Here you are!" he said, in a faint tone of relief. "I was hoping I'd have a moment or two alone with you. I understand you went to Meryton today. Do not tease me, Miss Bennet—if it is true, tell me so at once!"

"It is true." She made a great show of arranging the sheet music on the top of the instrument while she tried to tame her quaking fingers.

"And did you visit your aunt?"

"I did, but I beg you not to tell anyone. You see, I stole away while Miss Bingley and Miss Paget were shopping, so you mustn't betray me and tell them I was walking about the streets without a proper chaperone."

He smiled at her. "You must know by now that any secret

of yours is safe with me."

"I do know it. Of course I do! And I have much to tell—"

She stopped short as the door opened to admit Caroline and Helena, who were in the company of Mr. Penrose.

That gentleman first greeted Robert, then turned to Mary and said, cordially, "Please don't stop playing on my account, Miss Bennet. I heard your music upon my entrance in the house, and I must say, I think you have improved in your playing these past few weeks, if that is possible."

It was very nice to be complimented in such a way, for Mary rarely received encouragement to play from anyone outside members of her own family. She ran her tapered fingertips over the smooth surface of the pianoforte. "If I have shown improvement it is because of the instrument, I think."

"You are very modest, Miss Bennet."

Caroline moved around the pianoforte and quietly closed the fallboard over the keys. "It is always preferable to play a pianoforte over a spinet, is it not? Do come and join us by the fire, Miss Bennet. We rely so much upon your conversation."

This Mary divined as a sign that she was no longer invited to play; and she meekly followed Caroline and the rest of the party to the sofas arranged in front of the fireplace.

"What brings you here, Mr. Penrose?" asked Helena, as she arranged her skirts about her. "Did some divine guidance send you here to help entertain us?"

"Do you require someone to entertain you, Miss Paget?"

"Country life is very dull compared to life in town," she replied. "At times it is difficult to fill the days with anything

192

of interest."

"But country life affords many pleasures you cannot find in London, Miss Paget—especially when you consider the uncommon fine weather we have been enjoying this time of year. Nature has given us an invitation to spend our days out of doors while we can."

"I suppose that is true," she said peevishly, "if one enjoys shooting and walking and riding."

Mr. Penrose looked at her in mild surprise before his gaze shifted to Captain Bingley, who was standing close by the mantle. "I have heard a rumor *you* are a bruising rider, Captain. You, I think, must hold with a different opinion."

"I do, but only because I learned to ride at the age of five; I confess I feel more at home on the back of a horse than at an assembly or in a London drawing-room. Give me a good horse and a beautiful countryside to be explored, and I am a happy man."

It was then that Kitty made an appearance, just as the butler and a footman were placing the tea things on the table beside Jane's favorite chair. Charles and Jane entered soon after with Daniel; and for a time all conversation halted as the newcomers greeted Mr. Penrose.

"I hope this is a social call," said Jane, "and not a matter of church business. No one in the neighborhood is ill, I hope."

"Nothing of the kind," the vicar assured her. "I have come simply to satisfy my curiosity. I heard you have a new inmate at Netherfield, and I wish to make his acquaintance."

"This is Daniel Westover, sir," Jane said, as she drew the boy forward. "But how did you know of him?"

"News has a way of traveling quickly in a town like Meryton. It did not take long for a rumor to circulate that a young boy of uncertain age had taken up residence under your patronage."

"For once you have heard a rumor that may be relied upon as true," Charles said, as he placed a protective hand on Daniel's shoulder. "Daniel, you may be interested to know that Mr. Penrose is the vicar here."

Mr. Penrose extended his hand to the boy. "I have been anxious to make your acquaintance, Daniel. How do you do?"

Daniel looked up at him and immediately shook hands. "I am well, thank you, sir. My papa was a vicar."

"Was he, indeed? I should be very interested to hear about your father sometime."

"Thank you, sir."

Jane claimed Daniel's attention then, inviting him to sit beside her while she prepared the tea. "You look quite handsome this afternoon, Daniel. Do you like your new suit of clothes?"

"Yes, ma'am, very much so. And see?" He reached into the back pocket of his trousers from which he produced the wooden bilbo-catcher Robert had kept back from the Boxing Day offerings. "Captain Bingley gave this to me."

"Captain Bingley is very kind. I hope you thanked him properly."

"Yes, ma'am, I did." Daniel looked over to where Robert stood near the fire, close to the sofa on which Mary and Helena sat with the vicar. "I thanked him very thoroughly."

Jane bestowed on him her sweetest smile. "That was very

good of you. Now, you sit right here beside me while I pour you some tea." She had a sudden thought, and said, quickly, "I suppose I should have first asked if you drink tea? Some children, you know, don't like it very much. Tell me, Daniel, did you drink tea at the inn?"

"No, ma'am, but my mummy made tea; and I think I like it."

"You *think?*" she repeated with a smile. "We shall soon know for a certainty. Let me see if I can make a nice cup of tea that you will like." And she immediately employed her talents in the alchemy of concocting a suitable cup of tea for a child. "Weak, I think; with a good amount of cream. There! See if this is to your liking." She carefully handed him a half-full cup of a lightly-colored and generously-sweetened brew.

Daniel took a tentative sip and his eyes lit up. "I like it very much, thank you."

"I'm glad," Jane said. "I shall remember to make your tea that way from now on." She then turned her attention upon the rest of the party and spent the next few minutes serving her guests.

Mary had been watching Daniel's exchange with Jane, and said, "I have observed, Daniel, that you have very lovely manners. Have we your mother to thank for that?"

"Yes, ma'am."

"She must have been a very fine woman. Tell me, what was your mother's name?"

He thought for a long moment. "Mummy."

Mary heard a wistful note in Daniel's voice as he said the word, and her heart went out to him. There was so very much she wished to know about Daniel and she was glad

Jane had employed her sweetest charms to make him feel relaxed enough to speak of his family.

"What about your father, Daniel?" Mary asked, gently. "Do you recall his name?"

"Oh, yes, for he was named Daniel, too. I heard mummy call him so."

Startled, it was all Mary could do not to look at Robert's face. Still, she felt certain she could read his thoughts; knew, too, that he was now thinking that Daniel and his father shared a name. She thought back to their evening in the library, the words they had found in the *Debrett's*, and the seeds of speculation they had sown together. Were those seeds about to bear fruit? It was almost too much to consider, but there was a chance—a very real chance—that little Daniel just might be related to the Marquess of Rainham.

Mary did her best to show a calm face to Daniel. She leaned forward, as if closing the distance between herself and Daniel would somehow draw from him the very information she was so anxious to obtain. "Daniel is a very noble name. Have you any brothers or sisters? What are *their* names?"

"I had a sister once, but she had the influenza and died."

Jane wrapped a protective arm around Daniel's shoulders as Mary said, sympathetically, "That is a great loss and I am very sorry for you. I'm sure you miss her. Was your sister younger than you?"

"Yes, ma'am. Her name was Elizabeth." In the days since arriving at Netherfield, Daniel's initial reticence had abated; and though he still felt shy in the presence of a room full of adults, he was comfortable enough to share another morsel of information. "My mummy and papa had the influenza, too."

Kitty, who had been listening with interest, was anxious to lighten the mood of the people around her, and said, cheerfully, "I also have a sister named Elizabeth. She lives in Derbyshire now. I've never been there, but she writes that it's a lovely place and she wants me to visit her soon."

Daniel looked at her with a spark of recognition flickering in his eyes. "I have heard of Derbyshire."

"How do you know of it?" Mary asked. "Have you ever been to Derbyshire, Daniel?"

"No, ma'am, but my papa said he would take me there one day."

"And did he say *why* he would take you to Derbyshire?"

Daniel shook his head. "No, ma'am."

Kitty set her cup and saucer on the table and extended her hand to him. "Have you finished your tea? Then come with me for I purchased something for you in Meryton earlier today, and I think you will like it very much."

She led him to a corner of the room where she had left a parcel on the table; she presented it to him, and watched his reaction as he opened the package. Inside were a spinning top, and a flat of toy soldiers cast from pewter and painted in vivid colors.

Daniel let out an exclamation of delight, which drew Jane and Charles to join him and Kitty at the table to see for themselves the cause of his joy.

Robert took a seat on the sofa they had vacated. "As you see, Mr. Penrose, Daniel is a very unusual boy. We learn something new of him every day, it seems."

"I would be interested to know the boy better, myself," said the vicar. "Will you tell me how you met him and what you know of him?"

Robert opened his mouth to reply, but Miss Paget was there before him, saying quickly, "He is nothing but a stable boy. A dirty little stable boy who told a very sad tale to Captain Bingley. The poor man was caught in that urchin's web of pity before he knew what he was about!"

Mr. Penrose's hazel eyes examined her placid expression as he said, calmly, "Captain Bingley does not appear to me the sort of man who can be coerced into doing something he would as lief rather not. Wouldn't you agree?"

"Ordinarily I would concede he is a man of strong character, but you must know that men have no knowledge of children. They are no match for a child's cunning."

"I cannot agree there, either," Mr. Penrose said, smiling slightly. "I do not wish to shock you, Miss Paget, but I feel I must confess that I was a child myself once, and I do not recall being possessed of a *cunning* streak."

"Oh, you know what I mean," she said, in a more playful tone. "That boy has done very well for himself in a short period of time. Installed in the drawing-room at Netherfield! Why, his present circumstance is one I am certain he will not like to quit when the time comes."

Mr. Penrose's gaze strayed briefly toward Caroline's face before he said, "By that, I assume you mean, Miss Paget, that a more permanent situation must be found for the boy."

"Indeed, it must. And soon."

"But not just any situation," Robert said, frowning. "It must be suitable for him. I have pledged to take on myself the responsibility of finding him a home."

"I wish you well with that endeavor, Captain," the vicar said. "He seems a very nice young boy, and his manners are pleasing enough."

Helena sighed prettily. "Yes, he knows how to copy others, there is no question of that."

Robert's face flushed with resentment; he opened his mouth to speak, but thought better of it. Instead, he rose to his feet and said to Mr. Penrose, "I shall be glad to tell you what I know of him. Will you take a turn with me about the room, sir?"

Mr. Penrose agreed at once and the two men began a slow perambulation about the perimeter of the room.

"Oh, this is too bad of them!" Helena said as she watched Robert and the vicar pause, deep in conversation, near the windows at the south end of the room.

"Bad of *them?*" Mary repeated. "What have *they* done that is so very wrong?"

"Everything! Here am I wearing my prettiest afternoon gown and my newest ribband in my hair . . . and all for naught! For what have they done but walk away as if my efforts counted for nothing! What Bluebeards men are!"

Caroline placed a soothing hand on Helena's arm. "Let them have their talk, my dearest Helena; for I think Mr. Penrose may be able to exert an influence over my brother that you and I have failed to achieve. The vicar will talk sense to Robert, mark my words."

She spoke with such confidence that Mary couldn't help but wonder whether Caroline knew something she did not. "What do you mean, Miss Bingley? What is Mr. Penrose saying to your brother? And more important, how is it you are able to know of it?"

"I know nothing except that Mr. Penrose appears to me to be a man of good judgment," Caroline said calmly in the face of Mary's interrogation. "If the vicar has an interest in that boy and thinks he knows better what is good for him, would not Robert do well to listen to his advice?"

This was almost too much for Mary. She liked Mr. Penrose well enough, but he was a stranger in the matter concerning Daniel. How dared he think that within five minutes of making Daniel's acquaintance, he could make arrangements for his future and, possibly, his removal from Netherfield? Even worse was the notion that Captain Bingley would listen to such recommendations ... without *her!* Wasn't she just as invested in Daniel's welfare as the captain was? The mere thought that he would ignore her prior claim and cut her from any decisions about Daniel's future was hurtful in the extreme.

She tried to concentrate on what Caroline and Helena were saying, but her eyes kept straying to where the two men stood fast by the window. She tried to catch a word of their conversation but their voices did not travel far enough to be heard. She tried to divine the expressions on their faces, but the afternoon sunlight that poured through the window behind them left their profiles in shadow. Then she heard them laugh—a rich, hearty laugh of men enjoying a joke together, and she wondered what possible segment of poor Daniel's history they could find so amusing. Her patience diminished as her worry grew. At last she could tolerate the suspense no longer; she had to find relief from her anxieties in the only way she knew how. In the next instant she was on her feet.

"Please excuse me," she said to Caroline and Helena, "but I would like to continue playing now."

She didn't wait for their answer, but went directly to the instrument, carefully pulled the cover from the keys so as not to make a noise, and immediately began to play. Were she alone she would have given vent to her feelings with crashing chords in a storm of correct and incorrect notes; but despite her heightened emotions, she had enough mastery of herself to know that she could not play the beautiful pianoforte at Netherfield as she was used to playing her old spinet at Longbourn. She was compelled to play with restraint, yet she still found solace in her music. Soon she began to feel better, and her music softened in turn. For the remainder of the hour she played on, steadfastly refusing to look at anyone or anything but the keys before her; so she was very much surprised to realize that someone was standing close beside her at the instrument. She looked up to find Robert watching her.

"I did not know you played with such passion, Miss Bennet."

She stopped playing immediately and looked around to see that the hour for tea had gone by. Kitty was still in the corner with Daniel, helping him arrange his soldiers on the makeshift battlefield of the table top, but everyone else was standing near the fireplace, making good-byes, and preparing to go their separate ways.

"I did not realize the hour." She rose to her feet but refused to meet his gaze, still resentful over being excluded from his conversation with Mr. Penrose. "I hope my playing did not disturb you."

"On the contrary, your music helped the hour go by quickly. I have wanted to find an excuse to speak privately with you since your return from Meryton, and now I may finally get my wish."

That made her look up at him at last, and she searched his expression for some hint of his meaning.

He stepped a little closer and said in a low voice meant only for her, "Fetch the *Debrett's*, Miss Bennet, and meet me in the library in ten minutes."

With those tantalizing words the last of her worrisome feelings melted away, replaced by a sense of near breathlessness. Her heart, too, began to misbehave; it thumped erratically when he smiled at her.

"Don't be late," he said, then he went to join the group by the fire.

Mary watched him go, feeling the familiar heat of a blush advance up her neck—a blush brought on by nerves and anticipation . . . and an entirely new sensation she couldn't quite name.

14

Robert stood at the window of the library, looking out on the northwest prospect of Netherfield Park as he waited for Mary Bennet. The view before him was not as inviting as that to be seen from the south-facing windows of the drawing-room, but it was pleasant enough. He imagined the well-manicured lawns and the vast meadow beyond would green up nicely and make for a pleasing scene when spring came; but now the lawn and meadow lay dormant and colorless in the waning winter sunlight. By morning the landscape would be covered with frost—not the best weather for shooting, but Charles was keen to spend a morning out-of-doors, and Robert was keen to spend the morning with him. In the last few years the brothers had seen little of each other, and Robert knew that when he rejoined his regiment in a week's time, he stood a decent chance of receiving orders to some far-away post that would prevent him seeing Charles or Caroline again for months or even years. And if that happened, at least he would have the pleasure of taking with him memories of the time they spent together as a family at Netherfield.

He heard the library door open and looked over his

shoulder. It was Mary Bennet, prompt as always, and in her hand she held the *Debrett's Peerage.* Without a word she laid it on the table top, and carefully aligned the corners of the book with the straight edge of the table. Watching her, he couldn't help but smile; here was yet another example of her little eccentricities. Over the course of the last few days he had committed many of her quirks to memory; they had a certain charm he couldn't define, and he wondered fleetingly if she realized how much her quaint little habits revealed about herself.

"You were very gentle today," he said, from his place by the window.

She looked up at him, mystified. "Was I? When?"

"I am speaking of Daniel, and the manner in which you questioned him when we were in the drawing-room."

"Oh, yes. It seemed an opportune time. At first, I had no notion of asking questions of him, but when he mentioned that his father was a vicar . . ." Her voice drifted away as her eyes widened with a sudden thought. "You are not angry with me, I hope? You are thinking I should have waited—that I should have first allowed you to question him at a time you thought proper! Oh, I am sorry! I did not mean to over-step—!"

"No, no! That was not my meaning at all," he said quickly. "On the contrary, I have been standing here thinking how uncommonly kind you and your sisters have been to Daniel, in every possible way. I cannot help but draw comparisons to . . . to others of my acquaintance."

Suddenly shy, Mary looked down at the book and traced her finger along the embossed letters on the cover. "Jane has always had an extremely kind heart. And I probably should not say it, but Kitty rather likes toy soldiers—she played with them as a child when she grew tired of her dolls."

His lips curved into a soft little smile. "And what about you? Why are you so kind to Daniel?"

"I suppose I have had good examples. My mother and father, sisters and neighbors—they were my models. If I am kind, as you say, I learned by watching them."

"Would that we all could have had your family and neighbors to learn by." He left the window then and went over to place a chair for her at the table. "I am certain you heard everything Daniel said this afternoon, as I did. I have to tell you, I was a good deal shocked when he said he was named for his father! It was all I could do not to look at you."

"I had the same reaction," she confessed, as her cheeks colored slightly. "I was certain you shared my surprise, and I almost held my breath to hear what else Daniel might reveal about himself and his family."

He leaned back in a chair across from her, settled his gaze upon her face, and said, invitingly, "Tell me about your visit with your Aunt Philips. Were you able to learn anything?"

"A little, but it was difficult. I did not want my aunt to suspect a reason for my questions."

"What did she tell you?"

"She remembered Mr. Westover very well. She said he was a handsome young man, and many of the young ladies in Meryton were vastly disappointed to discover he was married and the father of two children."

"*Two* children? This afternoon Daniel told us he had a

sister, so that makes sense. Yet the *Debrett's* mentioned only Daniel."

Mary flipped open the cover of the book and examined the title page. "This *Debrett's* is out-dated; it was published in 1806, so if Daniel's sister was more than two years younger than he, she would not have earned a mention in this book; she would not have been born when this edition was published."

"Clever Miss Bennet!" he said under his breath. He reached over to pull the book in front of him, and turned the leaves over until he reached page sixty-seven—the same page they had examined together the night before. Aloud he read a portion of the entry that he now believed described Daniel's father:

> Daniel Eames, born Jan 19, 1780; married April 10, 1802, Anne Montgomery, daughter of William Montgomery, bart. by whom he had issue, Daniel, born Feb. 1, 1804.

"Did your aunt, by any chance, confirm any of the information written here? Did she mention Mr. Westover's middle name, perhaps? Or the Christian name of his wife?"

"No, and I did not ask it of her. But she did say that she had heard Mr. Westover was a younger son of a marquess— she didn't say which—and that there had been a great rift between father and son."

"What sort of rift?"

"Mr. Westover wanted to join the church, but his father wanted him to study law. He defied his father's wishes and sought ordination in the church, anyway."

"He sounds like a man who was committed to his

calling."

"His father hoped otherwise, for he went out of his way to make things very difficult for his son. The father hoped by throwing barriers in his way, Mr. Westover would relent and return to the family fold to take up law. The marquess even used his influence to prevent patrons from offering Mr. Westover a living."

"But those tactics didn't work, obviously."

"No. In the end Mr. Westover was given a living in Hertfordshire; but it was a poor living, to be sure."

"I wonder Lord Rainham didn't try to prevent that, too."

"My aunt suspects he did not know. She said Mr. Westover deliberately removed to Hertfordshire to put a good distance between himself and his father, thereby preventing interference from the marquess."

Robert was silent as he closed the cover of the book. "It is always a pity when a relationship between father and son comes to such a pass. If young Mr. Westover severed all ties with his father, it will be much more difficult for us to make the connection."

"There is one other bit of news I learned today that confirms a bit of Daniel's story," Mary said. "My Aunt Philips recalled there was a horrid influenza epidemic that swept the south of the county last year and took many lives. It is possible, I think, that Daniel's parents and sister may have been among the victims."

Robert sat back in his chair and looked at her. It was late afternoon and outside the sun was setting, casting deep shadows in the corners and niches of the room; but there was sufficient light for him to detect an expression of quiet concern on Mary Bennet's face that matched his own mood. He said, softly, "I am just now beginning to realize the responsibility I have assumed, Miss Bennet."

"You have always been mindful of it, I think. Daniel's welfare is not something you undertook lightly. Remember, I was with you at the start of it all."

A small smile tugged at one corner of his mouth. "Indeed, you were. And though it has been but a few days since we took Daniel from that inn, it seems a lifetime—and yet I am no closer to a decision about what is to be done with him. Were he just another boy without a family, it might be a simple matter to find a home for him where he can learn a trade or earn his keep; but everything we have learned from your aunt and from Daniel himself has only complicated matters." He frowned slightly with a sudden thought and asked, "How exactly did your aunt come by this history?"

"Bits and pieces, I think. She is a master of the puzzle. She collects crumbs of information from this source or that, arranges them, and fits them together to make a whole."

"That may pass muster for the drawing-room gossips, but it is, I fear, precious little to rely on in proving Daniel's identity. We need some facts—something credible that will establish without doubt who Daniel really is." He saw her frown and look away. "You don't agree?"

"I am unsure," she said, simply. "Perhaps it would be best if we look at the indisputable facts that we *do* have."

"We have a boy named Daniel."

She smiled shyly. "Indeed we do! A boy named Daniel Westover. And from Daniel we know his father, a vicar, was also named Daniel, and he had ties of some kind to

Derbyshire. On the other hand, we have *Debrett's Peerage*—which we both agree to be authoritative evidence—which lists Daniel Westover as a son of the Marquess of Rainham, whose family seat is in Derbyshire. Moreover, *Debrett's* tells us Mr. Daniel Westover—son of Lord Rainham—also had a son named Daniel, who was born about the same year as our Daniel."

"I am disposed to believe, Miss Bennet, that you studied law, for you have just made a very credible argument that could sway a jury."

She didn't answer, but he watched her earnest expression instantly change to one of uncertainty. Odd, for he couldn't remember the last time he had paid a young woman a compliment, only to have her doubt his intention. He was used to seeing young ladies blossom at the first hint of flattery—Miss Paget certainly did so!—but Miss Bennet's first reaction was wariness. He wondered over it, at the same time he realized that her countenance was very often the exact mirror of her thoughts. He said, in a gentle tone, "I merely meant that you have summed the situation to a nicety."

"Oh," she said, relaxing slightly. "Thank you."

"However, we must bear in mind that the similarities between Daniel's story and the facts in the *Debrett's* could be nothing more than coincidence. How are we ever to discover if our assumption is correct?"

"I suppose the only person who can determine whether Daniel is related to the Westovers of Derbyshire is Lord Rainham himself."

He gave her a long, measuring look. "Once again, we

think alike, Miss Bennet.

"We do?"

"You have voiced my thought exactly."

Her eyes widened. "What do you propose?"

"I propose that we write to Lord Rainham and ask if he has a missing grandson."

"*Dare* we?" breathed Mary.

"I can see no other way to confirm or deny our suspicions. Can you?"

"But what if we write to Lord Rainham and he does not reply?"

"Then we shall simply do our best by Daniel; it is all we can do, after all." He watched a series of expressions play across her face. "If you are of a mind to take a different path, I assure you, I am willing to entertain any suggestion."

"The truth is, I haven't one, yet . . ." She pressed her lips into a straight little line, and nervously resumed tracing her finger over the cover of the book.

"Yet . . . ?" he prompted.

"It is nothing—I simply wondered if, perhaps, Mr. Penrose had offered guidance." She fixed her gaze on the book, and continued in a rush, "I know it is not my place to ask, but I watched you speak to him of Daniel's plight, and certainly you are not obligated to relate to *me* your conversation, though I do have a very *great* interest in his welfare, and Mr. Penrose has none, for how could he when he has only just *met* the child—!"

Midway through her tumble of words Robert realized Mary Bennet was upset. He was surprised, for he never intended to worry her, nor had he thought that talking to Mr.

Penrose about Daniel would cause her the least anxiety. On impulse he laid his hand over hers, which was still resting on the book, and clasped her fingers meaningfully.

Startled, she stopped speaking; her wide eyes flew up to meet his, giving him a chance to say, "Yes, I spoke to Mr. Penrose about Daniel, but he offered no advice, nor did I ask him for any. You must know by now, Miss Bennet, that in matters concerning Daniel, you—and you alone—must always be my main advisor."

Even in the fading afternoon light he could see the distinct color of a blush advance up her neck to mantle her cheeks. She looked away, suddenly shy and uncertain, and would have pulled her hand away, but he held it captive a moment longer. If she needed assurance, he would give it to her.

"I cannot consider making any decision about Daniel's future without your approval, Miss Bennet. You believe that, don't you?"

She still could not bring herself to look at him, but she offered a little nod in response; then her soft fingers fluttered nervously beneath his. Slowly, reluctantly, he let go of her hand.

He leaned back in his chair again, putting a bit of distance between them, and said in a much different tone, "Shall we test your resolve, Miss Bennet? We have reached the point, you see, when the time for words has passed; it is now time to take action."

"What action do you propose?" she asked, still focusing her gaze on the book.

"It is time to write a letter to Lord Rainham."

She gave her head a little shake, and murmured, "Write to Lord Rainham! How does one begin such a letter?"

"Carefully . . . delicately! It must be a simple letter that lays the facts of the matter before Lord Rainham in clear, undisputable terms."

"Yes, I quite agree, but at the same time I cannot help but think the idea a wild one." She looked at him then, and said, a little apologetically, "I have spent my entire life striving to remain within the bounds of the conventional way of doing things, and to send a letter to a peer of the realm, without benefit of introduction—! Why, it is almost unthinkable!"

"Almost. But desperate times, as the saying goes, call for desperate measures. Well? Shall we write the letter?"

"Yes . . . but I suggest we send a second letter."

"To whom?"

"My sister. She is Mrs. Darcy of Pemberley in Derbyshire. While she has never mentioned Lord Rainham before that I am aware, there is a chance she is acquainted with the man, since his family seat is in Derbyshire, as well. I think it prudent to write her—first to ask what she knows about the family; and, second, to warn her of our intent in the event Lord Rainham contacts her or Mr. Darcy."

"An excellent suggestion, Miss Bennet!" Robert lit the taper on the table; then, from a desk on the other side of the room, he retrieved several sheets of paper, pens and an ink stand. "Shall we divide the work? You write your sister while I write Lord Rainham?"

"Gladly." With great deliberation Mary positioned a blank page squarely in front of her on the table, and, selecting one of the pens, began to write.

He watched her for a moment, impressed by the determined set of her chin and the way in which she applied herself to the task without hesitation. The thought occurred to him that she was a very singular young lady, and quite unlike anyone he had met before; but then he reminded himself that he, too, had a letter to write, and he set about accomplishing it. Very soon he had filled a single sheet of writing paper with close script; and when he looked up from his labor, he found Mary signing her name to the letter she had penned to her sister.

"Will you read this," she asked, "and tell me if I have stated the case to my sister in plain language?"

"Only if you will do the same for me." He pushed the letter he'd written across the table toward her. When he had finished reading her work, he said, "I cannot help but notice, Miss Bennet, that we have a similar writing style—succinct, polite, but to the point. What do you think—have I accurately laid our case before Lord Rainham?"

"You have." She folded the letter she'd written, and applied a bit of wax to hold the fold in place; then she turned the letter over to inscribe her sister's direction. "I hope Lord Rainham reads your letter with an open mind."

"He must, for Daniel's sake. I shall have these letters dispatched immediately." He watched her push her chair back and stand up. "Where are you going?"

"I promised to help Jane this evening, for she is growing anxious as the day of the New Year ball draws near."

He rose to his feet, frowning slightly. "But surely you are not obligated to attend her now. I thought perhaps we could . . ." *What?* He had no notion what to say to her; he only knew that he had spent a pleasant half hour with Miss Mary Bennet, and he was loath to see their time together end. He cast about in his mind, and said, with perfect sincerity, "I wish to thank you, Miss Bennet."

"For what?"

"For helping me; for your kindness to Daniel, for ... for so many things."

"You have thanked me already, and it is enough. Please say no more on that head. It is my pleasure to help Daniel in any way I can."

She was about to turn away again when he stopped her by saying, "Ride with me tomorrow." The words came out before he considered them, and he saw her expression change to one of mild panic.

"No—I mean, I cannot. Thank you, but I do not ride."

"So you have told me," he said, recovering his footing a bit. "I only thought you might learn to enjoy the exercise. Besides, riding will give us an excuse to speak privately about Daniel without inviting comment or suspicion. We cannot be forever sneaking off to the library, you know."

She frowned slightly. "Yes, I can see how that would be so, but I have never been in a saddle before; and horses are so large and *unpredictable!*"

"Some can be; but I am certain we can find a very docile mare for you—if not at Netherfield then we will hire one from Meryton's stables." He saw her hesitate, and that he took as a good sign that she was at least considering his invitation. "I wish you would think about it. I have resolved to teach Daniel to ride, and it would be a very good thing if you both learned together. You will lend him confidence.

And, Miss Bennet," he added, when she would have turned again toward the door, "I hope you trust me enough to know I will always keep you safe."

She gave the matter her grave consideration. "Yes," she said, finally. "Yes, I *do* trust you, Captain Bingley."

He had earned the trust of other young ladies throughout the course of his life, but Mary's admission was different; it moved him in a way that was strange to him. He rather suspected she did not trust many people and confided in considerably fewer. That was a shame, for since the moment of their meeting she had revealed to him her character: honest and kind, fair and thoughtful. It was unfortunate, then, that the passionate side of her personality—made so plain to him where Daniel was concerned—should be overlooked by others or hidden from view behind her wall of shyness.

But he had a feeling that Mary Bennet was becoming quite comfortable in his presence—comfortable enough to let down her guard and reveal that there was a charming young woman hidden behind her mask of blushes and stammers.

He went to the door and opened it for her. "You will, I hope, at least think about a riding lesson ... for Daniel's sake, I mean," he said quickly, when that doubtful expression appeared again in her eyes.

"Very well." She crossed the threshold into the great hall. "For Daniel's sake."

As he closed the door after her, Robert couldn't help but smile at the soft blow she had unwittingly dealt his ego. So she would not learn to ride to please him, but she would consider learning for Daniel's sake!

Salutary, Miss Bennet! he thought, with a shake of his head. *At least I always know where I stand with you.*

15

Mary could not reach her bedchamber fast enough. By the time she gained the safety and solitude of her private lair, a fresh patch of color had flooded her cheeks—not from embarrassment, but from the realization that she had come very close to losing the mastery of herself with Captain Bingley. Only the day before she had resolved to guard her heart against his attractions; yet as she sank down onto a chair by the window in her chamber, she recognized her resolve for the fraud that it was.

Even now she could focus her mind on nothing save their encounter in the library; the memory of it was fresh enough to make her breath catch in her throat. She had only to close her eyes to again feel the warmth of Captain Bingley's fingers as they covered her hand; and it took little effort for her to recall the tenderness in his voice as he asked her to trust him. Of course she trusted him! She trusted and admired and . . . *loved* him.

It was a frightening realization, but one she couldn't deny. She loved him despite her better judgment, despite knowing full well that his heart was pledged to another. Her mind told her to stay far away from the captain, but her heart yearned to be with him, to claim his attention where and when she could. She was sorely tempted to accept his offer of a riding lesson, knowing full well she would never consider such an offer had it been extended by anyone else. Why, she was even reading *Gulliver's Travels*—a book she never would have read of her own accord—only because *he* recommended it to her.

She reached over to the table beside her bed on which lay the book he had given her, and she held it close to her heart for a moment. Though she had read only a few chapters of the book so far, she'd been surprised to find the story engaging; but she deeply suspected that a good deal of her enjoyment of reading the tale resulted from knowing Captain Bingley admired it so. If he had claimed to enjoy a hive of angry bees, she would be willing to do the same. *That's how low I've sunk!* she thought.

In little time her pride once again came to the fore, and she resolved to keep a closer guard over her heart. She would behave toward the captain as she would toward anyone else, she told herself. But that resolution was sorely tested when she joined her sister Jane in the morning room an hour later.

Jane had asked for Kitty and Mary's help in finalizing the plans for the New Year ball. A disciple of neatness and organization, Jane had compiled a lengthy list of every task and detail associated with the grand event; and with Mary's help, she hoped to check off each item in turn, thereby satisfying herself that she had forgotten nothing, that no detail concerning the ball should be left to chance.

They were thus engaged—Jane at her ladies' writing desk with her list before her and a neatly-trimmed pen in her hand, and Mary ensconced in a chair close by with a box of receipts and merchant bills sitting on her lap. They were going over the list as planned when Jane had a sudden thought.

"Oh, I have forgotten to note anything about your gown, Mary! It was delivered by the *modiste*, was it not? What day did it arrive?"

"It was delivered yesterday, as was Kitty's."

"And is your gown satisfactory? Did the *modiste* make all the alterations we discussed at your last fitting?"

"She did indeed, and I like the gown very well. My old ball gown is white, and though I know white is the fashion, it does not suit me. I don't have your coloring, Jane, to creditably pull off a white gown."

"Simply because white gowns are popular does not mean they look well on a lady; I am afraid that is a lesson our mother has not yet learned."

Mary gave a soft sigh of resignation. "She *will* insist that fashion rule over practicality."

"Never mind. Your new ball gown is just the right shade of blue to bring out your eyes. With such an addition, your wardrobe is quite complete, I think."

Here was an opening in the conversation Mary had hoped for. With a cautious eye to Jane's reaction, she said, "Not quite. Unfortunately, my wardrobe is still lacking in one or two essentials."

"That cannot be," Jane said, in a light-hearted tone. "What could you possibly lack to wear, Mary?"

"A riding skirt."

The smile faded from Jane's face. "A what?"

"A riding skirt. I was hoping you had one I might borrow." Mary was pleased to hear how even her voice sounded as she said the words.

"A *riding skirt?*" Jane repeated, astounded. "Yes, I have a riding skirt—indeed, I own a full riding habit, but why do you wish to borrow it?"

"To wear, of course." Once again she was relieved to hear her voice maintain an even tone; but though her words sounded casual enough, Mary suddenly found she could not bring herself to look Jane in the eye. Instead she focused her attention on flipping through the bills in the box on her lap.

"But you do not ride, Mary."

"I intend to learn."

"You intend to *what?*"

Mary's chin rose to a defiant angle. "It is not so uncommon a plan, is it?"

"Uncommon? No—astonishing, more like! Forgive me, Mary, but I can hardly credit you are serious. You—who have been fearful of horses all your life—want to learn to *ride?* Why?"

"Many young ladies ride," Mary said, side-stepping her sister's question. "In polished society, I believe, a young lady who can ride with skill and grace is considered to be quite accomplished."

"That is true, but I am frankly surprised that you would come to that realization just now; you have never shown such an interest before. What has occurred to change your mind, Mary?"

The skepticism in her sister's tone surprised Mary so much, that her eyes met Jane's for an instant. Brief though it was, the look they exchanged was long enough for Jane to lay down her pen and say, in a voice of deep concern, "Did Miss Paget put the idea in your head?"

"Miss Paget? No, she did not; but I do believe she rides."

"Yes, but Miss Paget had an advantage over the Bennet sisters. The Paget family keeps their own stable of horses, and they undoubtedly employ a riding master. I imagine Miss Paget had riding lessons commencing at a very young age."

"But *I* intend to have lessons."

"From whom?"

At that moment one of Mary's unruly blushes betrayed her by commencing an insidious march across her cheeks. Before she could answer, Jane gave a soft little gasp and, turning in her chair to face Mary, she seized one of her hands.

"Oh, Mary, do not tell me—! Please do not say you will have lessons from Captain Bingley!"

"Why not?

"You know the answer already. Captain Bingley intends to marry Miss Paget."

"I know that, but is his impending marriage a reason he should not teach me to ride?"

"You know very well what I mean—" Jane was obliged to halt her words at the sound of the door opening.

Kitty entered into the room, saying brightly, "Have you begun without me? I would have joined you sooner, but I could not find a shawl that became this dress, so I stopped in your room, Mary, to borrow one of yours. Doesn't your green shawl look well on me? And when I was looking about, I found *this* in your room! What a good joke it is!"

She held up the copy of *Gulliver's Travels* Mary had left on the table by her bed.

Mary gave a little gasp and was on her feet in an instant to wrench the book from Kitty's hands. "Give me that! You have no right to help yourself to my things."

Kitty stared at her in surprise. "*Your* things! Do you mean you *knew* the book was in your room?"

"Of course I knew!" Mary said, deeply flustered, as she sat back down. "I am reading it. What *else* does one do with a book?"

"But it's a *novel*. You have never been interested in reading novels before, even after I have recommended title after title to you. You are quite full of surprises this week, Mary."

Having observed their exchange with a growing frown, Jane asked, "What is the name of this novel?"

"*Gulliver's Travels*," Mary said, staring down at the book in her lap.

"It is about a sailor," Kitty said, helpfully.

"It is not!" Mary declared. "He is a ship's surgeon! And it is a perfectly acceptable book for a young lady—unlike the novels *you* read!"

"What a termagant you are today!" Kitty retorted. "I only thought the book had somehow ended up in your room by mistake—that someone had given it to you as a joke. I should have known better than to think *you* capable of a laugh!"

"Kitty," Jane said, in a mildly warning tone. "Mary did not mean to react so angrily, I am sure; but it was wrong of you to remove the book from her room without permission.

Yes, I know," she said quickly, when Kitty opened her mouth to protest, "you borrow shawls and books from each other almost every day, but I would hazard a guess that Mary borrowed this book from the Netherfield library. Am I right, Mary?"

Mary nodded.

"There!" said Jane. "You know Mary takes her obligations seriously, and I'm certain she feels responsible for returning the book to the library in the same excellent condition in which she found it."

"Really, Jane, you make it sound as if I intended to throw it down the stairs or burn it to a crisp in the fireplace!" Kitty said. "It is not as if I do not know how to care for a book!"

"That is true, but you also know how particular Mary is about these things. Please, won't you put the book back where you found it?"

A look of strong indignation passed over Kitty's face as she drew herself up. "Why can't Mary take it when next she returns to her chamber?"

"Because I intend to keep Mary very busy for the rest of the evening and heaven only knows when she will have a chance to go upstairs again. Please, Kitty," Jane said, sweetly. "Please return the book, then come back and join us here; we will enjoy a nice coze and a bit of refreshment together— just we three Bennet sisters."

"Oh, very well," Kitty said, grudgingly. "Give me the book, Mary, and I'll put it back." She held out her hand and Mary gave the book to her; but as she went to the door, Kitty grumbled, "What a great fuss over a horrid old book!"

It wasn't until she found herself alone again with Jane

that Mary realized she had committed a strategic error by relinquishing the book; for now that Kitty had carried it off, there was nothing to prevent Jane from resuming the line of questioning she had introduced earlier.

Jane wasted no time doing so, and asked, solemnly, "Will you tell me how you came to select that particular book to read, Mary?"

"It was recommended to me."

"By whom?"

"Does it matter?"

"It matters a great deal if the person who gave you the book was Captain Bingley. Was it?"

Mary, who was never one to tell anything but the truth, was silent for a moment while she debated in her mind how to respond to a question she suspected would be best left unanswered.

Jane allowed her a few moments to consider the matter; then she reached over to grasp Mary's hand and said, earnestly, "Oh, my dear sister, you are treading on very dangerous ground."

Mary's chin went up a notch. "Why? Because I borrowed a book from the library?"

"No."

"Because I wish to learn to ride a horse at long last?"

"No; because you are becoming a little too fond of Captain Bingley."

"I am not!" Mary protested, even as her cheeks flushed scarlet.

Jane looked at her with sympathy. "Do you think I haven't noticed? You and Robert are in league together—Oh,

I know it is a shared wish to do right by Daniel that binds the two of you, but I have seen your reaction when he whispers to you—"

"He *has* to whisper, for Caroline and Miss Paget behave dreadfully whenever poor Daniel's name is mentioned."

"Perhaps he does have a reason to whisper; but if he is only whispering to you about Daniel's welfare, you should have no reason to blush in response."

There was a certain logic to Jane's argument Mary could not refute. "He is simply being kind to me," she said, in a strangled voice; then she caught her mistake and said, quickly, "I mean, he is being kind to *Daniel*."

"And we all admire him for it," Jane said, gently, "but you must not mistake his kindness for something else. Robert Bingley is a good man, but he has candidly spoken of his love for Miss Paget and his intention to marry her. He will not go back on his word. Not now—not ever. His honor forbids it. Do you understand?"

Of a sudden Mary could feel the tell-tale warmth of tears in the backs of her eyes, and she fought against them. "Of course I understand. Really, your concern is unnecessary, Jane."

"Tell me, Mary, has he given you any indication that he returns your regard?"

Mary dipped her head to hide the manner in which her chin had begun to tremble slightly. "No. He has done nothing. In all things his manner has been that of a gentleman. He is to me nothing more than a kind friend."

Jane relaxed her grip on Mary's hand. "Forgive me, but I had to ask."

"I understand."

"I dearly hope so. Guard your heart, Mary; I would not care to see it broken."

It was quite mortifying for Mary to discover that her efforts to hide her feelings for Captain Bingley had not been successful. She was still unable to look Jane in the eye as she asked, in a small voice, "What did I do to give myself away?"

"There was no single action or look that betrayed you; it was more of an overall change I have noticed in you. Since Captain Bingley's arrival at Netherfield there is a brightness to your eyes I have not seen before; your smile is sweeter and comes more readily; and I've noticed that your gaze follows him when he moves about the room."

"Oh, good grief!" Mary brought her hands up to cover her now flaming cheeks. "If next you tell me that everyone else has noticed such changes in me, I am completely undone!"

"Calm yourself, for I do not suppose any such thing. But if you continue on your present course, I believe it is only a matter of time before others—who know you not quite as well as I—will notice, too."

"Do you think—? Does *he*—?"

"No, dearest Mary, I do not think Captain Bingley suspects your feelings for him."

Relieved, Mary let out a little whoosh of breath she had been holding. "Thank goodness! If I have not betrayed myself to Captain Bingley, that, at least, is one bright spot in the wretched business."

"May I give you a bit of advice?" Jane asked very gently, and Mary nodded in response. "Begin now to repeat in your mind over and over these words: 'Captain Bingley is my brother-in-law and nothing more.' And resolve yourself to pull back a little from your interactions; do not be quite so ready to meet him, and do not initiate conversations with him."

"But he relies on me in matters concerning Daniel. We are partners—co-conspirators!"

"Robert is an intelligent man, a captain in the Hussars, and he is used to dealing decisively with troubles of all kinds. Don't you think he is capable of resolving Daniel's situation on his own?"

Mary's spirit sunk a bit further. "Yes, I suppose he is."

"It will be difficult for you at first to follow my advice, but I know whereof I speak. There was a time, you may remember, when I was obliged to hide my true feelings for Mr. Bingley, even though I loved him with all my heart. In my case, I did so because I was led to believe he did not care for me as I did him. In your case, you must hide your true feelings because Captain Bingley is pledged to another."

Though Jane spoke kindly and with the greatest sympathy, her words cut Mary to the quick. Once again she felt the tears gather in her eyes, and once again she resolved to stop them. Even as her eyes glimmered with unshed tears, she lifted her chin and said in tone of mock loathing, "Those *Bingleys!*"

That brought a smile to Jane's lips, and she leaned forward to wrap her arms around Mary's shoulders in a quick embrace. "Oh, my dear sister, what spirit you have! You *will* get through this, you'll see; and you may rely on me to help you. Remain strong and think on this: Robert will be here only another week; then he will return to his regiment, and you may rest easy."

Jane spoke with such assurance that Mary tried to please her by venturing a smile; but in her heart she rather doubted she would ever be able to rest easy again.

16

Despite the dull ache in her heart, Mary decided that Jane's advice was worth following. If Jane had noticed the state of her affections just by observing the light in her eyes whenever she looked at Captain Bingley, then she must do her best not to look at him at all, unless absolutely necessary. She lived in dread that anyone—especially the captain—should discover her secret, and pity her for it. That, she believed, would be the greatest possible humiliation, and she could not bear to think of it; so she adopted Jane's advice, and resolved to avoid the captain's presence as much as possible.

But first, she had to tell Captain Bingley that she could not accept his offer of riding lessons. This she was able to do when she came upon him in the hall as she was going out for a walk and he was coming from the stables.

She told him of her decision, and ended by saying, primly, "I thank you for your kind offer; and although it was good of you to volunteer to teach me, I have decided not to learn to ride at this time."

"Are you certain? I picked out a horse for you," he said, as if that fact might change her mind. "A docile mare that is the greatest slug that ever graced Meryton's stables. I am certain the ostler who hired her out to me thought I was renting the deplorable beast for my own use."

She couldn't help but smile at this. "I did not expect you to bruise your reputation for my benefit."

"*Bruised* is an excellent description of the condition of my ego! I don't know how I shall ever be able to hold my head up on High Street again." He gave her a speculative look. "You will not change your mind?"

"No," she said, clasping her gloved hands together in a determined knot. She had come to her decision with not a little heartache; but having made it, she would not veer from her course. Still, she felt the need to add, "Will it help if I confess I came very close to accepting your offer?"

His expression brightened. "A little."

"You will still give Daniel riding lessons, I hope."

"Of course! And if you ever change your mind, Miss Bennet . . ."

She said no more, but went on her way to take her daily walk. But the out of doors held no pleasure for her, as she realized she had completed only the first of several tasks ahead of her in her quest to limit her contact with Captain Bingley.

Her next order of business was to delay the time she usually breakfasted. It had been her habit to take her morning meal early; and from the day of Captain Bingley's arrival she discovered, by happy coincidence, that he was an early riser, too.

It was during those early-morning meals, when she found herself alone in the family dining-room with Robert and Daniel, that Mary felt closest to him. They comfortably conversed about anything and everything, from books to music, and any other topic that suited their fancy.

Mary had come to relish those breakfasts with Captain Bingley in which she could enjoy his attention; but since her emotional conversation with Jane the day before, she now concluded her mornings with Robert had to be given up. It was not a decision she made with ease, and she shed more than a few tears over the unfairness of it all; but in the end, she trusted Jane's advice and adhered to it.

The next morning she presented herself in the family dining-room at a time she knew Caroline and her sisters would be there before her. They all looked up at her entrance; and though Jane greeted her with a soft, sympathetic smile, Kitty chose to comment on her unexpected appearance.

"Are you just now come for your breakfast, Mary? Why, you are very late today. What kept you?"

"I fear I did not sleep well last night."

"You do look a bit bleary-eyed," Kitty said, after examining her sister's face a little more thoroughly. "Your eyes are puffy. You probably stayed up late reading that horrid book."

"What book is that?" asked Caroline, though she did not raise her eyes from her plate.

"Mary is reading *Gulliver's Travels*."

That revelation made Caroline look up with a mild expression of interest. "Is she? Pray, why is that so remarkable?"

"Because novels are not in Mary's usual line. She always reads treatises and biographies—dull, tedious things that are more like sermons than stories."

"If that is true, I congratulate you, Miss Bennet, on expanding your scope of reading."

"Do you *approve* of the book?" Mary asked, a little doubtfully.

"Indeed I do. I have read it myself."

Kitty stared at her. "*You* read *Gulliver's Travels*, Miss Bingley? I would never have guessed."

"I do not see why either of you should be so astonished. It was a very popular book some years ago. In fact, my brother Robert read it first, when we were much younger; and it was he who passed it along to me."

Mary dipped her head and concentrated on her breakfast, hoping no one would see the blush that rose in her cheeks at the mere mention of the captain's name.

"Still," said Kitty, "I would not have thought that kind of book would be to your taste, Miss Bingley."

"That is because you do not realize that the books we read as children are not at all the same as the books we read as adults. My choice in reading has refined considerably since my youth, a result, no doubt, of careful training by an exemplary governess and my vast experience in the world. It has given me a certain distinction and delicate discernment that one cannot acquire but through careful cultivation. Tell me, Miss Bennet," Caroline said, suddenly shifting her gaze to Mary, "do you read languages?"

"No, I do not."

"Then you must learn. No young lady may be considered truly accomplished unless she reads languages. I have mentioned to Jane several times that I cannot understand what your mother was about by not engaging a proper governess for you and your sisters. It was a gross oversight— but perhaps she did not know better, not having a governess herself growing up, and allowances must be made. Still it is a pity you and your sisters were not properly educated to take your place in the world."

Mary's blush flamed brighter in response to the implied insult. She looked across the table at Caroline and said, somewhat boldly, "I believe the Bennet sisters have done very well in taking their places in the world. After all, one sister is the mistress of Netherfield, and the other is mistress of Pemberley, even though neither reads languages. When I reflect on *their* circumstances, I can't help but think my mother prepared her daughters very well indeed!"

Caroline looked back at her in surprise for a long moment; then she put her chin up slightly and said icily, "I beg your pardon, Miss Bennet. My recommendations were kindly meant."

Mary already regretted her outburst, and answered in a contrite voice, "Please do not apologize, Miss Bingley. I was in the wrong, and I should never have spoken to you so. I humbly beg your forgiveness."

Caroline took a moment to glare at her, causing Jane to say, "We must remember that Mary is not herself this morning. She did pass a restless night and, like all of us, she is not her best without a good night's sleep."

"Normally," Caroline said, somewhat mollified, "I would suggest that Miss Bennet return to her chamber and try to sleep, but I shall not do so for fear of having my head bit off!"

Kitty laughed. "Who would have thought that Mary could

make Miss Bingley fear a scolding!"

"Kitty!" Jane said, warningly.

"Well, it is a great joke, after all. Imagine anyone being afraid of Mary."

"It is not my intent to make Miss Bingley afraid of me," Mary said, with a frown. "Perhaps my temper would be improved if I took Miss Bingley's advice and returned to my room."

"What you need," said Jane, "is some fresh air, which you will have in great abundance this morning."

"Oh? Will you take a walk about the grounds?" asked Caroline.

"No. Kitty, Mary, and I plan to drive to Lucas Lodge later this morning. Will you join us, Caroline?"

"But you cannot visit Lucas Lodge today," she said, with a look of consternation, "for *I* am driving to Meryton. I have planned the excursion since yesterday; so you see, I have a prior claim on the carriage."

"But we just visited the shops," Kitty said. "You were there but yesterday, and I'm sure you saw nothing to tempt you then. Why must you go back today?"

"For the very reason that I bought nothing yesterday," Caroline retorted, impatiently.

"I am certain," said Jane, "there is a way both our needs may be satisfied; it just takes a bit of managing. Why don't we all go to Meryton together and then call as one at Lucas Lodge?"

"That will not do." Caroline lifted her chin to a mulish angle. "I fear my schedule is quite fixed today."

"Will Miss Paget accompany you to the shops?" asked

Kitty.

"Why, no, she does not figure in my plans."

"Then is Miss Paget to remain behind here alone while *you* visit the shops and *we* call on the Lucases? And pray do not say that Captain Bingley must entertain her, for he and Charles left with Daniel over an hour ago for some shooting in the high meadow."

Caroline fixed Kitty with a look meant to deter further argument. "Then Miss Paget will go with you to Lucas Lodge. There, it is settled!"

"It is not settled at all," Kitty retorted.

"Caroline, you are being very mysterious this morning," Jane said. "What is going on?"

"Is it so unusual that I should wish for a bit of privacy while I execute a commission that concerns no one but myself?"

"I suppose not," Jane said, after a moment of careful thought. "If you cannot bring yourself to visit the Lucases, allow me to offer another solution: We will all drive to Meryton together, and set you down at the location of your choice. Then Kitty, Mary, Miss Paget, and I will drive on to Lucas Lodge, and we'll call for you later."

"Oh, very well," Caroline said, in a tone that lacked her usual grace.

"Thank you for understanding, Caroline," Jane said. "Yes, I think a bit of fresh air this afternoon is the very thing needed to improve all our spirits."

It was just before eleven o'clock when the ladies boarded the Bingley carriage and set off toward Meryton. Caroline's intention was to go directly to the vicarage. She would have preferred to arrive there in a well-appointed carriage with grooms to attend her and a tasteful hint of fanfare. That sort of display of wealth and status, she reasoned, just might prove to be the very thing needed to wipe that smug smile from Mr. Penrose's face once and for all.

But as the Bingley carriage neared Meryton, the thought crossed her mind that coachmen and grooms had a way of talking; and if word were to get back to Jane or Charles—or, even worse, that nosy Kitty Bennet—that Caroline Bingley had called upon the vicarage, she would be hard pressed to explain her purpose behind such a visit. Even now she regretted that she had ever promised Mr. Penrose that she would visit him again; and it was only her hope that he would help her rid Netherfield of Daniel's presence that drove her to keep her end of their bargain.

In Meryton Caroline was set down in front of one of the shops she had visited only the day before, where she was obliged to step inside until she was certain the carriage had moved on. While waiting, she purchased a small bottle of Olympian Dew so as not to attract suspicion for lingering there; and only when she was certain the Bingley carriage was out of view, did she tuck the bottle into her reticule and begin her walk to the vicarage, where she intended to come to terms with Mr. Penrose.

She had not gone many steps before she spied that very man walking on the other side of the street. Mr. Penrose was coming toward her at a brisk pace, with a large basket over one arm. She thought he looked like a man on an errand, which vexed her greatly, since he was supposed to be, at that very moment, awaiting her arrival at the vicarage.

She crossed the street and stood in his path; and she had the satisfaction of seeing his expression change to one of genuine surprise as soon as he caught sight of her.

"Miss Bingley! This is a delightful surprise. Are you visiting the shops?"

"No, I am not," she answered, crossly. "I am on my way to call at the vicarage—a call, I may add, we arranged yesterday at your invitation."

"Are you?" he asked, mystified.

"So you have forgotten! Oh, it is too bad of you!"

"I hadn't forgotten, I assure you; but I thought we agreed to meet later—after luncheon, in fact."

"That is true, but I find myself at the whim of other people's schedules today, and so I must insist we speak this morning . . . *now*, if you will be so kind."

He frowned slightly as he looked down at the basket he carried. "I'm afraid that will not do, for I have one more family to visit before I return to the vicarage. If I hurry I shall not be more than half an hour; then I will call for you at one of the shops—"

"No, that will not do at all. I haven't much time, and there is nothing in the Meryton shops to tempt me. Oh, this is quite disappointing, I must say!"

"Then perhaps you will consider accompanying me? We can talk as we go."

She considered his suggestion doubtfully. "But where are

you bound?"

"I am expected at Mrs. Doyle's. Perhaps you have heard of her?"

The name was definitely familiar to Caroline, but she could not place it. Since her arrival at Netherfield she had met all manner of persons with whom the Bennets associated. She met them on the streets of Meryton and at the assemblies, and several times she had been made to dine at the tables of Meryton's leading families—which she did only to alleviate the boredom of spending time in a country town. But while she could not clearly remember being introduced to a Mrs. Doyle, she was certain she had heard the name before on the lips of one of the Bennet sisters.

She lifted her chin and said, "Naturally I am acquainted with Mrs. Doyle."

He didn't try to hide his surprise. "Are you indeed? Then perhaps you will consider coming along with me. I am certain Mrs. Doyle will welcome you, and we can talk more about Daniel as we walk. Tell me, where is he this morning?" he asked, as he adjusted the weight of the basket on his arm and set off again at a brisk pace.

Caroline hurried to match his step. "As far as I know, the boy is with my brothers today."

"Doing what?"

"They have gone shooting or fishing or some such thing as men like to do together."

"Ah, the pheasants in the high meadow! I have gone shooting there with Mr. Bingley myself."

"I did not know you were a sporting man, Mr. Penrose."

"I dare say there are a host of things you do not know

about me, Miss Bingley. This way, please." He placed his fingers at her elbow and gently guided her around the next corner.

By this time they had left the main street and were walking, still at a winged pace, along a narrow lane with small houses on either side. Mr. Penrose stopped suddenly and mounted the steps of one of the stone cottages and rapped at the door.

"Mrs. Doyle! It is I, Mr. Penrose."

Caroline heard the rasping sound of a bolt being pulled back; then the door opened a few inches and a little girl peeped through the opening.

"Hello, Emma!" Mr. Penrose said in a friendly voice. "I've come to see your mother. May I come in?"

When the door swung wide, Mr. Penrose stepped to one side. "After you Miss Bingley."

Caroline glared at him and labored under the strong suspicion that she had been horribly deceived. The little stone cottage was not at all like the kind of home she was used to visiting, and she was now thoroughly convinced that Mrs. Doyle was not someone she had met in her travels through Meryton society. Why, the little house was really nothing more than a hovel, in her opinion, and she teetered on the brink of turning on her heel and fleeing the cottage as fast as her legs could carry her.

But Mr. Penrose was looking at her with a look of such guileless expectation that she found herself, before she half realized it, mounting the two stone steps. She entered a room that was quite small and extremely chilly. There was a pitiful fire in the hearth, near which was placed a wooden cradle.

The little girl who had opened the door at Mr. Penrose's coaxing had retreated to a position close beside the only comfortable chair in the room. On the other side of the chair was an even younger girl—no more than a toddler, really, and both children clung to the sleeves of the woman who was seated in the chair. That lady gave a small gasp as Caroline entered the room, and struggled to stand, but Mr. Penrose quickly stopped her.

"No, Mrs. Doyle, do not attempt to get up. Remember what the doctor said." He beckoned Caroline to come further into the room, saying, "This is Miss Bingley of Netherfield, you know. No need to stand on ceremony, since you are already acquainted, I understand."

Mrs. Doyle's eyes widened. "No, sir, I do not think so! Goodness, I am sure I would have remembered, if ever I had the good fortune to make *Miss Bingley's* acquaintance."

He looked at her curiously as he placed a chair for Caroline very near the woman. "Oh? I am mistaken then. No matter. I'll just tend this fire for a moment while you get to know one another." He set the basket on the floor and drew from it two pieces of wood, one of which he added to the meager fire; then he bent all his attention to coaxing the fire to burn more brightly.

Caroline, seated rigidly on the hard wooden chair near Mrs. Doyle, allowed her critical eye to travel the room. It was neat enough and certainly clean, but she was quite convinced that *this* Mrs. Doyle could not possibly be the same Mrs. Doyle of her imaginings.

After several moments of silent scrutiny, she looked again at the woman and found Mrs. Doyle and her daughters staring back at her with expressions of fear mixed with a good dose of curiosity.

She was quite unaccustomed to being stared at, and toyed with the notion of ignoring them altogether, when she decided that their lack of conduct was no excuse for lowering her own standard for good manners.

She cast about in her mind for something sensible to say, and asked, in her most majestic tone, "Are you ill? Mr. Penrose said the doctor was in, I believe?"

"Not sick, no, ma'am; but I hurt my back something awful, and it's so bad I can hardly move from this chair, that's how much it hurts."

"I see." She folded her hands in her lap and looked about the room again, all the while thinking how dreadful it would be to be imprisoned in such a small, dull space.

"There! I've finally got the fire up and you shall be more comfortable presently," said Mr. Penrose, as he claimed another wooden chair. He looked at Caroline; his eyes alight with amusement. "I take it you are not acquainted, after all?"

"No, we are not," Caroline answered, barely concealing her irritation. "I must have been thinking of a *different* Mrs. Doyle."

"No matter. Now that you ladies are known to each other, allow me to introduce the rest of the family. That," he said, with a small gesture toward the little girl who had opened the door, "is Emma. And the younger girl is her sister, Harriet. The little one in the cradle is John." He leaned forward a little and said in a kind voice, "Emma, may I present Miss Bingley to you?"

Emma inched closer to her mother, prompting that

woman to say, "Oh, don't shame me now, child! You must greet Miss Bingley proper, like I taught you!"

With a good deal of reluctance Emma let go of her mother's sleeve long enough to dip a curtsey and look up into Caroline's eyes.

The child was actually quite pretty, Caroline realized. She had a fair complexion and dark hair that, though slightly unkempt, almost matched the shade of Caroline's curls; and her eyes were almost the identical blue as her own. But she couldn't help but recognize the growing feeling that she had been tricked into coming to this place, and she had no desire to do anything but leave a soon as possible. That wish, however, was thwarted as Mr. Penrose picked up the basket again.

"I've brought some things for luncheon," he said, "and I've arranged for my housekeeper to come by later with your supper. No, no, you stay right where you are, Mrs. Doyle, while I see if I can make you a decent cup of tea."

"But I haven't any tea," Mrs. Doyle answered. "I am sorry for that, truly I am, and if I had any I would certainly offer it to Miss Bingley, here, but I haven't any at all. Why, there hasn't been a bit of tea in this house in months."

"Not to worry, for I've brought some." And so saying he carried the basket to the other end of the room, where there was a table and some shelves hung from the walls on which was arrayed a small collection of dishes.

Now, thought Caroline, was her chance to leave. She followed him to the other side of the room and said in a low voice, "Mr. Penrose—"

"Bless you, Miss Bingley, I *knew* you would want to help.

I'll go look for water if you will be kind enough to find a cup and fetch the kettle from the hob—"

"Do you actually expect *me* to make her tea?" she asked, incredulously.

"Isn't that why you are here? To help Mrs. Doyle?"

"I am here because you tricked me!"

"I assure you, I did nothing of the sort. You were the one who claimed a friendship with her, you know. Besides, now that you are here you must see the poor woman cannot very well make the tea herself. Why, she can barely stand without assistance. How can she ever hope to brew a soothing cup of tea and set a bit of luncheon on the table for her children?"

"Is her injury so very bad?"

"She'll recover, but it will take time. A small woman like Mrs. Doyle should never have tried to pick up those heavy bundles." He had been busy pulling a variety of covered dishes from the basket, but at this he paused and looked at her with that light in his eyes that Caroline now knew signaled his amusement. "So you really did not know Mrs. Doyle, after all?"

"Of course not; but I thought I knew the name somehow. It seemed to me I heard one of the Bennet sisters mention Mrs. Doyle, and I simply assumed . . ."

"Ah! That makes sense, for Mrs. Doyle works for the Bennets at Longbourn. She does their laundry, you see."

A flash of memory came to Caroline's mind—of Christmas and the Bennet sisters sorting through piles of trinkets and toys to deliver to their servants on Boxing Day. One of their parcels had been packed with a woman named Mrs. Doyle in mind. A widow, Mary had said, with three small children.

She looked over her shoulder at Mrs. Doyle and her gaze alighted on the younger daughter. She was still standing beside her mother, still clutching her sleeve; but in the child's other hand was a wooden peg doll dressed in a printed muslin gown—the very same doll she remembered Mary Bennet had carefully placed in a small box for delivery to the woman who did the family laundry.

So it was true! Caroline Bingley had been coerced into paying a call upon a washer-woman! She never felt more ill used in her life, and she was on the brink of telling Mr. Penrose so, when she felt a small tug on the fabric of her pelisse. Looking down she discovered Emma standing beside her.

"My mama says I am to help," she said, in a very small, very shy voice.

"Thank you, Emma, for we are especially in need of your assistance," said Mr. Penrose. "I shall fetch some water, if you will show Miss Bingley how your mother likes to put the kettle on the fire."

In the next moment he had picked up a bucket and was gone, leaving Caroline alone to deal with Emma.

17

Caroline Bingley was not a woman used to conversing with children, having no young nieces or nephews of her own. Finding herself alone with Emma—who was regarding her with wide, worried eyes—made her feel quite out of sorts and extremely uneasy.

"Don't you think," she said, after a long and uncomfortable silence, "you should return to your mother?"

Emma briefly looked over to where her mother sat, unable to move, and sorrowfully shook her head. "My mother said I was to help, because she cannot leave her chair, and if she cannot leave her chair, she cannot take care of us, and I don't know what we will *do!*"

Caroline felt a small trill of alarm as she watched Emma's blue eyes fill with sudden tears. Then, to her great horror, the tears began to spill over, and Emma began to sob as if her heart were breaking.

"Stop this instant!" she said, bracingly. "Don't you know that crying never solves a problem? Do you have a handkerchief? Of course not—whyever would I think you would! Here," she said, opening her reticule and withdrawing her own bit of lace-trimmed linen, "you must dry your eyes. Yes,

yes, take it!" she said, impatiently.

The remainder of Emma's tears remained unshed. She took the bit of lace and linen and examined it as if it were a specimen under glass.

"Oh, it is boo-tiful," she murmured. "I dearly love boo-tiful things."

"You may keep it."

Emma's eyes widened as her face went pale with pleasure. "*May* I?"

"I certainly do not want it back now."

"Thank you, Miss Biggy."

"Bingley!" Caroline said, impatiently. "My name is Miss Bingley." She was about to insist the child repeat her name back to her, but abandoned that plan when she saw Emma reverently touch the handkerchief to her face.

"It is very soft. Oh, and smell!" Emma thrust the hand-kerchief up toward Caroline's face. "How pretty it smells!"

"Yes, yes, take it away. Haven't you ever smelled rose water before?"

Emma traced one small finger over the pattern on the lace trim. "*I* would like to smell of rose water."

The wistful note in her voice brought to Caroline's mind the purchase she had made earlier. On impulse she pulled off one of her gloves and drew the bottle of Olympian Dew from her reticule. In the next instant she was kneeling on the floor in front of Emma.

"Here, give me your hand." She applied a bit of the lotion to the back of Emma's hand and used her own fingertips to spread it evenly over her skin. "There! Tell me what you think of that."

Emma tentatively raised her hand to her nose and gave a small gasp of delight. "It is boo-tiful, too! Oh, Mr. Penrose, will you smell my hand?"

Surprised, Caroline looked up to find the vicar standing only a few feet away. He was staring at her, an arrested look on his face she had never seen before. She scrambled to her feet as he set down the bucket of water he'd been carrying.

"Mr. Penrose, smell!" Emma said again.

He dragged his gaze away from Caroline's face, and bent over Emma's hand; then he drew an exaggeratedly deep breath and said, in a voice calculated to cause her the utmost pleasure, "What a charming perfume you wear this afternoon, Miss Emma. You quite cast all the other ladies into the shade."

Emma smiled delightedly. "*She* gave it to me. And look!" She held up the handkerchief in triumph.

"Did you remember the manners your mother taught you?" he asked, gently. "Did you thank her properly?"

Emma moved closer to Caroline and tugged at her pelisse again. "Thank you, Miss Biggy."

Bingley! The word of correction was on the tip of Caroline's tongue, but it died away unspoken as she peered down into the little girl's face. She really was an endearing little thing, Caroline decided, despite the fact that her appearance left much to be desired. Her hair, as Caroline had earlier noticed, was not particularly well kept; and on closer examination she saw that Emma's clothes were very worn, and her stockings had been mended by inexpert hands. To Caroline's mind, the child's situation left much to be desired; on the other hand, she certainly had an engaging little smile, and it was hard to find fault with any little girl born with an innate appreciation for beautiful—no, *boo-tiful*—things.

Emma tugged again at her pelisse. "I said, thank you *very much*, Miss Biggy."

"Yes, yes, run along now."

"But my mother said—"

Mr. Penrose halted her words. "Tell your mother to make herself comfortable. We shall serve tea presently."

He filled the kettle with fresh water and hung it back over the fire, which was now burning brightly. Returning to Caroline's side, he began to unpack the remaining contents of the basket and said softly, "Giving Emma your hand-kerchief was a kind gesture, Miss Bingley."

"She started to cry, and I didn't know any other way of stopping her," she answered candidly.

"Your instincts served you well. I think Emma is very worried about her mother. Mrs. Doyle wrenched her back something awful; and though she is confined to that chair and the doctor entreats her to stay immobile as much as possible, someone must care for her children. You don't know what torture a mother endures when she hears her baby cry and knows she is powerless to take the child up in her arms."

"Where is her husband?"

"He died four months ago, not long after little John was born. He was a laborer on one of the home farms, and since her widowhood, Mrs. Doyle has been supporting her little family as a laundress. It's not work she is used to, I'm afraid, and she miscalculated how heavy a pile of wet laundry can be—that's how she hurt her back."

Caroline looked over her shoulder at Mrs. Doyle, and for the first time she saw that, though the young woman sat very still, her lips were pressed into a grim line, signaling her pain. "Wouldn't she be more comfortable on a bed?"

"Perhaps, but Mrs. Doyle fears that if she were to lie down, she might not be able to get up again without assistance; and with two small children and a baby to look after, that would never do. Besides, installed where she is, in her most comfortable chair, she can at least watch over them; and Emma helps as much as possible."

Caroline did not think the poor woman's chair looked at all comfortable. "It seems to me there ought to be a better way to—Oh, that is all wrong, Mr. Penrose!" she exclaimed, after watching the manner in which he was arranging a plate of bread-and-butter sandwiches. She finished pulling off her gloves and placed them with her reticule on the table, saying, "Here, let me do it. And I imagine by now the water has heated sufficiently for tea, if you will be good enough to get it."

His brows went up, but this time the gesture was accompanied by a bright smile. "I *shall* be so good. And if you have any other commands for me, Miss Bingley, you will find me anxious to be of service to you."

In short order Caroline had arranged a tray on which she placed a plate of sandwiches and a nice slice of cheese, as well as a cup of strongly-brewed tea.

At her instruction Mr. Penrose delivered the tray to Mrs. Doyle; placing it across her lap he commanded her to drink every drop and eat every crumb or face the wrath of Miss Bingley.

Caroline heard him quite clearly, but since he spoke in that teasing tone he so often employed, she paid him no mind, as she busily began arranging similar plates for the children.

She had just finished serving the girls their meal at the table when there was a rap at the door. Mr. Penrose answered it, and invited in a middle-aged woman who knew of Mrs. Doyle's predicament and had come to help with the children. So the woman chattily told Mr. Penrose, but when she came further into the room and suddenly spied Caroline, she froze on the spot. Her eyes traveled over Caroline's frame, taking in every detail of her appearance—from the fur trim on her collar to the expensive kid of her shoes—and she gave an audible gasp.

"Let me introduce you," Mr. Penrose said, affably. "Miss Bingley of Netherfield, may I present Mrs. Henry to you? She lives but two doors down and has kindly come to spend the afternoon with Mrs. Doyle."

Mrs. Henry collected herself and made a deep curtsey fit for a queen; and Caroline let down her guard long enough to respond with a very civil nod of her head.

Once Mrs. Henry overcame her initial shock at finding a fine lady like Miss Bingley in such a humble cottage, she found her tongue, and explained that the women of the surrounding houses had formed a guild to take turns helping Mrs. Doyle. They had devised a full plan for furnishing meals and tending the poor woman's children. Mr. Penrose thanked her heartily, and Caroline added her own thanks, for she found, to her surprise, that in the short time she'd been there she had begun to feel a good deal of concern for Mrs.

Doyle and her children; but with Mrs. Henry's arrival, she felt the little family was being left in capable hands.

As she gathered up her gloves and reticule, Caroline was reminded of her earlier purchase. She knelt down beside Emma, who was still seated at the table, and presented the bottle of Olympian Dew to her. "This is for you to share with your mother and sister," she said. "All ladies of refinement use Olympian Dew—I am certain you have heard the Queen of France used nothing else—and once you have exhausted this supply, you must send word to me for more."

Emma was overcome by the unexpected gift; but Mrs. Doyle was more expressive with her thanks. She claimed Caroline's hand and held it to her cheek and thanked her so effusively that Caroline was immediately embarrassed, and looked to Mr. Penrose for help in making her escape.

Before long they were back outside, making their way down the narrow lane toward High Street.

"I am sure you know," Mr. Penrose said, with a laugh, "that your visit will be the talk of the neighborhood before the day is done. The other ladies will be quite jealous." He halted his steps and turned to look at her. "You were magnificent, Miss Bingley."

She felt an unaccustomed flush mantle her cheeks at the compliment. "How can you say so, when you know very well I was there grudgingly? If I could have found an excuse to leave, I would have."

"But you didn't. You stayed, and made a difference in their lives. They'll never forget it . . . nor will I."

There was something in the way he said those last three words that confused her and made her wish he would speak to her again in that teasing way he had. At least his teasings were familiar to her and she knew how to handle them; but when he spoke tenderly to her, as he did just now, she knew not how to react. She felt puzzled and flustered, and wanted nothing more than to return to an even keel.

This time it was Caroline who set off walking at a brisk pace, forcing Mr. Penrose to match her step.

"I am certain the hour is advanced," she said, "and there is a very good chance that Mrs. Bingley and her sisters will be waiting for me."

"I apologize for keeping you from your purpose today. We shall have to discuss Daniel's situation another time."

"No, that will not do. We must discuss it now, and quickly, for I cannot be forever devising excuses to visit you alone. As you said, people will talk, and how am I to explain my movements today? I am certain Jane and my brothers will be greatly surprised if word gets back to them that I visited Mrs. Doyle. How will I ever answer their suspicions?"

"You may simply tell them that you called upon a poor woman who was in need of help."

"Oh, you do not understand my meaning at all!"

"I think I do. You do not wish anyone to know that you have a kinder heart than you will allow; but I will keep that secret for you."

She heard that warm note in his voice again, and said, determinedly, "In the time we have left may we *please* discuss that boy my brother rescued? Tell me, have you found a family to take him?"

"No, I have not."

"Then a tradesman to whom he can be apprenticed?"

"I fear that is a possibility I have not yet investigated."

"But I told you," she said, sternly, "that a situation must be found for the boy immediately."

"Yes, you did."

"Then why do you delay? Surely you can understand why that stable boy must be removed from Netherfield with all speed!"

"My dear Miss Bingley, Daniel is no stable boy."

"Of course he is! My brother told me so."

"Your brother told you he found Daniel *working* in a stable; but he also told you, I am certain, that he knows nothing of Daniel's background."

"How you speak in riddles!" she said, with hot impatience. "First you say the boy works in a stable, then you say he does not—I never heard such nonsensical talk!"

"Then let me make it plain to you, for I was not in Daniel's company above three minutes before I realized he was not the boy you described to me. His manners are impeccable; I am certain you saw the poise with which he shook my hand yesterday—a sure indication that he comes of good family. And his diction is perfect, despite the exposure he has suffered over the last few months to the cant and foul language of ostlers and ruffians from all walks of life. In short, it is clear to me Daniel was very carefully reared until the unfortunate day that threw him into the power of a cruel innkeeper." His hazel eyes regarded her appraisingly. "Tell me, Miss Bingley, did you not notice those things about Daniel?"

She had not, but now that Mr. Penrose mentioned it, she had to admit that his observations had the ring of truth to them. She recalled Daniel's first appearance in the drawing-room. He had been utterly filthy from head to toe, but he had also been obedient, sitting in poised silence and speaking only when spoken to; and when he did answer, he did so with the utmost politeness.

And now that she thought on it, she recalled, too, that Daniel's voice had been quite pleasing; so pleasing, in fact, that had he been freshly bathed and more fashionably attired, she might have mistook him for a child from Lucas Lodge or some other worthy neighbor.

It pained her to admit he was right, and she said, a little grudgingly, "No, I had not noticed, and I cannot think why."

"It could be," he said, in a gentle voice, "you did not notice because you allowed your prejudices to rule your good sense."

This was too much, and her temper flared. "Prejudices! I have none, I assure you!"

"Perhaps not, but once you heard the words *stable boy*, I think you were blinded to every indicator that pointed otherwise. Your ears failed to hear his perfect diction, and your eyes failed to observe his excellent manners. Captain Bingley tells me the boy can read. Did you know it? Of course not, for your brother did not think you were interested in learning the news, and you did not think to ask."

Though his tone was pleasant enough, she felt very much as if he were scolding her. She gave an impatient twitch to the fur trim on the collar of her pelisse. "I did not ask because I am a very busy woman."

"Busy doing what?"

"Many things! There is a ball to be had at Netherfield in a

matter of a few days, you know."

"Yes, I do know. I have already received my card of invitation."

By this time they had rounded the corner of the main street, and in the distance Caroline could see the Bingley carriage approaching at a decorous pace. Seconds later they were standing in front of the shop where she and Jane had earlier agreed to meet. If she spoke quickly, she would have just enough time to ask the question that was suddenly and inexplicably burning the tip of her tongue.

"And will you attend? The ball, I mean."

She could have kicked herself, for her voice, as she asked the question, had sounded more anxious than she would have liked. She ventured to look up at Mr. Penrose, expecting to see that teasing look in his hazel eyes; but instead saw that he was looking back at her with a rather enchanting smile on his lips.

"I am looking forward to it. Attending, I mean."

The carriage pulled up before them. Mr. Penrose greeted the party of ladies with a touch of his gloved hand to the brim of his hat; and when the groom let down the steps, it was Mr. Penrose who handed Caroline up into the carriage with careful solicitude.

Jane put down her window to ask very sweetly if he would do her the honor of dining at Netherfield that evening, an invitation he quickly accepted.

"We shall send the carriage for you at seven," she said, just as they began to pull away.

Having claimed a place beside Helena, Caroline settled back against the carriage's comfortable interior, and focused her attention out the window at the passing scenery. She had made the drive from Meryton to Netherfield countless times before, and there was certainly nothing new to look at on this day in the dead of winter; but now that she was no longer in Mr. Penrose's company, she found herself thinking once again of the look she had seen on his face when he had come upon her on her knees before little Emma. She knew not what to think, for that look haunted her at the same time it appealed to her, and she couldn't help but wonder what he meant by it.

"Caroline?" Helena Paget touched one gloved hand to Caroline's shoulder to gain her attention. "Caroline, what are you thinking? The Miss Bennets and I have been talking an age, and I do believe you have not listened to one word of it."

"I beg your pardon," she answered, rousing herself. "I was only thinking . . ." She allowed her voice to trail away, unable to give voice to thoughts and questions that had filled her mind but a moment before. She looked across to where the three Bennet sisters were seated; and while Jane looked back at her with an expression of mild concern, Mary and Kitty regarded her with unmasked interest.

"Why do you stare at me so?" she asked, impatiently.

Kitty pointed to her hands. "Your gloves are soiled, Miss Bingley."

Caroline immediately looked down and saw a very distinct smudge on the back of her left glove. It surprised her, for she prided herself on her pristine appearance; yet thinking back on the events of the morning, she knew she must have stained it when she was at Mrs. Doyle's cottage.

"Kitty," Jane whispered in a warning tone, "do not be

impertinent."

"I do not wish to be, but you must admit that Miss Bingley always appears to advantage, and I do not think I have ever before seen her with a smudge of dirt on her gloves."

"Then it is a banner day for you indeed," Caroline retorted. She turned her gaze upon Mary. "And you, Miss Bennet? Have *you* any criticisms to make concerning my appearance?"

"None at all," Mary said, promptly, "for I have always found your appearance to be a point of envy and admiration; and if your attire today is less than its usual perfection, I am certain it must be the result of some great provocation."

Great provocation. Caroline turned the words over in her mind and decided that they fit Mr. Penrose very well. He provoked her and teased her and charmed her in turn; and if she was not careful, she rather suspected he would have her life at sixes and sevens in no time.

She was still mulling that thought over in her mind as the carriage entered the Netherfield gates and traveled the distance to the entrance of the house, where Charles and Robert stood waiting to welcome them.

"Here you are at last!" Charles said heartily, as he reached up to help each lady to alight. "Come in and warm yourselves. I have had the fire stoked in the drawing room and a warming punch awaits you there. Come in, come in!"

He led the way into the house with Jane on his arm, and the Miss Bennets scampered after them. Caroline was about to follow when she saw Robert step forward to intercept Helena.

"Will you do me the favor of taking a turn in the garden with me before you go into the house, Miss Paget?" he asked.

Caroline stopped and turned back in time to see Robert offer Helena his arm. She had worried that a divide had formed between them, but when she saw Helena smile up at Robert with just the right amount of coy shyness, she had her answer. Any rift that might once have existed had been of temporary duration.

She entered the house feeling well satisfied; she hoped Robert requested an interview with Helena so that that he might at last propose marriage to her. Of this she felt more hopeful than she had since her arrival at Netherfield, and she wished with all her might that the windows in her bed-chamber allowed her a view of the garden where Robert and Helena were walking.

The walls that surrounded the garden at Netherfield were clothed with climbing roses, wisteria, and clematis that bloomed with spectacular color in the spring and summer; but in the winter, those climbers were brown and bare of all color. Still, the garden was a delightful spot, with pleasant walks flanked by neatly-trimmed yews and ancient trees. It was to the garden that Robert and Helena walked under the mid-day sun.

Helena's gloved hand rested on Robert's sleeve as they made their leisurely way among the inter-connecting walk-ways in companionable silence.

After a few minutes of examining how nice her fingers

looked against the dark wool of his coat, she asked, "Do you like my gloves?"

"They are very pretty," he answered, looking down at her.

"And they were very expensive; my mother told me so. But then, pretty things are almost always expensive, and I cannot live without pretty gloves. But I must say, my hands do get so cold in them sometimes."

"Have you any fur-lined gloves, Miss Paget?" he asked, ready to be of service. "Shall I have someone fetch them for you?"

"No, thank you. I own a pair or two of fur-lined gloves, and they are comfortable, will grant you, but so ugly! They make my hands look like monsters. I cannot bear them!"

"You prefer to be cold?"

"Not necessarily. My solution is to stay indoors near a cozy fire; then I am not called upon to wear horrid gloves that make my hands look three times larger than they are. Why do you smile so?"

"I was merely thinking how delicate you are, and what a contrast there is between you and Mary Bennet. She is made of very sturdy stock."

"In what way?"

"I was recalling our drive together to the inn and back. The cold did not seem to bother her."

"I believe," said Miss Paget, "that is the way of country girls. As much as I endeavor to find common ground with her, I fear there remain some parts of Miss Bennet's make-up I cannot condone. The way she runs about Meryton alone, for instance. I am certain no true lady of breeding would dare contemplate such a thing. Country manners are so different than our London ways, are they not?"

He wasn't certain he agreed with her and said, "There is, in general, an ease of manners that can be found in the country, as you say; but I do not think Miss Bennet deliberately flouts convention."

"Oh, no," she said, innocently, "not deliberately. And we must remember that Miss Bennet has many fine qualities besides a hardiness for the cold, although I cannot think of one off-hand."

"I can," he said, promptly. "She showed an impressive amount of courage the day we brought Daniel back from the inn. By God, you should have seen her face that landlord! Her shyness was gone in an instant and for a moment she looked so forbidding, I thought she might try to draw the innkeeper's claret!"

Helena winced slightly. "That is high praise indeed. What young lady would not wish to hear herself so described?"

He laughed and said, "I merely meant that she seemed a completely different person than I first thought her to be. She was brave and caring and ripe for the challenge."

"You seem to have changed your earlier opinion of Miss Bennet."

"Perhaps I have, but that's to be expected, now that I have got to know her better."

"I suppose," she answered sullenly as she brushed at an imaginary speck of lint on his coat.

"It's a pity she is so shy. That kind of thing will hold her back in life. Fortunately, she has you."

She looked up at him. "Me?"

"You and your kind efforts. I recall what you told me on

Christmas morning; how you befriended Miss Bennet to help her out of her shyness. I hope you will continue to set an example for her."

Helena said, with a helpless little smile, "I can only be myself."

"That is more than enough, Miss Paget. But here—I do not wish you to be cold. Allow me to take you back to the house." He said this in a tone of great solicitude that caused Helena to reward him with a warm smile. She always smiled at him so whenever he took great care of her; and if she believed that he wished to take her back to the house because he was concerned for her comfort, so be it.

But the reality was that, despite her smiles and soft looks, he had detected in Helena's words a hint of malice that he had not heard before when she spoke of Mary Bennet. This, along with the unfortunate choice of words she had uttered against Daniel, puzzled him greatly. When they had been in London, in the places Helena knew well, and in the company of her family and closest friends, he had thought her charming; a lovely porcelain doll he wanted to please and protect. Yet since arriving at Netherfield, where the environment was new to her and where there was no one to curb her tongue, her delicate porcelain shell had begun to show a few small cracks; and through those cracks he had his first glimpse of the workings of his beloved's mind. It was a hard thing to admit, but he did not like what he saw.

Even as this thought occurred to him, he remembered what Charles had said: that she was young and impression-able; and that, under Robert's influence and guidance, she would soon alter her thinking and learn to speak with more care. He hoped it would be so. Then he immediately corrected himself: it *had* to be so.

18

When Robert first brought Daniel to Netherfield, he promised to devise a way of caring for him that would not inconvenience any member of his family. He was true to his word, and entered into one scheme after another to ensure that Daniel was kept busy and out of sight. The only exception was in the afternoon, when he presented Daniel in the drawing-room where Charles and the Bennet sisters made a great fuss over him and went out of their way to amuse him. That was not to say that Mary and Kitty saw Daniel only at tea time. Kitty often liked to play with him after presenting him with a new toy she had purchased in Meryton with her own pin money. Mary, too, often took possession of Daniel to walk about the grounds or to read to him in the library. In fact, she had grown close enough to Daniel that he had begun to call her by her Christian name.

Still, Robert remained Daniel's undisputed guardian and caregiver. In the mornings he took charge of Daniel himself; they breakfasted together, and then went to the stables, where Abbot amused Daniel while Robert exercised Ibis. If afternoon engagements prevented Robert from tending to Daniel, then he gave Daniel over to James, the footman who did double duty as Robert's valet; and since James had quickly realized that playing with a boy was far easier than fulfilling his duties in the household—and that he earned a very generous gratuity besides—he quickly became one of Daniel's willing playmates.

On this afternoon, Robert's time was his own; and since he had much to think about after his earlier walk with Helena, he took Daniel outside and allowed him to work off a bit of his pent-up energy.

He was thus engaged when Mary came upon them. She was trying to alleviate a sense of restlessness herself; and after walking the paths of the formal garden, she decided to circumnavigate the house. When she turned the corner toward the west, she saw Robert and Daniel together on the lawn, not very far away.

Robert was standing with his back to her, but Daniel, freed from his confines in the house, cavorted and skipped and ran. Then she saw him rush back to Robert's side, pepper him with questions, then set off running again intent on making some new discovery.

Before she could make a retreat he caught sight of her and waved. He ran toward her, saying, "Mary, we are on an adventure! Come with us."

Robert turned around then, and seeing her, went immediately to her side.

She tried to stop him, saying, "You must not feel obligated, Captain Bingley. I would not wish to intrude ..."

"Not at all," he said politely. "We are simply taking a walk to get some of the fidgets out of Daniel's legs. Please join us." He smiled and waved his hand in an inviting gesture that she could not resist.

She hesitated, wondering how she might refuse his invitation without appearing rude; but when she realized that she could keep Daniel close and thereby avoid being alone with Captain Bingley, she decided to join them on their walk.

"This way, Mary!" Daniel shouted. He ran ahead across the grass while she and Robert followed at a more sedate pace on the walking path.

Daniel gave another shout when he discovered a short length of a small, bare, broken tree branch, which he immediately began to swing at the grass as if it were a scythe.

"He has a lot of energy," Robert said.

"Which makes it all the more remarkable that he is so well behaved in the house. I have yet to hear him running through the halls or making a noise of any kind. He is a very good boy, don't you think?"

"I do, indeed," he said, thinking back to the arguments Helena had made that Daniel would somehow disrupt the peace of Netherfield. "Have you much experience with children, Miss Bennet?"

"I have nieces and nephews I love very much. I only wish they lived closer so I might see them more often."

Daniel raised yet another cry as he pointed to a small clearing in the trees. "There's a lake!" He gave a mighty swing of the tree branch and took off at a dead run toward the clearing.

"Do not go in the water!" Robert called back before he looked at Mary. "*Is* there at lake here at Netherfield? Should I call him back?"

"There is a small lake—more like a pond, really, but it attracts a good variety of birds, I believe, in spring and summer."

"Still, a pond can be dangerous for a boy if he cannot swim, and I never thought to ask him if he could or not."

He was about to head across the grass in pursuit of Daniel when he stopped short and looked back at her. "I beg your pardon, Miss Bennet."

"Whatever for?" she asked.

"Your shoes. I fear you will scuff them if you walk across the grass, and there are places here I can see are damp."

Mary looked down at her sturdy, worn walking boots and wondered why anyone would mistake her for being the kind of woman who worried about scuffed shoes. "I am not so particular as you think. Besides, I would like to see the pond, if you do not mind my company."

He lifted his brows in mild surprise. "I do not mind at all. This way, Miss Bennet."

They followed after Daniel; soon they were standing near the water's edge watching Daniel plunge his stick into the mud and peer down into the depths of the hole he had created.

"Be careful," Robert warned. "Some of that mud that is still in the shade may be slippery. It was cold last night, and the sun may not have melted all the ice."

"I'll be careful," Daniel said, confidently. "*I've* got a stick." He held it up in what he thought was a good representation of a soldier in bayonet position, then he ran off to search for hidden treasures in a cluster of nearby reeds.

"How different he is," said Mary, "from the fearful little

boy I first saw in the stable stall at the Bark and Bull. He has made remarkable progress, I think."

"He is still in need of fattening up, though. That will come in time." He looked at Mary and asked, suddenly, "Do you often walk alone, Miss Bennet?"

"Sometimes; not always. Today my sisters are engaged."

"Doing what?"

"They are huddled together with Caroline to talk about the ball and ensure all is in readiness."

"And you do not wish to participate?"

"I am not an expert in such matters," she said, candidly, "and I fear I annoyed your sister by making one or two ill-judged suggestions."

"I hope she did not speak unkindly to you!"

"No, nor did she utter a protest when I excused myself from the discussion. Do not be alarmed, for I have helped Jane with the planning as much as I am able; but the truth is that I do not care for balls very much, and all the talk and preparations make me feel a bit uneasy."

"You are a novelty, Miss Bennet! I did not think there existed in the world a young lady who did not like to attend a ball. Tell me, what do you dislike so much?"

"Many things. First, in order for a ball to be deemed a success, there must be more guests in attendance than the room can comfortably hold."

"I have heard the same. It is the hope of every hostess to hear her ball described as a *sad squeeze*. But doesn't the prospect of an overflowing ballroom increase a lady's chances of dancing?"

"You would think so, but I have not found that to be the

case. I am not very much in demand as a partner. Men only ask me to dance when they cannot help it."

Robert looked at her with an expression of concern mixed with sympathy. "I refuse to believe that is true."

"It is, and you will be a witness to it. Here is how the evening shall progress: I will sit out the first four dances at least, and I shall not be taken up as a partner until some compassionate gentleman turns his attention to the matrons and widows. I am in that class, you see."

He could detect no bitterness or sadness in her tone. He, meanwhile, was beginning to feel a strong sense of outrage. Mary Bennet did not deserve such treatment; and he had to wonder what the neighborhood cubs could be thinking to behave so shabbily toward her. Perhaps they did not know her well enough to realize that she was a very intelligent young woman who was extremely easy to talk to, once she set aside her initial shyness. But then he chanced to recall his own first impression of Mary Bennet. He had thought her plain and unremarkable; he had even said as much to Miss Paget, a misstep he now deeply regretted.

Looking back, he could not think when it was that his opinion of Mary had begun to change, but he realized that it was time he did her justice.

"No," he said, firmly, "you are not in that class. You are a young lady who deserves to dance the first dance and every dance, and I mean to see that you do so."

She looked at him doubtfully. "How?"

For answer he sketched a short bow. "Miss Mary Bennet, will you be so good as to promise the first dance to me?"

She stared at him with a look of astonishment that soon

268

softened into an expression of very becoming confusion. "I? The first dance?" In the next moment she was frowning. "But, won't Miss Paget expect—? Should you not lead Miss Paget out for the first dance?"

It was then his turn to be surprised—by his own lack of manners where Miss Paget was concerned, and by the quick flash of disappointment he felt when he realized he could not single Mary out for the attention he felt she deserved.

"You are right, of course," he said, clasping his hands behind his back. "Miss Paget has a prior claim. But that is no reason why I may not partner you in the second dance."

"You are very kind, but I must decline your request."

"May I ask why?"

"It has become a tradition in Meryton that the second dance at any assembly is a waltz."

"And you do not know the dance?"

"Oh, yes, I do, but I have never danced it in public, you see."

"Is there not, as the saying goes, a first time for everything?"

"I suppose. But though I know the steps, I have had very little practice. I might tread upon your toes."

"My boots are made of sturdy leather; I dare you to try to harm me."

"You see the humor in the situation, but I cannot," she said. "I may as well confess to you that I have had some rather *humiliating* missteps on the dance floor."

"And may I confide something to you? We soldiers are much more adept at marching than waltzing. I once whirled my partner in a left box turn and without thinking, finished by counting off a military marching cadence in my head that almost sent us trooping past the punch bowl as if we were on review."

She laughed and said, "I cannot think that ever happened! Not to you!"

"I assure you, it did. The young lady was taken by surprise, but I have decided to forewarn you of my penchant for mixing marches with waltzes, because I like you."

She had been regarding him with amusement, but his last words caused her smile to fade. "You . . . you do?"

"Yes, I do," he said, locking his eyes on hers. "And I mean to dance the second dance with you, if you will have me."

She looked down at the ground, still smiling, but blushing, too. The thought of dancing with Captain Bingley was much too tempting to resist. "Yes. I accept your invitation, Captain Bingley, and I will be pleased to dance with you."

"Thank you, Miss Bennet. Now, about those other dances—" he stopped, as he looked about and realized he could not see Daniel anywhere.

Concerned, he called his name. Daniel popped up from where he had been kneeling among the reeds, and ran to him.

"Look what I found," he said, opening his hand to reveal several smooth stones of varying colors.

"An excellent find," Robert said. "Do you know what those stones are good for?"

Daniel shook his head.

"Skipping. You know how to skip stones, don't you? Here, I'll show you." He took one of the stones from Daniel's hand, turned slightly, planted his feet firmly, and threw the stone with a flick of his wrist toward the water.

Daniel watched the stone bounce one, two, three times before it sank. His eyes lit up.

"Let me try! Here, Mary, will you hold these?" And without thinking she opened her gloved hand to take possession of the remaining very wet and rather dirty stones.

"Like this?" Daniel asked, mimicking the stance he'd seen Robert take. Then he let his stone fly, and was immediately disappointed. "It only skipped once."

"Try again," Robert said after spending a few patient minutes showing him the quick hand movement needed to make the stone skim across the water.

Daniel obeyed and let out a whoop of victory when his stone skipped three times. "Did you see that, Mary?"

"I did indeed," she said, with a bright smile. "Now let me see you do it again."

As Daniel took another stone from her hand, Robert leaned toward her and said in a quiet voice, "I fear, Miss Bennet, you have ruined your gloves."

She followed his gaze and saw that her glove was dirty from handling the stones. "Oh, I don't mind. I am more interested in seeing if Daniel can throw his stone farther this time." She looked up and saw an odd expression on Robert's face that immediately put her on alert. "What is it? What have I done to make you look at me so?"

He thought a moment before he answered. "Forgive me, but are you not upset that your gloves have been ruined?"

"But they haven't been—at least, I don't think they have. I will ask Kitty to help me when I return to the house. She

271

will know if they can be saved. There is no purpose in being upset without cause, you know. "

He looked at her curiously but said no more; and when Daniel urged him to throw another stone, he immediately complied.

Daniel also took another turn, but when there was only one stone left in her hand, Daniel said, "Mary, you try it."

"Oh, no," she said, half-laughing as she shook her head. "I do not know how to throw."

"But haven't you been watching? Captain Bingley will show you how. Here!" And without warning he clasped Mary's hand and thrust it toward Captain Bingley.

"Do you feel you need a lesson, Miss Bennet?" he asked.

She pulled her hand back, blushing. "I—No, I don't. Perhaps I will simply . . ."

"Throw it, Mary," Daniel urged.

She turned a little to the side, as she had seen Captain Bingley do, and drew her arm back. In one quick movement, she brought her arm forward at the same time she shifted her weight to her other foot. The stone left her hand, the heel of her shoe began to slide, and in the next instant she was on the ground. It all happened so quickly, she was given no time to react, and she landed with a little yelp of surprise.

"Miss Bennet!" Robert rushed to help her up. "Are you hurt in any way?"

She wasn't, but she was a good deal surprised and embarrassed. She felt Robert's strong hands pull her to her feet, and he held her by the shoulders to ensure she was steady before he let her go.

"I should have watched where I was stepping," she

murmured, still trying to make sense of what had happened.

It was then that Daniel, trying to be helpful, brought to her attention the fact that she had sat down in a patch of mud.

"Oh, dear!" She twisted her head from one side to the other, trying to see down the back of her pelisse. "Is it very bad?"

She looked up then at Captain Bingley, counting on him to break the news to her; instead, he said with a stricken look on his face, "I beg your pardon, Miss Bennet. I should have paid better attention—"

"But it was my own fault! You warned us of the damp and ice." She grasped the skirt of her pelisse and tried to draw the back of it around her legs to give her a better view. "Perhaps it is not so bad as I thought. I cannot see the damage—how much disgrace am I in?"

He didn't answer and she looked up at him, bracing herself to hear him laugh or tease her over her discomfort. Instead she found him looking back at her with a frown.

Her heart sank as she tried to interpret his expression. Perhaps he thought her unladylike. At the very least he probably thought her clumsy, and since she had been described so often enough in her life, she could not very well argue the point.

Still, she was sorry for the state of her pelisse, but there was no use regretting what could not now be undone. She swatted her already-soiled gloved hands at the back of the skirt in a vain attempt to remove some of the dirt and mud. "At least I can be thankful I am not wearing my sister's pelisse! That is a silver lining, I think."

273

"You aren't angry, Mary?" Daniel asked.

"Not at all. It was a stupid thing to have done, but you see, I wanted to throw a stone, too. Tell me, did the wretched thing skip at all?"

"No," Daniel said with a regretful shake of his head.

"Then I shall have to practice, and in a few days I will show you how much I have improved."

Daniel's expression brightened. "I'll practice, too. Then we can have a contest!"

"Very well. A contest in one week's time to see who can skip a stone the farthest across the pond."

"Can Captain Bingley be in the contest, too?"

"If he wishes," she said, afraid to look at him again, for fear of seeing a look of disapproval on his face. She picked up her skirts a little and began to walk toward the clearing in the trees.

Daniel followed her, having reclaimed his stick. "Maybe," he said, with a grave expression, "we should not let Captain Bingley enter our contest, after all. He will win, won't he?"

"No he will not, for you and I will insist he must throw with his left hand."

She was finding it difficult to walk, for the heels of her boots had been caked with mud when she slid, and with every step she felt as if she were wearing weights on her feet instead of her comfortable walking boots.

Without warning she felt Robert's hand at her elbow to help steady her steps. The warmth of his fingers burned through the wool of her pelisse, and for a moment she didn't know whether to enjoy the sensation or yank her arm away. She looked up at him and saw his previous frown had disappeared and he was smiling slightly.

"Conspiring against me, Miss Bennet?"

"More like assigning you a handicap," she managed to say in a no-nonsense tone, even as her spirit soared. "Daniel and I are amateurs while you have had years to practice skipping stones."

"But not with my left hand!"

"Then what do you suggest?"

He cast his mind about for a solution and said, "I'll spot you five points."

"Hmm," she said, pretending to consider his offer. "What do you think, Daniel?"

"*Ten* points!"

Robert burst out laughing. "You drive a hard bargain, young man! I shall have to be very careful when I negotiate with you in future."

By this time they had begun to retrace their steps across the lawn. When they reached the house, Mary stopped and carefully drew her arm from Robert's grasp.

"I will wish you a good day, Captain Bingley."

"Will you not continue on with us?"

"I think it would be best if I returned to the house to see if I can repair some of the damage to my pelisse."

"Yes, of course." Still, he didn't move, and after a moment of steadily looking at her, he said, "If you will do me—That is, Daniel and me—the honor of walking with us again, I pledge to take better care of you in future."

"You are too hard on yourself. It was nothing but a stupid accident. Pray do not think of it again."

"You are very good, Miss Bennet. I cannot help but think

there are other ladies of my acquaintance—*They* would not be so forgiving."

"I cannot think why. After all, what is the damage? A bit of dirt on my gloves, some mud on my pelisse, which I have worn three seasons already by now. Of course, my *pride* suffered the greatest damage, but that will soon be mended, too."

He said nothing, but he was watching her with an expression she had not seen before. She puzzled over it until a distant movement caught her eye. Pointing to a spot just past his left shoulder, she said, "I must warn you that Daniel has just disappeared from view around the far corner of the house. If you run, you may be able to catch up to him."

His expression changed. "Scamp!" he uttered in a tone that promised playful vengeance on his runaway charge; and with one last look at Mary and a hurried good-bye, he set off in pursuit of Daniel.

19

Jane arranged for the Bingley carriage to deliver Mr. Penrose to Netherfield at the appointed hour for supper. An attentive hostess, she presided over a well-appointed dining table; in turn, Mr. Penrose was an appreciative guest, who helped carry the conversation along in an easy manner, and paid unerring attention to the ladies.

When their meal was at an end they eschewed Town customs, and removed—ladies and gentlemen together—to the drawing-room.

Walking beside Robert to the fireplace, Mr. Penrose said, "I hope I will have the pleasure of seeing Daniel again this evening. Tell me, Captain Bingley, how does he go on?"

"Very well . . . considering all he has been through. He is still a boy without an identity, you know, but he seems happy enough."

"He should be more than *happy enough*," Helena said, as she claimed a chair near the fire and arranged her skirts about her. "I am certain he has never lived so well as he does now. I cannot think he has done anything to deserve his good fortune."

"Perhaps not," said Mr. Penrose, "but if good fortune

only falls to those who deserve it, I fear many of us would find ourselves living completely different lives than the ones we now enjoy."

"True enough!" said Charles. "But Daniel is a good boy and eager to please. Robert and I took him out to the high meadow this morning—You know the place, Mr. Penrose—and I never enjoyed a morning of shooting more. You should have seen him running and playing. I do believe he scared up more pheasants than the dogs."

"And when he is with the ladies," said Caroline, thinking instantly back to her conversation with Mr. Penrose, "his manners are very pretty."

Her comment was met with a moment of stunned silence, until Helena turned to her with an expression of wide-eyed innocence and asked, "Of whom do you speak, Caroline? *Who* has pretty manners?"

"I speak of . . . of Daniel, of course," she replied, with her chin up and the slightest hesitation before saying his name.

"How funny you are!" Helena exclaimed.

Caroline shot her a look of cold hauteur. "In what way?"

"Why, you have attributed good manners to a boy who has lived his life in a stable! Really, Caroline, how would such a boy come by pretty manners?"

Caroline ignored her, and casting her eyes about the room, she saw Jane sitting quietly, as she often did. Caroline moved to the seat beside her, laid her hand on Jane's arm and said, "You may not yet have heard the news, I think, that Mrs. Doyle is ill."

Jane looked back at her in surprise. "Mrs. Doyle?"

"Yes. She hurt her back dreadfully, you know."

"No, I did not know. *Mrs. Doyle?* The woman my mother employs at Longbourn?"

"How many Mrs. Doyles could you possibly know?" Caroline asked, with some irritation. "Yes, the very same Mrs. Doyle who does the laundry."

Jane did not try to hide her astonishment. "But how do *you* know her? Have you met her?"

"Indeed I have. I have also made the acquaintance of her children—charming little girls, especially the older one, Emma. She is a dear little thing."

"You—! I—! Forgive my astonishment, Caroline, but I can hardly credit what I am hearing! How did you come to—?"

"It is a simple explanation: when I was in Meryton today I came upon Mr. Penrose who had just received news of Mrs. Doyle's injury. Of course, I accompanied him to determine whether I might be of assistance."

"And *were* you of assistance?"

"Indeed I was; I made tea; but that is beside the point. Let us return to the issue at hand. Mrs. Doyle is in need of help and a good deal of rest if her back is to heal properly. And since she is a dependant of Longbourn, I feel it is our duty to call upon her, in your mother's absence, and provide what assistance we can."

"Yes, of course!" Jane answered, gathering her wits. "Caroline, you are very good to be in sympathy with Mrs. Doyle's plight."

Caroline gave a dismissive wave of her hand. "A handful of women in the neighborhood have united to provide food and tend the children while Mrs. Doyle's back heals, but I observed there are very few comforts in the home. Why, the poor woman has not even a pillow on which to rest her feet. And now that I think on it, a few warm quilts will do much to help bring some comfort into her little cottage."

Jane stared. "So you *did* visit her!"

"Did I not tell you as much? But about Mrs. Doyle's injury—I think it is very painful to her, though she tries very hard to pretend otherwise. Do you know, her back pains her so much she cannot lift her arms to comb her daughters' hair?"

"This is a serious injury, indeed. Of course I will immediately arrange to deliver blankets and firewood and anything else the poor woman needs."

"We must also find some little things for the children that will keep them occupied while Mrs. Doyle rests."

"I will speak with my housekeeper this very night to make arrangements, and I will visit Mrs. Doyle myself tomorrow. Would . . . would you care to accompany me, Caroline?" Jane asked, cautiously.

"Thank you, I will."

Mary, who had been quietly reading in a nearby corner of the room, looked up. "May I go, too? I should be glad of a chance to do a kindness for Mrs. Doyle; she works very hard for the Bennets."

"Too hard," Caroline said. "She is a very small woman who never should have tried to pick up heavy wet bundles. You must see to it, Mary Bennet, that you do not overtax her again in future."

Mary's eyes widened as a protest formed on her lips, but Caroline would hear none of it. Instead, she ordered Mary to the small writing desk and charged her to write a list of each item she and Jane thought of to be delivered the next morning to Mrs. Doyle.

When the list was complete, Jane got up to look over Mary's shoulder to see if any small comfort might have been missed. It was then that Caroline sensed Mr. Penrose's presence.

He had been standing behind her and as soon as she was alone, he placed his hands on the back of her chair and leaned forward to whisper, "I am proud of you, Miss Bingley."

She felt his breath tickle her neck and every nerve in her body sprang immediately to life. She turned her head slightly, hoping to catch a glimpse of him from the corner of her eye, but he had already stepped away to the fireplace, where he declined Miss Paget's invitation to sit beside her, saying he preferred to stand; but in the next moment his gaze was fixed upon Caroline. In his expression she saw neither a hint of his loathsome sense of humor, nor censure. Then, without warning, she saw him smile ever so slightly, and her heart gave a tiny lurch.

She almost blushed, but caught herself and looked away, even as she wondered how the approving glance of a simple country vicar could manage to fill her heart with so much happiness.

The next morning Mary, Jane and Caroline drove to Meryton. They had sent ahead a job carriage laden with all the items they had enumerated the evening before; items they were convinced would greatly advance Mrs. Doyle's situation.

But as they drove up High Street Caroline had a sudden thought that more could be done to pamper Mrs. Doyle. She ordered the coach to stop in front of the very same shop in which she had purchased the bottle of Olympian Dew only the day before.

"We shall only stop a moment," she said to Jane, as she alighted.

Inside the shop she was immediately confronted by two annoyances. The first was the realization that Mary had followed her into the shop; the second was the discovery that other shoppers were there before her, and she was obliged to wait her turn to be served.

Determined to ignore Mary's presence, she began to idly examine the wares on the tables; her attention was caught by a child's toiletry set. There was nothing remarkable about it: comb, brush, and hand mirror clad in plated silver, it was an insignificant and cheap version of a lady's dressing table essential. Yet she found herself staring at it and thinking of Emma, and how nice the little girl would look if her hair were properly combed and styled.

She looked up at the clerk, who had just finished serving the customer before her, and asked, imperiously, "Have you any blue ribbands? The kind a little girl may wear in her hair?"

Very soon she was standing before an array of ribbands of every imaginable shade a blue. With Mary Bennet's interested gaze trained upon her, Caroline selected a nice but serviceable ribband that she hoped would match the color of little Emma's eyes. To that purchase she also added a selection of lace-trimmed handkerchiefs for Mrs. Doyle.

"I will take that, as well," she said, pointing to the dressing table set. "You may wrap them together, please." Then, for the first time since entering the shop, she turned to Mary with a challenging look. "Yes, Miss Bennet? You wish to comment on my purchases, I believe. Please, be my guest, and say what you wish!"

"I would not presume to do so."

"So say your lips, but I can tell from the look in your eye that you have one hundred and one questions with which you wish to plague me."

"Not at all."

Caroline pressed her lips into a tight line of irritation. "So you mean to deny me the satisfaction of even that? I must say, I do not know who is more provoking—you or that extremely slow clerk. How long does it take to wrap a simple gift, I wonder?"

"Oh, it is a *gift*, then?"

"Of course it is—for little Emma and her mother and sister. You did not think I purchased those items for myself, did you?"

Mary's expression softened. "Mrs. Doyle and her daughters are fortunate, indeed."

"Why, because I am giving them a simple dressing table set?"

"No. They are fortunate because they have won your sympathy and friendship. You have a kind heart, Miss Bingley."

"Nonsense!" she scoffed. She had never before heard

herself described as *kind*, and she wasn't certain she knew what to make of it. In taking up Mrs. Doyle's cause she found herself in unfamiliar territory. Had she never visited Mrs. Doyle's cottage she might have blithely lived the remainder of her years with no thought whatsoever to the manner in which people of the working class lived; but Mr. Penrose—whether he intended to do so or not—had opened her eyes to it; and having seen Mrs. Doyle's suffering and the look of unhappy worry on little Emma's face, Caroline was unable to shake from her mind the images of the cold, spare cottage or its inhabitants.

She was quite satisfied that the practical gifts of blankets and food and firewood she and the Bennet sisters bore would make a great difference to Mrs. Doyle and her children; but it was up to Caroline Bingley to bring a bit of extravagance to the party. After all, she thought, as the clerk delivered the wrapped items she had purchased into her hands, what woman or little girl did not like to have her hair brushed and be made to feel pretty every once in a while?

They arrived at the cottage to find Mrs. Henry there. She was warming a pan of soup to set before Mrs. Doyle and her children when Caroline greeted her and made her known to Jane and Mary. Then she turned her attention to directing the men in unloading the boxes and bundles from the job carriage.

While Mrs. Henry cared for the family, Caroline, Jane, and Mary set to work. It took a good portion of the morning to set the cottage to rights; but by the time they had finished, Mrs. Doyle—who alternately cried and smiled as so many needed items were arranged about the room—was comfortably settled in her chair with a cushioned stool beneath her feet. A fire burned bright and warm in the hearth, and beside it, arranged in a neat pile, was a good supply of firewood. The cupboard was stocked with food and tea (a result of Caroline's insistence), and warm quilts were draped across the bed and over baby John as he lay in his cradle.

The crowning touch, presented just before the ladies took their leave, was the presentation of the toilet set and ribbands. Caroline herself brushed out Emma's hair while Mary plied the comb to Harriet's curls; and by the time they were done both little girls looked, in Caroline's words, quite fetching. Mrs. Doyle thought so, too, and thanked Caroline, Jane, and Mary so often and in such effusive terms as to make Caroline suspect that her ears would begin to burn.

Still, she couldn't help but feel satisfied when she and the Bennet sisters stood up to take their leave. Mrs. Doyle made one last attempt to express her thanks, but a rap at the door halted her words. A moment later Mr. Penrose entered and, taking in the changes that had been made to the room with one quick astonished glance, said, "Why, this is remarkable! I think you must have had some angels visit you, Mrs. Doyle!"

That lady laughed for the first time since her injury. "I have indeed, sir!"

He saw the ladies drawing on their gloves. "I hope you are not leaving now on my account. Won't you stay a bit longer?"

"I fear we are expected at Netherfield," Jane said gently. Then she made her good-byes and led the way to the carriage.

Mr. Penrose followed them, and handed Jane and Mary up; but when he took Caroline's hand to do the same, he added a bit of pressure to her fingers as he clasped her hand, and said softly, "I know this is your doing. Thank you!"

She meant to protest, but he stepped back, allowing the groom to take up the step and close the door. As the carriage pulled away, Caroline chanced one last look at him, hoping to see a hint of that soft smile on his lips. He did not disappoint her.

20

Mary moved restlessly about her bedchamber and wondered how many more days she would be required to spend in solitude in order to avoid Captain Bingley's presence. She had already passed two days since her last encounter with him near the pond, and since then she had devised one reason after another to ensure she was never alone again in his presence.

She missed him, and she rather suspected he had noticed her absence; he undoubtedly noticed, too, that she no longer took a daily walk or ate her breakfast at the same time he and Daniel did; yet he did not question her.

Sometimes, when she dared to look at him, she saw that his smile was not so ready as it had once been, and he seemed to be preoccupied with some great and weighty matter.

She paused in her travels about the room to look out her window. She had a view of the garden, and as she looked down and wondered if she might safely walk its paths without encountering Captain Bingley, there came a rap at her door.

One of the upstairs maids entered with a small silver tray

on which rested a letter. Mary instantly recognized her sister Elizabeth's handwriting. As soon as the door closed and she was once again alone, she gently pried the pages apart and settled in a chair near the window to read her sister's letter.

My dearest Mary, your letter arrived today and I read it with great interest. How brave you were to rescue that little boy! But I always knew you to be a young woman of firm conviction, so I cannot say I was surprised to read your account of the story. You displayed as much courage as Captain Bingley, and I relished telling Mr. Darcy of your adventure.

I fear I must admit Darcy is a little skeptical of your theory that Daniel may be related to Lord Rainham, for it would be a fantastic coincidence to find the grandson of a marquess living among ostlers, but stranger things have happened in this world, I suppose.

Darcy is now on watch for any communication from Lord Rainham. We are a little acquainted with him and admire Captain Bingley's courage in commencing a correspondence, for Lord Rainham is a formidable man. His holdings in the county are vast, and his home is a great deal grander than Pemberley, although he lives there quietly enough. He takes great pleasure in carrying out his ceremonial duties as steward, but he does so, I think, with the sad remembrance of happier days long ago.

If you did indeed view his entry in Debrett's as you mentioned in your letter to me, then you know by now that he has endured a father's greatest loss. His daughter Catherine died in infancy and another, Anne, in childbirth. He was given three sons: Thomas, his heir, died last year without producing a child after twelve years of marriage. His second son, John, died as a youth years ago; and Daniel, the third son, defied his father by joining the church instead of making a career in the practice of law. Lord Rainham has never spoken of what happened next to Darcy or me, so I cannot verify the veracity of the story, but neighborhood lore will have it that Lord Rainham was so vexed with his youngest son that he set about thwarting the young man's efforts to secure a living, hoping his son Daniel would relent and return to the family and follow his father's wishes that he practice law. Instead, Daniel disappeared; that was twelve years ago and Lord Rainham never saw him or heard from him again.

Following this there was a great blotch of ink, as if Elizabeth had thoughtlessly allowed her pen to drip ink upon the page, while she considered how best to relate the rest of her news. When she did resume, her handwriting was much less carefully formed, giving Mary the impression that she was laboring under a great agitation. Elizabeth wrote:

Oh, Mary, you shall never guess! Just as I was

about to close my tidings to you, who do you think was announced at our door? Lord Rainham himself! I was quite astounded to receive a visit from the very gentleman about whom I was writing you. I will confess he is a man who cuts an impressive figure, and I felt my heart thump a time or two as I greeted him with my best and deepest curtsey, for he is a man who naturally inspires a bit of awe in everyone he meets. Mama was quite speechless—for which I was sincerely glad—and father performed most creditably.

Well! Lord Rainham spent a little time in making pleasant talk, then dove into the heart of his visit. He said he had received a letter from a Captain Bingley of Netherfield, Hertfordshire, and was anxious to know if Darcy was acquainted with the man. Of course, Darcy had to admit he had never met Captain Bingley in his life, but was acquainted with the captain's brother vastly well. He then told his lordship that he was somewhat aware of the circumstance through another party—his sister-in-law Mary Bennet—and could vouch for the sincerity of Captain Bingley's overture.

I believe—although I cannot be certain—the old marquess was greatly moved by this news, for he was silent for a long time. Then he asked Darcy if he thought it possible that Captain Bingley and Miss Bennet would confuse the matter? He asked, were they of steady character or were they the sort of people who jump to conclusions? After Darcy assured him that both of you were possessed of sound judgment, Lord Rainham was very quiet again. I think he paled just a bit as he reflected on Darcy's claim, but he then rallied and said he had hopes of meeting us all again in the new year and wished us happy. After a bit of talk about county events he took his leave. I imagine the poor man has much to think upon if Captain Bingley's letter to him contained even a fraction of what your letter divulged to me.

Oh, Mary, I cannot foretell what will happen next in this business you and Captain Bingley have begun, but I hope you will inform me if you do hear from Lord Rainham. I am anxious to learn if this story ends happily for all concerned. Do write again soon.

Give my love to Jane and Kitty, and tell Captain Bingley he has earned Darcy's and my admiration.

The rest of Elizabeth's letter was filled with news concerning their parents and accounts of the different entertainments they had enjoyed throughout Derbyshire—accounts which Mary only scanned, for it was her intention to show Captain Bingley the letter without delay.

In very little time she was properly dressed for the out of doors and making her way directly to the stables. She was keenly disappointed to discover Captain Bingley was not there. Abbot, reading her crest-fallen expression to a nicety, suggested that the captain could not have gone far, for Ibis was still in her stall. Mary thanked him and, armed with this information, set off in search of Robert.

She skirted around the front of the house, where she caught sight of Caroline and Helena walking the garden paths. From there she went to the west lawn, where she had come upon him two days before with Daniel. In the distance she spied Robert far off near the grove of trees. He was walking away from her while Daniel and Charles' dogs cavorted about him. Immediately she began to move his direction at a rapid pace; at the same time she called his name.

Robert stopped and turned about; and upon catching sight of her, he altered his course and began walking her direction. With his long legs, he very soon closed the distance between them.

"Hello, Miss Bennet," he said, but his friendly expression quickly changed to one of concern. "Why, you are out of breath! Are you well? Tell me what has occurred to upset you."

"It is nothing! I have simply been walking too fast after receiving the most astonishing news! You see," she said, trying hard to catch her breath, "I have received a letter from my sister, Mrs. Darcy. Oh, here, you must read it." And with that she thrust the letter into his hand and watched for his reaction.

Robert immediately unfolded the sheets of paper. It did not take long for him to master the letter's contents.

"So he knows!" he said, raising his eyes to Mary's face. "Lord Rainham knows."

"Knows what?"

"Knows there is truth to our theory about Daniel's lineage! Why else would he immediately seek to verify our characters?"

Mary's brow furrowed slightly. "I think we have piqued Lord Rainham's interest, but nothing more. We must not try to divine Lord Rainham's intentions until we hear from the man himself."

"Oh, no, Mary Bennet, I will not allow you to be sensible in this. Not now when there is the glimmer of hope that we have found a family for Daniel at last!" he said. Then he bestowed upon her a smile so dazzling she felt the day warm by degrees.

"Well. . ." she said, hesitatingly.

"Come now, say you will be optimistic." He folded the letter and reached out to put it back in her hand, but instead of releasing her, he kept hold of her hand in a strong grip. "Say it!"

His unexpected touch seemed to burn through the soft kid of Mary's glove like electricity; and that, combined with the happy and hopeful light in his blue eyes, made her succumb to his mood as nothing else could. She was caught up in his enthusiasm before she knew what was happening, and said, with a little laugh, "Oh, very well. I will not be practical; instead, I will be *hopeful!* There! Are you satisfied?"

"Thank you, Miss Bennet, for I know how much such an admission cost you."

She would have drawn her hand away then, but he prevented her; and instead lifted it to his lips and lightly kissed it.

It was a gesture made in fun, she was certain of it, but the pressure of his lips on the back of her hand immediately robbed her of breath. It even made her feel a bit light-headed, and it took several precious moments for her to gather her wits and slowly draw her fingers from his grasp.

She clutched the letter to her chest and tried to speak sensibly, but she had a difficult time making her tongue behave. "The letter—I still think—Oh, dear!" This last was uttered as she saw a change come over Robert's face. She realized he was no longer looking at her, but at a point just past her left ear. She turned to follow the direction of his gaze.

There, a short distance away, stood Caroline looking back at her with an expression of deep censure; and at her side Miss Helena Paget looked very unhappy indeed.

21

No, Caroline!" Charles said, with unaccustomed force. "By God, no! What reason have I to insist that Mary leave Netherfield?"

"But if you had only *seen* Helena's face you would understand!" Caroline said, pleadingly. Her voice seemed to echo off the walls of the little morning room where she had demanded a private interview with Charles and Jane in order to recount to them the scene she had witnessed. But Charles had immediately balked at Caroline's description of Mary Bennet as a scheming seductress, and made it clear he intended to defend her.

Caroline turned her arguments on Jane. "If you have any regard for me, Jane—Any regard at all!—you will take steps to separate your sister from my brother."

"I have already done so," Jane answered quietly.

"You . . . you *have?*" said Caroline in great surprise.

"I spoke to Mary about her friendship with Robert a few days ago, and pointed out to her the perils of being seen too often alone in his company. Mary promised to be more circumspect in the future; and since Mary is a very good girl and not at all the sort to defy my advice, I must believe that something extraordinary occurred to cause her to behave as you described."

"Hold on, Jane," Charles said, "for it was not Mary who kissed *Robert's* hand! If there is any blame to be attached to their meeting on the lawn, then we must look to Robert."

"So that is the sort of brother you are!" Caroline said, her color much heightened. "How like you to blame *him*, but then, it has always been so!"

"I attach blame to neither Robert nor Mary . . . only to you, Caroline, for bearing tales! You know very well that Mary Bennet would no more try to come between Robert and Helena than I would."

"But I saw her," Caroline insisted, still trying to make a case against Mary, "and I very distinctly heard her laugh."

"Then I recommend you ask Robert to tell you what he said to Mary that was so remarkably funny, but I will not. And I will not have Mary banished from Netherfield."

It was not often that Caroline found herself close to tears, but worry for her friend Helena and her own mounting frustration almost made her want to cry out loud. "Am I the *only* member of this family to recognize the danger here? If Helena decides she will not have Robert, what will become of us?"

"If Robert and Helena do not marry," Jane said, reasonably, "I am certain Robert will recover. He will be able to find a suitable wife and—"

"But not a wife with an *earl* for an uncle. Do neither of you see that?"

"If you think," said Charles, "that Robert singled Helena out as the recipient of his affections simply because she had a nobleman in her family, you are glaringly abroad!"

A hasty retort quivered on the tip of Caroline's tongue, but the sound of the door opening forced her to bite it back.

Kitty entered, and she did not try to mask her curiosity. "What is going on?"

"Does *she* have to be here?" demanded Caroline with a burning look toward Jane.

But Kitty would not be deterred. She closed the door and came further into the room. "Don't bark at me. I only ask because Captain Bingley has had a great row with Miss Paget." Her announcement had the desired effect of surprising her listeners.

"Kitty," said Jane, "how do you know this?"

"You were listening at a door!" Caroline said, accusingly.

"Not at all, nor would I. But I could not help overhearing, for they were in the great hall and voices do have a way of echoing about there, you know. I was just coming down the stairs when I heard them speaking quite angrily to each other, and with every word their voices got louder. I've never seen Captain Bingley in such a state, and Miss Paget was angry, too, for her face was quite red, and then she stomped off."

Caroline anxiously sprang to her feet. "Did Robert go after her?"

"No, he went in the opposite direction. And when I asked where he was going, he said quite savagely that he was going to the northeast corner of Jericho and Nowhere. Then he left the house in a fury—and had a footman not been there before him, I am certain he would have slammed the door on his way out, for that's how angry he was."

"Thank you, Kitty," Jane said in a composed voice. "Now,

will you excuse us, please?"

Kitty showed her disappointment. "Then I am not to know what they were arguing about?"

"It is a private matter, Kitty, between Captain Bingley and Miss Paget."

"But I would just as soon stay here with you."

"I'm afraid we were in the middle of a conversation when you interrupted. You will excuse us, I know."

With a great deal of reluctance, and an audible mumble that she was never allowed to know anything, Kitty left the room.

Caroline immediately renewed her pleas to Charles that Mary be made to leave the house. She maintained her opinion that Mary had deliberately attempted to lure her brother into an illicit flirtation; and Charles stood equally firm in his belief that the scene Caroline witnessed was nothing more than playful antics between two friends.

As the storm in Jane's sitting room came to a close, a storm of a different kind began to brew outside. By the time the sun set in the late afternoon, a light rain had begun to fall and gusts of wind howled faintly at the windows on the west side of the house. Later, as the Netherfield party retired for the night, the temperature outside dropped considerably and the mild days they had recently enjoyed faded into a wintery scene.

Mary awoke the next morning to the sound of rain—a gusty, cold, turbulent rain that lashed at bare trees and scratched their limbs against the outer wall of her bedchamber. The rain drove into her window when she was foolish enough to raise the sash ever so slightly, and she closed it quickly before donning a heavy shawl about her shoulders to ward off the cold.

In the family dining room she found only Kitty and Jane at breakfast. She was relieved, for she was rather fearful of facing more of Caroline's anger or Helena's displeasure. There was no doubt in her mind she was in disgrace with both ladies, but she did not know how to apologize to them or, indeed, whether she even should. She knew only that she felt uncomfortable and a little embarrassed that they had witnessed her encounter with Robert and wished that the entire episode had never happened.

She rather thought her best course of action might be to avoid the presence of everyone involved in the little drama that occurred on the lawn. Toward that end, having finishing her morning meal, she invited Kitty to her bedchamber for a game of backgammon. Kitty accepted, and the sisters passed the remainder of the morning together.

By afternoon when everyone gathered for tea, the storm outside had picked up strength. The sky was heavy with dark, greenish-grey clouds, which seemed to match the mood of everyone confined to the house, for they were generally out of sorts.

Mary entered the drawing-room with her copy of Fordyce's *Sermons* in her hand and took up a place by the window, hoping to make herself as inconspicuous as possible as they waited for the tea tray to be brought in. Kitty stifled a faint yawn, and Charles took a seat at a small writing desk, announcing his intention to pen a letter he had been meaning to write for an age. Caroline impatiently leafed through a book of hand-colored prints of flowers that Jane had procured for her from the library; and Robert chose to stand at the window and moodily watch the falling rain turn to heavy wet snow.

Only Helena moved about the room. She fluttered from chair to sofa, from window to door like an uneasy bird in a cage. At last her gaze alighted on Mary, and she said, in a bright little tone as she sat down beside her, "My dear Miss Bennet, you are very quiet here."

Mary looked up from her book. "I am always quiet when I read."

"Of course you are! I believe you prefer reading to anything else. You have patience in abundance, Miss Bennet."

Mary sensed the time had come to try to explain to Helena what had passed between her and Captain Bingley. She slowly closed her book and said, "Miss Paget, I hope you will allow me to explain about yesterday—"

"Yesterday? I can think of nothing—Oh, do you mean the moment Caroline and I came upon you and Captain Bingley on the lawn? Pray, do not think of it again, for I assure you, I do not. Tell me, is that a book of poetry you read there?"

Mary shook her head, feeling a bit confused by Helena's rapid change of topic. "No, it is a book of—"

"Miss Bennet, why don't you frizz your hair a bit about your forehead? The style would be very becoming on you."

"Frizz?" She blinked several times in confusion and instinctively reached up to touch her fingers to her brown hair. It was dressed in a plain style that she had always considered to be neat and appropriate. "I had not thought of it. I've never worn my hair any other way."

"And isn't that the best reason to make a change? I promise it will look well on you." Helena took hold of her arm and hung upon her confidingly. "My maid is very adept at styling my hair, as you see, and I have a new curling tong that will do the job nicely. Everyone compliments me on my artistic abilities when it comes to my hair. You do like the way I have my maid arrange my own, do you not?"

Mary's eyes swept over Helena's bright golden curls, styled so enchantingly about her face, and said honestly, "Yes, I do."

"Then come to my room after tea and let me take you in hand. It will be such an improvement, you'll see. I am certain you will like it immensely."

Mary accepted her invitation with a good deal of misgiving. She had been initially surprised that Helena would speak to her in so friendly a manner, for she frankly thought that Miss Paget might be angry with her. The last time she had seen Helena, she had a very shocked and disapproving look upon her face, and Mary had already prepared herself for the prospect that she might have to beg Helena's forgiveness on bended knee in order to make things right between them. She was, therefore, a good deal surprised that instead of harboring vengeful thoughts, Helena was willing to let bygones be bygones, for nothing in Miss Paget's manner seemed anything other than her usual bright, frothy self.

Mary's attention shifted to the sound of the door opening to admit Daniel, who had grown accustomed—thanks to Captain Bingley's insistence—to taking tea every afternoon with the adults.

Daniel went immediately to Robert's side. Robert drew his brooding gaze from the scene outside to look down at Daniel with a fond smile and ruffle his hair; but Kitty instantly laid claim to Daniel. She drew him to a place near the fire and invited him to sit beside her while they looked at the book Caroline had abandoned but a few minutes before.

Immediately after tea Mary accompanied Helena to her bedchamber and put herself into that young lady's power.

Helena's maid, once she understood her assignment, gave a low grunt and immediately sat Mary down at Helena's dressing table and began to unpin her hair.

"Her hair is just like yours, miss," the maid announced as she ran strands of Mary's hair through her fingers. "Fine with a bit of natural curl. Yes, it should do very well I expect."

"Good!" said Helena as she clapped her hands together in delight. "That means you should be able to dress Miss Bennet's hair just like mine. You are in capable hands, Miss Bennet; just leave everything to my Nell."

Helena then drew a chair beside the dressing table so she could sit next to Mary and observe every detail of her transformation; through it all she maintained a remarkably steady stream of chatter. "I am so happy you agreed to do this, Miss Bennet, aren't you? I am convinced you will like the outcome and—Dare I say it?—you may not recognize yourself once we are done."

"Won't I? But I do not wish for a *drastic* change." Mary said, as she heard the first snip of the maid's scissors and a long tendril of her brown hair fell into her lap.

"Sometimes it takes a drastic change to make a thing of beauty. But I should warn you here and now, Miss Bennet, that he will appreciate any change we make here today, no matter how small."

"He? Who do you mean?"

"I am speaking of Captain Bingley, of course," Helena said, looking back at her with an expression of abject innocence. "Changing your hair was his idea, you know."

Mary was stricken to silence by these words and she knew not what to make of them. At last she said, "Did—Did Captain Bingley *ask* you to change the arrangement of my hair?"

"Not directly. He merely asked that I suggest a few alterations to your appearance ... suggestions any true friend would make."

Mary felt her mouth go suddenly dry and her heartbeat slowed to a dull, uneven tattoo. "He suggested—But I don't understand."

"It is so simple, really. He told me of the day he made your acquaintance and how he mistook you for a governess—or was it a lady's companion? I don't suppose it matters, for men are always judging women by their looks, you know, whether they mean to do it or not."

"He mentioned my appearance?"

"He did, but do not worry, Miss Bennet, for I defended you in the strongest terms—We were already on our way to being fast friends by then, you'll remember. 'No,' I said to Captain Bingley, 'I will not allow that Mary Bennet is dull and unremarkable.' Of course, he said no more, for he could not continue on in that vein when I was so firmly set against him!"

Mary could practically feel the color drain from her face

as Helena chattered on. Helena's voice sounded honey-sweet, but to Mary the words she spoke left a hundred little knife cuts upon her heart.

Dull. Unremarkable.

She knew the words applied to her—indeed, she'd known it all her life—yet they stung so much more when they were uttered by someone else. Someone like Captain Bingley.

She hardly heard the snip of Nell's scissors as she stared at her own reflection in the looking-glass and realized she had been very foolish to think that Captain Bingley would ever think of her as anything more than a relative by marriage. And all those times Mary had thought she'd seen a look in his eyes—that special look she imagined that he saved only for her—she now realized had been nothing more than a piece of fiction conjured by her own wishful thinking. But, oh, how she had cherished that fiction; and for the short time it had lasted, his words had made her feel smart and his look had made her feel beautiful. Now she was to understand that she meant nothing to him. In Mary Bennet he saw a governess, a drudge, a woman not tempting enough to attract him. In the face of these revelations her spirits sank and she wished with all her might that she had never followed Helena to her chamber.

"*Voila!*" said that young lady as her maid tucked a final pin into a braided row of Mary's hair. "Well, Miss Bennet, tell me what you think! Do you not look as charming as I predicted?"

Mary examined her reflection in the glass. The maid had fashioned a row of curls about her face that accentuated the shape of her eyes and brought out a piquant little point to her chin that she had never really noticed before. Never before had her hair been so fashionably dressed, and she thought the style was, as Helena promised, rather becoming to her; but the thought gave her no satisfaction.

She thanked Helena and voiced admiring words for her maid's talent; but all the while she wished she had never gone to Helena's bedchamber in the first place, and had never heard the hateful words that young lady had uttered with blithe unconcern.

As soon as she was able Mary made her escape. She flew down the stairs to the drawing room, and went directly to the pianoforte. The first touch of her fingers on the keys resulted in a crashing chord, followed by another, then she began to pound the keys in a manner that almost made her fingers hurt. After a minute of this she stopped; only then did she realize she was not alone.

"Miss Bennet?"

Startled, she spun around on the music stool to find Captain Bingley seated in a comfortable chair near the fire, a newspaper open in his hands.

"Miss Bennet, are you well?"

In her fury she had not stopped to see if anyone else was in the room, but had flown to the pianoforte, her source of comfort, as she was used to do when she was at Longbourn. But instead of comfort she now found herself face to face with the very person she least wanted to see.

She pursed her lips together and turned back to the instrument.

He stood up and without taking his eyes from her, abandoned his newspaper and advanced a few steps toward her.

"Has something happened to upset you?"

"Not at all." Her voice was curt and she refused to look at him.

His blue eyes scanned her face and hair. "What have you done?"

"I? *I* have done nothing."

"But your hair . . . You changed it. Why?"

"Don't you approve?" she asked, resentfully. "Or do I still look like a governess or a poor relation?"

"A governess? What do you mean by—" His posture stiffened. He asked, carefully, "Who spoke of you in those terms?"

"You did—at least, that is what Miss Paget told me. Do you not recall saying as much to her on the day you arrived at Netherfield?"

"She could not have told you so," he said, as a dull flush appeared above the white lawn of his shirt collar.

"She did, and more. But I do not blame Miss Paget, for I have always known myself to be dull and unremarkable, but to hear it said *about* me . . . *that* is a very different thing, I assure you."

Mary turned her face away as her teeming emotions almost got the better of her. She raised her hand to dash away a teardrop, and said in a voice that trembled, "I do so *hate* to be talked about."

"As you should." He reached out his hand to her, but he immediately thought better of it and allowed his arm to drop. "I apologize, Miss Bennet. Miss Paget should never have repeated my words—No, wait. I said that wrong. The truth is, I should never have said such a thing to Miss Paget in the first place. I am to blame. I cannot excuse myself or explain why I spoke so cruelly. I can only beg your pardon and ask you to forgive me."

She did not answer, for it took every ounce of control she possessed to keep from dissolving into a torrent of tears. As it was, she had to pull her handkerchief from the sleeve of her gown and hold it up to cover her suddenly trembling chin.

He moved to the side of the pianoforte, the better to see her face. "I humbly apologize to you, Miss Bennet. What I said then—it was thoughtless of me."

"Oh, do not talk anymore! Can't you see I am too upset and too—yes, too *angry?* Only tell my why you thought you must discuss me with her. Don't you think I, more than anyone, know I can never measure up to Miss Paget's standards? I assure you, I have known since I was a child that I am not a beauty, and I have known for many years that I am dull and unremarkable, as you say, but—"

"You are none of those things," he said, decisively. "Surely you know my sentiments have changed since the day I first met you. Those words I used—I would never attribute them to you now, not to the Mary Bennet I have come to know."

He spoke so earnestly and looked so concerned, that she wanted to believe him very much. But she was still deeply hurt to think that he had talked about her in less than flattering terms with Miss Paget. She couldn't help but wonder what else they might have said about her; and when the thought occurred to her that they might even have laughed as they discussed her appearance, she heartily wished that the floor might somehow open up and swallow her whole. But the floor did not magically open up, and Mary was obliged to remain where she was.

"I've asked too much," he said, regretfully. "Very well, do not grant me your forgiveness, but for God's sake at least allow me the chance to prove I am worthy of earning your good opinion again."

She heard the note of strain in his voice and instantly felt herself respond to it. A quick glance up at his expression convinced her of his regret. He'd hurt her terribly, but she sincerely doubted that she would feel any better by hurting him in return. Besides, a seed of suspicion was slowly beginning to develop in her mind that Helena Paget's innocent disclosure had not been as artless as Mary had first supposed; and she was beginning to believe the entire episode of dressing her hair had merely been Helena's method of punishing her for allowing Captain Bingley to kiss her hand.

Very well, Miss Paget! she thought. *You have had your revenge, but I will not be embittered by it.*

She looked up at him. "Are you *very* sorry?"

"Yes. I could not be more so."

"Very well, if you are intent upon being contrite, I suppose I cannot be so disobliging as to fly into a pelter."

His body, which he'd been holding in rigid check, relaxed a little. "You are very good Miss Bennet. Thank you!"

"I have never believed it wise to carry grudges." That much was true, but she was uncertain whether she would be able to trust him again or look at him in the same way she did before. Even now she could barely meet his eyes, and when she did chance to look up at him again, she saw that his gaze had strayed once again to her hair. She felt as if he were examining every curl, every tendril that had been so painstakingly arranged about her head. She vaguely wondered if he liked it, but quickly decided his opinion did not matter, for she had already developed a decided distaste for the entire business; and those fashionable curls—which seemed so attractive in the looking-glass in Helena's room— were now nothing but an unpleasant reminder of the hateful words Miss Paget had uttered. Mary knew what she had to do.

She stood up and smoothed her skirts. "I beg you will excuse me now. I must go to my sister."

"Of course. Allow me, Miss Bennet," he said as he walked with her to the door and opened it for her. "And Miss Bennet?" he said, just as she was about to pass the threshold.

She stopped and looked back at him.

"Allow me to say once again how truly sorry I am."

She knew he was; she could read it in his expression. "Please do not mention it again; I know I will not."

She went immediately upstairs and rapped at the door of Kitty's bedchamber and went in without waiting for an answer.

"Kitty, I need your help."

"What, again? Didn't I just spend an entire morning with you playing—Good gracious, what have you done?" she asked, as she looked up and saw Mary's hair for the first time.

Mary touched her fingertips to the hated fringe and

asked, "Is it so very different?"

"Of course it is! Why, you look lovely, Mary—not like yourself at all! But how did this happen?"

"Miss Paget had her maid do it." She stood very still as Kitty walked a circle around her in order to see the full effect of the change.

"Well, I must say she did a splendid job of it. It's very becoming on you. I like it."

"So did I . . . for about six seconds."

"What do you mean?"

"I confess, my fingers are itching to undo it all from its pins. I don't like it anymore. I want to arrange my hair in the way I am used to wearing it."

Kitty squinted her eyes as she took a closer look at the delicate little curls that framed Mary's face and brushed against the nape of her neck. "It looks like she used a pomade to keep the curls in place. You will have to wash it out."

"Will help me?"

"Are you certain that's what you want? The style is very pretty on you."

"But I do not feel like myself. Besides, you know I haven't the patience to dress my hair every day and pin up these curls every night before I go to bed."

"Very well," Kitty said reluctantly, "if you're certain that's what you want . . ."

Mary crossed the room to give a tug to the bell pull. "What I want is to feel like myself again before we sit down to supper."

A maid responded to her summons, and a short time later Mary had the satisfaction of seeing all the curls that

Helena's maid had so patiently arranged, float away in a bath of warm water.

"We shall have to wash your hair at least once more if we are to get all the pomade out," said Kitty.

"But at least we have gotten rid of most of it," Mary said, "and I feel so much better already." It was true, for washing her hair made her feel as if she were also washing away some of the hateful little words Helena had said to her. Some, but not all.

She knew Miss Paget must have been deeply shocked to witness the little scene between herself and Captain Bingley; and as she thought about it, she realized that Miss Paget certainly had a reason to be upset. She might even have a reason to confront Mary about her behavior.

But what she could not understand was the manner in which Helena had exacted her revenge. Had Helena railed at her, she would have happily suffered the scolding. Had Helena chosen to punish her with icy silence she would have accepted the slight and gone about her business. But Helena had done neither, opting instead to execute a plan designed to drive a wedge between herself and Captain Bingley.

That realization made Mary pause, and as Kitty worked to dry Mary's long hair before the fire, she asked, thought-fully, "Do you think Miss Paget is glad she came to Netherfield?"

"She is glad enough when there are people about to flatter and adore her. Otherwise, she is very discontented, I think."

"That is a severe assessment."

"It is an honest assessment," Kitty said. "I once overheard Miss Paget tell Caroline that she abhors country towns. That was the word she used—*abhor!* She claimed there was little to do and no society to do it in and, even worse, no one to admire her when she does it."

That convoluted admission made Mary smile. "She does like to be admired, I think."

"Well, she has one less person to admire her now."

Startled, Mary looked up at her. How could Kitty have known of the cruel things Miss Paget said to her? "Do you mean me?"

"No, I mean Captain Bingley. Do you not remember the row they had? What *was* it that made them both so angry?"

Mary dropped her eyes so Kitty would not detect any of the guilt she felt. "I cannot say."

"Cannot or will not?"

"Please do not ask questions. Isn't it enough to know that both of them are unhappy right now?"

"I suppose. But I cannot help but think it might turn out for the best that they did argue about something. I have thought for some time now that Captain Bingley and Miss Paget do not seem to suit each other. They are very different people, you know."

Yes, Mary did know, for she had long ago formed the same opinion in her mind; and she could not help but wonder if Captain Bingley would make an effort to mend the rift with Helena Paget.

22

When Robert went searching for Miss Paget a short time later he discovered her in a most unlikely spot; she was in the library alone, flipping through the pages of a slim volume of poetry. Fleetingly he wondered what might have drawn her to this particular room above all others. She had never, to his knowledge, been a great reader; and in his mind he had become so used to associating the serenity and comfort of the library with Mary Bennet, that he couldn't help but feel a small flash of resentment at finding Helena intruding upon the space.

He closed the door with a decided click, and she looked up with an expression of bland interest.

"So you have found me at last," she said, turning her attention back to the book. "I am glad, for I did not wish to wait here for you much longer."

"Is there some reason you wished me to find you in this particular room?"

"There is a quiet atmosphere to it, don't you think? And since I was rather certain Miss Bennet would immediately run to you, I thought it best that I find a secluded place where you would feel comfortable saying the things you wish in private." She closed the book and placed it on a nearby table before she folded her delicate hands together in her lap. "I am ready. Please say what you will."

This was not the manner in which he had envisioned beginning their conversation. He remained in the center of the room, and said, frowning, "I hardly know *what* to say. Tell me, Miss Paget, what did you hope to gain by speaking to her so?"

"Gain?" she said with an artificial little laugh. "Why, what could I possibly gain from Mary Bennet of all people? She has no breeding, she has no manners, and she has no conversation. I feel nothing for her but the deepest pity, I assure you. What could I gain from her?"

"A bit of revenge, I think. I told you very clearly yesterday, but you would not listen, so I will say it again: If anyone was at fault for what passed between us yesterday afternoon, it was me. *I* took her hand. *I* teased her and kissed her fingers. Miss Bennet was not at all to blame."

"So you told me."

"Yet you still decided to wreak havoc upon her by saying hurtful words and trying to drive a wedge into the middle of her friendship with me. Well, you have had your revenge. I hope it gave you satisfaction."

It had not, but Helena was not prepared to admit it. She raised her chin to a defiant angle. "I *knew* she would run to you with the tale."

"She did not. I came upon her quite by accident and forced her to tell me what occurred. Frankly, Miss Paget, I am at a loss to understand your reason for repeating to her the ill-advised words I said to you in confidence."

"In confidence! When you spoke those words to me we were standing in the front hall with half a dozen footmen nearby. Pray, what made you think that anything we said to each other under those circumstances was the least bit confidential?"

He frowned. "I would like to think that anything I may say to you is for your ears only and will not be repeated."

"That sort of thing is, I believe, a privilege reserved for married couples, or men and women pledged to marry," she answered coolly. "We are neither of those things, you and I."

"If I understand your argument, you need feel no scruples in repeating anything I might say to you because we are not formally engaged to be married!"

"Naturally. Of course, *if* we were formally engaged the circumstance would be altered." She unclasped her hands to smooth an imaginary wrinkle from her skirt.

"Tell me, Miss Paget, if I were to share with you a secret about myself right now, would you keep that secret?"

"I would consider it, but—with circumstances as they are between us—I cannot pledge to maintain silence on a matter that might beg to be shared in future—under the right circumstance, of course."

"Handsome of you!" he said, with a darkling look. At the same time he was giving vent to his irritation, he was reminded that Mary Bennet was at that very moment scrupulously guarding a number of secrets for him. Never once had she broken their pact and blurted out to anyone their suspicions concerning Daniel's lineage; nor had she told anyone—even her sisters—of the letter he'd written to

Lord Rainham and the hope they shared every day for his reply.

To Mary Bennet, too, he had once shared his hopes for the future, of his plans for his career, his desire for a promotion and the obstacles in his way toward achieving that ambition. Mary had listened without judgment, and even encouraged him. And never once had he harbored a moment's concern that she might repeat his words to anyone.

Now, as he looked down at the woman he had planned to make his wife, he felt as if he were seeing her for the first time. Oh, there had certainly been signs all along—signs he had stupidly ignored because they did not suit his notion of the way a woman of Miss Paget's beauty and poise might behave. But little by little the scales had fallen from his eyes, and though he still thought her physically beautiful, he saw nothing else about her to beguile him. All the little things he had once cherished about her—her feminine gestures and musical voice; the way she held her head and the dainty way she walked—suddenly held no attraction for him.

"You are angry now, Captain Bingley, but you will not be for long."

"Won't I?"

"You will soon forget Mary Bennet. I assure you, I never intend to give her another thought."

"You are very blunt!"

She raised one finely-arched brow. "I merely state a fact."

There was a coldness in her tone that repelled him; but it also prompted him to think the time had come for them to have an honest conversation about their future together.

"I think it is time for us to speak plainly, Miss Paget. What exactly do you want of me?"

She did not hesitate to answer. "*Plainly speaking*, I want you to put an end to your ridiculous entanglement with Mary Bennet."

"It is not an entanglement," he said, irritated. "It is nothing more than a friendship."

"You may call it friendship, but after seeing the look on her face when you kissed her hand yesterday, I assure you she would not agree with you."

"What a great piece of nonsense! If you are suggesting that Mary Bennet is in love—" he broke off suddenly, and his body tensed.

"Yes, I am suggesting such a thing. I had no suspicion of it myself but there was no mistaking her expression as the two of you enacted that little scene on the lawn. You ask what I want? I want you to break it off with her. Send her somewhere—I understand she has an uncle in Cheapside. She will go to him if you tell her to. Yes, I think London should do very well for her this time of year. Tell her she must go."

But Robert was no longer attending to her words. He moved to the fireplace and stared down into the flames as a sudden, blinding thought sprang to his mind. If it were true that Mary Bennet was in love with him—No, that was too much to contemplate, he thought, preferring to think any feelings she had were little more than mere affection—surely he would have noticed it. Conscience-stricken, he made a quick mental inventory of his interactions with Mary, trying to pinpoint a look or action on his part that might have inadvertently given her the wrong impression. At first glance he found none.

But then he chanced to remember the evening he had discovered her on the ladder in the library, and how she'd blushed as they turned the pages of the *Debrett's* together. He should have noticed her embarrassment but he'd been too caught up in the moment, too busy admiring the way she had plied her nimble mind to reasoning out the mystery of Daniel's parentage.

And then there was that day by the pond, when she'd slipped in mud. She'd blushed then, too, as he helped her up, but at the time he'd been more taken with the realization that she had handled her misfortune with a healthy dose of good humor; and he vividly remembered that at the time he could not help drawing a comparison between Mary's reaction and Miss Paget's response upon finding a scuff of dirt on her new kid boots.

The devil of it was that with each recollection, his conscience began to cloud. He had not, he now realized, been blameless in his dealings with Mary Bennet. With each encounter and every conversation, he had felt more and more drawn to her, until he came to the point when he realized he no longer saw Mary Bennet as others did. To him, she was a delightful companion, with a self-deprecating sense of humor, and a natural manner that he found genuine and unpretentious. There were many times when he had had the unique pleasure of being seated across from her at dinner, and looked at her in time to see her reaction when Caroline made some fatuous remark with perfect sincerity; then he would catch Mary's eye and watch her smother a smile, and know that she was appreciating the joke as much as he. That was an example of a camaraderie he had never shared with Miss Paget. And while others saw her as little more than a shy, retiring female who resisted all efforts to call attention to herself, he knew Mary was capable of acting bravely when her principles demanded. In short, he liked Mary Bennet—he had since the morning of their curricle drive to the inn—and the more he saw of her, the more he had come to realize how much he would miss her if she were to suddenly vanish from his life.

All these thoughts swirled about his mind in a fleeting instant, but their effect was profound. He'd behaved very foolishly not to see where his friendship with Mary had been leading; and he was equally foolish not to realize that his own feelings for her had undergone a significant change. He wasn't yet ready to admit he was in love with Mary, but he was at least honest enough to now realize that he had developed a very deep affection for her—an affection that threatened to grow stronger the more he saw of her.

He looked over his shoulder to where Helena sat with calm composure, and asked, "What will sending her away accomplish?"

"For one thing, she will cease to be a daily reminder to me of your lapse in judgment."

"Or the blow to your ego. That's what this is about, isn't it? You do not wish anyone to think that a man—any man—might prefer Mary Bennet over you."

"How *dare* you!" she breathed.

"Come, Miss Paget, we said we would speak plainly with each other."

"Very well!" she said, clasping her hands together again in a tight grip. "If you wish for plain talk, Captain, I will give it, and remind you, at the same time, that there is an understanding between us of a future life together. Isn't that the reason you and I came to Netherfield in the first place? So you could pay court to me and, when the time was right, propose marriage? Everyone knows it to be so. My mother and father gave their tacit approval when last you saw them in London; and certainly Caroline and Mrs. Bingley anticipate a match between us. Our engagement is expected; our marriage, a foregone conclusion."

"But I have not offered marriage to you yet."

"You will," she said, complacently adjusting a bracelet on her wrist. "You are, after all, a gentleman. After making your intentions known so publicly you would not cry off now."

"No, I would not. But you could."

"And stand by while the world watches you run straight into the arms of Mary Bennet? I think not."

"Would you really marry me under such a circumstance? I begin to wonder, Miss Paget, if you have any tender feelings for me at all!"

"Of course I do. You are very handsome and you look well enough in your uniform to turn the heads of ladies as you pass by. That, you can be sure, I find very gratifying. You are also a man possessed of an ample fortune, and that must also reflect well on me."

"That is your idea of love?" he asked, incredulous.

"Love! *Love* is a word actors throw about on the stage. Gently-bred people such as you and I do not *fall in love*, Captain Bingley. That is an emotion in which only the lower classes indulge."

"I see," he said, grimly. "And you will be happy in a marriage based on nothing more than pleasing looks and a sufficient income?"

"Oh, now you are willfully misunderstanding me. Surely you know we have more in common than that. For example, your tastes in music and conversation are completely compatible with mine—that is important, I think, for a marriage to prosper. I have my own good parents to look to for example in this; and my dear uncle and aunt, Lord and Lady Berkridge have enjoyed a marriage of many years built on mutual esteem and respect."

"Ah, yes—Lord and Lady Berkridge," he murmured, realizing for the first time how very often Miss Paget mentioned their names.

"I am glad we had a chance to clear the air," she said as she stood and shook out her skirts. "I feel better, don't you?"

In silence he watched her cross the room to the door, and as she took hold of the knob, he said, quietly, "What you did to Miss Bennet . . . it was cruel of you, Helena. I had not thought you capable of such behavior."

She raised her slim shoulders in a gesture of helplessness. "It had to be done. Now you and I can go on as we were before Miss Mary Bennet decided to interfere. In time you will agree with me." She opened the door, but had a sudden thought. Turning back to him she said, "The sun has gone down, but I think the moon is bright enough to lend sufficient light outside. Would you like to take a walk through the garden before the evening turns too cold?"

"Thank you, no."

"Then I will see you at supper," she said in a pleasant tone that was so completely at odds with the conversation they had just had as to jar his sensibilities.

When Helena entered the drawing-room a few minutes later, her veneer of calm resolution had vanished. She was visibly agitated. To her good fortune she found her friend Caroline to be the sole occupant of the room.

Caroline was established in a comfortable chair near the window with a dish of tea and the latest edition of a ladies' fashion periodical; but upon seeing Helena's flushed expression, she immediately abandoned both her tea and her reading material.

"My dear Helena! Come sit beside me and tell me what has occurred to distress you so."

"This *place* distresses me!" Helena said, hotly. "Indeed, I wish I had never come here!"

"But what has happened? Why do you say such things?"

"A better question would be, why should I not? Sometimes I wonder, Caroline, how you can *bear* to come to this place. You must agree there is no society to speak of and little to do. Oh, when I think that I might, even now, be in Essex with my parents and sister, enjoying the company of truly *worthy* individuals, I could cry in vexation!"

Now alarmed, Caroline reached out to seize Helena's hand in a firm grip, and said, soothingly, "Calm yourself, my dear friend! I am convinced you are unwell."

"Oh, no, I have never been better, for my eyes are quite

open now!"

These words struck an ominous chord in Caroline's mind. "Tell me what has occurred."

"Have I not been clear? I want to leave! I want to go now. I want my mother!"

"But I don't understand. If you do not tell me what has happened to distress you, how can I make it right?"

Helena hesitated, and pressed her pink lips into a resolute line. She was not at all certain that she wished anyone—even her dear friend Caroline—to know that Robert Bingley might actually prefer dull, stupid Mary Bennet over her. A light sheen of angry tears brightened her eyes as she said, "I don't think you can do anything at all. In fact, I am quite convinced you hold no power over your brother, despite all your assurances to me in the past."

"My brother? Robert? What has he done?"

"He has—Oh, I cannot bear to say it! *I* will certainly never speak of it! You must ask *him*."

Caroline stared at her, wondering what to make of these incredible words; and when the thought occurred to her that Helena was on the brink of breaking off relations with Robert, she felt a sickening tinge of dismay.

"I will," she said, resolutely. "I will ask my brother what he has done to distress you, and you can be equally certain, my dear Helena, that I will personally see that he makes amends to you. Leave everything in my hands."

Caroline spent several more minutes uttering similarly soothing words to her friend, until, as last, she had coaxed Helena into a better mood. Still it was another thirty minutes before Caroline felt she could leave her friend alone and go in search of her brother.

Having gained the knowledge that he was last seen leaving the house, she donned her warmest cloak and tied the ribbons of her most serviceable bonnet beneath her chin, and set off to find him.

It was cold outside, to be sure, and rather windy, but she soon found Robert near the stables. He was standing at the paddock fence, his hands and forearms resting on the top rail of the enclosure, as he watched the grooms exercise the carriage horses.

"Here you are at last!" she said, wrinkling her nose at the smell. She never could abide the unique odors of a stable. "I hope you are not thinking of riding now. It is almost dark."

"No, I'm just out to get some fresh air. But what are you doing out here? Aren't you in danger of losing your bonnet?"

"I've been searching for you, naturally."

"Why? Is someone in need of me?"

"No, but I wanted to speak to you alone. I heard what happened. Helena told me you argued—" She stopped short as he let out a bark of ironic laughter.

"Argued? I think we have gone past simply arguing, Caroline! I don't know how I ever supposed that Miss Paget and I would suit."

These were the last words she hoped to hear. Now thoroughly alarmed, she said eagerly, "I can tell something has occurred to upset you, but when your temper has cooled, I think you will see that Miss Paget is still the same sweet, lovely girl you met in London a few months ago."

"You are right, Caroline. She is the same person; it is I who have changed. No, not changed—Let us say, come to my senses. I see now how foolish I have been."

"Robert, you are the least foolish person I know."

"Then you cannot be acquainted with a great many people."

"How *can* you jest at such a moment?"

"But I am not jesting, my dear sister," he said, quietly, his eyes still focused on the horses trotting in a wide circle around the paddock. "I am ashamed to have to admit it, but I am perfectly sincere. I've behaved stupidly, abominably— even now I cannot explain it very well, even to myself. I thought somehow that a woman of so much beauty must be possessed of an equally beautiful soul."

"You are speaking nonsense, and I think you are being very hard on Miss Paget."

"No, I am being very hard on myself. I have been the greatest gull—so dazzled by her looks and connections that I never thought to learn whether or not we would suit."

Caroline stared at him; but instead of seeing his face, she was envisioning the collapse of her dreams. She was not yet ready to give up her plans to see her best friend happily married to her brother, or—more importantly—being able to claim that young lady's noble uncle as an in-law. "Only tell me, Robert, for I must know: Have you broken off with Helena?"

"No, I have not."

She let out a small breath of relief. "So you will still marry her!"

"So it seems. I cannot do otherwise. You know the code by which gentlemen must live. It is she who must break it off, and she has assured me she will not do so." He gave an odd little laugh and uttered, "God, I have made a great mess of it."

That odd little laugh did not fool her for an instant. She was close enough to her brother to recognize by his expression that he was suffering under the weight of a good deal of regret; but she also recognized that there was more to his present mood than the simple realization he had nothing in common with the woman he had publicly courted for months.

She was suspicious of the change in him and asked, slowly, "What exactly did you and Helena argue about just now?" He didn't answer right away, but gave her a speaking look that made a bit of the color drain from her face. "Oh, no! Pray tell me you did not argue again over Mary Bennet! Robert, this is too bad of you! But I do not blame you! Oh, no, it is Mary Bennet who must answer for her own conduct. *She* is to blame for everything that has happened since you arrived. How, I wonder, is it possible that a . . . a *country dowdy* should be able to cause so much trouble in less than two weeks' time?"

He flicked a sharp look at her. "If you were a man, Caroline, I'd knock you down for saying that. I advise you not speak of Miss Bennet in that way to me again."

She gave a little gasp. It was not so much his words that shocked her as the manner in which he'd said them. He may not be willing to speak about Mary, but the fact that he would brook no criticism of her told Caroline all she needed to know. Robert no longer considered Mary Bennet as nothing more than a sister-in-law; nor did he see her as merely a friend. No, there was something much more compelling going on—something deeper that she could barely bring herself to name. Her dear brother, whom she loved to distraction, had, it seemed, fallen in love with Miss Mary Bennet. And it had all happened right under her very nose.

"I do not understand you," she said in a voice that shook. "You have sat in Helena Paget's pocket for the better part of these last four months and now—after little more than a fortnight's acquaintance—you have thrown your heart at Mary Bennet! It is not to be borne!"

"Try for a little sense, Caroline. I have *not* thrown my heart at anyone."

"Then why do you stand here with a blue cloud over your head, when all the time you should be pleased with your good fortune? Why, you are practically engaged to marry a lively, beautiful girl—"

"With whom I have not one thought in common. You may believe she is aware of it, too, but she insists that *mutual esteem* is a sufficient foundation on which build a marriage." He looked over at Caroline. "Again, we disagree, Miss Paget and I."

"Would that be such a very bad thing? Many long and comfortable marriages have begun with less."

He shrugged his shoulders. "I suppose so."

"Then why are you so unhappy?"

"I'm not unhappy; I'm simply ... disappointed with myself mostly. But fear not! I will do my duty, Caroline. I will marry Miss Paget, since she is so keen to go through with the business, and I will do my best to be a good husband and ensure that she will never have cause to regret it."

"And what of Mary Bennet?"

"Miss Bennet," he said in a voice of dull resignation, "does not figure in my plans in any form. Are you satisfied?"

Caroline felt a twinge of guilt—but only a twinge. In her heart she believed Robert would soon snap out of whatever foolish mood had taken hold of him. Soon he would come to his senses and see that his initial attraction to Helena Paget had been the lure worth following, and that Mary Bennet had been nothing but a momentary distraction to him.

The situation only called for a bit of steady management to make it right again. Soon Robert would be married to Helena; soon the Bingleys would welcome an earl into the family, and when that time came, everyone would thank her; and the entire unfortunate business concerning Mary Bennet would be nothing but a faded and disagreeable memory.

23

When Mary entered the drawing-room before supper, she was neatly attired in her favorite green evening dress and her hair was carefully arranged in the plain style she had worn before Helena decided to take her in hand.

Helena looked up when Mary entered and flushed slightly, but she made no comment concerning the change. Neither did Robert, but there was an undeniable gleam of appreciation in his eyes as he looked at her.

Caroline, seeing the look, sensed danger. She had already decided to study Mary Bennet with a new sense of awareness to see what tricks she employed to wreak her havoc. But despite her vigilance, she saw no artifice in Mary's behavior, no lure to capture Robert's attention. At dinner Mary focused her eyes on her plate except for one or two instances when someone directed a question specifically to her which she was compelled to answer. After supper she spent only five minutes in the drawing-room before excusing herself and disappearing for the remainder of the evening.

The next day progressed along the same lines: Mary appeared for meals, but absented herself whenever there was a chance her path might cross with Robert's.

Caroline could not help but feel a sense of relief. Perhaps she had judged Mary too hastily. Perhaps Robert's developing feelings for her had been purely one-sided and she did not return his regard at all.

Still, she remained vigilant when everyone gathered in the drawing-room the very next afternoon. Mary was the last to enter, having stopped to collect a book she wanted to read; and as soon as she entered the room, she retreated to a chair in the corner and opened her book. Robert, seated beside Helena, merely looked up when she entered, and immediately turned his attention back to Helena.

Watching them, the last of Caroline's suspicions subsided. To judge by the quiet occupations of everyone around her, she might never have known there had been any arguments or discord the day before. Charles was buried behind the pages of a London newspaper that had arrived earlier in the day. Jane and Kitty were seated on the sofa with Daniel wedged between them; Kitty, pretending to work a bit of embroidery, spent most of her time trying to keep her embroidery silks from tangling; and Jane, listening to Daniel softly read aloud from a book, interrupted him once or twice to correct his pronunciation of a word. In such a tranquil atmosphere, Caroline began to think the trouble that threatened to come to a head the day before had been vanquished.

It was then that the Bingley's excellent butler entered the drawing-room carrying a small silver tray on which reposed a letter. He stopped in front of Captain Bingley.

Charles lowered the pages of his newspaper and frowned. "Came by express, did it? That cannot be good news."

Caroline sat up a little straighter in her chair. "If it is an order to return to your regiment, I will toss it into the fire myself."

Robert took the letter and saw, with a sinking heart, that he did not recognize the hand that had written the direction. If it was indeed an order from his colonel, then he must obey, but he was in such a foul mood, he was greatly tempted to follow Caroline's advice and chuck the thing into the flames.

"Oh, look!" Helena said, pointing at the letter in his hand.

He turned the letter over and saw what had excited her interest. On the back of the letter was a large seal of blue wax with a beautiful impression. He stared at it a moment, for he'd seen the design before; a profile of a swan set against a pair of crossed swords. It was a portion of a family crest—a crest he had seen replicated on page sixty-seven of *Debrett's Peerage*.

Instinctively his eyes flew to Mary's face; she looked back at him, her expression questioning and hopeful. In that instant he knew her thoughts, and he wished with all his might that he had been alone with her when the letter had been delivered, that they might have shared together the letter's contents in private. He wanted to read it aloud to her and absorb its meaning, then discuss it together and hear her speak her opinion in her sensible way. He saw her hand flutter up toward her neck for a nervous moment—he had seen that same gesture countless times since the beginning of their acquaintance—before she caught herself and controlled her emotions by clasping her fingers together in a tight grip around her book.

"That swan," said Helena, still pointing, "looks like part of a coat of arms, but the question is whose? Who do you know, Captain Bingley, to write you such a letter?"

"I . . ." His voice trailed away, for he had not planned to tell anyone about his communication to Lord Rainham until he as certain of his lordship's reply; but there was no way to hide the letter now.

In her excitement Helena bobbed up and down in her chair and said eagerly, "Well? Aren't you going to open it?"

"Yes, of course." He made a move to slip his finger between the sheets of paper, but Kitty stopped him.

"Oh, take care!" she said. "That seal is much too lovely to be broken. Here, cut the paper." And she passed her embroidery scissors into his hand.

With the knowledge that everyone was watching him and anxious to learn the contents of the letter, Robert cut the paper and unfolded the sheets. He looked first at the signature.

Rainham.

He stared at that word as his heart began to beat a little faster. It was the letter he'd been waiting for; in the next moment he would know Daniel's fate—Would Lord Rainham acknowledge Daniel or not?—and he wished with all his being that he was alone with Mary, instead of sitting in a drawing-room with seven pairs of eyes trained upon him.

He drew a steadying breath and scanned the writing above the signature, then he looked up at Daniel. He owed the boy a quiet moment, just the two of them, in which to relate to him the contents of the letter; and he cast his mind about for an excuse to send him from the room.

"Daniel," he said, with one of his careless smiles, "I seem to have forgotten my quizzing glass. I fear this writing is too small and fine for me to see properly without it. Would you be good enough to fetch my glass for me? I cannot do justice to this letter without it."

Daniel obeyed immediately and as soon as the door was closed upon him, Kitty said, scoffing, "Quizzing glass! What bit of nonsense was that? I am sure I have never seen you read with a quizzing glass before."

"I thought it best to send him from the room while I explain this letter. You see, it is from Lord Rainham."

There was a long moment of surprised silence, which Charles broke by asking incredulously, "Rainham of Derbyshire? I did not know you were acquainted with the man!"

"We are not acquainted. I have not had the pleasure of an introduction."

"Then why does he write to you?"

"Because I wrote to him first. He simply responds to my letter, you see."

Caroline rose to her feet, her body almost quivering with surprise. "You wrote to Lord Rainham—a *marquess?* Robert, what possessed you?"

"It was a matter of some urgency. We—I had information that I thought should be made known to him."

"*We?*" Caroline repeated, in an ominous tone.

"Perhaps you should tell us the whole story," Jane suggested. "Start at the beginning."

"Yes, well, the story is simple enough. I wrote to Lord Rainham about Daniel. You see, I have reason to believe Daniel may be his . . . his *grandson*."

Helena gasped. "That dirty little urchin? You must be mad!"

"You, of course, would think so," Robert answered calmly, refusing to look her direction, "but it was not caprice that drove me to make such a claim. I had a very good reason for thinking that Daniel's father was the lost son of the Westover family."

"*What* reason?"

Robert's glance strayed toward Mary for the briefest of moments. "I shall tell you presently, but first—May I read to you a portion of Lord Rainham's letter?"

"Of course!" Charles said, and almost in unison, each listener leaned a bit forward in anticipation of learning the contents of the letter.

Robert began to read, pausing after each sentence to allow his eyes to scan ahead and master the next written revelation. He didn't want to read aloud any portion of the marquess's letter that might refer to Mary Bennet, for he did not think it wise to drag her name into the business if Lord Rainham did not intend to acknowledge the possibility of Daniel's relation. With that in mind, he was obliged to skip one or two sentences.

"Ah, here is the portion of Lord Rainham's letter I think will be of interest to all," he said.

> *You will understand my feeling, Captain Bingley, that I am unable at this time to make any*

determination concerning the child you know as
Daniel, without seeing him and making inquiries
of my own. I therefore request the honor of
waiting upon you and your family Tuesday next,
when I am hopeful of meeting the child for myself.
I shall trespass on your hospitality for only three
days, for duty requires my immediate return to
Derbyshire. I remain, etcetera, Rainham.

Robert looked up to find everyone staring at him in astonished silence.

Jane was the first to recover, saying with confusion, "Tuesday next. But when did he write the letter?"

Robert turned over the page. "Three days ago."

"Goodness! Then he will be here the day after tomorrow! He will arrive the day before the ball!" She stretched out her hand to her husband and, grasping his sleeve, said in a breathless voice, "Oh, Charles! We are to welcome a marquess to our home!"

"I hope," said Kitty with a laugh, "he will not be too surprised when he learns he will be expected to dance while he is here."

Helena clapped her hands together as she often did to signal her delight. "Oh, do you think he *will* dance? I am certain he must be very old, and probably infirm. I am told that great men of his age often have gout, you know."

"Whether he dances or not, you may be certain," said Caroline, "that Lord Rainham will be a most excellent guest." She sank down onto a chair, and murmured, "A marquess at Netherfield! Oh, my cup is full; it is to run over!"

335

"Never mind all that, Caroline," said Charles, still trying to get to the root of the matter. "What I want to know is, how the devil did you come to suspect that Daniel was somehow related to Lord Rainham?"

Since he had finished reading the letter aloud, Robert had been sitting in silence, his gaze focused on Mary, and wondering how he would answer that very question should someone pose it. He still did not like the idea of dragging Mary's name into the story until he was certain of Lord Rainham's intent. He said slowly, "I cannot say exactly how—"

"Yes, you can," said Mary. He frowned at her and she said, encouragingly, "They might as well know the whole of it. Besides, it would be better to learn the truth from us right now than to be surprised by hearing bits and pieces of the story when Lord Rainham arrives." Still, he hesitated, prompting her to quote to him the very words he had once spoken to her: "Remember, we are in this together, you and I. Co-conspirators!"

With that reminder he let down his guard and recounted the entire story, beginning with Mary's initial suspicion.

When he was finished, Charles said, in an admiring tone, "Well, isn't Mary the clever one!"

Jane thought so, too, saying, "Oh, Mary, I am so proud of you. Only think: if this is all true and Daniel does belong to Lord Rainham, they will be reunited as a direct result of your efforts."

"I shall be glad for Daniel if he is Lord Rainham's grandson," said Kitty, "but how I will miss him!"

"As will we all," said Jane. "But I am still very impressed

with you, Mary, for putting the pieces of the puzzle together."

Miss Paget had heard enough praise heaped on Mary, and said, dampeningly, "But there is a very good chance Mary Bennet is wrong! I, for one, cannot believe that boy you found is Lord Rainham's *lost grandson!* What utter nonsense—as if Lord Rainham would lose a child in the same fashion one might lose an earring or a handkerchief. Why, the very idea is preposterous, if you stop to think about it."

But the idea seemed a little less preposterous a moment later when Daniel entered the room and handed Robert his quizzing-glass. Helena, with a good deal of anxiety in her expression, decided to make up for her past treatment of Daniel—in the event he was indeed related to a peer of the realm—and patted the place beside her on the settee, saying, "Do come and sit here beside to me, *dear* little boy."

Her tone, Robert thought, held the same quality as a spider coaxing a fly into its web, but since he was seated close enough to ensure that no harm would come to Daniel from sitting in close proximity to Helena for a few minutes, he did not interfere.

Helena's haltingly uncomfortable attempts to engage Daniel in conversation did not last long; for very soon the footman, who served additional roles as Robert's valet and Daniel's companion during those times Robert could not be with him, arrived to take him upstairs.

The mood of the assembled party had altered significantly as a result of Robert's revelation. Where they had been quiet before, they were now talking all at once, trying to make sense of the circumstances and reveling in the thought of entertaining a noted peer of the realm for three days.

"You realize," said Helena, "that once word spreads that Lord Rainham traveled all the way from Derbyshire to attend a ball at Netherfield, your reputation as a hostess will be quite made, my dear Mrs. Bingley."

Jane's eyes widened. "But Lord Rainham's visit has, at its heart, nothing to do with the ball. Why, he does not even yet know there is to be one!"

"Still it will do you a great deal of credit if he is willing to be coaxed to make an appearance in your ballroom. I must say, his presence is more than any of the local families could ever wish for, do you not agree, Caroline?"

Caroline hardly attended her. Since learning the news that she would soon make the acquaintance of Lord Rainham, her joy knew no bounds. Restlessly, she moved about the room until she came to the window. Looking out she was in time to see Mr. Penrose walking up the drive. She gave a little gasp and murmured, "Excuse me, please" in a distracted voice, and left the room with the intent of intercepting him.

She met him in the front hall where he was divesting himself of his hat, coat, and gloves.

His smiled at the sight of her. "Hello, Miss Bingley. I've come to see how Netherfield fared the storm."

"Oh, Mr. Penrose, I am in great need of you."

"I am happy to hear it," he said, with an unmistakable light in his eyes as he looked down at her. "How I may be of help?"

She linked her hand through the crook of his arm and forced herself to ignore the charming manner in which he smiled down at her. "We have just had the most astonishing news," she said, leading him toward the drawing-room. "It is about Daniel."

His playful expression immediately changed to one of concern. "Is he ill?"

"No, not at all." She stopped, her hand on the door knob. She looked up into his face poised so close to her own, and said with a small throb in her voice, "You were right, Mr. Penrose. Oh, it seems you are *always* right!"

"About what?"

"About Daniel. You must come in and hear the news for yourself." And she turned the knob and led him into the drawing-room.

Kitty, owing to her proximity to the door, was the first person to greet him. She dipped a quick curtsy and whispered, eagerly, "What a good time you have chosen to call, for we are all in uproar! Captain Bingley and Miss Paget have had a horrid row—"

"Oh, do be quiet!" scolded Caroline.

"—and Lord Rainham is due to arrive Tuesday. Only fancy—A marquess here at Netherfield!"

He bent his head toward Caroline. "A marquess? My, my, Miss Bingley, you are about to realize an ambition!"

She heard the faintly teasing note in his voice, but instead of railing against it, she found his tone oddly comforting. She was given no chance to answer him, for Charles and Jane came forward at that moment to greet him.

They ushered him to a chair they knew to be a favorite of his near the fire; and in a very short time they had apprised him of not only the contents of Lord Rainham's letter, but of the roles Robert and Mary had played in determining the possible connection between Daniel and Lord Rainham's family.

"What you have just described is quite extraordinary!" said Mr. Penrose, as he looked from Robert to Mary and back again.

"But we do not yet know if Lord Rainham is at all connected to Daniel," Mary said, reasonably. "Indeed, I beg you will not repeat this news to anyone until we can be certain."

"Naturally I shall not, but I hope you will allow me to say it was very ingenious of you both to put the pieces of such a puzzle together. I congratulate you."

"It was Miss Bennet's doing," Robert said. "If anyone deserves praise it is she."

"Oh, yes, Miss Bennet walks on water," said Helena, acidly. "We all cherish an extraordinary regard for her, don't we, my dear Caroline?"

Caroline preserved her silence, but Mr. Penrose said, with a gentle smile and a glance at Mary, "One thing I have learned in this life, Miss Paget, is that we all have our good qualities . . . as well as bad. It is up to each of us to decide which quality we want to put on display each day. Tell me, Mrs. Bingley, what do you think of all this?"

"I think I will miss Daniel immensely," Jane said. "We enjoy his company so much that I have come to think I should like him to remain with us forever. It will be difficult to put my own feelings aside if Lord Rainham does indeed lay claim to Daniel."

"I had not thought of that," said Kitty, frowning. "If Lord Rainham takes Daniel off to Derbyshire, we shall never see him again!"

"That is not necessarily true," Charles said. He moved closer to Jane, grasped her hand in a meaningful grip, and asked in a low voice, "I think it is time we told them, don't you?"

"I suppose," Jane said. "Oh, I so wanted to wait until after the ball to speak, but with these developments—Yes, Charles, I think they should be told."

"Now you have piqued our interest," said Robert. "Come, out with it! What do you have to say to us?"

"It is the purpose of the ball, really," Charles said. "We wanted to bring everyone together—all our family and friends—in order to . . . Well, to say good-bye, really."

"Good-bye?" Caroline echoed. "What do you mean?'

"I mean to say that we—Jane and I—are leaving Netherfield."

"You're removing to London?" Kitty asked. "But that is not so unusual."

Charles shook his head. "Not London. I have purchased an estate in Nottinghamshire—a place of our very own. Jane and I will leave Netherfield in the spring."

This pronouncement was met with stunned silence, until Helena murmured, "Good heavens!"

"But why?" demanded Caroline. "What reason could you have for wishing to leave Netherfield?"

Charles laughed. "That is an odd question from you, Caroline! More times than I can count you have said to me, 'My dear Charles, whatever possessed you to lease a house in the wilds of Hertfordshire?'"

"But I never encouraged you to—! Nottinghamshire is so far away."

"Not so very far, after all," he said, in a cheery voice. "I tell you what—we shall all enjoy next Christmas together there, all of us. How does that sound?"

He received no answer to his question, and as he cast his eyes about the room, it quickly became clear that no one was gladdened by the news he had imparted. His gaze fell upon Mary.

She had not moved from her place in a corner of the room since Mr. Penrose's arrival, hoping that, by remaining quiet, she might escape the censorious notice of Caroline Bingley and her friend Helena. But once she had grasped the meaning of Charles' announcement, her startled gaze had immediately flown to Robert's face. He looked back at her, his expression somewhat grim; and she wondered if he was thinking along the same lines as she—that once Charles and Jane removed to another county, there would be no occasion for her to meet Robert again. As long as Charles and Jane resided at Netherfield, she had cherished a hope that Robert might visit Netherfield in future, and his path would cross with hers. Or, even better, he might claim the rights of family and while making a visit to Jane and Charles at Netherfield he might call upon the Bennets at Longbourn. These thoughts she clung to, even though she knew that by the time he next visited Netherfield he would be married to Miss

Paget. But now, with the news of Charles and Jane's removal to Nottinghamshire, those pathetic little dreams she had nurtured vanished.

"What do you say, Mary?" Charles asked. "Does not a Christmas in Nottinghamshire sound fine?"

She felt her lips go dry, but managed to say, "As Miss Bingley reminds us, Nottinghamshire is quite far away. I fear," she added, as her eyes strayed once more to where Captain Bingley was sitting, "I will never see you again."

"No, no," said Charles, "you needn't worry about that! Jane and I have talked about it already, and we've agreed that you must come to us—you and Kitty—and make a stay. You will enjoy it immensely, for Pemberley is very close by, you know—less than thirty miles!—and you will see your sister Elizabeth and Darcy quite often. Come, Mary, say you like the idea."

She forced a smile for Charles' benefit. "I do, indeed. You surprised me, that is all. I will soon grow accustomed to the notion, and in the meantime, you must tell us all about the estate. Is it very large? What is the house like?"

Her questions helped turn everyone's attention back on Charles and Jane, and gave her a moment to marshal her emotions. But she dared not look again at Robert for fear of losing the mastery of herself and dissolving into a flood of unhappy, and very disappointed, tears.

24

The news that she would soon be welcoming a peer of the realm into her home sent Jane into a flurry of excitement. Her best bedchamber, once assigned to Mr. and Mrs. Dauntry, who were close friends of Jane's mother and father, was instantly given over to Lord Rainham. That, of course, meant her second best chamber must be given to the Dauntry's, and every other guest chamber in order had to be re-thought and re-assigned.

So much activity and changes to Jane's plans necessitated long meetings with her housekeeper, and she begged Caroline's help in planning the little details that might make Lord Rainham's stay more comfortable. She did not have to ask twice. Caroline was in her element, and was confident in her ability to add those charming little comforts that a man of his wealth and position would expect.

By the time Tuesday came, the family were in high spirits, and as they waited for Lord Rainham's arrival, Jane confessed that her heart was fluttering to such a degree, she worried that it might leap from her chest at the first sight of the great man.

Mary, too, was nervous, but for a very different reason.

In the time since receiving Lord Rainham's letter, she had begun to entertain certain doubts about the entire affair. She worried that Daniel had grown too comfortable at Netherfield, and would be loathe to leave. She worried that Lord Rainham would judge Daniel harshly and refuse to acknowledge him as his grandson, or, worse yet, would accept Daniel into his family and whisk him off to Derbyshire, never to be seen again. Her greatest fear was that Daniel would go from his happy situation at Netherfield to a less than desirable existence. In fact, that was her chief concern, for she knew nothing of Lord Rainham and doubted that a three-day stay would be sufficient to take his measure. How could she be certain, she wondered, if he would be kind to Daniel? How would Lord Rainham prove that he intended to do well by the boy? All these thoughts were tumbling through her mind when the announcement came that a traveling carriage had entered the gates and was fast making its way up the drive to the house.

Charles and Jane led the way into the great front hall, where everyone assembled to greet his lordship. Only Charles stepped outside to watch his arrival.

Lord Rainham had traveled in state; four great black horses, gleaming from their exertions, drew his chaise, on the side of which was emblazoned a coat of arms bearing the very same image of a swan's head and crossed swords that had been embossed into the sealing wax of the marquess's letter. A liveried coachman sat up on the box, and two liveried grooms rode behind. In addition—as if the entire affair was in need of a bit more distinction—a pair of outriders flanked the carriage astride two additional black horses.

When the chaise came to a halt one of the footmen sprang into action to let down the steps. A moment later the great man himself appeared. He was possessed of a fine figure, standing slightly over six feet tall. His body was lean, his posture was erect; his brown eyes were keen and alert as they swept over the front façade of the house and took in every detail of his surroundings. In his sixties he was still handsome, with only one or two tiny lines at the corners of his eyes to signal his age; and though a few touches of silver streaking marked his dark hair, they only added to his overall air of distinction.

"Welcome, sir!" Charles said, stepping forward to shake hands. "Do come inside. It's dreadfully cold out here."

In the front hall Charles made all the necessary introductions. Lord Rainham's piercing eyes examined Robert's face once he was made known to him; and when Charles introduced the ladies, Rainham said, looking down on Mary, "Ah, Miss Bennet!"

In the drawing-room, Charles invited Lord Rainham to claim a seat nearest the fire, and said, "You must have enjoyed good roads between here and Derbyshire, for you made excellent time, I think. Would that all journeys should be equally trouble-free!"

Then he and Lord Rainham spent the next few minutes discussing the state of the roads, the chances of foul weather impairing one's speed, and the relative lack of snow compared to previous winters of his recollection.

For his part, Lord Rainham responded politely, but several times his eyes strayed toward the door, on watch in case someone else should enter the room.

At last he said, "You'll forgive me, I hope, if I come directly to the point of my visit. I am an old man, as you see, and time is something I cannot take for granted. Mrs. Bingley, I beg you and the other ladies will excuse me if I ask for a private interview with your husband and Captain Bingley."

Jane immediately gave her permission, and Charles led Robert and their visitor to the library.

As soon as the door closed upon them, Mary said, anxiously, "Oh, I *wish* they would have remained here with us. Why did you allow them to go?"

"I could not very well deny his request," said Jane. "Indeed, he struck me as the sort of man who never allows anyone to deny him anything. I must confess, I am quite in awe!"

Caroline, her cheeks glowing with happiness, said, "And so you should be, my dear Jane. It is not every day that you have opportunity to meet half such a man!"

"He is very handsome for an older gentleman," Kitty observed.

"He is," Helena said, "but still there is something about him I cannot quite like. I don't think he smiled at me once, although I did my best to engage his good opinion."

"We must remember," said Jane, "that this is probably a difficult time for his lordship, and he may be a little distract-ed. I am certain he will more genial once the business concerning Daniel is concluded."

"What do you think they might be saying?" asked Mary, nervously clasping, then unclasping her hands.

Jane reached out to still her movements in a firm grip. "You may trust Captain Bingley to tell Daniel's story with fairness and accuracy."

"Yes, but why must they speak in private?" Mary pulled her hand away and began to pace the room, as all her previous worries came crowding back. "If only I could hear what they were saying!"

She was to have her wish. The door opened; a footman announced that Mr. Bingley requested the pleasure of Miss Bennet's presence in the library, if she would be so good.

The moment she had half-hoped for, half-dreaded had come. She forced herself to walk sedately to where the library door stood slightly open; and upon entering, her heart beating fast, she heard Charles say, "Ah, here is our Mary!"

But it was Robert who drew her further into the room. He went to her immediately and, tucking her hand into the crook of his arm, led her to one of the comfortably upholstered chairs she knew so well.

"This way, Miss Bennet," he said softly; then he smiled at her and placed his warm hand over her fingers as they rested on his sleeve. His voice, his touch, his smile all worked in concert to quiet her turbulent thoughts; and by the time Robert had seated her with great solicitude, she felt a bit more comfortable.

Lord Rainham claimed a chair beside hers and smiled slightly. "Will you allow me to shake your hand, Miss Bennet? From all I have heard, it is you I have you to thank for rescuing the boy from the inn; and it was you who first discovered a possible link between the child and my family. Is that true?"

She felt the familiar warmth of a blush mantle her cheeks. "Yes, but it was the merest coincidence that I should recognize Daniel's last name."

"*If* it is his last name," Lord Rainham said kindly. "You appreciate my reluctance, I think."

"I suppose it is natural for you to be wary." But even as she said those words, she settled the matter of Daniel's claim to the Westover name for herself. It was clear to her that Daniel was related to Lord Rainham, for she saw a very distinct resemblance between them. They were both possessed of the same brown eyes, the same aquiline nose and strong square chin. Surely, she thought, once he saw Daniel he would see the similarities for himself.

"No matter what happens here today, Miss Bennet," his lordship continued, "I will forever be mindful of your bravery in rescuing an unhappy boy from a barbarous landlord."

Although she murmured her thanks, she was mindful that this was not at all the speech she had hoped to hear from Lord Rainham. She looked questioningly up at Captain Bingley and asked, "Have you already told him everything we know about Daniel?"

"I have," said Robert, "and it is agreed between us that we shall not reveal anything to Daniel quite yet. I have sent for him to join us, but for this first meeting, Lord Rainham wishes to simply meet him and see if he notices any resemblance."

"I do not wish to frighten the lad," said his lordship, "and I rather think—"

He stopped speaking as the door opened and Robert's valet ushered Daniel into the room. Lord Rainham's eyes fell upon him and held. He uttered a sound that was half between a cough and a gasp and slowly rose to his feet. "Why, he looks exactly like . . ." He bit back the rest of his words as Daniel, standing before him, executed a very proper bow Kitty had taught him the day before.

"Lord Rainham," said Charles, "may I present Daniel Westover to you?"

Towering over Daniel, Lord Rainham reached down to shake Daniel's hand, and held it a moment longer than was necessary. He said, striving for a friendly tone, "I am very pleased to make your acquaintance, young man. Your friends here have told me quite a bit about you. I'm curious: do you know anything about me?"

Daniel clasped his hands together behind his back as he had seen Captain Bingley do. "No, sir."

"Well, then, we shall have to get acquainted, you and I," said his lordship, sitting down again. "Tell me, how old are you?"

"I was nine years on my last birthday."

"And when was that?"

Daniel thought for a moment, and said in some confusion, "I don't recall, sir."

"That is not so unusual, I think." He leaned forward a little and smiled kindly at Daniel. "I understand that your family name is Westover. Is that right?"

"Yes, sir."

"By coincidence, my name is Westover, too. I wonder if we might be related? What do you think?"

"I should like to be related to someone," Daniel said, after giving the matter some thought.

"Why don't we find out?"

"I should like that, but how, sir? *How* shall we find out?"

"There is a family trait—a birth mark of sorts—that belongs only to the Westovers. I have it and my sons had it after me." He motioned for Daniel to come closer. "Will you hold up your left hand for me?"

Daniel responded instantly for it seemed to him like a reasonable request.

"Now, make a fist and show me that thumb of yours!"

"My *thumb?*" Daniel repeated, wrinkling his nose. Still, he obeyed; he clenched his fingers into a fist and examined his own thumb as if he were seeing it for the very first time. It looked perfectly normal to him.

But Lord Rainham, upon seeing it, drew a quick breath. For several seconds he said nothing while the muscles in his jaw clenched and unclenched. At last he said, in a strained voice, "Thank you, Daniel."

Daniel looked down at his thumb again and frowned. "Did my thumb tell you if we are related or not?"

"It did, indeed."

"And *are* you?" Robert demanded impatiently.

"We are."

"But how can you tell?"

By this time Lord Rainham had recovered his composure and invited Daniel to sit beside him. "This young man has the Westover thumb. Show us your left hand again, Daniel. See how every finger on his hand is perfectly formed with a deep, round nail bed? But now look at his thumb! It is short—half the size of his other thumb—as if some fairy came in the night and lopped off the tip while he was sleeping. Look!" And he held up his own hand so his thumb was next to Daniel's.

Mary leaned forward to examine the evidence for herself. "Why, your thumbs are the same!"

"It's a family trait—the mark of a Westover. I have one short thumb, as did my father before me—as did your father before you, Daniel. Do you see it, my boy?"

"Yes, sir," Daniel said, as he turned his hand first this way then that to view his thumb from all angles. "But is it really a fairy who makes it so, sir?"

"So I have been told, and I cannot think of a better explanation, can you?"

This made Mary smile. There was a gentleness to Lord Rainham's voice that pleased her, and all the concerns she had harbored about whether Lord Rainham could be trusted to take good care of Daniel suddenly melted away.

"I suppose," said Lord Rainham, "you know what this means, don't you?"

"I think," Daniel said slowly, "it means we are related, as you said."

"Not just related, but *closely* related. In fact," he said as his voice grew suspiciously deep, "I wouldn't doubt that I may very well be your grandfather. Would you like to have a grandfather?"

"I should like it very much."

"And if you've no objections, we might spend some time together, you and I, and get to know one another."

"I should like that, too." Daniel looked up at Robert. "He can stay in our room, can't he?'

"He can if he'd like to," Robert said with a laugh, "and he

will be most welcome. But I think Mrs. Bingley has already ordered a bedchamber for Lord Rainham that he might find more to his liking."

"Tell me, Daniel," said his lordship, indulgently, "what is your favorite thing to do in the whole world?"

"Ride a horse. Captain Bingley is teaching me, and one day I will ride as well as he does, and I will have a horse just like Ibis."

Lord Rainham agreed his was an admirable ambition; and when he asked Daniel if he would be good enough to show him what he had learned so far, Daniel's eyes lit up, and he rushed off to don his riding clothes and coat.

As soon as the door was closed upon him, Lord Rainham slowly drew one hand across his forehead. "This has been an eventful day," he murmured.

"It has indeed—for all of us," Robert said. "News like this naturally takes some getting used to."

Mary, who was seated closest to Lord Rainham, could see that he was laboring under the weight of a strong emotion, and asked gently, "Lord Rainham, would you like to go up to your room? After your journey I am certain you must wish to refresh yourself before you go with Daniel to the stables."

"Thank you, Miss Bennet. An excellent idea; I should like it very much."

Charles pulled the bell, and within a few minutes Lord Rainham was making his way up the stairs to Netherfield's finest guest chamber.

"I don't mind telling you," Robert said, when he was alone with Mary and Charles, "that as much as I suspected— or hoped—that Daniel was related to the man, it is still a stunning thing to learn the truth. What do you think, Mary?"

"I think," she said, looking up at him with a suspicious moisture in her eyes, "that I shall miss him very much!"

Robert claimed the chair next to hers and pressed her hand between both of his. "But not for long. Remember, you shall visit Jane and Charles in Nottinghamshire. Why, you'll be practically close enough to stand on Rainham's doorstep. Isn't that right Charles?"

Charles, watching them both with frowning fixity, said, slowly, "Yes, that's right."

"So you see?" Robert said, encouragingly. "You shall be reunited with Daniel soon enough, and in the meantime, you know just as well as I do that Lord Rainham will be very good to Daniel."

She nodded and brushed away a tear and tried very hard to smile. "Yes, I think he *will* be good to him. Did you see how his emotions overcame him? It was a very good sign, and I think in that moment he began to love Daniel as his own."

"I saw it, too," Robert said, softly.

They were silent for a few moments, content to sit quietly, their hands entwined, their heads very close together, thinking over the enormity of what had just occurred. It was Mary who first uttered something sensible.

"Should we join the others in the drawing-room? I'm sure they are anxious to hear the news."

"No need," said Charles, rousing himself from his contemplative mood. "I will break the news to the ladies while you try for a little control, Mary. You know that if Jane sees you are about to burst into tears, there will be no stopping her from doing the same. Take all the time you need." And with another curious look, he left the library, and she was alone with Robert.

25

Mary came to her senses as soon as she heard the door click closed behind Charles. As delicious as it was to be alone with Robert in her favorite room with her hand in his, she was keenly aware of the peril of her situation. She told herself that he was merely trying to comfort her; that he was only being kind because she had allowed her emotions to get the better of her. Despite these admonishments, she knew the state of her own heart, and knew, too, that her feelings for Captain Bingley had not diminished. She had to tread carefully whenever she was around him in order to keep her secret safe; but it was a bittersweet resolution, for even now she wanted to store away in her mind this moment with him, and to savor its memory as a treasure beyond price.

With a good deal of willpower she slowly pulled her fingers from his grasp and stood up. "We should join the others. I do not think Charles should have to shoulder all the responsibility for making explanations to everyone."

He rose to his feet beside her. "Is that all that was troubling you—the fear that Rainham will whisk Daniel off to Derbyshire and you will never see him again?"

"No. Indeed, I am very happy that Daniel will have the chance to be comfortably established in a great house."

"Then what worries you?"

"I am not worried about anything."

"Very well, then, *concerned*."

When he spoke to her in just that way she was very nearly tempted to pour her heart out to him. But a single woman had no business confiding her fears and hopes to a man who was almost engaged to be married to another woman.

Resolutely, she began to move toward the door, saying, "I am only being stupid and sentimental, but I can't help but feel as if our family is breaking up. We all seem to be going in different directions—Daniel to Derbyshire, Charles and Jane to Nottinghamshire—"

"What about me? I'm not going anywhere."

"Not yet, but you will leave here when your colonel commands you. It is only a matter of time, you know."

They stepped into the hall together, but when Mary passed the door to the drawing-room and set a course for the stairs, Robert asked, "Where are you going?"

"To my chamber."

"But you are needed here. Everyone will have questions and—"

"You and Charles can tell everyone the story of what occurred in the library; you don't need my help for that." And with a good deal of resolve she went quickly up the stairs to her room.

She didn't see Captain Bingley again until later that afternoon. He had arranged for Daniel to display his riding prowess for Lord Rainham and his lordship, in turn, invited Mary to be one of the party. Together they walked to the stables, where Robert delivered Daniel into Abbot's keeping.

"How is his seat?" Lord Rainham asked.

"Fair enough," said Robert, "although he is still in beginning stages. Still, I can tell you with a bit of pride that he is something of a natural. I think he will make a bruising rider in time."

Robert had modified his earlier assessment concerning the hired mare he had once labeled a slug; she was now assigned to be Daniel's hack, for she possessed the perfect temperament for a novice rider.

A few moments later Daniel entered the exercise ring, smiling broadly as he held the reins and set the mare on a slow, deliberate circle around the yard; all the while with Abbot riding protectively beside him on a nimble bay.

They walked a full circle around the yard, then, at Abbot's instruction, Daniel urged the mare to quicken her pace. He bounced in the saddle only one or two times before he regained control and circled the enclosure twice more. Mary clapped her hands, and Robert called out encouraging words.

Lord Rainham looked on proudly and said, "I think he has the makings of regular out-and-outer. I shall purchase a pony for him first thing. A bit more practice is all he needs."

Robert looked at him. "Will you be taking Daniel with you when you leave for Derbyshire then?"

"That is my plan. You have no objections I hope?"

"No objections—but I do have questions."

"Ask them if you'd like. Feel free!"

"Very well," Robert said, squaring his shoulders slightly. "I would very much like to know, Lord Rainham, why you did not go looking for Daniel on your own. He would have been easily found, and you might have saved him from having to endure the brutality of that brute of an innkeeper." His spoke in an even tone that he hoped held no hint of judgment, but it was a question that had plagued him since Mary had first suggested the idea of Daniel's lineage.

Lord Rainham thought it a fair question, and said so. "But by the time I discovered Daniel had been orphaned, it was too late to find him. Don't think I am not mindful of the fact that every decision I made concerning my son and his family was a wrong decision. When Daniel—my son—first came to me with the idea of joining the church, I forbad it and never gave the matter another thought. But when he persisted, I knew not what to think. Perhaps he did feel a genuine calling for the church; I chose to believe he was simply rebelling as younger sons are wont to do. I could have helped him, but instead I made the way difficult for him; I used my influence to deny him livings throughout the county. And when he took his wife and child and left—without my knowledge or consent, mind you!—I thought he would return, if I was patient and bided my time. I cannot tell you how difficult it was to hear the sound of a carriage on the road and feel the disappointment of hearing it drive by the gate instead of turning in. I knew he was stubborn, but so was I; then days turned to weeks and weeks into years. I made inquiries through the bishop and learned he'd been given a church in Hertfordshire, and a very poor church it was. I was heartened by the news, for I felt certain he would not stand the hardship and would return to me of his own accord. But when many more months went by without a word, I again made inquiries, only to learn I was too late. My son had died, along with his wife, and I could not discover what happened to my grandson. Some reports came to me that he had been taken in by a local family; but another report said he had been apprenticed to a wheelwright. Neither report proved to be true."

"I can tell you," Robert said. "that Daniel has confided bits and pieces of his story to me. He was indeed apprenticed to a wheelwright, who was very badly injured in an accident and could no longer care for him. I still don't know how he ultimately ended up at the Bark and Bull."

"You may wish to know, too," said Mary, "that Daniel had a sister. He told us her name was Elizabeth and she died at the same time as Daniel's parents."

"I was unaware of that," said Lord Rainham, grimly. "It seems I have made more wrong turns than I knew." He had a sudden thought and looked sharply at Robert. "Will he go with me, do you think? Will he gladly leave you and Miss Bennet if I offer to take him home with me to Derbyshire?"

"If he is your grandson, as you say—well, then I suppose he must."

"No, no! I don't want to *compel* the boy! It was that very sort of thinking that sent me sideways in the first place with the child's father! Tell me what you recommend, Captain Bingley."

"You have already made a good beginning with Daniel; and he is very desirous of having a family to call his own. If you will use your time here at Netherfield to become better acquainted with Daniel, you may rely on me to use my influence to encourage him in the right direction." He looked over at Mary. "Miss Bennet?"

"I shall do the same," she said promptly.

"You are both very good," said Lord Rainham. "I owe you both an enormous debt, and I have wracked my brain for ways in which to repay you for all you've done for Daniel and for me."

"That is not necessary, sir."

"But it is—it must be. My eldest son Thomas died only last year, which means Daniel is my heir; he'll inherit one day. Now, I'm an old man and I may be gone tomorrow, for all the world knows. Daniel will need a good man to guide him and help him grow up to be as strong and kind as you have been to him. What do you say? Come to Derbyshire, Captain Bingley; there is room for you at Cottesmere—or, if you prefer, there is a small estate that neighbors mine. Say the word and it is yours."

"You do me a great honor!" Robert said, surprised. "But I am a soldier, sir. I have never wanted to be anything else."

"Then let me help you there. Who is your colonel?" And when Robert named the man and his regiment, Lord Rainham shook his head. "I know your colonel. He takes a page from Wellington's book, does he not?"

"Indeed, he does."

"What does that mean?" asked Mary.

"It means," said Rainham, "he only promotes those officers who come from noble families and can, in turn, elevate his own social standing."

She looked up at Robert. "Is this true?"

"It is, unfortunately, the way of the world sometimes," Robert said. "I once hoped to climb the ranks through hard work and faithful obedience, but I quickly discovered that no amount of skill or loyalty could make up for the plain circumstance of my birth. I have been passed over by less qualified men who come from higher ranking families than we Bingleys, and I recognized long ago that I must be satisfied as a captain."

"Well, I have never heard of anything so abominable," she said, ready to be angry on his behalf.

"I can rail against the injustice of it, I suppose," he said, "but in the end, I will still be a captain."

"Perhaps *you* see no way to alter your circumstance," said Lord Rainham, "but I do. In fact, I think I am the very man who can smooth the way for you."

Robert, torn between interest and pride, said, "You, sir? How?"

Lord Rainham said confidently, "Once your colonel realizes that I rely on you and have entrusted you with my grandson—something along the lines of a favored uncle or a godfather—he will change his mind, I am certain of it. I have only to put the word about town. And in the spring, when I open my house on Grosvenor Square and hold one or two very select parties, your colonel may find his name on my guest list."

"That is very generous of you, sir! But surely you need not go to so much trouble!"

"I do not think of it as trouble at all, I assure you. And now, Miss Bennet" he said, turning his attention to her, "how may I show my appreciation to you?"

"There is no need, sir."

"But I insist. There must be something I can do for you."

"Well," she said, even as she wondered if she should mention the matter, "your arrival was very timely, for tomorrow evening there is to be a ball here at Netherfield. I hesitate to ask . . . would it be too much to request that you make an appearance at the ball? I have been told by someone who knows such things that if a man of your rank were to attend, you would *quite make* my sister's reputation as a hostess," she said, repeating the very words Helena had said the day before.

"Is that all?" he asked. "Why, it would be my great honor to attend the ball, Miss Bennet. And if you will do me the favor of allowing me to lead you out for the first dance, I shall consider myself fortunate, indeed."

This was much more than she expected. She blushed slightly and protested there was no need, but Lord Rainham laughed and said, "You do not wish to dance with an old man when you have a younger, more handsome partner in mind, eh? Very well, Miss Bennet! Grant me the first dance and I promise not to claim another, for I'm quite certain you would rather have Captain Bingley squire you about the floor all night than a stodgy country gentleman like me."

She gave a little gasp. "Captain Bingley—? Oh, no, you quite mistake the matter!"

"How so? Do you not dance, Miss Bennet?

"Yes, I do, but—"

"But not with him, eh? I see how it is! Never fear; once you two are married, he will change his ways and whirl you about the dance floor as often as you like, mark my words."

Mary blushed a fiery red and said, in a strangled voice, "But I am not—! That is, *we* are not—!"

"What Miss Bennet is trying to say," Robert said, quietly, "is that we are not engaged to be married. We are friends. Her sister married my brother, and therein resides the basis of our relationship; nothing more."

"Is that so?" Lord Rainham asked, surprised. "Then I do beg your pardon! After seeing you and Miss Bennet together, I would have thought otherwise. Perhaps it was wishful thinking on my part, for it seems to me that two people as kind and honorable as you have proved to be would no doubt make each other very happy. Well," he said, as Daniel joined them at the fence rail, still astride his compliant mare, "you are quite an impressive rider, Daniel! I've no doubt you will be galloping over fields and meadows in no time! I'm proud of you, my boy," he added, with an unmistakable warmth in his brown eyes. "Very proud indeed! You have the makings of becoming a first-rate horseman when you grow up."

"That is my ambition," said Daniel, "if I am to join a cavalry."

"So you want to be a soldier, do you?"

"Yes, sir, I do. I want to be just like Captain Bingley."

When they returned to the house a while later, Robert found yet another letter waiting for him. This time he did recognize the hand that had written the direction, and he broke the wafer with a feeling of impatience.

"Bad news, Captain?" asked Lord Rainham. "From the

look on your face, it cannot be good."

His eyes quickly scanned the contents of the letter and he frowned. "My leave has been cut short, and I am ordered to return to my regiment sooner than anticipated."

"How much sooner?" Mary asked, wanting to know yet dreading the answer.

He raised his eyes to meet hers. "Only a day. Still, it is one less day that I can spend with . . ." He stopped, caught himself in time, and finished, ". . . with the people I care about."

Mary, looking grave, said nothing; but Lord Rainham suggested he lose no time in making his family aware of the change in his plans. Robert acted on the advice, and in very little time the entire household had heard the news.

Caroline, returning from a leisurely walk about the grounds, learned of the change in Robert's orders from Jane, and she lost no time in hurrying to Helena's side. She found her pacing the floor of her bedchamber, her cheeks faintly tinged with angry color.

"My dear Helena!" she said, consolingly, "I knew you would be unhappy at the news!"

"Unhappy? Oh, I am more than merely unhappy, I assure you! To think I ever considered pledging myself to a man capable of such treachery!"

This was hardly the reaction Caroline expected. "Treachery? I cannot understand what you mean—although I suppose one might consider Robert's colonel to be very underhanded in what he has done—"

"Oh, no, not his *colonel!*" said Helena, scornfully. "It is your brother who has behaved abominably. I can never forgive him!"

"What has he done now?"

"He has received a very fine offer from Lord Rainham!"

"*What* offer?" Caroline asked, mystified.

"Then you do not know? Brace yourself for astonishing news, Caroline. Lord Rainham offered your brother a living—a fine estate to call his own in Derbyshire and all the prestige that comes with as close an association to the house of Cottesmere as one can have without blood ties!"

"Did he?" Caroline asked in a voice of wonder. "But this is extraordinary! All my hopes—all my dearest wishes for my family! Can it be true?"

"Of course it is true! It is also true that your brother *refused* his lordship's offer!"

Caroline's spirits, which had soared a mere moment before, quickly plummeted. "He could not have done so."

"He most certainly did, and he took a perverse amount of pleasure in telling me about it, I am certain."

"But, why? *Why* would he refuse?"

"For no good reason that I can see. Oh, he made ridiculous excuses—Honor and pride and his career in the army! It was all utter nonsense!"

"I had no idea," said Caroline, sinking limply onto a chair as she tried to marshal her thoughts, "that Robert could be so stubborn."

"Stubborn and inconsiderate. He never gives a thought to me," said Helena. "Why, he turned down Rainham's offer without even thinking of consulting me first. Had he done so, I would have counseled him most strenuously to agree to anything Rainham proposed. But, no! He will insist upon remaining in the army. Do you know what he said? He told me he expects me to be an army wife! He wants me to travel the world with him like a gypsy! I will not have it, Caroline!"

That lady immediately agreed that poor Helena had been badly used, and with soothing words, she did her best to comfort her friend.

"So we are in agreement that something must be done?" Helena asked, hopefully, after a few minutes of receiving Caroline's ministrations.

"We are indeed."

"Then you will speak to your brother for me?"

"I shall go to him immediately. Robert is behaving very foolishly."

"And selfishly," Helena said. "He thinks only of himself and his desires. What about mine? I don't ask for so much, I think, and if he will only make one small change and resign his commission, he will bring a good deal of happiness to a great many people. And yet he will think only of himself!"

"I could not agree with you more, my dear friend. In fact, now that I consider it, I believe my brother Charles will help us once he is presented with the facts. Charles will convince Robert to change his mind." She reached over to pat Helena's hand consolingly. "You may leave everything to me, my dear Helena. I shall see that Robert is brought to heel in short order."

But when she presented her case to Charles a little while later, his response was not at all what she had hoped.

"Ask Robert to resign his commission? Quit the Army?" Charles uttered with an appalled expression. "Have you lost your senses, Caroline? I shall do no such thing!"

"But you must!"

"Why?"

"Because Lord Rainham has made Robert a very generous offer."

"What sort of offer?"

She clasped her hands together and said, her eyes shining, "He wants to set Robert up with his own estate in Derbyshire!"

Charles listened patiently as she recounted the details as she knew them, and he shook his head. "He'd never accept such a circumstance. As fond as he has grown of Daniel, I do not think for a moment that he would abandon his career in the army for the life of a country gentleman."

"But he must! Why, he would have Lord Rainham's ear and a fine estate of his own. Only think of the society we would enjoy! Only think how many doors would open to us!"

"*Us?*" he repeated with a pointed look.

"Naturally, we shall all benefit, too. Aren't we Robert's nearest and dearest? It is only right that you and I should enjoy the fruits of his good fortune."

"So you will make our brother live a life you know he will despise just so you may attend a few more parties every year? I did not think you capable of such mercenary behavior, Caroline!"

She felt her temper rise. "I resent that. My chief motive has always been to have Robert here in England close to us and far away from the daily dangers of army life. If he can live safely in Derbyshire, out of harm's way, while you and I enjoy an elevation in our social standing, can that be so wrong?"

"Yes, it can."

"How? *How* can it be wrong?"

"Because it is not what *he* wants. Oh, Robert wants his family to be happy, of course; but he also wants to make his own way in life. He wants to travel the world, and be a good officer, and . . ." He turned to Caroline and squared his shoulders, adding bravely, ". . . and marry Miss Bennet."

Caroline raised her hand to her heart as if she'd just been dealt a mortal wound. "No! He does not want to—! Oh, it is not true!"

"I assure you, it is," said Charles, calmly.

"But she is unsuitable!"

"She is just as suitable to be Robert's wife as Jane ever was to be mine. Must I remind you how much you have come to love Jane as a sister? You will soon feel the same for Mary."

"I will not!"

"But Robert loves her. I will be the first to admit, it took a little while for me to recognize the signs, but now that I have, I cannot help but wish that some way might be found for Robert to marry her. She will suit him very well, I think."

To Caroline's mind this sort of talk bordered on treason. After all her efforts to see Robert married to Miss Paget, she now, for the first time, began to think her plans might actually be in jeopardy. But after turning the problem about in her mind for the remainder of the day, Caroline began to think that it may not be so bad a circumstance that Charles refused her pleas to intercede with Robert. As much as she disagreed with everything Charles had said, there had been a kernel of truth in one of his arguments: The matter of

Robert's marriage to Helena could only be resolved by the parties involved. Robert could not break it off, and Helena *would* not; and as long as that was the case, there was nothing else required of her to ensure the wedding took place; and with this realization, Caroline went to bed that night a very happy woman.

26

The Netherfield ball was to begin at nine o'clock, but long before the appointed time the household was awake and in motion. There was a good deal of bustle downstairs in the kitchens, for Mrs. Bingley had ordered a supper for midnight as well as two breakfasts: one of which was to be served just before dawn to provide fortification for those guests who would embark for home at first light; and the second to be served at ten o'clock for anyone fortunate enough to have spent the night in one of Netherfield's comfortable guest chambers.

The family was to gather in the drawing-room at eight o'clock, and when Mary and Kitty entered the room, it was already filled with family and guests. Mary paused on the threshold; she had never been one to do well in crowds of people, having never mastered the art of small talk or general conversation; but Kitty, made of sterner stuff, clasped her hand and led her into the fray, smiling to people she knew, saying a word of greeting to others, while Mary allowed herself to be carried along, blushing all the while.

They set a direct course for Charles and Jane, who were standing near the south-facing windows.

"My dear sisters, how lovely you look!" Jane said when she saw them for the first time. "Your hair, Kitty, frames your face very well; and Mary—why, the gown you chose could not be prettier. Charles, what do you say?"

"I say there were never two lovelier girls in all of Hertfordshire!"

Mary had received compliments on other occasions, but tonight, for the first time, she was almost inclined to believe them. She knew her new gown to be very becoming, with its tiny puffed sleeves and seed pearls embroidered into a floral design across the bodice. More pearls hung gleaming from her earlobes and at her throat, and in her hair glittered a lovely decorative comb chaced with silver and mother-of-pearl. A long pair of pristine white gloves and an exquisitely painted fan completed her ensemble. She knew she was looking her best and with that knowledge came a sense of confidence that brought a soft glow to her cheeks and a light of anticipation to her eye. She couldn't help but wonder whether Captain Bingley would like her new gown. Perhaps he might even find her pretty, and the suspense of discovering his reaction when first he set eyes upon her made her nerves flutter with anticipation.

Caroline, who had been standing near enough to hear their exchange, said, "I must also add my compliments, for you both look very nice. In fact, I am quite pleased with everyone present. Being in the country, I half expected to see a good number of green velvet waistcoats and dreadful paste jewels on display."

"Oh, Caroline," Jane protested, with a small laugh. "You have been at Netherfield often enough to know we are not the savages you like to think us."

"True enough," said Charles. "I never saw a handsomer assembly of people. I would not have your critical eye for all the world, Caroline!"

"Then you can imagine my delight in finding your guests so handsomely turned out! Jane, my dear, I think the time has come for you and Charles to lead the way to the ball-room and prepare to receive new guests. This drawing-room has already become too close, and if even one more person joins us here, I fear we shall all be crushed!"

"But we cannot go yet," Mary said, as her eyes scanned the room full of people. There was no sign of the one person she wished to see above all others. "We are not all yet assembled."

"Who is missing?" asked Charles.

"Miss Paget is not present. I see neither her nor—"

"Do not worry, Mary." Jane said. "They will be along presently, you can depend upon it."

"But it does not seem right to go through until we are all together, does it?"

"I think," said Caroline, with a slight gesture toward the door, "we need not fear that anyone will get lost on their way to the ball-room. Miss Paget shall find her way, never fear."

Jane and Charles led the procession of guests through the great hall to the back of the house where the ball-room was located. As Mary made a move to follow them, Caroline linked her gloved hand through Mary's arm.

"You need not fear for Miss Paget's tardiness," she said, ignoring Mary's startled expression. "I happen to know she is not alone. You see, Helena and I came down together, but we met my brother Robert in the hall, and he begged a moment's conversation with her in private. I believe," she added, bending her head toward Mary's and lowering her voice, "he was waiting for her and has something very *particular* he wishes to say to her."

Her words had the desired effect. Although Mary Bennet certainly did her best to cover her consternation, Caroline could tell that she was upset by the news.

As soon as they entered the ball-room, they parted ways, and Caroline, quite satisfied with her efforts to drive yet another wedge between her brother and Mary Bennet, went off in search of someone worthy of her company.

Her quest ended almost as soon as it had begun when she spied Mr. Penrose. He was across the room, speaking with a young couple Caroline did not know, and she halted her steps while she tried to decide whether she should join them or not.

Mr. Penrose was dressed in his usual conservative style of black coat and pantaloons, but on this evening, there was something different about him—an air of quiet elegance Caroline had not notice before. And when she saw him bend his head slightly, the better to catch the words of the young woman chatting beside him, there was a gentleness in his expression that Caroline found charming.

Studying him, noting his every movement and gesture, she began to wonder why she had never before noticed how handsome he was, or the manner in which his presence somehow seemed to fill the room. In fact, in that moment her attention was so fixed upon him that all the colors of the ball-room seemed to fade away; there was only Mr. Penrose; and when he turned his head and caught sight of her, a soft wave of happiness seemed to wash over her and she smiled shyly at him.

He immediately ended his conversation, and began to make his way toward her. By the time he reached her side, her eyes were softly glowing.

"Good evening, Miss Bingley," he said, in a voice that was now comfortably familiar to her. "Am I too late?"

"Too late for what?"

"To beg the honor of a dance with you this evening?"

Without warning Caroline's heart began to beat a little bit faster. She looked up at him and thought that his brown hair, neatly combed in its usual style, looked rather more lush and unruly under the lights of the many candles that lit the room; and his hazel eyes that had so often looked down on her with that teasing glint, on this night bore a soft expression that she liked very much.

She raised one brow and asked, lightly, "*Can* you dance, Mr. Penrose?"

"That," he said, "sounds very much like a challenge! Very well, Miss Bingley! *En garde!* It will be my pleasure to show you just how talented I am in that quarter."

"I look forward to it," she said, enjoying the sight of one of his very charming smiles.

After a long moment, he dipped his head closer to hers and murmured, "Is something wrong, Miss Bingley?"

"No, not all. Why do you ask?"

"You do not often stare at me in silence. What, I wonder, have you been thinking? Have I offended you by the manner in which I have tied my cravat?"

She flushed slightly, for she had not realized she'd been staring. "Your cravat is a model of propriety, but I cannot help but wish that you might have found a way to add just a *bit* of color to your attire this evening."

"As much as I desire to please you, Miss Bingley, you must be content to accept me for who I am. I cannot be otherwise."

So he desired to please her! She was not certain whether she should be delighted or frightened by his words. She was very much intrigued and was beginning to wonder where this new, mild flirtation would lead, when she saw a footman bearing down upon her. In the next moment he was beside her, conveying to her a message from Miss Paget, requesting her immediate presence in Mrs. Bingley's morning room.

With a good deal of reluctance she excused herself and went to see Helena; but when she entered the morning room, she found a scene that was not all the one she expected. Robert, attired in full military regalia, was standing near the window, a scowl on his face and his hands clasped behind his back.

Helena, too, was dressed for the ball, but she was pacing the room in an agitated manner until she saw Caroline. Then she rushed to her, her hands outstretched, and said, in a voice of distress, "Thank God you have come! You must speak to your brother immediately for he vows he will not quit the army, and if you do not make him change his mind, now—this instant!—I vow I will not have him!"

"Calm yourself, my friend," Caroline said. "Robert, is this true?"

"It is," he said, in a voice of steely calm. "I have explained to Miss Paget, yet again, that I am a soldier. That is my profession; it's what I love; and I will not be shackled to an estate with nothing to do but count the number of deer in the park and select what blend of tobacco I will put in my snuff box each day."

"Do you hear how he speaks to me?" Helena demanded, very close to tears. "You must bring him to heel immediately, Caroline, if you ever wish to see us married!"

"Bring him to *heel?*" Caroline turned the phrase over in her mind and decided she did not care for it one bit, especially as it had been applied to her brother. Robert had always been the independent one in the family, the adventurer; and she did not think that anyone—even her friend Helena—should be allowed to clip his wings.

"Well, Caroline?" There was a challenge in Helena's tone and a confidence in her expression that told Caroline she expected her to fall in line and do her bidding.

Caroline looked beseechingly at her brother. "Robert, can you not consider making one or two small sacrifices—"

"This is no small sacrifice, Caroline. I am soldier; I have never wanted to be anything else; and if Miss Paget truly cared for me, she would recognize that truth and be content to accept me for who I am."

In Robert's words Caroline was immediately reminded of a similar sentiment Mr. Penrose had spoken to her only minutes before. For so many weeks it had been her ambition that Robert marry her friend, she had never stopped to consider what their married life would be like. But now, with Mr. Penrose's words echoing in her mind, she had a sudden realization that aside from good looks, fine manners, and blue eyes, her brother and Miss Paget really had little in common. Since his arrival at Netherfield Robert had spent more time with Mary Bennet than he had with Helena, and those times he did seek out her company, their conversations had been marked by disagreement and discord. And now, to make matters infinitely worse, she realized that a marriage with Helena would consign her brother to a future without adventure, without exploration to those foreign lands he had always talked about visiting, without the merest hint of the things Robert took pleasure in.

Robert deserved better; he deserved someone who loved him, someone whose eyes lit up the moment he entered a room . . . much the way her eyes lit up whenever Mr. Penrose was near to her.

She blushed at the thought, but took no steps to hide it. There were more important matters to attend; her brother needed her and she meant to protect him as she always had. All her dreams, all her brilliant plans and schemes for her family's future and her own social benefit she cast to the winds without a murmur of regret.

"My dear Helena," she said, "have you considered you are being rather hard on my brother? You ask him to give up an honest occupation—one he has dreamed of since he was a child."

"No true gentleman," Helena said, mulishly, "engages in an *occupation*. My uncle, Lord Berkridge, has said so to me many times, and I cannot help but—"

"Perhaps there is the rub," Caroline interrupted, wishing that she might never have to hear Lord Berkridge's name again. "Perhaps Robert is not a gentleman who can measure up to your uncle's standard. And if that is the case, my dear Helena, he cannot possibly timber up to yours."

"I don't understand."

"It is simple, my dear friend. If your uncle would not wish you to marry a man who has engaged in a profession— even a profession as noble as the military—you must not defy him. Why, it would be unthinkable. I advise you most strenuously to break off all ties with my brother and only think of what is best for *you*."

Helena furrowed her lovely brow and decided there was a good deal of wisdom in what Caroline said, especially the last part. "But if your brother will leave the army, he will then be acceptable to my uncle."

"Will he?" asked Caroline, clearly doubtful. "Robert has been engaged in a profession for many years now. There is no telling what odd and—Shall I say it?—*distasteful* habits he has adopted as his own. Don't you think your uncle will be able to detect those small, subtle, *ungentleman-like* flaws in Robert's character?"

"It is true," Helena said, thinking it over, "my uncle is a man of extraordinarily refined taste!"

"I know how unselfish you are, my dear Helena," she said, although the words almost choked her, "but the time has come, I think, for you to consider what your family will want. Think of them. Think of yourself!"

"Oh, Caroline, you always give me the best advice!"

"Then we are in agreement? You will end your engagement to my brother?"

"Why, there is no engagement at all, for he never asked me to marry him, I assure you! And even if he got down on one knee this very minute, I would be obliged to refuse him, I think, in light of what you have said."

Robert, realizing his best response was grateful silence, simply offered Helena a low bow as she began to move toward the door.

"I wish to leave tomorrow," she said, pausing with her hand on the knob. "You'll come with me, won't you, Caroline?"

"Where do you intend to go?"

"To London first, and then to Essex. My sister will have had her baby by now, and I dare say there will a celebration of some sort that might be entertaining. You'll accompany me, of course!"

Caroline said she would be glad to go with her as far as London; and with this arrangement fixed, Helena went upstairs to consult her maid and order her trunks packed for the journey.

"Why did you do it?" Robert asked in a gentle voice as soon as the door was closed again.

"I am certain you know the reason," Caroline said, evasively.

"But I thought my marriage to Miss Paget was your dearest wish."

"It was. But I have an even stronger desire to see you happy in life. Haven't I always been your most ardent champion?"

"Indeed you have," he said, smiling warmly.

"I realize now—As much as it pains me to say it—that I have been forcing you together with Helena. I was wrong to do so. You should not be made to marry where your heart is not genuinely engaged."

"First of all, you did not force me to court Miss Paget at all. I was to blame for that; I was smitten at first sight of her, and acted foolishly from that fateful moment on. Second, when—If I may be allowed to ask—did you become sentimental? Marry for love? You have never uttered such a thought before in your life."

"I believe," she said, lifting her chin, "it is not so unusual in these days for people to marry where their heart is engaged. The world is changing, Robert, and we must keep up with the times. Why, even Charles and Jane married for love, and you see how well suited and happy they are."

He gave a quick bark of laughter, followed by a brief kiss upon her cheek. "I, more than anyone, know just how much that admission cost you. Thank you!"

"Oh, do stop speaking nonsense and go to her!"

"Her?" His smile froze then faded from his lips. "Who do you mean?"

"Why, Mary Bennet, of course. She is the woman you love, is she not? You will find her in the ball-room—probably looking miserable and dejected, but *your* presence will soon brighten her mood."

"How did you know where my feelings lay?"

"How could I not? You have been mooning about Netherfield since the day of your arrival, brightening when Mary Bennet enters a room and glumping about under a dark cloud whenever she disappears from your sight. Why, I never saw anyone so wounded by Cupid's dart!"

He laughed again. "It is a strange wound, to be sure—and altogether different from what I thought I felt for Miss Paget. I can only hope you will one day know what it is like to be struck by a similar arrow!"

On this point Caroline could not agree. As she walked back to the ball-room with Robert, she realized the words he had spoken in fun had come dangerously close to gauging her own feelings where Mr. Penrose was concerned. Like Robert's affection for Mary Bennet, Caroline's attraction to Mr. Penrose had begun before she knew it, and grown steadily ever since. At first she had seen him as nothing more than a poor country vicar with an odd sense of humor and a penchant for telling others what to do. But at some point— when she did not know—she had begun to see his kindness and observed the little ways he showed his care for her. This was a revelation to her. Her own feelings for him, which she had tried so hard to shroud and deny even to herself, now appeared without disguise: she was very much attracted to Mr. Penrose, and if they continued on their present course, she suspected she would be at risk of losing her heart to him altogether.

She was given cause to test that theory a moment later; for no sooner did she enter the ball-room on Robert's arm than Mr. Penrose was there to claim his promised dance.

His voice was a deep murmur as he said everything that was proper. He offered his arm; she placed her gloved hand over his and allowed him to lead her to where a number of couples were forming a set. The music began and they made their way through the beginning figures before she said, in a casual tone, "Miss Paget leaves for Essex tomorrow."

His brows went up. "Does she? That is rather unexpected, is it not?"

"She and my brother have decided they will not suit."

"I see. I cannot say I am surprised, and I dare say there is one person here tonight who will be glad of the news."

Without thinking Caroline's eyes strayed to where Mary Bennet was standing with her back to the wall behind the dowager's row. "There are actually two such people," she said, "for Miss Paget does not care for Hertfordshire at all. She has mentioned several times since her arrival that she is tired of meeting only farmers and shop merchants. I do not think she would care to set foot in Hertfordshire again."

"Poor Miss Paget!" he said, as a spark of unholy humor lit his eyes. "Has she had such a difficult time of it?"

"I shall simply say her visit to Netherfield did not progress as she hoped it might." She drew a deep breath as she realized the moment for disclosure had come. "I must tell you that I plan to accompany her."

Her voice sounded admirably even. *Good*, she thought. He wouldn't be able to tell just how difficult a time she was having controlling her emotions. She waited for his reaction and when she finally could stand it no longer, she looked up. In his expression she saw none of the regret or disappointment she had hoped for. He merely looked back at her and blinked several times.

"Why must you go?"

"She cannot very well travel alone with only a maid and some hired coachmen to accompany her."

"How long will you be gone?"

"I cannot say. Tell me, what news have you of Mrs. Doyle?"

He looked at her curiously, but answered, "I saw her this morning. Her back is healing nicely, and she charged me most ardently to once again convey to you her heart-felt thanks. Are you simply going to run away?"

Startled, she said, "Run away? Not at all! I just explained to you that—"

"Come, Miss Bingley, you are a clever woman. I am certain with a bit of ingenuity you could devise a method to convey Miss Paget to Essex that will not require your removal from Netherfield. Have I frightened you so much?"

There it was again—that blunt way he had of speaking that had the power to disconcert her. "I am not running away," she said. "My friend needs me now."

"What of the people here who need you?"

"They will all go on very well without me."

"Not all of them."

Again the movement of the dance drew them apart, and when they found themselves once again united, he said, "Naturally, you must do as you think best, Miss Bingley. I am aware there are times in our lives when our hearts can sometimes lead us into situations that are new and frightening. I could not live with myself if I ever thought I frightened you."

There was a note of compassion in his voice that she appreciated; but she also recognized that he was holding himself in check—that there were many more things he wished to say to her, if only she would give him permission to do so. As curious as she was, as much as she wanted him to go on talking to her in the same low, beguiling tone, she knew she could not allow him to continue; for once he said his peace, and once his thoughts were uttered, she knew their relationship would be forever altered.

It took every bit of will-power she possessed to look up at him and say, in an even voice, "Thank you. You are very good, Mr. Penrose."

"John. My name is John Penrose."

John Penrose. It was a nice, solid, old-fashioned name. She liked it. She liked him, and suddenly she wasn't at all certain she wanted to leave Netherfield in the morning.

"Very well, John Penrose," she said, secretly marveling at how nice his name sounded on her lips, "I wonder if you would be good enough to take me to my brother Charles. I should like to tell him the news about Robert and Helena myself before the rumors begin to circulate."

"With pleasure, Miss Bingley." And true to his word, he offered his arm and, with the utmost solicitude, escorted her to her brother's side.

27

Mary Bennet found Lord Rainham to be an attentive and charming dance partner. He appeared at her side just as the orchestra struck up a warning to alert the assembly that the first dance was about to begin. He chatted amiably with her about commonplace topics, and when the time came for them to join others in making up the numbers, he extended his hand to her and asked pleasantly, "Shall we take our place in the set?"

She allowed him to lead her to where the other dancers were assembled, and when the music began, she acquitted herself very creditably; but all the while, as she smiled and did her best to make pleasant conversation with his lordship, Mary's attention was fixed upon the door of the ball-room. More than once her gaze swept the room, on watch for a sign that Captain Bingley had joined the party, but each time she was disappointed.

He will be along presently, she told herself, for he was pledged to partner her in the second dance, and he was not a man to hold such promises cheaply. But even with that dance to look forward to, she had hoped to see him before the ball commenced. She had hoped for a brief interview—even as little as one minute—for him to see her in her finery without the noise and distraction of other guests, that she might see the expression on his face. Would he approve of her looks? Would she see admiration in his eyes? Would he think her— Dare she say it?—*pretty?*

Lord Rainham had told her she was. She even saw a hint of admiration in his eyes as they waited for the music to begin. But even as she dipped a curtsey and made her first opening step in the first figure, she couldn't help but send yet another searching look toward the door.

When their dance was over, Mary sought a place beside Kitty, who, having danced the first set herself, was standing near a row of chairs, fanning herself with vigor.

There was no doubt in Mary's mind that Kitty was enjoying herself immensely. Her cheeks glowed and her eyes were bright as she observed aloud to Mary all the sights she found most entertaining, from the height of one gentleman's collar points, to the brilliant glitter of another lady's jewels.

"But still I have not seen the one thing I wished for," Kitty said. "What could be keeping Captain Bingley? He promised to wear his dress uniform tonight and it is most unkind of him to tease me and make me wait so long to see him. Do you know where he is keeping himself?"

Mary could honestly say she did not. Unlike Kitty, she already knew, thanks to Caroline, that Captain was secreted away with Helena Paget in order that he might propose marriage to her. From there it was a simple matter for Mary to believe they were even now murmuring pledges of love and fidelity to each other, mindless of the guests now crowding the ball-room.

Since the moment of her acquaintance with Captain Bingley, Mary had always known it would happen, for Robert had never tried to deny that he intended to propose marriage to Helena; but the thought that he might actually have done so—that his future was now irrevocably tied to Miss Paget's—almost brought the tears to Mary's eyes.

"Lud, how can you dance, Mary, and not become over-heated?" Kitty asked, fanning herself. "Help me!"

Mary obediently unfurled her fan and began to gently wave it in the direction of Kitty's flushed face. In a few minutes Kitty was satisfactorily cooled, and announced herself ready for the next dance.

As if on cue the orchestra sounded a warning chord. Elegantly-clad couples began to assemble in the center of the room; and when Kitty's partner came to claim her, Mary was left to stand alone near dowager's row. It was certainly not the first time she had been left so, but it was definitely the most painful, and she realized she had no one to blame for her circumstance but herself.

She had allowed herself to conjure in her mind a deeper friendship with Captain Bingley than actually existed; she had teased herself into believing he cared more for her than he truly did. And when he had suggested partnering her in a dance, she had grabbed hold of the notion like a starving kitten clinging to a stranger's promise of a dish of milk.

Never again, she told herself. Never again would she sink to such pathetic depths over a man, or harbor the mistaken notion that he—or anyone, for that matter—might actually find her attractive.

These thoughts and many like them tumbled through her

mind as she watched the couples take their places for the beginning of the second dance—the dance she had pledged to Captain Bingley. Instead of taking her place with him, she was made to watch as a whirl of waltzers went by her. One pair after another, in blue and white and pink gowns, flew and flashed before her; each lady holding a man's hand; each man embracing a lady's waist.

When the set was ended, Kitty once again returned to her side. She was full of gossip and descriptions of the other guests and Mary did her best to pay attention. She even managed to smile when Kitty recounted how her partner had missed his steps twice and turned in the wrong direction once, thereby ruining her pleasure in the entire dance; but as Kitty chatted on, some sixth sense made Mary look toward the door. She was in time to see Robert enter the ballroom with Caroline on his arm; she watched them part almost immediately—Caroline walking toward the orchestra with Mr. Penrose, and Robert going in the opposite direction.

"Oh, Mary!" breathed Kitty, in a tone of deep awe. "Here is Captain Bingley at last, and only *look* at the coat he is wearing! I cannot think a red tunic has ever looked so well on a man! See how it shows his shoulders to advantage?"

Mary's heart had begun to thump wildly, and she knew not where to look, except that she knew she would not look at Captain Bingley.

"I beg you will not *stare*, Kitty," she said, through suddenly dry lips.

Kitty was not to be deterred by such a mild rebuke. Not only did she continue to gaze appreciatively at the captain, she began to wave at him as well, hoping to attract his attention.

She was successful. Within a minute's time he was standing before them, providing Kitty a close view of the impressive array of medals pinned to his tunic.

"What has kept you?" she asked eagerly; then before he could answer, she said in a rush, "No need to tell us—you have been with Miss Paget, I am certain. But what was so important that could have made you miss the *first two dances?*"

"Miss Paget and I had some things to say to each other in private—"

Kitty gave an audible gasp. "Say no more, Captain Bingley! We quite understand, Mary and I. Only tell us your news!"

His smile faded slightly. "My news?"

"Of your interview with Miss Paget. Did you come to an understanding at last? Was your conversation satisfactory?"

"Kitty!" Mary said, blushing hotly. "Why must you ask such impertinent questions?"

"Our conversation," he said, his eyes fixed on Mary's face, "was most satisfactory."

"That is good to hear," Kitty said. "I did not mean to be impertinent. I asked only because I wanted to know if I should wish you well."

"I hope I may always have your good wishes, Miss Catherine." He looked at Mary. "And yours, too, Miss Bennet."

It was clear to Mary that he expected a response from her. She said, looking down at the embroidered pattern on the toe of her dancing slippers, "Captain Bingley may always be assured of my good wishes."

He smiled slightly. "Captain Bingley thanks you."

Kitty laughed. "Well, now you are here you may be assured all the ladies will want to dance with you, myself included; but I fear I am already promised for the next dance."

"That is a disappointment I will struggle to overcome," he said. "Do you know where to find your partner, Miss Catherine?"

"No, but I am certain he must be somewhere in the ball-room."

"Perhaps you should go in search of him."

"Oh, he will be along to claim me presently; and if he does not, I will look forward instead to a dance with you."

"I will happily dance with you a dozen times if you will go away now so I may speak with your sister."

"Oh!" Kitty said, with dawning understanding. "You wish to speak to Mary? Very well, but do not be long, for I dare say I am not the only lady in this room who will look to you for a dance on this night!"

She left them, on the search for her next partner as Robert had suggested, and he was at leisure to once again turn his gaze on Mary.

"Miss Bennet, I believe you promised me a dance."

"I did," she said, still refusing to look up at him; "the *second* dance, which has come and gone."

"Are you engaged for the third?"

How much she wished she could tell him that she was! "No, I am not."

"Then I hope you will allow me to atone for my bad

manners."

That, she thought, would be impossible. "I do not care to dance, Captain Bingley."

"Very well. We'll simply talk. Shall we walk as we do so?" He held his hand out to her.

She hesitated, weighing in her mind the benefits of accepting his offer against the more satisfying prospect of refusing him and causing a scene. At last she decided to take his arm. He claimed he wished to speak with her. *Very well!* she thought. *Let him say his peace and get it over with.* She already had a very good notion of what he intended to tell her. She could almost hear the words already in her mind:

Miss Paget has accepted my proposal of marriage.

We will wed in the spring with an earl and his countess, and the whole of London society in attendance.

I will resign my commission in favor of becoming the gentleman of leisure Miss Paget always wished me to be.

With these thoughts plaguing her, she allowed Robert to lead her through the crowd of guests; and it wasn't until she found herself passing into the great hall near the front of the house that she was suddenly brought to attention.

"Where are we going?"

"To the library."

"But why? Why can you not speak to me in the ball-room?"

"I like the library better," he said, opening the door and ushering her inside. "Does the lock on this door have a key?"

She had gone directly to the table in middle of the room, but at this she whirled about to face him. "Why do you ask?"

"What I have to say to you must be said in private. I

should not like having some wandering guest blunder in to interrupt us." His search for a key was unsuccessful, and he had to be content with leaving the closed door unlocked. "Will you sit down, Miss Bennet?"

"Thank you, no," she said, clasping her hands together in a nervous grip. "Please say what you wish so I may return to the ball-room."

"I have a number of things to tell you. First," he said, moving leisurely toward the fireplace where a small blaze lighted the room in a mellow glow, "Lord Rainham has decided to leave tomorrow. He plans to take Daniel with him."

"I know."

"Did he tell you so himself?"

"He did . . . *while we were dancing*." She saw no reaction in his expression, prompting her to add, "At least *he* did not forget his commitment."

"Very true. Lord Rainham seems a man of high principle, and I think he will quickly turn into an affectionate and doting grandfather. Only think how quickly Daniel managed to twist you and me around his little finger!"

Mary turned away to hide a smile. "I did grow very fond of him in a short amount of time. I will miss him."

"You have an open invitation to visit him at Cottesmere any time you wish."

"That is true." But even as she said those words, she knew she would probably never see Daniel again, for what opportunity did she ever have for travel? "And your other news?"

"Lord Rainham promised to write to my colonel as soon

as he returns to Derbyshire."

"Oh? Is that necessary?" she asked, in some surprise. She had supposed that if Captain Bingley intended to leave the army to please Miss Paget, there would be no need for Lord Rainham to write such a letter.

"It can do me no harm, and it might do a world of good. You will remember I mentioned to you once before how difficult it has been for me to rise in the ranks."

She remembered. Indeed, she recalled almost every conversation she ever had with Captain Bingley, and the confidences they had shared.

"Then you do not intend to resign your commission, after all?"

"No, I don't," he said. "I am a military man at heart, and in the military I intend to stay."

"I admire your commitment, Captain Bingley," she said, primly. "And I hope you achieve your heart's desire to one day claim the rank of major."

He dipped his head slightly. "I shall strive to be worthy of the promotion, if it comes."

"It will come; but you must not be deterred or despondent if you do not achieve it right away. There is a saying I read once: 'When the road proves rugged, or is in danger of growing tedious—'"

"'—one successful method of beguiling it, is for the travelers to cheer and amuse one another.'"

Startled, she raised her eyes to meet his. "*What* did you say?"

"Shall I repeat it?"

"No! But how did you—?"

394

"I believe I read it somewhere. Where was it? A book, I think, with a long and tedious title. Ah, yes! It was Reverend Fordyce's *Sermons for Young Ladies, Volume One.*"

"*You* read Fordyce's *Sermons?*"

"Why not? You read *Gulliver's Travels.* I cannot tell you how gratified I was that the first novel you ever read was the one I recommended to you. If you'll recall, until you met me you had never read a novel before, nor had you ridden in a curricle or skipped stones across a pond."

She blushed slightly, and sat down on a nearby chair. "I am sure you think I have led a very boring life."

"Oh, no. You, Mary Bennet, are the least boring woman I've ever met. You dash with abandon about the countryside in curricles; you thoughtfully assemble gifts for your neighbors like an angel; and you dream of traveling to exotic lands like any self-respecting adventuress would."

"Me? An adventuress! You do not really think so!"

"I *must* think so. You see, I have always wanted to marry an adventuress."

In one quick movement Robert left his place by the mantel and pushed an ottoman in front of her. He sat down, his knees almost touching hers, his face very near.

"Mary," he said in a low voice, barely above a whisper, "will you ever be able to forgive me?"

Something told her he was not speaking of the dance he had missed. "Forgive you for what?"

"For being the greatest fool in the world; for being so stupid I could not recognize where my heart was leading me until it was almost too late. Tell me honestly: *am* I too late?"

She stared as the meaning of his words began to sink in.

"Surely you don't—! You cannot mean—!"

"That is *exactly* what I mean," he said, taking possession of her hands.

"But you are to marry Miss Paget!"

"No, my dearest."

"But she is beautiful and well-connected and—"

"Never," he said, sternly, "compare yourself to Miss Paget again."

"How can I not? You love her."

"I *thought* I loved her, but the truth is, I was so besotted by her face and figure and voice, that I never bothered to look any deeper. I'm not proud to admit it, I can tell you; but then I met you and realized how foolish I'd been."

"Is this true?" she asked, a little dazed.

"Upon my honor."

"I never imagined!" She gave her head a small shake. "I cannot think what you saw in me."

"Then I will tell you," he said, as he began a slow, inexorable pull upon her hands to draw her closer. "I saw your intelligence, and I was intrigued. I saw your humor, and I was charmed. I saw your soul, and it was beautiful. I am in love with you, Mary Bennet."

By this time he had drawn her near enough that her lips were within a very close proximity of his own, a fact he immediately took advantage of by kissing her tenderly.

"Oh, we shouldn't!" she said, as soon as he drew back a little.

"Why not?"

"Don't you recall how much trouble I was in the last time you did such a thing? And that was only a kiss upon my hand!"

"There is an old adage: If I am going to be in trouble, pray let it be for doing something I like."

"There is no such adage!" she protested, trying not to giggle.

"I am certain I read it in a book somewhere. One day I will have to show it to you. Meanwhile, I am having a devil of a time taking you in my arms. Let me ask you to join me here on this very comfortable ottoman."

Before she knew it, Mary was seated close beside Robert, his arms were about her and he was kissing her quite thoroughly.

Her response was immediate and natural. Her arm slid up and around his neck; her fingers plunged into the soft waves of his lush brown hair; and when he raised his head after one long, delicious kiss, she heard him let out a soft, soul-shuddering sigh.

She clung to the front of his tunic, and tried to catch her own breath. At last she understood what Kitty had been talking about when she described ladies being swept off their feet in the pages of her favorite novels.

"We have plans to make," he murmured as he held her close.

"Do we?" she answered through a happy fog. "What kinds of plans?"

"The usual kind: Where shall we be married—?"

"At Longbourn, of course."

"And where shall we go on our wedding trip—?"

"Somewhere exotic. China, I think!"

"And what shall we tell our families about this sudden

turn of events?"

"Oh, dear! Our families!" she murmured.

"You need not worry that we shall have to tell them very much. They have already guessed my feelings for you."

"Have they? But what about Caroline? She, I think, will be greatly disappointed you are not to marry Miss Paget, after all."

"And you would be wrong for thinking so. Who do you think helped me honorably extricate myself from my courtship of Miss Paget, once I discovered we would not suit?"

Mary pulled a little away from his embrace, the better to see his face. "*Caroline* did that? But she was so determined to see you marry her friend."

"She is even more determined that I should be happy in life. She is a very good sister—as protective of me as a tigress for her cubs. And so she will be toward you once we are married."

"I shall have to thank her for putting your welfare over her own schemes and plans."

"I think that is a very fine notion, as long as you do not wish to thank her *right now*," he said, drawing her back into the circle of his arms. "Did you mean what you said about China? Would you really go there?"

"I would willingly go anywhere in the world if I am by your side."

"I'm a soldier," he said, unnecessarily. "I go where I am commanded; and sometimes my home is nothing more than a tent; and sometimes I live in places where the food is very bad."

"That," she said, grabbing hold of his epaulet and drawing his lips once again toward hers, "sounds heavenly."

The End

About the Westover Thumb ...

The story of *Mary and the Captain* sprang wholly from my imagination, with one notable exception: the family trait that identified Daniel as a member of the Westover family!

The Westover thumb that I described in the story is real; it's a physical trait found in generations of my family. My grandfather had it, as did my Lawrence uncles; but when it came to my generation, something began to happen to the Lawrence gene pool. Only one in three of my cousins have the short Lawrence Thumb that I described in this story. As for my little branch of the family tree, neither I nor any of my siblings have it.

I have never been in a position where I had to prove that I was a member of my family, like Daniel had to; but in my heart, I always wished that I had inherited the Lawrence Thumb. Instead, I got the family nose, which is as long as The Thumb is short. I can also tell you that noses aren't nearly as interesting or as much fun to write about as thumbs!

Thank you!

Thank you for reading *Mary and the Captain*. I hope you enjoyed the story. Please consider writing a quick review of *Mary and the Captain* on your favorite bookseller's website or on Goodreads to let other readers know your thoughts about this book.

I hope you will visit me at my website ...

www.NancyLawrenceRegency.com

... friend me on Facebook at

https://www.facebook.com/nancy.lawrence.712/

... and follow me on Twitter at

@NLawrenceAuthor

I'd love to hear from you!

Printed in Great Britain
by Amazon

37884300R00229